Praise for
ONE DROP OF BLOOD

"Holland's debut novel is a riveting read—filled with duplicity, cover-up, mystery, and the realities (and frustrations) of forensic science. This is an engrossing thriller that immerses the reader in an historical injustice that only *One Drop of Blood* can resolve."

—Dr. Michael Baden and Linda Kenney,
authors of *Remains Silent*

"This is the best first novel I've read in years. Thomas Holland has solid forensic science credentials—he's a leading expert in his field. That might get you to pick up this book, but block out some time—you won't want to put it down. Engaging characters, high-octane suspense, and Holland's remarkable storytelling skills combine with a voice that's fresh, strong, and true to provide a terrific read."

—Jan Burke,
author of *Bloodlines* and *Bones*

"A unique take on the genre . . . Holland has created a couple of highly believable investigators in Levine and McKelvey, and draws a colorful description of the small-town South, with dark secrets." —*Toronto Sun*

"A dandy tale, wonderfully told . . . Holland dishes up local color that's as flavorful and genuine as the pecan pie at the small-town diner." —*St. Louis Post-Dispatch*

"*Mississippi Burning* meets *CSI* as a forensic anthropologist and a down-on-his-luck FBI agent join forces to unravel a 40-year-old civil-rights crime in [this] well-done debut. The author . . . proves a steady hand at maintaining the story's momentum, slowly escalating the tension."

—*Kirkus Reviews*

continued . . .

ONE DROP OF BLOOD

A C.I.L. NOVEL

THOMAS HOLLAND

BERKLEY BOOKS, NEW YORK

THE BERKLEY PUBLISHING GROUP
Published by the Penguin Group
Penguin Group (USA) Inc.
375 Hudson Street, New York, New York 10014, USA
Penguin Group (Canada), 90 Eglinton Avenue East, Suite 700, Toronto, Ontario M4P 2Y3, Canada
(a division of Pearson Penguin Canada Inc.)
Penguin Books Ltd., 80 Strand, London WC2R 0RL, England
Penguin Group Ireland, 25 St. Stephen's Green, Dublin 2, Ireland (a division of Penguin Books Ltd.)
Penguin Group (Australia), 250 Camberwell Road, Camberwell, Victoria 3124, Australia
(a division of Pearson Australia Group Pty. Ltd.)
Penguin Books India Pvt. Ltd., 11 Community Centre, Panchsheel Park, New Delhi—110 017, India
Penguin Group (NZ), 67 Apollo Drive, Rosedale, North Shore 0745, Auckland, New Zealand
(a division of Pearson New Zealand Ltd.)
Penguin Books (South Africa) (Pty.) Ltd., 24 Sturdee Avenue, Rosebank, Johannesburg 2196,
South Africa

Penguin Books Ltd., Registered Offices: 80 Strand, London WC2R 0RL, England

This is a work of fiction. Names, characters, places, and incidents either are the product of the author's imagination or are used fictitiously, and any resemblance to actual persons, living or dead, business establishments, events, or locales is entirely coincidental.

ONE DROP OF BLOOD

A Berkley Book / published by arrangement with Simon & Schuster, Inc.

PRINTING HISTORY
Simon & Schuster hardcover edition / May 2006
Berkley mass-market edition / August 2007

ISBN: 978-0-425-21693-4

BERKLEY®
Berkley Books are published by The Berkley Publishing Group,
a division of Penguin Group (USA) Inc.,
375 Hudson Street, New York, New York 10014.
BERKLEY® is a registered trademark of Penguin Group (USA) Inc.
The "B" design is a trademark belonging to Penguin Group (USA) Inc.

PRINTED IN THE UNITED STATES OF AMERICA

10 9 8 7 6 5 4 3 2 1

How shall a man escape from his ancestors, or draw off from his veins the black drop which he drew from his father's or his mother's life?

—R. Waldo Emerson,
Conduct of Life, "Fate" (1860)

PROLOGUE

Quang Nam Province, Republic of Vietnam
THURSDAY, 6 OCTOBER 1966

He could smell them.

When he first arrived in Vietnam, the old-timers said you could smell them, but he hadn't believed it. He couldn't. How could anybody smell anything? You smelled everything. And it was all the same: smoke, fish, rotting meat, decaying plants; sour—everything sour.

Now Jimmie Carl Trimble was the old-timer. Eleven months in-country, nineteen years old, and an old-timer. Now he could smell them. The smoke and fish and decay were still there, but now his nose could tease out subtleties. The vinegar smell of sweat, the reek of fear, the sour musk of unwashed cotton clothing.

You smelled it, or you died.

And Jimmie Carl hadn't died—at least not in Vietnam.

The mission was supposed to be about as uncomplicated as it got, but it had screw-up written all over it. They were to helo in, make their way from some map coordinate here to some map coordinate there, and then wait for further instructions. Jimmie Carl had been on enough of these goat-ropes to know that the instructions were almost always the same—return to where you started and don't ask any goddamn questions. And though they obviously were venturing into Indian country, the Intel guys had assured them that no bad guys were supposed to be between the here and the there, which, of course, is exactly where the bad guys proved to be. Bad and in strength.

It was a little past midday. The men were all strung out—a few in more ways than one—as they snaked and looped through the waist-high elephant grass. They'd been walking for well over an hour and had cleared the available cover provided by a thick stand of eucalyptus and gum trees and were now exposed. The stinging sun and heat were already taking effect, and that worried Jimmie Carl. Worried him enough that he'd worked his way to the front of the column to talk to the lieutenant. As the medic, it was Jimmie Carl's responsibility to watch the men closely for signs of heat stroke or dehydration or anything else that would fray the fabric of the platoon. He'd been telling the lieutenant that they needed to slow their pace and reform or they were going to be in a world of hurt. That's when they got hit. The hammer fell in the center—snapping the already disjointed column into two writhing bloody clots of confusion. The tail-end stragglers, including the platoon's senior NCO, were dead within the first thirty seconds.

The young lieutenant had shown tremendous maturity under the gun, and with gestures and shouts and physical manhandling had managed to pull his remaining lost lambs into a loose defensive knot from which they could assess their situation. Only the tree line offered any hope of survival. The decision was easy. The lieutenant initiated a fighting withdrawal back toward their Landing Zone. He assumed the point in the hell-bent sprint across the open ground, and Jimmie Carl brought up the rear. That's when Private Chester Orel Evans, running directly in front of Jimmie Carl, took a single AK-47 round near his belt line. There was a moist slap, like the sound of wet hands clapping, and then he collapsed as if his body had no momentum or inertia, as if the strings had been cut. He went down with all the subtlety of a bag of odd-sized rocks. The medic dropped to the young man's side and surveyed the wound, probing it with his index and middle fingers.

It was mortal.

The single bullet had entered in his back, just below his right kidney. It was a small circular puncture that had already closed upon itself—hardly even bloody, but in the front, where it had tumbled out of a jagged hole to the left of his navel, the accompanying shock wave had liquefied everything in its path. Jimmie Carl jabbed him with a morphine syrette and looked into his eyes. Ordinarily, he'd have painted a big "M" on his forehead with Mercurochrome to alert the docs at the aid station about the morphine, but this time it didn't matter. This one wasn't going to make it that far. Jimmie Carl stuffed the wound with a thick wad of gauze and then stripped off his belt and cinched it tightly around Evans's middle to try to at least hold his guts in till he could get him somewhere better to die.

Better to die?

Jimmie Carl knew he should leave Evans and try to rejoin the other men now nearing the covering trees; Evans was dead, he just hadn't stopped breathing, and there was nothing that was going to change that, but the lieutenant and the other men—however many were still alive—would be needing all the help they could get.

Jimmie Carl knew all of this, but he also knew that it didn't matter. This was his day of atonement. That moment, that one crystalline point of Time when you are granted the opportunity to put the mistakes of the past to rest and square your soul with God. Jimmie Carl wasn't going anywhere. He wasn't leaving Evans.

Hoisting the young private onto his back and shoulders, Jimmie Carl recalled a series of bomb craters that the platoon had passed on its way in from the LZ, before they were hit. They offered the best cover. The only cover. They also were five hundred meters away—a stroll on a good day; a lifetime today.

Jimmie Carl picked up the wounded Marine's heavy M-14 and began running. As he did so, Evans bobbed up and down on his shoulders; each time the young private expelled a strained grunt of air, like some huge, human bagpipe. And each time the grunt grew quieter as more and more air was squeezed out and wasn't replaced. Jimmie Carl ran in a straight line; the shortest distance to the end zone. Razor grass shredded his shins. The heat and wet were oppressive and sat on his chest like a sack of moistened concrete, and Evans, small as he was, was deadweight—wet, sticky, dying weight.

Jimmie Carl could smell bowel, and his sunburned neck and back prickled and stung from bile and stomach acid that leaked from Evans's shredded gut. The far bomb crater they had passed, the one closest to the tree line, the one that offered the best hope of survival, kept receding as he ran, farther and farther away with each step, and he felt like he was treading in waist-deep sorghum, and all the while, automatic weapons fire kept stitching a path in front of him.

His lungs bursting, Jimmie Carl dove into the first crater he came upon, throwing Evans in before him. The wounded private hit the ground and lay still, no longer even groaning. Jimmie Carl quickly pried open one of the boy's half-closed eyes with a muddy thumb; the iris had shut down and it was dark and unresponsive and clouding up like it had been buffed with steel wool, either from death or from the effects of the morphine, yet he was still breathing. A wet, stuttering, bubbling sound percolated from deep within.

Evans was a skinny black kid from a shotgun shack outside Greensboro, North Carolina. He stuttered and got tongue-tied when anxious, which was most of the time, and had opted for the Marine Corps only when it was presented as the option to another run at the state pen—three-to-five for grand theft auto. Three-to-five versus one-and-out in a place he had never heard of—the Republic of Vietnam. He'd chosen the unknown, but when the time came he reconsidered and went AWOL from the induction center. Two SPs had found him in a snooker hall four blocks away and educated him on the Marine Corps' lack of a sense of humor in such matters. Things hadn't improved much after that. The four months of basic training that followed had been one long, un-interrupted stretch of disciplinary guard duty, and then came the RVN.

Evans had been universally disliked by the other men from the beginning. He'd been nothing but trouble to them since setting foot in Da Nang, and the lieutenant had been working on the necessary paperwork to get him transferred, but given personnel shortages and the ever-increasing mission tempo, the paperwork kept getting lost at headquarters. What no one in the unit could comprehend was why Jimmie Carl had be-friended the boy; had sought him out when all others had turned a shoulder. It made no sense to anyone.

Now, sitting in six inches of fetid red-black muck at the bottom of the shallow crater, Jimmie Carl inventoried his op-tions: He had the boy's M-14 with maybe a full clip of ammo, maybe less. He didn't think Evans had gotten off a shot before he caught the stray in his gut. He also had his meds kit. Evans appeared to have two high-explosive M-26 grenades and an M-18 smoke canister clipped to his suspenders, and he also was carrying one of the unreliable hand-held PRC-6 "handi-talkie" radios that no one else in the squad had wanted to lug around due to the weight and so had foisted on the unpopular private.

Options. Options.

There were no options. In this case there was only one out-come—Jimmie Carl Trimble was dead and unlike the mo-tionless Evans, he knew it. Even now, in the time that it had taken to examine the kid and survey his vitals, they had closed the distance.

Above the oily pall of cordite and dust, above the leaking, mortal stench of Evans, he could smell them now—they were that close. In about five minutes Jimmie Carl Trimble, who-ever he was, whoever he had become, would cease to exist. Maybe that wasn't a bad thing; maybe it was all for the best. Maybe it didn't matter, but just as certain as his own death was the fact that ten minutes after that, maybe even less, two companies of well-trained North Vietnamese regulars would fall upon the fractured remnants of his platoon, and they too would cease to exist.

Unless someone did something, fast.

Jimmie Carl looked again at the radio slung around Evans's shoulder. Maybe there was an option.

"Dwayne, Dwayne, can you read me? Over." The heavy, piece-of-shit PRC-10 on his radioman's back snapped and hissed as First Lieutenant Dwayne Crockett reached for the handpiece to reply. He'd gotten his men well back into the trees and was establishing a tight perimeter that he hoped they could hold until the helos got there. The radio handpiece was packed with mud, and he had to smack it repeatedly against his thigh to clear it. He could tell from his medic's tone of voice and minimal radio formality that things were going critical. The use of his first name on the radio rather than a call sign or code words; the raw desperation; it added up to a grab-ass situation, and Jimmie Carl wasn't the type to panic without reason. Since arriving in Vietnam almost a year ago Jimmie Carl had proven himself pragmatic to the point of fearlessness. Dwayne Crockett keyed the microphone and responded with the same informal efficiency. "I'm here, Jimmie Carl, what's your situation? Over." He fought to keep his voice calm and even; to not betray his surprise that Jimmie Carl was still alive.

"Up a creek . . . got Evans with me. Over." Even with the hiss and static of the radio, the thick honey in Jimmie Carl's slow southern drawl was discernible.

"Hope your paddle's bigger than mine, buddy. What's your position? Over."

"That third bomb crater we passed on the way in from the LZ; the small one. It's bad, Dwayne; Evans's probably already gone. Poppin' some smoke. Over." Jimmie Carl flicked the smoke grenade over the lip of the crater. It sputtered momentarily and then began ejecting a thick stuttering plume of rust-colored smoke.

"Got your position—break," Dwayne Crockett replied as

he craned his head over the tall grass. Over the last six months he'd allowed himself to get close to the quiet navy corpsman. He'd come to rely heavily on him, his maturity and sound judgment. Now as he watched the plume of smoke rise in the distance, he took stock of his remaining men, gauging what they were really capable of doing. He looked back over his shoulder—no sign of the incoming helicopters. He keyed the microphone again. "Sit tight, Jimmie Carl, we're going to work our way back down the tree line and lay down a covering fire—you'll need to come to us—break—leave Evans, I say again, leave Evans. Over."

"Negative, Lieutenant." Jimmie Carl responded quickly. "There's a whole lot of bad guys here that want to have a talk with y'all, and they'll be crawlin' up your skinny coon ass soon enough. Do not, I say again, *do not* advance this position. You read me, Dwayne? Over." Jimmie Carl had no intention of letting Dwayne expose the remaining men to any more heat than was necessary for their own survival, and he also had no intention of leaving Evans, even if it would have made a difference. It was time to end the secrets and the lies and the sleepless nights. It was that crystal-clear moment.

"I hear you, Doc. Maybe you got a plan I don't know about? Over." Dwayne rose up again to mark Jimmie Carl's location as the smoke began to dissipate and drift away.

It was a matter of who would put voice to the plan first. Jimmie Carl could delay until the helicopters arrived and hope that Dwayne and the rest could withdraw faster than the NVA could shoot at them. "Y'all need a head start—break—y'all got to buy some breathin' room. Only one way to make that purchase, and you know it. Make the call, Dwayne. Over."

"Say again? Over." Dwayne was stalling, and Jimmie Carl knew it. And there wasn't time.

"You heard me, Dwayne . . . make the call. Put it on my head. Y'all read that, Lieutenant? On my head. Over."

"Negative. We'll figure something out. Over." Dwayne continued to stall.

"You heard me, Lieutenant. Nothin' more to figure. Make the friggin' call. For God's sake, make the call, Dwayne—while there's still some smoke for a marker. Over."

Dwayne found it hard to answer, but he knew Jimmie Carl was right. He knew what had to be done. The helos were still ten minutes out, the NVA maybe five. "Hold one. Break," Dwayne finally responded. He spread the mission map out on his knee and used his finger to trace the map coordinates from the edges. He switched frequencies and made the radio call, and then two long minutes later he rekeyed the mic for Jimmie Carl, "Forgive me, buddy . . . Over."

"Semper Fi, Do or Die," Jimmie Carl said gently. "No forgivin' necessary, Bubba. Over."

Dwayne had no response. He gripped the handpiece tightly and scanned the sky for any sign of the incoming helos. The race was on. If only they'd arrive. *If only.*

The radio popped and hissed for several seconds and then Jimmie Carl's voice broke through again, strange and lacking the calm decisiveness that it had held moments before. "Dwayne?" It was hard to hear him. Already overhead was a vibrating roar, like a bed sheet being torn quickly in two.

"Yeah, buddy, I'm here. Over." Dwayne found himself shouting into the microphone.

"Dwayne . . . ain't no time to explain . . . been too long . . . I need to hear it again, Dwayne. You hear me? Can't die this way. Aw, Jesus, Dwayne . . . you hear me? I need to hear it again. One last time . . . can you call me . . ."

"Call you what? Jimmie Carl, call you what? Over . . . goddamn you, Jimmie Carl, call you what? Over."

But Jimmie Carl Trimble never finished his sentence. He looked up just in time to see two silver-colored napalm canisters come tumbling in, ass over elbows.

CHAPTER 1

Split Tree, Arkansas
FRIDAY, AUGUST 12, 2005

Split Tree was a simple town of great complexity.

In the big, wide scheme of things, it had never seemed to rise to the occasion. Even in the boom days before imported cotton had bottomed out the local market, Split Tree hadn't really amounted to much; just a flat, even-tempered, east Arkansas collection of ramshackle that even its most ardent bred-in-the-bone supporters sometimes had to admit was a waste of good dirt.

And nowadays it seemed to have even less working in its favor.

Dirt was actually the word most appropriately used when you needed something to finish a sentence that started with Split Tree. The whole town was like fine grit in the teeth. Grit and silt and dry, wind-blown floodplain clay. *Dirt.* In fact, the community gave the impression of having collected about the county courthouse in much the same manner that dirt and cotton lint seem to drift up around a tree stump in the middle of a field—not organization as much as lazy convenience.

Like many southern river towns devoid of troublesome topography, Split Tree was organized like a checkerboard with a baseline that ran straight east to west, from sunup to sundown. The eastern anchor was the three-story red-brick and limestone courthouse, the seat of county political affairs for over 150 years; to the west, on Tupelo Road, was the Bell Brothers Cotton Gin, the seat of gossip and economic business for even longer. Long-fiber cotton was on the wane, and the Dew family—who'd purchased the Bell gin during the Depression but kept the name out of deference to tradition—had been forced to expand the business to one of general agricultural supply. It had even started selling Japanese-made tractors with long, funny names, but increasingly it was having a hard time competing against the co-op, and there was a persistent rumor of imminent closure.

Split Tree was not a bad town, but somehow it woke up one morning on the wrong side of the century. It was a place where most folks still found it rude to be rude; where the women retained a quiet sense of grace and composure and men still visited their mothers every Sunday afternoon. The kind of place where people still knew the name of every dog in town.

A place where very little seemed to happen, and very little had ever happened.

Almost.

In the late summer of 1965 Split Tree, Arkansas, hit its high-water mark of excitement when two bodies were found; one black, one white; one identified, one unknown. And as they say in Split Tree, that sort of thing don't happen just any old day.

The identified body created the most stir—at least at the time—as it proved to be the physical remains of one Leon Jackson, late of Natchez, Mississippi. The unidentified remains certainly caused their fair share of head-scratching, but as Split Tree was a small community and since none of her native sons were known to be missing, conjecturing as to the identity of the unknown body soon subsided into little more than a stray barbershop topic.

But Leon Jackson wasn't so easily forgotten, no matter how much some wished that he were.

Leonidas Stephen Jackson was either a civil rights martyr or a goddamn Negro that had no business west of the Mississippi River; your particular view depended largely on whether you lived in lowland east Arkansas in the 1960s or wrote for big-city newspapers along the Atlantic seaboard. Regional perspectives aside, the reality was that Mr. Jackson was a would-be civil rights organizer who lacked the physical presence or visceral charisma of a Medgar Evers or Martin Luther King, and even by the most generous historical reckonings, was decidedly second shelf. Which is precisely why he ended up in the floodplain of eastern Arkansas in 1965 rather than Mississippi or Alabama or Georgia or one of the more racially charged crucibles of that era. Arkansas was on the periphery of the civil rights movement—Governor Orval Faubus and the forced integration of Little Rock's Central High School notwithstanding—and an obscure Negro championing the cause of backwater Arkansas cotton farmers and black share-croppers who wanted little more than to be left alone did not fire the imagination of eastern publishers the way German shepherds and fire hoses and lunch-counter sit-ins did. In fact, when Leon Jackson disappeared after last being seen at an African Episcopal Methodist church on the outskirts of West Helena, no one, not even his family over in Natchez, realized he was missing for several weeks.

If the truth were told, Leonidas Jackson became a historical footnote not because he was murdered, but because his body had the singular good timing to wash out of a flooded, earthen levee less than a year after the bodies of Goodman, Cheney, and Schwerner were found in an earthen dam in Neshoba County, Mississippi. Across the river. Even then he would have faded into complete anonymity had the eastern press not opportunistically connected the two incidents, despite the obvious differences—not the least of which being that they occurred a good two hundred miles apart.

Split Tree's second body was found almost a month later in September, when the rain stopped and the Mississippi River flood clay dried up enough that the FBI was able to dig up more of the levee. The fact that the second body was that of a young, white male—like Goodman and Schwerner—

seemed to confirm to all the northern fire-eaters, whose limited knowledge of Arkansas had been gleaned from *Lum and Abner* radio shows, that something fell shadowed the whole South. But try as the authorities might, the second body was never identified, and the case was never closed.

Which is precisely why Special Agent Michael Levine found himself in Split Tree, Arkansas, on a blister-hot August afternoon forty years later, specifically in the office of Locust County Sheriff Waymond Ray Elmore.

"Holy shit. Can it get any frigging hotter?" Levine said as he walked into the office. The comment was directed at his own discomfort more than at anyone in the room. A mumble as he plucked at the front of his light-blue cotton shirt, tugging it away from his moistening chest. Little rivulets of sweat were snaking down his skin and pooling at his belt line in the small of his back, making it hard to keep still. It was early in the day, but already the thermometer at the Farmer's Bank showed 102 degrees, and the humidity was well over 80 percent for the fifth straight day. The air had the sullen feel of an impending storm, but the skies were clear and the sun shone down unmolested. Levine had endured long, painful summers growing up in a two-story brick walk-up in Brooklyn; he'd humped the jungle in Southeast Asia with a forty-pound rucksack on his back as an eighteen-year-old ground-pounding infantry grunt, but this heat was different. It had a personality and a closed agenda. It had been bad enough in Memphis, where he had been transferred four long months ago, but the heat in this little east Arkansas toaster oven was physically assaulting. Its presence closed in around you and hugged you tight, sitting on your chest and catching your breath like some unforgettable shame.

"Excuse the language, Sheriff. Probably not the most appropriate introduction. Special Agent Michael Levine, Federal Bureau of Investigation," Levine said, flashing his tin as he settled into a modern plastic-and-fabric spring-backed of-

fice chair that looked as totally out of place in the old building as did the sheriff's modern wood-laminate desk. An un-
derstrength, asthmatic box air-conditioner rattled and clicked
in a nearby window and was managing to take some edge off
the heat—but only the edge.

"Understandable. Yeah, it's some kind of hot all right,"
said Sheriff Elmore as he watched his visitor take a seat. The
whole room had been renovated recently with a dropped
acoustic-tile ceiling and the contemporary palette of the
neooffice that seemed designed to erase the character from
historic buildings. Waymond Elmore hated it. Even more, he
hated the fact that his office had been one of the first to un-
dergo the facelift. "Would of thought y'all be used to this,
though. From Memphis, ain't that right?"

"Not by a long shot, Sheriff, just temporarily detailed to
the field office there." Levine reflexively distanced himself
from anything Dixie—not that he could be mistaken for a
local. He still hoped that his time in the South was a temporary unpleasantness, kind of like a summer cold that could be
cleared up in a short time if only you took proper care of yourself. That was the problem, however; Levine had made a career of not taking care of himself.

The agent surveyed the sheriff's office. The desk was relatively clean and indicated either a lack of work or a surplus
of efficiency. Levine's natural inclination when dealing with
what he viewed as red-faced molasses suckers like this one
was to assume utter incompetence, and therefore, the former.
In his short sojourn in southern culture, he had come to take
this as axiomatic. The walls were painted a thin chocolate-
milk brown—a color that he still called beige despite its current reclassification as taupe—and were as bare as the desk
except for a framed picture of grizzly wading into frothy
white water to snag a leaping salmon. Above the picture was
the word *Determination*; there was something written under it
as well, in dark blue script, but he lacked both the eyesight
and the interest to try to discern it. He had seen the same

picture in an advertisement in an airline magazine recently. There was a single, framed photograph of two small, tow-headed boys on the sheriff's desk—too young to be current unless they were grandchildren—next to a plastic twenty-ounce Dr Pepper bottle that contained a half-inch of something resembling diluted coffee grounds. From the lump visible under the sheriff's gum Levine surmised that it was what he grew up hearing his grandfather call snuff, but was now marketed as "smokeless tobacco."

"Just what is it I can do for y'all now, Agent . . . I'm sorry . . ."

"Levine."

"That's right, Levine . . . now, what can I do for y'all, Mr. Levine?" Despite his upbringing, Sheriff Elmore was in no mood to be cordial and was hardly even inclined to be polite to a man that smelled of big-city smug. He was ready to get this meeting over with, although, truth be told, he had virtually nothing to do for the remainder of the afternoon, but he had taken a visceral dislike to this federal yahoo at first glance—this tall man with his necktie and his sport coat and his lined face that was starting to flush a dull, mottled red. Elmore was anxious to set him on his way on principle alone, not to mention the unpleasant fact that the FBI agent had mentioned the Jackson/John Doe murder earlier on the telephone, and he certainly didn't welcome walking that dog no matter how long the leash.

Levine had to swallow hard to avoid a wave of nausea brought on by the heat and the smell of stale cigarette smoke and Elmore's old hair tonic. Since moving to Memphis he had spent more time eating and less time exercising, and now as he leaned forward in his seat the slight movement made him realize that his shirt collar was fitting too tightly. He felt like his eyes were bulging with each pulse. "Well, Sheriff, as I mentioned to you over the phone, the Bureau has decided to take a fresh look at the Leon Jackson/John Doe case . . . you're familiar with it, I'm sure."

"Yes, sir." The *sir* part was clearly said out of local custom and not deference. Elmore almost defied his upbringing and left it off. "Course I would be, just like anyone else around here my age. Don't say I remember much, though. Believe it happened the summer I graduated high school. It was news . . . at the time. But then you boys solved that one, as I recall. Klan related, so y'all said." He smiled as he spoke, but it was a look that conveyed no amusement.

Waymond Elmore's voice was high-pitched and sounded something like a car skidding on hot asphalt. It crackled and skipped with a nervous energy that belied his slow demeanor. He was a tall man, not a giant, but good-sized, with shoulders as wide as a yellow broom handle, and the muscles stood out on his body like knots on a branch of weathered driftwood. His once silty-brown crew-cut hair had long ago salted into a pale cement gray that matched his eyes, and deep furrows plowed by over fifty years of river basin sun etched his face. He'd been a handsome man at one time, but that time was over and now there was a profound weariness shadowing his looks, like a man who'd reached the end of his options and saw no content in his future.

"Well, that's not quite accurate," Levine corrected for the record, though he suspected that the sheriff was well aware that the case had never been closed. One of the worst aspects of his posting to Memphis was that he had to spend an inordinate amount of time with tin stars like this one. He absolutely hated having to dick-dance around with these backwater good ole boys, and in five minutes he had made this one out to be a colossal putz. "You're right that the Bureau established a circumstantial link between Jackson's murder—and that of the John Doe found with him—and the Ku Klux Klan, but no one was ever brought to trial." Levine tended to avoid using the pronoun *we* when he referred to the Bureau. He figured there was some degree of symmetry in the matter since he was absolutely positive that the Bureau avoided using *we* when they referred to him.

He continued, "In fact, as I mentioned earlier when we spoke on the phone, that's precisely why I'm here. As I'm sure you're aware, there's been a string of convictions recently in some of the unsolved cases from the sixties. Cherry and Blanton in the '63 Alabama church bombing, de la Beckwith for the Medgar Evers murder, and most recently the arrest and conviction in the Goodman, Cheney, Schwerner murders over in Mississippi. The Emmett Till killing has been reopened, and the Bureau believes that with some of the new forensic technology that's available, it may prove worthwhile to reopen the investigation into the Jackson case as well." Levine knew this was utter bullshit. Certainly new forensic techniques—notably DNA testing—were sometimes applicable in older cases like this, but that wasn't why he was here. The reality was that Levine had jammed up an influential senator from Pennsylvania on some insider trading and hadn't backed off when the Bureau told him to permanently file the evidence. Instead, a reporter for the *Philadelphia Inquirer* got an anonymous package filled with classified FBI case memoranda. The result was predictable: The senator announced that he had decided to spend more time with his family and would not stand for reelection, and Levine was detailed to Memphis to work on what he suspected was the Bureau's equivalent of a snipe hunt. He was a white-collar crime specialist—bank fraud, money laundering—with no training in murder investigations except for a few courses at the Academy, years ago. Given the right case, it was a matter of when he stepped on his dick, not if. In a forty-year-old unsolvable crime, the Bureau was baking up a payback pie. He'd even figured out the recipe: Send one asshole Levine to jerkwater Crackerland, run him around in useless circles until thoroughly mixed, bake his nuts at 110 degrees for six months, and serve with voluntary retirement papers.

"Very interestin', Agent . . . ?"

"It's Levine, same as it was two minutes ago, Sheriff. Special Agent Levine." He was really starting to work up a case of the ass for this guy. There was something about him that made Levine want to punch his lights out, though he couldn't articulate precisely what.

"That's right, that's right . . . seems to be a hard name for me to remember, Agent Levine. But tell me . . . Agent . . . Levine . . . that case over in Mississippi . . ."

"Goodman, Cheney, Schwerner."

"That's right. That one. In case you don't read the newspapers, that one was tried in state court. You Feds had your shot at that fella way back in the sixties and couldn't make it stick."

Levine took a deep breath. "You're correct, Sheriff. The point is, these old cases, like the Jackson case, are still prosecutable—no matter what jurisdiction officially takes it. But it seems that sometimes the . . . the local authorities need a push."

"And y'all here to push?"

Levine returned a humorless smile. "If need be."

Elmore nodded slowly, as if he were considering what Levine had said. "So what has any of this got to do with the Locust County sheriff's office? Course, we certainly would like to hep y'all in any way we can, but we have a pretty busy caseload of our own to tend to."

Yeah, Levine thought, *I'm sure you do, Sheriff, got to catch all those Colombian drug lords who are putting cherry bombs in Farmer Pudd's mailbox.*

So much for the get-to-know-you courtesy call. After only a few minutes Levine figured he knew this guy's type well enough, and Elmore's attitude was making him feel anything but courteous. That and the heat. Even with air-conditioning, the sheriff's office, which was on the southwest corner of the second floor of the old county courthouse building, was probably pushing eighty-five degrees—though Sheriff Waymond Elmore didn't seem to notice. As he'd been driving to the courthouse that morning, Levine had already decided that today might be a good day to get drunk, or strangle somebody, or both. In fact, he could have envisioned any number of things, but sitting in this sweatbox talking to this little uniformed redneck jerk had not made it onto the short list. Levine decided to start pulling this meeting to a close before he did something that the Bureau would try to make him apologize for later.

"Glad for the offer of . . . *hep*. Look, Sheriff, the Bureau has some jurisdictional involvement in certain aspects of the case, namely the civil rights angle, but the victims' bodies were found in Locust County, and I believe that makes this case yours, technically. Always has been. The reason I'm here is basically to take a fresh look at it. You know, review any new information your office has; talk to some residents in the area to see if there are any new leads; shake the tree and collect the nuts. I will tell you, however, that we have initiated DNA testing on some of the evidence found in 1965 and that avenue looks very promising." Levine hated forced civility, absolutely hated it, and this was as forced as it got.

Sheriff Elmore looked at the special agent with a silent derision he normally reserved for avowed evolutionists and female sports anchors. After a moment, he rocked his chair back and unscrewed the cap of the Dr Pepper bottle. Without breaking eye contact with Levine he put his lips to the bottle, dribbled a long rope of muddy brown saliva into it, and recapped it before speaking. "And just what sort of promisin' evidence might'n that be? This here evidence from 1965 that y'all are testin'."

Levine stared hard at Elmore's face, trying to read the concentric lines around his eyes as if they were tree rings. He'd mentioned that the murder had occurred the summer that he graduated from high school. *That would make him about my age, a year older probably,* Levine thought to himself—*midfifties, give or take a couple.* Of course that was assuming that the sheriff graduated in twelve years, which Levine was beginning to seriously doubt. Levine had finished high school a year after the murder occurred, Erasmus High class of 1966.

The year Sandy Koufax won twenty-seven games and hung up his spikes. The year the Supreme Court made Miranda a household name. The year before the U.S. Army awarded Levine a full-ride scholarship to the University of Reality in Phuc Me Long Province, South Vietnam.

"As you may recall, the second body—the John Doe—was found with some bloody clothing, and not much else. No identification materials, no wallet, no jewelry. The remains were too badly decomposed to identify back then. The Bureau retained samples of the shirt and pants for trace evidence analysis—there were some hairs found on the shirt at the time that were of interest to the folks in Trace. So far that hasn't panned out, but now the interest has shifted to the blood. All they could really say in 1965 was that it was A positive. Chances are that the blood is his—the John Doe's, that is—at least that's always been the assumption, but there's always a chance that it may be some sort of castoff from the perpetrator. The hope is that DNA testing may shed some new light on either the identity of the victim or the identity of the murderer. Either way . . ." He paused to give Sheriff Elmore time to respond or even show a spark of interest.

He did neither, so Levine continued. "And that's the other reason I'm here; since we had the clothing in our custody, we were able to initiate the testing on that. The body, however, or more accurately, what I've been told I can assume is probably a skeleton, is assumed to be here in Locust County—I presume still at your medical examiner's office." Levine thought he detected the slightest flicker behind Elmore's eyes. Quick, then gone. "I need to obtain some samples from the remains so the lab can compare the DNA from the clothing to them."

"Well now, Mr. . . . Levine," the sheriff said as he leaned forward, placing his elbows on this desk and interlacing his fingers on top of a large, outdated 2001 write-on desk calendar that read *"Bing Bros. New and Used Automobiles."* His chair creaked under his shifting weight. "In the first place, Locust County doesn't have a medical examiner. This here's a coroner state, and that's just what we have—a coroner—and in the second place, I can almost guarantee you that he doesn't have no bones left over from 1965."

Levine sat silently for a moment, until he was sure that Elmore had finished, and then he responded. "Sheriff, I'm sure you can appreciate that that information isn't exactly what the Bureau wants to hear. There is no statute of limitations on murder, and as I reminded you a few minutes ago, this is an open homicide—a rather high-profile homicide—and the expectation in an open homicide is that important evidence will be retained. Now, I suspect that you may simply be mistaken about the whereabouts of the remains." Levine knew virtually nothing about homicide investigations, and he was wondering if this small-town sheriff would know enough to call his bluff. "I'm sure your coroner is aware of this case. I guess he's the one I should really be talking to. I'm here as a professional courtesy only. I need to pay him a visit." Levine had no prior experience with small-town America coroners, but he'd been debriefed at the office not to expect too much. Unlike medical examiners, coroners usually were elected positions that did not require a medical degree, simply a voter's card and a felony-free record. In fact, the coroner system originated around the time of the Magna Carta and was more concerned then with tax collection than anything else. In the United States, coroners often were funeral directors who supplemented their income with a county paycheck.

"Knock yourself silly, Mr. Levine, but I'm tellin' you that you're wastin' your time down here in Locust County tryin' to sniff out anythin' on that old case. I truly am sorry that that Mr. Jackson fella came down here and got hisself killed and all, but that was almost forty years ago. Don't serve no purpose to be whackin' that hornet's nest—don't matter what kind of new scientific stick y'all got to do it with. And it don't matter what exactly the Bureau wants to hear." Sheriff Elmore focused on Levine's eyes and didn't blink. His look took on a sharpness that was almost feral in its hardness. "My advice is to let dead men rest in peace, Mr. FBI Special Agent, just let them sleep."

"And killers? Mr. Locust County Sheriff." Levine hadn't given a real damn about this case ten minutes ago, but that was beginning to change. He rose from his chair faster than he intended. His head swam with the movement and the heat, and he was forced to steady himself by leaning on the edge of the sheriff's desk. The effect was primal. "Do we let killers sleep?"

The sheriff looked down at his fingers momentarily and then brought his eyes up again to meet Levine's. The contempt that had blazed from Waymond Elmore's face throughout the meeting had burned out and been replaced by something else. Something that Levine couldn't get a quick handle on. "What makes you think a killer can ever sleep, Mr. Levine?"

CHAPTER 2

U.S. Army Central Identification Laboratory, Hawaii
FRIDAY, AUGUST 12, 2005

"D.S., how about you callin' a staff meeting in about five minutes or so . . . it'll be a short one," Robert Dean McKelvey didn't slow his pace, but rather called out over his shoulder as he walked by the deputy laboratory director's office. It was Friday morning, but already the day was shaping up to be nothing but a sack of serious headaches. It had started almost immediately. The commander had greeted him at the front door with the news that the secretary of defense was thinking about paying the Lab a visit next week. His plane was scheduled to refuel in Hawaii on his way back to Washington from a visit to China, and his aides thought he could make use of the downtime by visiting the Lab. McKelvey knew that visits like that always added up to nothing short of a painful waste of time and patience. The perfect start to his first day back at work.

Most people at the Lab called him *Kel*. Actually, he had been called Kel pretty much his whole life, at least by those on familiar terms, and even some that weren't. Robert had been his father's given name and his grandfather's before that, and while his parents gave it to their youngest son for sentimental reasons, the family also had intentionally shied away from using it with reference to him to avoid the inevitable confusion that would follow. There would be no *Big Bob* and *Little Bob* for the McKelveys. The problem, of course, was that it didn't leave many options when you needed to call him for dinner. His middle name, Dean, wasn't at all a serious contender for casual use.

It was an unrealized childhood aspiration hung on him by his three older brothers almost fifty years earlier. They had lived and breathed St. Louis Cardinal baseball at that point in their lives and wanted the newest addition to the family to grow up like one of the famous Arkansas Dean brothers. The sobering reality was that if his parents had not intervened to the extent that they had, he'd have been named Robert *Dizzy* McKelvey for sure—or even worse, *Daffy*. Kel always reckoned that by comparison to those two very real possibilities, Dean wasn't so bad—so long as no one used it, which no one did. But the basic problem remained: Ex-out Robert and Dean from the usable list of names and that didn't leave much by way of an option except Mac—which everyone hated. In the end, he was called Kel. Had been for as long as he could remember.

"Jesus F. Christ, we need a visit from the SecDef like I need someone to piss in my left ear," Kel muttered to himself as he unlocked his office door and stepped square into a pile of memos and brown case-file folders that people had been feeding under his door while he'd been gone. A few skated out from under his foot. It was like stepping into a puddle of slippery brown mud. Kel had just flown in from spending a week in the communist time warp of North Korea, and thanks to the combined magic of jet travel and the International Date Line he had managed to arrive thirty minutes before he'd taken off. As if five workdays in a week were not sufficient, he now had the opportunity for an encore performance. Not only that, but days at the CILHI must be measured in dog years, he often thought; one week gone somehow added up to seven weeks of accumulated work. Certainly there appeared to be at least seven-weeks' worth of folders piled on his floor.

And now the secretary of defense.

Nothing personal against the SecDef, he had seemed to be a nice enough guy the few times Kel had met him, but VIP visits to the CILHI were like putting your tongue in an electric pencil sharpener—a novel enough experience the first time around, but not something that needed frequent repeating. And lately they were repeating much too frequently. Besides, Kel knew that the chances were quite high that the only productive thing to come out of this visit would be the first sergeant getting all the cigarette butts policed up out of the parking lot—which was not a bad thing—but more often than not, visits of this level began with the commander having everyone jumping through flaming hoops of shit, and then ended, at the last possible moment, with the entire visit being canceled.

Kel stood looking at the folders scattered underfoot. In one shining epiphany it occurred to him to simply close the door, go home, and never return. Then it passed, and he knelt and began scooping the pile into his arms. That's when Davis Smart poked his head in.

"Everyone's ready and waiting in the conference room," D.S. reported as he glanced at the accumulated paperwork. He smiled. "I promised everyone you'd keep it short. Told 'em you had lots of work to do."

Kel looked up at his deputy. His eyes were much too bright for any workday morning, Kel decided, especially if you were starting your second one in the last twenty-two hours, and he couldn't help but notice the *it-sure-is-crap-to-be-you* tone that edged itself into his voice.

"Can you believe all these files?" Kel asked.

"Wait till you open your e-mails—I was out sick for two days and I had over five hundred waiting for me when I got back. I'll bet you have a thousand, fifteen hundred, easy."

"Great," Kel said, standing up. He was normally taller than D.S. by a couple of inches, but he was still kinked up from the long airplane flight, and they were now leveled almost eye to eye. "That's what I need, and, oh, by the way, are you ready for some really good news? The commander snagged me on the way in. It seems that the SecDef has decided that the CILHI is an absolute must-see. This comin' Friday's what I'm told. We continue to be the hottest tourist attraction on the island."

"Yeah. But look on the bright side, at least we'll get all the cigarette butts picked up." D.S. smiled. "C'mon. Staff's ready."

CHAPTER 3

Quang Nam Province, Republic of Vietnam
Wednesday, 12 October 1966

First Lieutenant Dwayne Crockett found it hard to get his bearings. His head was swimming, and the overpowering smell of kerosene and scorched earth stung the lining of his nose and made him salivate as if he were going to vomit. Everything had changed, and he hadn't counted on that. He closed his eyes and he could see it; the image was seared into his brain, and he knew he would never forget a single detail. Not a single, life-rending detail.

But now everything was changed.

The napalm strike that had killed Jimmie Carl Trimble— the napalm strike that Dwayne Crockett had called in on his medic's head—had accomplished its purpose of buying enough time and space for him to extract his remaining men. Successive flights of Air Force F-l05 Thunderchiefs and Marine Corps Corsairs had then thoroughly relandscaped the area into the oily, blackened moonscape that Dwayne now surveyed.

Everything's changed.

He'd lost seven men, including his medic and friend; there were another five injured. And those were just his men. Two other platoons had been hit a couple of klicks away. All totaled up, Operation Snap-Dragon, as some chair-warmer at Headquarters had named the mission, had spent the lives of thirty-one Marines and one navy corpsman—Dwayne Crockett's navy corpsman. Predictably, the SITREP, the daily situation

reports sent out by headquarters, established for the record—
lest the facts somehow confuse the matter later—that the operation had been an overwhelming tactical and strategic success.
The enemy had been sorely hurt; set back months, if not longer;
its will broken. Perhaps that was all true. All Dwayne knew was
that he and his men had successfully had their asses handed to
them in a shiny paint can, and he had the ghosts of seven dead
men to hang around his neck for the rest of his life.

Initially the commander hadn't wanted Dwayne to lead the
recovery mission for the bodies. He was too junior and too
personally involved, the Old Man had said, but that was before Dwayne had insisted almost to the point of physical in-
subordination, and now he was here—on the surface of
friggin' Mars trying to piece together his bearings. He'd
wanted to come back immediately. So had most of his men.
Gear up and get back. Same day. Instead, they were told to
wait. They waited. And waited. It had taken six days for the
area to cool off—figuratively if not literally—during which
time Dwayne had slept very little. He'd lost men before—too
many in his short commission—but never like this. Never had
he so plainly anted-up another man's chips to save his own
life. Everyone said that he did what was right; everyone said
he'd done what he had to do; everyone said that he'd saved
the lives of his men. He was even up for a medal. But he
would always wonder.

Had he done it to save them?

Had he done it to save himself?

For six long days the radio conversation replayed itself
over and over and over in his brain. He heard it waking and
sleeping. *"Make the call, Lieutenant . . . Semper Fi . . . No
forgiving necessary, Bubba . . ."* Over and over and over. And
then that last cryptic—what was it? He had barely been able
to hear it over the searing rip of the incoming jets. Had it been
a request? A plea? What was it? *"Call me . . ."* Jimmie Carl
had asked him, and then nothing but static and a wall of heat
and the greasy smell of kerosene.

Call you what? Jimmie Carl, call you what?

That had been six endless days ago. Now they were back, and in force this time. They'd come back with a purpose and a will that had been lacking before. Dwayne's small recovery team was phalanxed by two reinforced Marine infantry companies and enough air support circling overhead to level the eastern Tennessee foothills of his youth.

Predictably, the first five bodies had been located relatively quickly. They were in the open, and in the heat and humidity they had started going fast. Decomp was in an advanced stage for only six days; yellow-brown bones with soft, unrecognizable lumps and masses of wet tissue. And maggots. Everywhere. Millions of them. The bodies were found near the small grassy clearing near where the Vietnamese had first struck Dwayne's men less than a week ago. The majority of the shitstorm unleashed by the Thuds and Corsairs had been almost half a klick to the south and southwest. Some ordnance—mostly antipersonnel bombies—had scattered its way here, and a couple of the bodies were partially fragmented. There were some Viet bodies here as well, but from the looks of the injuries they probably had been killed by Dwayne's men and not by the metal rain unleashed from above.

It was farther to the south that Dwayne was having a difficult time getting his landmarks. Jimmie Carl had taken cover in a small bomb crater near a cluster of trees and elephant grass. But where were the trees? They were all gone to splinters, and the whole friggin' field was nothing but craters now.

One huge, blackened sea of bomb craters for a hundred meters in every direction.

Everything had changed.

It took the better part of three hours to locate the spot, during which time the men of Dwayne's protective umbrella grew increasingly anxious. The talk grew louder and more rapid-paced as adrenaline levels increased beyond the level of fighting efficiency. Few men relish the idea of dying to recover the already dead, even never-leave-a-buddy-behind Marines, and every minute spent on this moonscape was another roll of the dice, in their eyes. Steadily the talk grew louder and more pointed, but Dwayne didn't want to hear it. He had already decided to shoot the first sonofabitch who tried to pull the plug on this mission—regardless of their rank. He'd abandoned Jimmie Carl Trimble once; he wouldn't do it again.

As it turned out, it was a young Hispanic lance corporal who first spotted the body. He had followed the sound of an electric buzz, almost like that given off by an old neon light about to flame out, and it turned out to be an enormous swarm of flies.

His other senses took over from there.

When Dwayne reached the crater, it took him several moments to realize that what he saw the men working with was a human body and not one of the many burned tree trunks that had been tossed like wheat straw so randomly about the clearing. Jimmie Carl Trimble's lower body, the legs and hips, were gone. Never to be found. His upper body, the head and torso, was charred and weeping a clear yellow fluid, and the muscles in his arms had contracted in the heat so that his arms were pulled up in front like a dog begging for table scraps. But it was a body. Once your brain patterned the features it was unmistakable. And it was Jimmie Carl's body—Dwayne didn't have to bend over and examine the blackened dog tag visible amid the burned chest wall. It was Jimmie Carl's body—the pair of surgical forceps fused to the left breast tissue, right where Jimmie Carl carried them in his left pocket, told him what he needed to know.

Dwayne Crockett turned away as two of his men used their rifle butts to roll and tip the remains into a green body bag.

"Call you what? Jimmie Carl, call you what?"

CHAPTER 4

"You be Mr. Levine?"

Special Agent Levine had been so royally pissed off when he left Sheriff Elmore's office that he could have taken a bite out of an anvil and crapped nails for a week. That, combined with the absolutely brain-melting heat, had conspired to make him feel like he'd been spun around very quickly in circles and snapped on the back of the head with a wet towel. He had purchased a can of Pepsi Cola from the overweight blind vendor who ran a gum-and-cough-drop store in the corner of the courthouse's main lobby and was taking a seat at a small, unstable, cranberry-colored Formica table when the young deputy sheriff approached him.

"I'm Special Agent Levine, Federal Bureau of Investigation, and what can I do for you, Deputy?" Levine kept his eyes focused on the beads of sweat forming on his can of Pepsi and readied himself for what appeared to be the start of Round Two. "Can I assume Sheriff Elmore sent you to find me? And what might be on his game plan? Going to try and give me a body cavity search?"

The pie-faced deputy eyed Levine with that proprietary blend of awe and disdain that small-town cops reserve for federal agents. He tried tilting his head sideways in hopes that a change of perspective would enhance his understanding. It didn't. "No sir, can't rightly say I'm into that sort of thing—but then I'm just a small-town sheriff's deputy."

Levine looked up at the deputy for the first time. He was a young, chubby kid, with short cotton-blond hair and deep blue eyes the color of roadside chicory. His face was shiny and moist, but not sweaty, just moist. He was average height, maybe a shade smaller, and he adequately filled out a tan uniform shirt similar to the one that Sheriff Elmore had been wearing. His name badge read BEVINS, and aside from a six-pointed star over the left pocket, an American flag on one sleeve, and an embroidered Locust County sheriff's patch on the other, his uniform was relatively plain and stood in sharp contrast to his glossy black leather gun belt, from which hung a vast array of all of the latest crime-fighting accessories that the county budget could handle.

"Sorry. Mike Levine, FBI," he extended his hand and flashed the first smile he'd allowed himself since he'd arrived in Split Tree. "Can I buy you a soda?" He nodded his head at the Pepsi can in his left hand.

"Y'all make it a Coke Cola and you got yourself a deal," the deputy said enthusiastically as he pumped Levine's hand twice and drew up an adjacent chair. As he leaned forward, the small table canted in his direction. "Jim Bevins, glad to make y'all's acquaintance. Just about everyone here calls me Jimbo, no reason for you to be the exception now."

"Don't be so sure . . . about being glad to meet me, that is." Levine raised his arm and made a motion, the way you would in a city restaurant—but not the way you would to a blind vendor in Split Tree, Arkansas. He immediately realized that that was going to be about as productive as talking to the sheriff had been and pulled his arm in, hoping that no one else had seen him.

"Don't think that's goin' get you too far there, Mr. Levine." Jimbo Bevins smiled and stretched the syllables of Levine's name out to an astonishing length. "Larry Lee there don't see so good, no more. I'll get this here one, and you can owe me another one later on," he said as he got up and went to the counter. When he returned he again cocked his head to one side and looked at the FBI agent as if his facial features weren't arranged in the same order they had been before he got up.

Levine took a long drag of his rapidly warming Pepsi, swallowed hard, rocked his chair back onto two legs, and returned the inquisitive stare. Finally he spoke. "So, tell me, Deputy Bevins, who'd you go and piss off to get assigned as my keeper? You are my keeper, aren't you, Jimbo?"

"Well, sir, let's just say that the sheriff thinks you might could use some assistance, not bein' from around here and all."

"That's right, I'm definitely not from around here. So, you're to be my assistant?"

"Yes, sir." Jimbo took a slug of his Coke and set his can down with a determined clank. The table shifted its direction again. "Yessir, I am."

Levine smiled a second time before responding. "And what if I was to tell you that I don't need an assistant? It's sort of like what the army used to tell me in Vietnam, if the Bureau had thought I needed an assistant they'd have issued me one. And since they didn't—I can only guess I don't."

Jimbo knit his forehead as if this was really a question that required some measured thought. Then he returned the smile as he answered. "Well, as I see it, the sheriff ain't your Bureau, he's the sheriff, and he's pretty sure you're gonna."

"I'm sure he is." They'd been alternating drinks and now it was Levine's turn to take a swallow. As he did so, several beads of sweat dripped off his can and spotted his tie. He brushed at them with his free hand, turning them into dark smears. He took a deep breath and held it momentarily before exhaling. "All right, Deputy Jimbo Bevins, we'll play this game for a while." He stood and retucked the parts of his shirttail that were working their way out of his khakis, then he tugged the lapels of his blazer, straightening the shoulders. "First order of business, Mr. Assistant, I want to talk to the local medical examiner—I believe you'd call him the county coroner. You know where I can find him?"

"Sure." Jimbo grinned. "He's my cousin."

"Then let's roll, Kato."

CHAPTER 5

U.S. Army Central Identification Laboratory, Hawaii
FRIDAY, AUGUST 12, 2005

"Well, I guess this really will be a short one," Kel said as he stepped into the wood-paneled conference room adjoining the Lab's library. It was large enough to seat forty but was now almost empty. Counting himself and D.S. there were only seven people available to attend the hurriedly called staff meeting: two dentists and three other anthropologists, including a stranger that he assumed was one of the Lab's new interns who had been scheduled to arrive while he was in North Korea—James somebody or other. *God, he looks like a kid,* Kel thought.

Kel knew he shouldn't have been surprised by all the empty chairs in the room. After all, he had just returned from visiting six of the Lab's recovery teams in North Korea, each one headed by one of his anthropologists; added to that were another five finishing-up sites in Vietnam, four cutting their way through the jungles of southern Laos, two responding to a terrorist bombing in the Philippines that had taken out a nightclub full of tourists, one team somewhere in eastern Europe looking for a long-lost World War II crash site, and a couple more humping buckets of sand around on some God-forsaken coral atolls in the Pacific. That made twenty, and of course there was always one or two on leave, at a conference, sick, or otherwise occupied; still, the U.S. Army Central Identification Laboratory, Hawaii, was the largest forensic skeletal identification laboratory in the world, with over thirty forensic anthropologists, three forensic dentists, and eighteen search-and-recovery teams. With over two hundred personnel, it never ceased to amaze him when there wasn't enough scientific staff around for a pickup game of basketball.

The CILHI is unique within the Department of Defense—for that matter unique in the world. It is the only forensic laboratory with jurisdiction to recover and identify missing and unaccounted-for U.S. war dead. It has worked cases as varied as the Vietnam Unknown Soldier and the sailors of the Civil War ironclad the USS *Monitor*. And then there were the humanitarian missions and emergency responses like those following the 9/11 attack on the Pentagon and the Christmas tsunami of 2004. With its current staffing, the laboratory was identifying almost two men a week—an impressive statistic until the numbers were placed into perspective: There are almost 5,000 men still missing from World War I; 78,000 from World War II; 8,100 from the Korean War; 120 from the Cold War; and 1,800 from the Vietnam War.

"All right," Kel began, taking in each face. Like D.S., they all somehow managed to look fresher than they should at the end of a long week. "I just got in an hour ago, and I freely admit that I don't have a clue as to what's goin' on." Someone started to snicker. "I know, I know, what's new, right?—so I won't keep y'all here long. Just wantin' to touch base; see what's up. In fact, I intend to be headin' home about noon—if I don't fall asleep sooner—so if you have anythin' you need to talk about or need me to sign, see me before then, otherwise have D.S. take care of it or hold it until Monday. Okay? Ahhh . . . let's see, no big news from the field, except that the guys in the Workers' Paradise of North Korea are having a wonderful time and wish each and every one of y'all were there in place of them. Startin' to get cold there already, at least at night. Otherwise nothin' from my trip that can't wait till Monday's regular staff meetin'. But here's the news du jour—in case y'all haven't heard—the SecDef may come pay us a visit next Friday."

Kel waited for the staff to register its predictable opinion with a harmonious groan before continuing. "Now, now, my feelin's exactly, but let's not get too spun up quite yet. I suspect it may still fall through, but just in case, it'd probably be a good idea to start pickin' up the Lab a little, empty the wastebaskets, clean the coffee cups, make sure Paul doesn't wear one of his god-awful Hawaiian shirts. Let's not wait until next Thursday afternoon to get started. I'll let you know the details as I get them, but wanted to give y'all at least a heads-up." He looked around the conference table. "Other than that, I'm tapped out for today . . . Anythin', Dr. Smart?" Kel pointed to D.S.

"Yeah," D.S. answered. "Ahhh . . . what I've got can wait till Monday if you'd rather, but I got a quick update on a case you were interested in before you left." He paused as he shuffled through some notes on his lap, "It's REFNO 145-66." The REFNO, or reference number, indicated a Vietnam War loss. It was a numbering system established during the war to track men who went missing in action. "Wanna wait till Monday or not?"

"Go ahead."

"Well, you'll remember this one. Two guys involved— Evans and Trimble—ground loss in Quang Nam Province, up by the DMZ. Fairly early on in the war; 1966. Marine private and a navy medic . . . make that navy corpsman . . . anyhow, Trimble's remains—he was the corpsman—were recovered fairly soon after the incident and identified by dental records. Evans, however, was never found. He's still carried on the books as unaccounted for."

"Trimble got the Navy Cross, right? Am I rememberin' the right case?"

"That's the one. Real Audie Murphy stuff, by all accounts. We surveyed the loss location in '96 and again in late '99 with no luck. Finally got some good witness information in the form of two Vietnamese who were involved in the fight—on the other side, of course."

"All the better to know what happened."

"Exactly. Anyhow, these two showed us an area that we excavated late last year. Very disturbed site—lots of bomb craters. Had to dig up half the province, but we recovered some fragmented skeletal remains and some material evidence—boot sole, couple of fatigue buttons and, most important, an identification tag for Evans."

"That's good."

"That's very good; it tells us we were in the right spot, at least. So much for the good news. On the flip side, most of the bone is pretty badly burned, but four fragments were in good enough shape for DNA testing, so we sampled them last April."

"I remember," Kel responded. He leaned back in his chair and closed his eyes, rubbing the jet lag from his eyelids with his thumb and forefinger. He still had his eyes closed as he continued. "What's the update? We get the results back?"

"Sort of," D.S. answered. "Like I said, good news, bad news type of thing. We got results, but unfortunately we didn't get the results we were hoping for. Two of the samples were inconclusive—and the other two," he shrugged his eyebrows at the same time as he shrugged his shoulders, "don't match the family reference sample for Evans."

"That figures. Evans is the only guy unaccounted for from the area?"

"Yep. And it ain't him—despite the dog tag."

"How about Trimble? You say his body was recovered and identified at the time, right? And that was when—1966? Question I'd ask is: Was he recovered intact? Maybe some fragments of him were left on the battlefield—any chance that what we recovered is just additional parts that they didn't find durin' the war?"

D.S. puffed his cheeks and blew them out. He cleared his throat. "We thought the same thing, so we pulled the Tan Son Nhut file for him. From what I can tell, yes, he was missing some body parts when they recovered him in 1966, all lower body—so the leg fragments that we recovered could be him."

During the Vietnam War, the U.S. Army ran two large identification mortuaries in-country, one at the big airbase at Tan Son Nhut on the outskirts of Saigon and a smaller one at Da Nang. The CILHI had the complete wartime file for each of the fifty-thousand-plus American servicemen identified through the two mortuaries including body diagrams that showed what was present and what wasn't.

"I sense a *but* . . ."

"The *but* is the biological profile. From the fragments we recovered, we could get a rough stature estimate. It's acceptable—within two inches of both guys—it's the age estimate that's a little bit of a problem, though. The epiphyseal caps are unfused on the femur and the tibial fragment, so it's a young guy, under twenty—that matches Evans okay—he was like nineteen or so—but it's a bit young for Trimble, who was midtwenties. But, then again, the remains aren't in the best of shape, so . . ."

Kel drummed his fingers on the conference table while he thought. "So you're sayin' that while it could be additional parts of Trimble, it's not very likely. Okay, so where does that leave us now?"

"That's the question, isn't it?"

"Yeah, that's the question, and here's my suggestion. Correct me if I'm wrong, but we should have requested a family DNA sample for both Evans and Trimble, right? Or am I wrong? We would have wanted a blood sample from the Evans family to compare to what we thought were goin' to be his remains, and we should have requested one from the Trimble family for exclusionary purposes, right? Check on it. If we requested a blood sample from the Trimble family, then have the DNA lab compare it to the remains. Shouldn't take too long if the samples are already in. We'll see how it shakes out. We know it's not Evans, so either it's more of Trimble or we got us a real puzzle on our hands."

"Ahhh."

"What?"

"Nothing. Never mind, we can talk later."

"What?"

"Nothing . . . it can wait for Monday." D.S. waved Kel off.

Kel verified with a look that D.S. had nothing else to add, and then he continued around the table, nodding to each staff member in turn and asking if they had anything that needed to be discussed. They all indicated that they had no information for the group, but most needed to see him after the meeting for one thing or another. The last one to answer was the new guy—*James? John?*

"And I'm guessin' you're . . ." Kel stalled for time by drawing out the last word as he half-rose from his chair and leaned over the table, extending his hand to the newest member of his staff. The stalling paid off.

"Matt Hardy, glad to meet you, Dr. McKelvey," the new kid replied quickly.

Matt? So it wasn't James or John, but he really was a kid, nonetheless. Kel guessed he couldn't be much over twenty-seven or twenty-eight. They seemed to get younger with every hire—a fact that lately only augmented Kel's growing sense of professional burnout.

"It's Kel. We try to not use *Doctor* very much around here. Don't know about the others, but it makes me feel like I should be takin' out your appendix or somethin'. Anyhow, welcome. All settled? Let's talk for a few minutes after this."

The young staffer nodded and smiled.

Kel sat back down and surveyed the staff again. "That about it? Anybody got any alibis or saved rounds?" He caught himself using the military slang for last-minute comments at staff meetings.

"Yeah," said D.S., trying to restrain a smile. "Matt, tell Kel here how old you are."

Matthew Hardy looked at D.S. and then at Kel. "Twenty-four," he replied.

"Oh goddamn," Kel muttered.

CHAPTER 6

Split Tree, Arkansas
FRIDAY, AUGUST 12, 2005

"So, tell me, Deputy, I assume you know why I'm visiting this happy little shit pile of rural America? I'm sure the good sheriff must have filled you in on the animals before making you zookeeper-for-the-day," Levine asked as he settled into the passenger seat of the Locust County Sheriff's Department cruiser and fastened his seat belt. He was careful not to touch the brown vinyl trim that skirted the seat any more than was necessary, for fear of searing any exposed skin.

Jimbo Bevins squinted at Levine. He was still having trouble understanding him. "Don't know if you're shinin' me on, Mr. Levine, or if you're just tryin' to be a dick, but if we got to spend this here time together, we might as well stop kickin' each other in the shins. Fair?"

"Fair enough." Levine expended some effort in biting back any other comment and extended his hand as an offering of truce, but Jimbo Bevins simply cranked the ignition and the green-and-white Monte Carlo came alive. The air-conditioner exploded on as if startled from a deep sleep and blasted Levine with warm air. So warm that it was hard to take a breath and it made him blink hard in reflex.

Jimbo muttered something.

"What was that?" Levine asked. He couldn't have sworn to it, but it sounded like *Jew* to him.

"Didn't say nothin'."

"You sure about that?"

"Quite sure, Mr. Levine. But to answer your first question, no sir, I don't know the nature of your business down here in Locust County." Jimbo looked out the back window as he reversed out of the courthouse parking lot. The car was still coasting backward when he flipped the transmission lever into drive. With a jerk they soon were headed west on Tupelo, one of the town's two major streets. "But I 'spect that y'all be a'tellin' me soon enough."

Main and Tupelo crossed at the courthouse. Main Street ran north to south and connected up to County Road 1, which angled up to Helena and West Helena; Tupelo ran east to west. Old-timers still called it Old Gin Road because it would take you to the Bell Brothers gin, if you followed it out west far enough. In fact, as you drove west out of town you began encountering more and more stray wisps of cotton lint blowing across the road—locals could gauge their proximity to the gin by the density of cotton waste clinging to the weeds lining the shoulder.

There had once been a time when you could stand at the southwest corner of the town square and look to the horizon in any direction, assuming you had nothing better to do—which in fact, most people around town didn't. A few buildings erected since the *Late Unpleasantness* of the Civil War had defied local convention and towered to a cloud-scratching three stories, and that partially obstructed the panoramic view, but they were limited in number and effect.

"Deputy Bevins, you remember the Leon Jackson murder in 1965?" Levine finally picked up the thread of their conversation after a minute or two of quiet driving.

Jimbo hesitated only long enough to blink hard as an aid to recollection. "Black fella. Came lookin' for trouble and found it. Got hisself killed and buried in the second levee out by the Rumsey property south of town. Seems like they was a white boy found with him—don't think they ever did figure out who he was, though. He weren't from around here, I know that."

"You're right, he wasn't . . . identified, that is," Levine

replied, taking note of the *Got hisself killed* comment. "Although the Klan was implicated in it, no indictments were ever handed down, no arrests, no convictions—no real suspects, even. That was 1965. Now, here we are forty years later, and the Bureau has decided to take another look at the case and see what shakes free after all these years."

Jimbo smiled and squinted one eye as he looked at the man next to him. His eyes were off the road for a long time and it took Levine a moment to realize that the road, being as straight as a twelve-gauge shotgun barrel, didn't need a great deal of attention. "You believe that, Mr. Levine, or are y'all shinin' me on again?"

"I'm not tracking here, Deputy, do I believe what?" He could see his own face reflected in the green teardrop-shaped lenses of Jimbo's glasses, and he found it unsettling. He wondered if his inexperience with homicide cases was as obvious as he sensed it was. Stenciled on his forehead for all to see.

"That there Klan bullshit. Y'all don't really think the Klan was responsible, do you?"

The FBI agent now shifted in his seat so that he was more directly facing the deputy; if Jimbo wasn't going to look at the road, neither would he.

"Shit," Jimbo continued. Most of the words that came out of his mouth seemed to have a surplus of syllables, or at least required an uncommonly long time to get them completely sounded out. Cuss words were no exception. "Your people see boogie men everywhere."

"My people? You mind telling me who *my people* are?"

Jimbo finally bounced a quick glance off the road, verified that he needed no midcourse correction, and returned his attention to the museum curiosity sitting next to him. "Wouldn't think I'd have to."

"Maybe you do."

Jimbo smiled. "Big city." He checked the road again. "That's what I meant. This here's east, now-don't-you-go-botherin'-me-and-I-won't-be-botherin'-you Arkansas, Mr.

Levine. Y'all got to go clean acrosst the river to find yourself a real Klansman in these parts."

"I'm not sure I'm hearing you correctly, Deputy Bevins, you're telling me that there's no Klan activity in this area? None?" Deputy Bevins wasn't far off the mark. Like most northeasterners, Michael Levine religiously believed everyone living south of the Ohio River had a spare bed sheet or two that they reserved for midnight recreational wear.

"Not like y'all mean, no sir."

"And how do I mean, Deputy?"

"Shootin's, lynchin's, crosst-burnin's, whatever you're a-thinkin' in that brain of yours. Not here. No, sir. We don't take to that here. Don't think we ever really did neither . . . not to speak of, no, sir. Some of the old-timers were John Birchers, for sure . . ."

"But there is Klan activity in the area? Or was at one time . . . in the 1960s at least . . . you aren't denying that?"

"I'm not denyin' nothin'. All I'm sayin' is that guys sometimes get together to drink beer, tell about the fish and women that got away from 'em, argue about SEC or Devil football. Call it what y'all will. The guys that do that 'round here are too lazy to get into any real trouble. That's a fact, for sure."

Now it was Levine's turn to study his companion's face. "You make them sound like a civics club . . . kind of like the Rotarians."

"Well . . . kind of like a gentleman's club, exactly," Jimbo replied, seemingly oblivious to the irony wickered in Levine's voice. Now he turned to face the federal agent as he slipped the cruiser into park and killed the engine. It took Levine a second to realize that they had stopped. He looked out the window to see what appeared to be a recently constructed red-brick and white-clapboard house with a sign in the front yard that read *Pacific Funeral Home*. "We're here, Mr. Levine," Jimbo said.

The wall of heavy, wet heat that met Levine when he opened his car door caused his lungs to catch. He forced a breath. He couldn't fathom how anyone could live and function in such an environment.

Jimbo noticed Levine reading the sign in front of the house. "Kind of a hoot, ain't it?" Jimbo stated more than asked. He was seating his hard, waxed-cane cowboy hat onto his head by working it back and forth. It made his ears look particularly enormous.

"What is, Deputy?"

"That there sign," he indicated with a small jerk of his head. "Here we are, about—what? I dunno—maybe like ten thousand miles from the ocean, and they go and name it *Pacific*." He smiled broadly. "*Pacific*, Donnie just hates it."

"It means peaceful." Levine closed the door. He instantly regretted saying anything that would prompt unneeded small talk, and he closed his eyes hoping to reel his comment back in before there was a bite.

"Yeah, maybe, but we're still a long way from the ocean."

"Sure are, Deputy, sure are. So, who's this Donnie character?" Levine wanted to change the subject as much as anything else. The lawn was green and obviously well-watered, and some bright, late-summer yellow dandelions were equally distributed amid the grass. Crepe myrtle bushes stood sentry beside the walkway, their color mostly gone but still looking healthy despite the heat.

"My cousin, Donnie Hawk, the coroner. He owns this here place."

Levine wasn't surprised that the coroner was an undertaker. He'd almost expected as much, but for some reason that he couldn't figure, he hadn't expected to come to a funeral home to do business. "Why's he call it that if he hates it?"

"*Pacific?* Some dang company policy; Donnie says they pulled it out of their corporate ass, don't you know? It was Hawk Mortuary and Funeral Home all while I was growin' up. Hell, been that since old Granddaddy Hawk started the business almost a hundred years ago. But 'bout two years ago, Donnie Junior—he owns it now that his daddy's done gone—

he went and sold part of the business to some big undertakin'
franchise down in Texas. He said it seemed like a good idea
at the time. Good marketin', he said. Not sure he still feels
thataway no more. Anyhow, they's the ones that renamed it."
Jimbo smiled broadly again, obviously enjoying his cousin's
frustration. "And Donnie just hates it."

They mounted the front steps two at a time. The front
porch, though new, was designed to be Old South. It wrapped
around the front and two sides forming a gallery, and there
were three spindle-backed rocking chairs patiently waiting for
either company or a breeze to give them movement. The
tongue-and-groove decking was hard and firm and painted a
shiny battleship gray, and there was sand mixed in the paint
by the steps and front door to keep it from getting slick in the
winter.

A heavyset, jowly man opened the door for them. His complexion was red with splotches of off-white folded in un-
evenly, and his skin glistened. He probably was only about
fifty years old but appeared to be working as fast as he could
on sixty. Dark-framed glasses magnified his brown eyes to
twice their size, and the part in his hair had migrated south
over the years. It now abutted his right ear and could go no
farther. The hair that still showed up for work was grown long
and was applied to his crown in a swirling fashion that made
him resemble a sticky cinnamon roll. He was wearing a pair
of Sansabelt chocolate-colored pants that were of a glossy sort
of fabric that Levine didn't recognize, and a half-sleeved
white shirt. His dark-wine-colored tie was far too wide for the
part of the country where Levine was from.

"Hey there, Big Jimbo," the man's tone was loud and
cheerful and the complete opposite of that of every funeral director Levine had ever encountered back east. His voice betrayed a lifetime of exposure to cigarette smoke and volatile
chemicals. "Long time . . . now, how long's it been, again?"

"Hmmm," Jimbo made a dramatic show of pondering this
query, pulling off his sunglasses and going squinty eyed for

the purpose. "Hmmm, now I think that would be . . . hmmm . . . that'd be last Friday night."

"Boy-oh-boy," the jowly man said. "Time sure flies for the wicked, and you're a wicked one, that you are, Jimbo. Mercy me."

Both men good naturedly punched and shadow-jabbed each other's arms like they were in high-school gym class and the coach was out sick. It continued until Jimbo's eyes flashed and he struck his cousin on the shoulder so hard that it made a popping sound. The fat little man winced, rubbed his shoulder, and distanced himself from the deputy before turning his attention to Levine.

"Donnie Hawk, Junior." The fat man shot a hand in Levine's direction, causing the FBI agent to flinch in anticipation of being punched in the arm. "Now, what can I hep you with today?"

Hawk's hand looked like it had been inflated with a bicycle pump, but it was soft and pliable. "I'm Special Agent Michael Levine, FBI, temporarily out of the Memphis Field Office." Levine briefly thought about getting his credentials out, but realized that the presence of Deputy Bevins was all the identification he needed in this setting.

"This here's Mr. Levine of the F-B-I," Jimbo added anyhow, as if one introduction might not inoculate properly and a booster shot was required. His eyes had returned to their soft, clear blue, and there was also a hint of this-is-my-brush-with-greatness in his voice.

"F, B, and I, mercy, don't get many of them types around here, no sir. No sir. F, B, and I. Mercy. Hope you're not here to arrest someone I done buried, they got a right to be silent, ya know . . ." Donnie shot a glance at Jimbo, who smiled and threw a lazy jab at Donnie's shoulder. Donnie forced a smile and returned a tentative feint.

"Actually, Mr. Hawk, I was hoping to ask you a few questions. You are the Locust County coroner, is that correct?" Levine shifted the tone of his voice in an attempt to impose an

air of professionalism on what had become a porchside fra-
ternity party. He swore to himself that he'd cap the first one
of these bastards that tried to punch him in the arm.

"Surely am. Took over 80 percent of the vote last three
elections."

"Yeah, and what he ain't tellin' you," Jimbo chimed in
quickly, his voice failing to suppress his enjoyment, "is that
he was unopposed in two of them."

"Now, Jimbo Bevins, that ain't right, and you knowed it."
Donnie Hawk shot a glare at Jimbo.

"And he ran against a man with a glass eye in t'other."

Donnie Hawk turned quickly and invited them both into
the funeral home before his big-mouthed cousin could continue. "Lettin' all the cool air out, we are. Come on in here,
Mr. Levine. Mercy, it's a hot one today, that's to be damn
sure."

Damn sure, thought Levine.

The interior was cool and dark. The floor was carpeted in
a conservative wheat-colored short-napped carpet that was
emotionally comforting but also easy to clean. The walls were
a sensitive dull tan with cream-colored trim. There was a large
grandfather clock ticking rhythmically beside the door, and
beside that was a waist-high, walnut-stained wooden stand
with an open guest book. The top page was empty.

Donnie Hawk directed them to the visitation parlor off to
their right. It too was cool but brighter thanks to a wide, twelve-
paned window that opened onto the gallery. Along the wall
under the window was a plumped-up sofa, and opposing that
were some comfortable-looking padded chairs covered with a
flowery pattern. The remaining space was occupied by vases of
gladioli and roses and mums, and the walls were covered with
spiritually uplifting mass-market pictures of Jesus Christ and
rainbows and clouds rent by gracious shafts of light. Along the
back was a dark, lacquered, cherry-stained bookcase filled with
Reader's Digest condensed books, various Bibles, and volumes
of contemplative poems—all arranged quite carefully and rev-

erently around a twenty-seven-inch Sony Trinitron television
with on-screen programming and picture-in-a-picture capability.
Currently, but presumably temporarily, parked in front of the
bookcase was a big-boned young man with sandy brown hair
and a disagreeable complexion. He was slumped deeply into
one of the overstuffed chairs, and the tattered black bill of his
red Arkansas Razorback cap was pulled down low over his
brow. He was utterly hypnotized by an attractive young couple
who appeared to be arguing on an afternoon soap opera. The
volume was too loud.

Donnie Hawk, Jr., walked over to the young man, picked
up the remote from the arm of the chair, and muted the television; he then grasped the back of the boy's neck—pinching
it firmly but affectionately. "Skeeter Boy, why don't you run
across the street there and get us a six-pack of ice-cold Coke
Colas?" he directed the youth. "Coke Colas 'right with you
boys?" Donnie asked his visitors.

Both men nodded.

The boy responded immediately but without an outward
sign of acknowledgment, and apparently not without some
practice, walked backward out of the room, never taking his
eyes from the TV despite the now absence of sound. As
Skeeter Boy stood, Levine noticed that his T-shirt was too
short and exposed a light-brown leather belt with the name
"Donnie" ornately tooled into it. *Another Donnie. Donnie
Hawk the Third? Sure beats Skeeter Boy,* he thought.

With a generous, sweeping wave of his arm, the elder Donnie Hawk indicated that his guests should have themselves a
sit. Jimbo took the chair vacated by young Donnie, scooting
it around a quarter-turn so that it faced the other two a bit
more and the television a bit less. He leaned back and crossed
his legs, ankle to knee—properly, as he'd been taught a man
should. He had on ribbed white socks, and as he sat back, he
adjusted his gun belt so that he wasn't sitting on it.

"Now, Special Agent Levine, what can I do for you as Locust County coroner? You don't seem to be all that dead." He

flashed a grin at his cousin. Donnie seemed intent upon keeping within Jimbo's good graces, but he also clearly had shifted occupational hats and was speaking now as an elected official.

"Mr. Hawk, the FBI has decided to take a fresh look at the Leon Jackson murder case, do you recall it?"

Donnie shot another quick look at his cousin. Levine didn't follow his look but kept his eyes focused on the coroner.

"Why, of course I do, Mr. Levine," he said. He pronounced the name slowly and with the wrong stress, the same way that both Deputy Bevins and Sheriff Elmore did—LEE-vine. "I was in elementary school then, of course, not the county coroner, but I reckon just about everyone around here remembers it quite well. Big news it was, in its day . . . but then that was in its day."

"I wouldn't be so sure about everyone remembering it, Mr. Hawk. Your esteemed Sheriff Elmore seems a bit rusty on some of the details—most of the details, really." Levine couldn't avoid the "esteemed" part of the comment. He still had a piece of that jerk-off sheriff stuck in his teeth and felt the need to publicly floss. Besides, he doubted Donnie Hawk caught the tone of sarcasm.

Donnie Hawk smiled. Maybe he did; maybe he didn't. This time his eyes didn't leave Levine's. But he also didn't answer.

"What I was really hoping you could help me with . . . Mr. Hawk . . . is locating some evidence. As you will recall, there was a second body found with Mr. Jackson's. A young Caucasian male. That individual was never identified, and the Bureau is hopeful that new technologies available might prove useful in this case. We've already submitted some blood-stained clothing recovered in association with the body for DNA analysis and we're hoping to test the remains as well."

"That's very interestin', Mr. Levine," Donnie Hawk responded. "Me and my boy watch all them forensic science shows on the cable television, and I know all about the new technologies and gadgets y'all got at your disposal. Quite impressive what y'all can do. Mercy."

"So, you can provide the Bureau with some assistance?"

"Absolutely, Mr. Levine, you just tell me who, what, where, when, and the by-God how. Not every day that the Locust County coroner gets to hep the F, B, and I. Mercy."

"Well, you can help by allowing me access to the remains."

"You bet, Mr. Levine. Y'all bring your remains here, and I'll hep in any way I can."

"I appreciate the offer of *hep*, but I think we may have a disconnect here, Mr. Hawk. I was hoping you'd tell me you had the remains here."

"You mean of that white boy that got hisself killed along with that Jackson fella?"

"That would be the one."

"No." Donnie Hawk looked genuinely confused to be asked such a question.

"Do you know where they might be? The remains . . ." *Why don't we see if we can pull these teeth out one at a time, shall we?* Aside from putting the barrel of his Sig Sauer to his head and ending his misery, Levine felt his options waning by the second.

"Hell no, Agent Levine, I assumed you did. No, sir, don't know nothin' about any remains."

"But Mr. Hawk," Levine's patience still hadn't had an opportunity to scab over from his meeting with Sheriff Chucklehead, and now this guy was doing his best to gall it up again, "this is an open homicide—as in never solved—as in no killer ever caught. That body is evidence. The main evidence, technically. Evidence in an open homicide that occurred in your jurisdiction. You don't simply lose evidence in open homicides."

"I didn't lose no dang evidence, Mr. Levine, and I'm not at all sure that I take kindly to what you seem to be implyin'— hell's bells, you're not even implyin' you're sayin' it direct to my danged face, ain't ya? Don't know y'all from Job's one-eyed cat, but you're a'sittin' here in mine own business and sayin' it to my danged face." Donnie Hawk had bowed-up in his chair, his chest crowned out aggressively, and he now cast a look at the silent Deputy Bevins, making sure his support could be counted on.

Levine also turned to see whose side of the fence Bevins was on, as if he had to guess, but to his surprise he found that the deputy had inched his chair away and now was intently watching the muted television, seemingly oblivious to the conversation in the room.

"No offense intended, Mr. Hawk—I assure you." Levine quickly softened his tone, realizing that backing the waxy little coroner into too tight a shoebox was bound to be counter-productive. "However, since this is in your jurisdiction, I simply thought that you might have some ideas as to what could have happened to the remains. That's all. You know, like where they might be?" He made circle motions with his hands as if trying to conjure up an answer. "What's the normal procedure for storing of remains? Protocols? That sort of thing."

"In that case, I won't take no offense." Donnie Hawk seemed eager to back down, and he gauged Levine, trying to get a handle on whether he was being sincere in his apology. "To answer your question, there ain't no normal procedures, as such, Mr. Levine. Fact of the matter is that we don't get many unclaimed remains down here in Locust County. Not many open homicides neither, but you're correct, if it is an open homicide, then it falls square within my jurisdiction as the duly elected coroner of this county—at least with regard to cause and manner of death. And to that end I will take all measures prudent and proper in the lawful execution of my duties, so hep me God." Donnie's tone and vocabulary had ratcheted up a professional notch, but he was still ready to bow-up for a fight if necessary. "The actual responsibility for any homicide investigation in this here county, of course, falls to the Sheriff's Department."

There was a pause while Donnie Hawk waited for his message to soak into Agent Levine. "But, you do understand that

I was not the coroner at the time that case was active. That was nigh on some forty years ago."

"Of course, of course, understood," Levine answered. "But am I correct in assuming that you do know who the coroner was at the time?"

"Hell, Mr. Levine, anybody from 'round here knows that. Locust County only had but one coroner all the time I was growin' up. That would be Doc Begley, a real doctor too—served almost seventy years, he did—but I'm afraid he's done dead and buried . . . oh . . . what you thinkin', Jimbo," he looked to his cousin, "about seven years?"

"'Bout," Jimbo replied.

So, Levine thought, *Deputy Bevins wasn't completely lost in the soap opera.*

"What about his records?" Levine continued pressing Donnie Hawk. "Notes? Files? I assume he passed on any official records to you when you were elected."

"Yes sir, gave me everythin' he had—might have included somethin' from that case—but if he did, they all done blowed away in a tornado five years ago when I lost my first funeral home. This here one," Donnie gestured grandly to make sure that Levine understood he was referring to the structure they were currently sitting in, "is only 'bout four years old. I'm afraid I don't have a single record left over from Doc Begley's term."

Levine sighed. "And the remains, they were destroyed?"

"No. Now I don't mean to give you the run 'round, but I sorely think I'd recall if he'd given any remains to me. I'd have to have found someplace to store them and all." Donnie looked intently at the far corner of the room, his eyes moving about as if he half-expected to find some of the skeleton caught in a cobweb. He twisted his face in concentration as if he was wringing out a wet towel and it was somehow painful.

"Look, Mr. Hawk, unless they were destroyed in your tornado, they should be somewhere." Levine's temper started to flare again. He took a quick breath and momentarily held it.

"You're an educated man. You must have some educated guess as to what Doctor Begley might have done with those remains. Stored them, buried them, ground them up for herbal tea . . ."

Donnie Hawk continued to run his face through a series of facial contortions intended to convey that some serious mental gears were meshing. "If I was you, now," he finally announced, "I might check with them Boy Scouts."

"Boy Scouts?" The words just absolutely popped out of Levine's mouth as if he'd Heimliched up a piece of lodged food. Suppressing his incredulity, he repeated, "You did say *Boy Scouts*, didn't you, Mr. Hawk?"

"Yes sir, I sorely did," Donnie replied with absolutely no sense of the absurd. "Them bunch that meets at Oak Glen Baptist Church on . . . when'd they meet there, Jimbo?"

"Thursday nights, seven-thirty to nine," Jimbo replied, still lip-reading his soap opera.

Levine took a deep breath and thought back to the Lamaze class he had taken with his wife before their first child was born. *Breathing, slow, controlled breathing . . . that's the key, controlled breathing.* Even now he could envision his case report being Xeroxed and passed around the break room along with the page of latest blonde jokes. *Hey—you read Levine's last report? What a hoot. Boy Scouts . . . Let's put it on the Internet. Who's Levine? You mean that guy they transferred to the field office in Bismarck?* He closed his eyes and inhaled slowly. Slow, controlled breathing.

"Mr. Hawk, I'm sure all this makes absolute perfect sense to you." He smiled at the coroner, after he regained some composure. "But, as I keep being reminded, I'm not from around here. I don't have a frigging clue as to what you're talking about. A little help would be appreciated."

"Really not that complicated, Mr. Levine. Doc Begley used to loan skeletons to the high school and whatnot for study. Usually they was Indian skeletons that someone would turn up with a bull-tongue or a Ditch Witch, or somethin'. I remember that them Boy Scouts had one for a while, they went and wired it all together real nice—now, I'll be honest with you, I'll be totally honest, I doubt it's the same one you're lookin' for. But I'd still check with them if I was you."

They rode in silence for a few minutes after leaving the Pacific Funeral Home. Levine sipped his soda—one of the six-pack young Donnie the Skeeter Hawk had finally returned from the store with—and stared out the window trying to wrap his brain around the events of the last hour.

What an absolute Hatter's tea party.

He took another sip, hoping that the caffeine would help clear his head.

They were headed east, back into the center of town. Levine had asked Deputy Bevins to drop him off at the courthouse so that he could collect his car. The day had seriously mushed his brain, and although it was still early he had decided to skip town. It was worth the two-hour drive back to Memphis for a long weekend. *With any luck,* he thought, *I can run my car into a concrete bridge abutment along the way. No, what am I thinking? I'd end up in Donnie Hawk's jurisdiction. Then again, I might finally get to make Eagle Scout, provided the Boy Scouts can wire me all up real good . . .*

"Sir," Jimbo Bevins interrupted Levine's cannonball into the crazy pool. When the FBI agent continued staring out the window, scanning the countryside for a suitably sturdy bridge abutment, Jimbo simply continued. "I wish you wouldn't be so hard on W.R., he's got some weedy patch to hoe just now."

"W.R.?" Levine roused himself and looked at the deputy. He had Donnie Hawk, Jr., and Skeeter Boy and the BSA fresh on his mind, and the initials "W.R." weren't registering.

"Yes, sir, W.R. The sheriff. Sheriff Waymond. He's got a terrible load on his mind." Jimbo took his eyes off the road and caught Levine's. For the briefest moment. He'd put his sunglasses back on, and it was hard to see where his pupils were focusing, but Levine figured it was on his face.

"Ahh, right, the good Sheriff Elmore. Almost forgot him. Well, tell him to get in line, Deputy Bevins, we've all got a seven-course plate of shit on our table. Me? I've only got a forty-year-old unsolved murder that the director of the goddamn *F-B-and-I* claims that he needs solved PDQ when in reality he couldn't give a shit, a coroner who gives bodies to the Boy Scouts so they can wire them 'all up good,' and Sheriff Andy of Mayberry who wants to play stump the monkey." He exhaled sharply through his nose and returned to looking out the window. "Well, guess what, Deputy, I'm not in the mood to be anyone's goddamn monkey."

Jimbo continued to look at the federal agent next to him. He had a look on his face as if he was trying to recite the twelve-times table in his head and had gotten to the last few hard ones.

They rode on in silence for a little longer.

"What sort of weeds?" Levine finally asked. Deputy Bevins seemed like a good-enough kid, a little volatile, perhaps, but good enough, and he didn't warrant a whipping because other people had tied a half-hitch in Levine's ass.

"Sir?"

"You said he had weeds to hoe—the sheriff—W.R.—you said he has some weeds . . . a weedy patch."

The deputy puckered his lips as if he was fixing to blow a spit bubble. "Yes, sir, he does. Meanin' no offense to your problems. The sheriff's, well, they's the usual ones, I suppose—but more of 'em than most right now. Kids are all growed and don't have much to do with him no more. Haven't even spoken to him in six years or so. Wife done left him a few months back . . . ran off with that big Honda dealer up there in Blytheville. Course his father, Big Ray, he got hisself killed almost fifteen years ago now and that was a blow; mother died a few years back, brother never came home from Vietnam." He shrugged as if further elaboration was unnecessary.

"Let me get this straight," Levine said. "There's this Ray, you call him Big Ray . . ."

"Big Ray. He's the daddy. He's dead."

"The father. And then there's a brother who died in Vietnam . . ."

"The sheriff's twin, yes, sir. That'd be Ray Junior. He's dead too."

"A twin. And then there's the sheriff. W.R. He's not dead."

"Yes, sir. Waymond Ray. He ain't dead." Jimbo Bevins shook his head to punctuate his words. "A terrible load."

Levine noticed a wet ring had formed on his trousers from the sweat snaking down the side of his drink can. He took another drink, emptied the can, crunched it, and dropped it to the floor between his feet. *All God's children got problems,* he thought. He wiped his hand on his trouser leg and looked out the side window.

"How'd his father die?" he asked, as much out of courtesy as curiosity. He was still looking out the window at the convenience stores and metal-frame buildings that had grown up on the periphery of the old downtown. Metal and glass weeds. Video stores and gas stations. Even one that advertised "Liquor, Guns, and Ammo" all in one drive-through location.

"Sir?"

"How'd his father die? You said the sheriff's father was killed? Accident, murder, alien abduction?" Levine asked. He now directed his attention at his driver.

Jimbo checked the road and then turned his head to Levine. He clearly was having some difficulty getting a straight handle on this guy—interested, not interested; prick, nice guy; hot, cold. "Respondin' to a domestic dispute," he replied after a pause. Cop-speak.

"He was a sheriff too?" Levine's flagging interest had suddenly been jabbed with a sharp stick. He ran some quick calculations in his head. If Sheriff Elmore was about Levine's age—midfifties give or take a couple—that would make his father midseventies, maybe a little older if he was alive. And if he'd been a sheriff, that would have been thirty-five or forty years ago, about the time of the Jackson murder, give or take a couple of years. The problem was, Levine didn't recall seeing a Sheriff Elmore mentioned in any of the case file documents he'd read.

"No, sir," Jimbo answered.

Levine bobbed his head at Jimbo a couple of times trying to elicit a continuation. He stopped himself when he realized it made him look like a pigeon.

"He was chief of police—for Split Tree," Jimbo Bevins said before taking a long swallow of his own drink. His cheeks puffed as he vented some carbonation. "Big Ray was chief of police all the whiles I was growin' up, leastways until 1985 or so when he retired. Year or so later he got his head all caved in and died."

Levine's mind began trying to put these new puzzle pieces in place. Jackson's and the John Doe's bodies had been found outside city limits in Locust County, so it would have been outside Split Tree police jurisdiction—technically. That might explain "Big Ray's" name not appearing in the documents he'd read. But still . . . Levine recalled reading something about Jackson having had a small run-in with the Split Tree police a couple of months before he disappeared. American Civil Liberties Union got briefly involved. Nothing ever came of it, as he remembered, and it was more of a footnote in the Bureau's file than anything of substance.

Still . . . what are the chances that a chief of police—even if it were in Frog's Ass, Crackerland—wouldn't have some official involvement in the biggest homicide case to ever hit this part of the state?

Slim, that's what the chances are.

And what are the chances that that same chief's son, a cop himself, would barely remember the case?

Astro-goddamn-nomical, that's what.

"You said he got his head 'caved in'?" The deputy's words

had been slow to sink through to Levine's brain. "How'd that happen? They ever catch the guy?"

"Oh hell yes. He done turned hisself in right after he done it. Felt real sorry for it. He and Big Ray knowed each other all their lives, almost." Jimbo's tone of voice implied that he thought Levine should have learned all this in grade school.

He continued. "See, Booger Red had caught his wife in an act of . . ." Jimbo leaned slightly toward Levine and affected a conspiratorial tone, "intimacy with one of them older Mooney boys—don't recall which one—Hell's they're all the same, ya know. Anyhow, he caught 'em together and took to whuppin' up on his ass with a ball-peen hammer. Well, Jennerette, Booger's wife at the time, she runs out to the road and commences to holler and holler that ole Booger was goin' to kill that Mooney boy—which he probably woulda. Anyhow, away 'bout then Big Ray comes drivin' by . . ." Jimbo cast an unsure look in Levine's direction. "You sure you're interested in this?"

"Booger Red . . . ball-peen hammer," Levine cracked a genuine smile. "Absolutely."

"Well, Big Ray, he goes in and starts to put Booger in a bear hug, ya know—to calm him down—but by this time ol' Booger, he's in an absolute ass-whuppin' frenzy, and just as Big Ray makes his move, Booger done swings his arm back to let fly and—*pop*—if he don't catch Big Ray right smack on the side of his head." Jimbo indicated the approximate location with his index finger. "Punched a hole the size of a peach pit right through the bone. Course, back then we didn't have no hospital that could fix that sort of thing and by the time they got Big Ray to the one in Helena, half his damn brain had leaked out." He sighed and took a couple of deep breaths.

He checked the road again and then Levine.

"WR. was with his daddy when he died," the story continued. "Big Ray weren't right at the very end, ya know, he thought W.R. was Ray Junior, his other son, finally come home from the Vietnam. W.R. took it real hard, real hard—his daddy not knowin' him and all."

Levine had been looking at the deputy as he talked. Jimbo kept on with his story, about W.R. and his brother Ray Junior and a host of other things, but Levine wasn't listening any longer. He turned his gaze out the passenger window and watched the brown, flagstone buildings of old downtown Split Tree slide by. The five-and-dime, the dry-goods store, a Rexall drugstore. Many closed. Brown empty shells. He folded his thoughts inward, thinking about his own return from Vietnam so long ago. It had been a hot summer then, too, early evening in the city. He'd gotten out of the taxi a couple blocks from home so that he could walk the old neighborhood and soak up the sounds and the smells and the familiar of home. But it hadn't worked. The buildings were the same—Garfield's at the corner of Church and Flatbush, Loew's Kings Theater—the smells were the same—chicken fat and cinnamon rugalah and Fox's *U-bet* syrup—but it was all different somehow. The sense of easy comfort and taken-for-granted security were forever gone. Lost in the sawgrass outside Bien Hoa and in rancid silt settling along the banks of the Mekong and in the damp darkness of the tunnels of Cu Chi. "Where you been?" his father had asked him when he walked in, his duffel bag slung over his left shoulder because his right arm was slow to heal and still tired easily. *"Where you been?"* this old man who'd never strayed more than a mile from Flatbush Avenue had asked. As if his son had simply been gone delivering groceries. As if he hadn't gone to hell and back. Had his old man even looked up from his newspaper? His mother had quietly stood to the side kneading her hands and smiling as if she could apologize for her husband.

Had his father really not known, or had he simply not cared?

CHAPTER 7

Tan Son Nhut, Saigon, Republic of Vietnam
Wednesday, 12 October 1966

Somehow, Specialist Fourth Class Thad Dawkins always seemed to get the stinky cases. The real messes. The ones everybody else found some way to avoid. He'd been given a heads-up that this was a particularly ripe case, despite being what the identification techs irreverently called a "crispy critter." Usually they were better—smellwise.

He'd also been given a heads-up that this one was a real glass ball—as in don't screw up and drop it.

The helicopter had brought in a dozen or so body bags right before lunch. That seemed to be normal for his shift; always right before lunch. Most of them were recent kills—within a couple of hours of catching it, and some were still warm and wet. You could tell just by the way the body bag flexed and bent and the sound it made when it hit the table—a soft thump rather than a clunk. But this one was a week or so old judging by the maggots—the cheese skippers—crawling all over the bag. He'd heard that it was burned, and that seemed right from what he could tell through the plastic. You could feel hard knobby stumps through the bag, and that usually meant burned. This one was particularly small and hard and very stumpy. He caught himself wondering what could have happened to this guy to get so fried—something pretty dang hot, that was for damn sure. He brushed some of the maggots onto the floor and stepped on them.

Good thing if it was burned, it'd be a real mess otherwise.

Spec-Four Thaddeus J. Dawkins had enlisted right out of R.W. Mann High School in Thacker, West Virginia. With his grades, the possibility of college was more like a nonpossibility, and rather than take a roll of the dice with Uncle Sam's Selective Service System, he had voluntarily signed on the army's dotted line with the iron-clad promise of becoming an MP—badge, baton, and barking out orders. Of course, that was before his Military Occupational Specialty test scores and the results of his physical came in. Thaddeus Dawkins was given the choice of being a cook or joining Graves Registration—and Thad Dawkins wasn't cooking food for nobody.

He'd arrived in sunny South Vietnam three and a half months ago, and so far, he couldn't figure out what all the whining and puling were about. This shit was great. Better than great. Eighteen years old, with a rock-hard piece of dangle, plenty of script for spending money, and all the LBFMs—Little Brown Fucking Machines—that he could handle. And he could handle a bunch of them. Hell, he'd put up with a thousand dead bodies for this assignment, even the stinky ones, and in the three months he'd been at the U.S. Army Mortuary at Tan Son Nhut, a thousand wasn't far off what he'd handled. It was okay for the most part, as long as he didn't think about the fact that all those dead Joes were the same as he was. Exactly like he was, really, except dead, that is.

The mortuary at Tan Son Nhut Airbase on the outskirts of Saigon had been running for only a month or so when Spec-Four Dawkins arrived. The army, with its losses mounting daily, had taken over the identification operation from an overtaxed air force. The air force was glad of it. It would be months before the cramped facility was expanded and another year before the army got the smaller Da Nang Mortuary into operation. Now, in the early fall of 1966, Tan Son Nhut was crowded and understaffed and overworked.

The goal was simple on paper and noble to the ear. *Concurrent Return* is what it was being called in Pentagon briefings and press releases and testimonies before Congress. It was official Department of Defense policy. No more hoarding up lost souls in temporary graveyards a half-globe away, waiting for the end of the war so that they could be returned home. There might not be an end to this war; Korea had taught the country that little historical fact, if it learned nothing else. Now the goal was different; now the goal was to get the body from the battlefield to the flight line as quickly as a chopper could fly it; from the flight line to the mortuary in another thirty minutes or so; ID it in an hour; embalm it in two, maybe two and a half if it was messy; finalize the paperwork over the next eight hours and check to see the embalming took; load it up, and ship it out.

Concurrent Return.

Total time at the mortuary, less than thirteen hours—*on paper.*

Time from death to funeral, about a week—*on paper.*

If the rice paddies of Vietnam were the bloody killing factories of the war, then the mortuary operations at Tan Son Nhut certainly could pass for an assembly line.

Thaddeus Dawkins examined the muddy green body bag on the table. From the outside, the bag looked like the other thousand he'd unzipped; as uniform as the bloody hamburger he knew would be inside it.

Another young spec four was standing at the foot end, having accompanied the bag on the "meat run" in from the field. Another 57-Foxtrot. His green-and-black nametape read HUS-TON, and he looked less than enthusiastic about being there. Truth be known, Huston was trying to recall the exact words that the army recruiter in Columbia Falls, Montana, had used to motivate him into signing up. Whatever he'd said, he doubted that "Join the army, and you'll get to accompany stinking, bloated, dead bodies to a warehouse filled with other bloated, stinking bodies" had been any part of it. Somehow, it had sounded much more glamorous and exciting at the time, but then a great many things sounded more glamorous and exciting than staying in Columbia Falls after high school.

Dawkins grabbed a yellow paper tag at the head end of the body bag and flipped it over so that he could read it. It was muddy and smeared with dirt and body grease.

BTB TRIMBLE, Jimmie C., HM.

"Know him?" Dawkins asked the escort.

"No," Huston replied. "Simply got the honor of sorting the maggot bags at the collection point."

"HM?" Dawkins asked, looking at the paper tag again. He had reluctantly learned the army ranks—you had to or some pissant officer would have you holding a salute through your lunch break—but this wasn't an army rank. It was navy, and he was rusty on navy ranks. They didn't see many of those, and then never the same two twice. He looked at Huston for help.

"Hospital something-or-other. A corpsman . . . you know . . . like a medic," the young soldier replied. "He was with some Marines that got their asses handed to them up near Da Nang last week. A dozen or so others came in on the same bird."

"Oh yeah?" Dawkins responded. "I wonder if this is the one the captain was telling me to be on the lookout for. He said some medic was coming in with a load of shot-up Marines . . . apparently they're writing him up for like a friggin' Congressional Medal of Honor or something."

"Dunno," Huston said. "I'm just the delivery boy."

Dawkins shrugged. Medal or no medal, the guy was dead now. He bent to work.

The exterior of the bag was greasy and covered with little crusty pieces of black, charred tissue. There was a faint smell of cooked meat that lasted until Dawkins cracked the zipper. Then all the pent-up smells of six days of jungle heat working on burned, shredded human tissue were released.

Dawkins flinched.

Huston didn't.

Despite his working at the mortuary for three months, heavy decomp cases still evoked a slight gag reflex in

Dawkins; not because of how they looked—hell, a burned, decomposed body is about as abstract as a piece of modern art—no, it was a normal reaction to the incredibly powerful smell. Like something absolutely unholy. And this one was bad. It was greasy and wet and bubbling and so loaded with crawling and jumping maggots that it seemed to ripple. Dawkins took shallow breaths through his partially cracked mouth. He wasn't even going to take this guy out of the bag; just unzip it enough to fill out his charts and leave it for the embalming guys to deal with. Nothing bothered those friggin' zombies.

Specialist Dawkins gloved-up and gingerly picked at the remains. He took hold of a short stiff stump that looked to have once been a left arm and levered the torso to its side so that he could examine the back. Nothing jumped out at him, except the maggots. He wiped the grease from his gloves on the side of the body bag and picked up his clipboard. On top was Department of Defense Form 893, *Record of Identification Processing, Anatomical Chart*. He checked the tag on the zipper again—*Believed-To-Be TRIMBLE, Jimmie C., HM*. He transferred the information and then slowly began to shade in the diagram of the body to show what was missing—everything from about the waist down. There was a charred stub of spinal column sticking out of the bottom of the blackened mass of cooked organ tissue and muscle. The arms were pulled up like he wanted to fight—the morticians who ran the place called that the "pugilistic pose"—common in burn cases. The muscles had actually contracted so much that the forearms snapped in two and were folded over amid the knot of muscle and tendon. The fingers were burned into short rounded knobs that looked like radio buttons; so were the facial features. The tongue had swollen and was sticking out like it was mocking the living.

Dawkins manipulated the arm stumps, stiff and hard from burning, unrolling the muscle and bone so that he could account for both hands. He was looking for a watch or ring. He found none. "No personal effects?" he asked Huston.

"In the PE bag," Huston said, referring to a small green bag buried at the foot of the pouch. The Graves Registration guys at the field collection point had already segregated the personal items.

Dawkins unzipped the body bag further and retrieved the small PE bag, turning his head to the side to avoid the newly stirred smell. It contained a ball-and-link chain with two dog tags that had once been taped together with hundred-mile-an-hour tape that had melted into a green-black glue. He peeled the tags apart:

TRIMBLE, JIMMIE C.
4410597
A POS
PROTESTANT

The bag also contained some stainless-steel Kelly forceps— either the guy really was a medic or he liked a toke now and then.

Maybe both, Dawkins thought. *Hey, no problem with that.*
There was nothing else.

"Not much to work with. Can't estimate stature very well with the arms busted up and the legs missing. Maybe get something off a humerus—it'll mean cutting it out, though. Looks like a white boy," Dawkins was commenting for himself as much as for Huston's benefit. "Looks young, maybe my age—our age."

Specialist Dawkins completed coloring his form and looked over at his tool tray. "Hand me that pry bar, will ya, Ace?" he asked Huston. Huston responded by picking up a small metal bar from the tray and holding it for Dawkins to take. "Trade you," Dawkins said as he handed the clipboard to the young soldier and took the bar in his right hand. He always hated this part—splitting the jaws—but you had to see the teeth. Had to make the ID somehow, and there sure weren't any fingerprints left on this stubby charcoal briquette.

With his hand placed on what was left of the face, Dawkins used his left thumb to spread the charred lips; they crumbled into oily yellow and black flakes. He paused to wipe them away before he slowly levered the bar past the swollen, protruding tongue, prying it up and down until he was able to open the mouth. Sometimes, if the tongue wasn't out and the mouth was closed, you chipped the teeth all to hell—especially if rigor was bad, and then the morticians got all bent out of shape and chewed on your ass.

Screw them. Friggin' undertakers. Nothing but goddamn ghouls.

But not this time. This time the mouth resisted only momentarily and then opened easily as the charred masseter muscles crumbled and fell away. Dawkins traded the bar back for the clipboard. He wiped his glove on the exterior of the bag again and then turned to the second page: Form 891, *Record of Identification Processing, Dental Chart*. He picked up a pencil and started charting the teeth, drawing in each restoration that he saw. He honestly liked this part—probably because he was good at it. He started with the lower right jaw and used his finger to wipe the grit and ash off the teeth.

Number 32—present, virgin; Number 31—occlusal amalgam; Number 30—looks like a mesial-occlusal amalgam . . .

"This guy's got a shitload of dental work. Should be an easy ID if he's got any antemorts," he commented as he colored his diagram of a mouth. Huston looked on quietly.

And it was. The identification specialist—one of the morticians—working that shift took less than two minutes comparing the charting that Dawkins had made and the antemortem dental records for HM Jimmie Carl Trimble, 4410597, U.S. Navy, that had come down from Da Nang by special escort. It was him. No doubt. Perfect match. Didn't really need to do much else except type up the paperwork and have a dental officer initial off on it.

Thad Dawkins made it a point to check the status of the case when he reported for duty the following morning. Usually he didn't give a rat's stinky ass, but this case had all the officers and the GS-mucky-muck-12 morticians all spun-up like it was General Patton or something. He opened the large paper logbook and flipped back to yesterday's cases. His glass ball was gone. The casketed remains of HM Trimble had been on a C-141 headed for Travis Air Force Base in under twelve and a half hours.

"Shit. Maybe not a record," Dawkins told himself, "but pretty damn good."

CHAPTER 8

U.S. Army Central Identification Laboratory, Hawaii
MONDAY, AUGUST 15, 2005

It was a little after six o'clock in the morning, with the sun just showing in an otherwise clear, blue Hawaiian sky, when Kel arrived at the CILHI. He was still jet-lagged enough that he had been wide awake and staring at his bedroom ceiling for the last several hours, so he figured he might as well go to the office and get a head start on his backlogged work before the rest of the staff began filtering in after seven o'clock. Once that started happening, he'd be chasing his tail until at least midafternoon, and perhaps even longer. He often told people that a normal CILHI workday was something like having your hair set on fire when you first walked in the door; you then got to spend the rest of the day trying to damp down the flames.

The first trouble sign was visible as he neared the end of the long, palm-lined straightaway that led to the CILHI—his deputy's car was already in the main parking lot. That ordinarily wouldn't set any fire bells to ringing, since D.S. usually got to work before him—but 6:00 A.M. was early even for D.S.

Kel swung his own car into his parking space and switched off the ignition. He rested his hands in his lap and sat while the engine cooled and ticked, looking out the window at the entrance to Pearl Harbor less than two hundred yards away. This was becoming a ritual, and he remembered enough of his freshman cultural anthropology class to recognize avoidance behavior when it presented itself. If he avoided eye contact with the Lab, maybe it wasn't real, if even for a moment. Instead, he watched the coconut and date palms slowly ripple and frill in the early morning breeze. By midmorning the trade winds would be kicking up and the leaves would be rattling, but at this hour it was a gentle ripple. The sound was hypnotic, and the sky was a soft mixture of gold and blue, devoid of any clouds this early, devoid of any strife and problems. You could smell the salt even with the windows rolled up. Warm and comfortable and full of promise.

It really was a magical place to work, he reminded himself, both the place and the mission. That too was telling. He didn't use to have to remind himself. In the almost fifteen years since he first arrived at the CILHI—first as a junior worker bee and for the last twelve years as the scientific director—he had never once rolled out of bed and not wanted to come to work, and while that was still true, lately he'd found himself sitting in his parked car longer and longer in the morning. Slow to initiate the day. Slow to engage the storm. Having to remind himself that what he did was worthwhile. The unflagging pace of the Lab was taking its toll, both on him and on his family, and he felt the numbness of burnout starting to chill his limbs. It was like the slow onset of frostbite, and the question was becoming one of life versus limb. Maybe it was time to consider life after the CILHI. Maybe it was time to sever the limb.

Maybe. But not today. Today there was work to do. Worthwhile magic still to perform.

Kel finally entered the building. The duty sergeant at the front desk, thinking it might be the CILHI commander, started to rise and call the almost empty building to morning attention. With obvious relief she saw that it was the scientific director, and more important, a civilian not requiring military formality. She settled back into her chair and simply smiled and waved in acknowledgment. Kel waved back out of reflex. He didn't recognize the woman. She was very young and black and looked totally out of place in her camouflaged uniform and her slick, conked hair. The organization had outgrown the cozy little family atmosphere that had prevailed when he first started and now was large, and complex, and formally efficient, and largely staffed with a host of dedicated young men and women that Kel couldn't have picked out of a police lineup if they'd mugged him first.

He shot a quick look at the commander's office as he entered, to verify that it was indeed empty. Admittedly, it was early for the colonel, and his car hadn't been in the parking lot, but sometimes he rode his bike from his nearby quarters so his car wasn't always the most accurate weather gauge.

Kel was relieved to see that the office was still dark. He wasn't in the mood to have his chain jerked this early in the morning, and the commander was an acknowledged master of tying your dick tightly in a knot exactly when you needed it the least. Like this morning. It hadn't always been like this. The previous commander, Jim Costello, had been a good guy, supportive of the Lab, smart, decent, dedicated, and hard-working, despite being slightly rotund and having a predilection for taking frequent naps. His only real fault was an acerbic sense of humor that left a wake of victims in his path, each one of them plotting some unique form of revenge. But his replacement, Colonel Boschet—more commonly known to the staff as *Inspector Botch-It*—was a different story. Ring-knocker Adjutant General branch, and borderline moron.

But so far so good. Neither the commander nor the deputy were in yet, and Kel made it all the way down the hall to the double glass doors that opened into the Lab without seeing anyone, except the duty sergeant. He shifted his backpack to his left shoulder and held his identification card against the electronic reader by the door. It beeped its verification, and he waited for the soft metallic click that signaled the lock opening. He pulled the door open.

He knew it was too good to last.

The examination floor was completely lit up, and he saw that the light on the alarm box was showing a solid green, indicating that the Lab's security system had been disarmed.

D.S. hadn't left his car parked here over the weekend; he was in extra early as well.

Open Zippo, light hair.

"Morning." D.S. smiled as he gophered his head out of his office. He'd heard the door lock click open and wondered who else was venturing in so early. "What brings you in at this hour—gluttony or dedication or something else? My money's on jet lag."

"How about some combination? But I could ask you the same question, couldn't I? A bit early for a Monday mornin', even for a lark like you, isn't it?"

"Like you gotta ask," D.S. said as he shrugged in resignation and returned to his desk. It was awash with memos and reports. Davis Smart removed his "Deputy" hat and became the acting scientific director in Kel's absence, which meant, among other things, chasing a seemingly endless pile of paper around and around the tree in administrative circles until they turned to butter. Now that Kel was back, D.S. would wash his hands of it as quickly as he could—even if it meant coming in extra early to get it accomplished.

Kel had to smile at the sight of D.S. and his desk. "Better you than me—if only for a few more hours," he said. He was still smiling as he fished the noisy tangle of keys from his pocket and unlocked his office door. His smile faded immediately.

"Good God," he said as his door swung partially open to reveal a new pile of accumulated case files and paperwork. Predictably, he hadn't gotten out of the office at noon the previous Friday as he'd intended; it had been closer to three o'clock when he finally closed his door, but before he left he'd managed to clean the mass of files up off his floor. Now it had reappeared in his doorway, or another pile exactly like it—if not larger. He'd left work the Friday before right in time to catch the vanguard of Hawaii's famous *pau hana* rush-hour traffic. It had taken him an hour and fifteen minutes to drive the seventeen miles home, and that had provided more than ample time to think. And one of the many stray thoughts that coursed its way through his mind as he sat inching along toward home was whether or not the office elves would be active over the weekend. The *Menehune*, as they call them in Hawaiian, little elflike creatures that build monumental structures overnight. Legend said they worked with lava rock and coral. Kel knew that stacks of administrative paperwork were an equally creative medium. That he opened his door to discover that they'd indeed been active didn't really surprise him, but the size of the newly created pile of work did. Sometimes instead of *Menehune*, he envisioned sooty, sweaty men stoking coal into a blast furnace, only their shovels were piled with brown file folders and the firebox was the inch-wide gap under his door.

"You looking at that impressive pile of case folders?" D.S. asked, his amused voice wrapping around the wall adjoining their offices.

"Yeah, I can't even get my damn door all the way open. You gotta come see the size of this."

"Don't have to; who do you think put most of them there?"

Kel stood for a moment before tossing his backpack across the room onto a small couch—it, too, was piled high with administrative past-dues and research projects put on indefinite hold. Not a day went by that he didn't promise to give it some long-overdue attention as soon as he finished with whatever bag of cats he was currently sewing up. The problem seemed to be that there was an endless supply of cats and a finite source of bags. He eased around the door, kicking the accumulated folders enough to the side to open the door fully, and then he stepped over the pile and walked straight to his desk. He wasn't even going to pick the case files up, he decided. He'd often wondered how high the pile could grow if left untouched; maybe it'd start to compost and the bottom layers would turn to potting soil. His wife would like that. She was from the country and had not quite adjusted to the poor volcanic, almost pure iron oxide, soil around their home in Hawaii.

As he was settling in behind his desk, trying vainly to rec-
ollect where he'd left off on his office-reclamation efforts on
Friday, D.S. called out from the next room.

"Hey, Kel, you have the sound of a man who needs some
good news," D.S. said as he casually walked around the corner, hands in his pockets, into Kel's office. He stepped over
the pile of folders on the floor as if they were a rain puddle on
the sidewalk and pulled up a chair in front of his boss's desk.
In addition to being a little shorter, D.S. was also a little older
than Kel. They had little in common, aside from blue-collar
roots and having started work at the Lab within a few months
of each other. Still, they had gotten along well from the start,
and had come to rely on each other both personally and
professionally.

"You want the good news or the not-so-good news first?"
he asked. "Your choice."

"I don't believe you said anythin' at all about bad news,"
Kel said, looking up momentarily.

"I didn't say 'bad,' that's your term. I prefer to call it, 'not-
so-good.'"

Kel didn't respond, at least immediately, and he took his
eyes off D.S. Instead he scanned his desk slowly back and
forth trying to find the loose thread that would successfully
unravel the Gordian knot of mounded paper. There was none.
He thought of Alexander. What had he done? He'd cut the
knot. With that inspiration, Kel took his left forearm, raked a
corner of his desk free—calving a small avalanche of papers
to the floor—propped both feet in its place, leaned back in his
chair, smiled, and said, "Give me the good first."

D.S. nudged the pile of paper tailings on the floor with his
toe. "Well." He cleared his throat. He cleared his throat frequently, not so much out of need or nervousness, but out of
habit. "Getting back to the Trimble and Evans case. Evans is
still missing, and the DNA from the remains here in the Lab
doesn't match him . . . remember?" He paused and nodded his
head forward, arching his eyebrows.

Kel mimicked the gesture and replied, "I believe I remember."

D.S. gave a look to suggest this was not an unreasonable question on his part. "Just checking. You were pretty zombiefied last week when you got off the plane."

"Zombiefied, perhaps, lobotomized, no. Please go on. And remember, this is supposed to be the good news."

"Right. Good news." He cleared his throat again and crossed his arms. "Remember that you wanted the DNA sequence from the bone here in the Lab compared to the Trimble family DNA. In case we were dealing with left-over parts of that guy." He paused again.

"Please, D.S., do try and take all day with this—it's not as if either one of us has anythin' else to do this mornin'."

"Be delighted. The fact is, we requested AFDIL make the comparison last week, right after we got the no-match to Evans. Figured, like you did, that if it isn't Evans, then it's probably unrecovered parts of Trimble. And the good news—because you said you wanted the good news first—is that the results are in. We had an e-mail from AFDIL waiting for us first thing this morning. How's that for efficiency?"

"Consider me impressed. That's the good news?"

"Ahhh, yeah, that would be the good news. That we got an answer."

"And the bad news would be?—I think I can see this one drivin' straight down the center of the road."

"Yeah, you probably do. The bad news is that the DNA from the remains we have here doesn't match the Trimble reference either. Both Evans and Trimble can be excluded on the basis of the DNA."

"Not extra parts, huh? How do you explain that?"

"Don't know that I can."

Kel considered this briefly and then asked, "How good was the recovery? Do we feel good about the archaeological context?"

"I feel very good—Caroline did the recovery, and she

knows what she's doing. It's the right grid coordinates, squares up with a good after-action report by the Marines who policed up the battlefield in 1966 a couple of days after the loss. We were definitely in the right spot. On top of that, we got a dog tag for Evans at the site, remember? That confirms the location. The recovery is solid."

"Anybody else lost at the site? Or just Evans and Trimble?"

"Just those two. Some other guys—a half-dozen maybe— lost in the firefight, but they were some distance away, according to the wartime report, and despite some advanced decomp, they were found in pretty good shape. No chance of a misidentification, as far as I can tell. No chance of leaving behind any parts either."

"How about the DNA? Any chance it was contaminated?" It was always a small chance. Both the CILHI and the Armed Forces DNA Identification Laboratory had stringent protocols that minimized the potential for contaminated DNA samples, but it was always a remote possibility.

"AFDIL says no. Controls are good, all four bone samples we submitted gave the same sequence—with full sequence data—and it doesn't match the DNA from any of our staff or theirs, so it doesn't appear to be the result of contamination. DNA looks as solid as the recovery—which is solid."

Kel leaned back and stared at the acoustic ceiling tiles as he thought. The DNA lab was working with mitochondrial DNA, and that presented problems. Mitochondrial DNA— mtDNA—is the redheaded biological step-molecule when it comes to the press and public. Cable television is filled with news stories and documentaries involving the extraordinary power of nuclear DNA to fight crime, right injustice, and cure genetic disorders. Consequently, most people have absorbed at least a rudimentary understanding of nuclear DNA's shared origin—how half comes from the father and half from the mother—which is why it is of such use in forensic settings; a little bit of this, a little bit of that, shake and bake and scramble a bit more, and the result is an individual with such genetic rarity that it approximates uniqueness. But mtDNA is different. Floating around in the watery cytoplasm outside the nucleus—largely unnoticed by the press and cable television viewers—are little bean-shaped organelles called mitochondria, whose function is to supply energy to the cell. Each carries its own circular ring of DNA—mtDNA. The difference between nuclear and mtDNA is not in its structure but in the latter's lack of a shared parental origin. As the fertilized egg cell divides, the nucleus divides and so does the combined maternal and paternal nuclear DNA. But the cytoplasm contains only the mother's mitochondria—the father's mitochondria being discarded in the tail of the sperm the way a Saturn rocket discards its booster stages—and when the cell divides, only the mother's mtDNA is available. The result is a mitochondrial identity that is not unique but is shared through maternal lines, in much the same way that last names follow paternal lines. Individuals sharing maternal blood—mother, siblings—have the same mtDNA, barring the occasional mutation.

It is this shared bloodline that presents the promise and the problem for forensics. The stability of mtDNA allows it to be applied to very old cases; cases for which no direct reference sample may be available. It is ideal for helping to identify U.S. soldiers who died thirty, fifty, even sixty years ago, and for whom direct or parental blood samples may no longer be obtainable. Using mtDNA, maternal relatives not even born when a soldier was lost can supply a blood sample for comparison.

"How about the family references?" Kel knew he was grasping, but sometimes a family member turned out to not be related quite the way they thought they were. It was a delicate issue, but one that cropped up nonetheless. "Any chance one of the relatives isn't a real maternal relative?"

"Brian doubts it," D.S. continued, referring to Brian Smith, the CILHI's DNA coordinator. "AFDIL does too. The samples for Evans are from his mother and brother; the Trimble samples are from his mother and a maternal aunt."

"Yeah," Kel considered, "but if one of those mothers isn't the birth mother, then the other relatives don't matter. Maybe one of them—Evans or Trimble—was adopted. We had a case like that a few years ago, in 1997 or '98, remember it? . . . air force lieutenant shot down in Laos . . . you remember? Turned out he was adopted, and his elderly adopted mother didn't realize it made a difference for DNA—just sent the blood sample in and didn't think twice about it. Took almost a year to put that puzzle together, as I recall. Why don't you have Brian e-mail the marine and navy casualty offices and get them to double-check on whether we might be dealin' with a situation like that?"

"Okay, but . . ."

"But what? You don't think the chance of an adoption is very good? Well, neither do I, but we need to tie that loose end up just to make sure. I'm not hearin' any other explanations, am I? You know as well as I do that sometimes these older parents don't really understand why they're givin' a blood sample, and if the casualty reps didn't fully explain the procedure to them, they may not have realized the need to divulge an adoption. With that generation, adoptions are sometimes very private matters."

"It'll probably take awhile, but sure, I can have Brian do it. You know as well as I do, though, that it's unlikely either of these guys was adopted. That isn't going to answer this one. It simply isn't them, either one of them."

Kel leaned back farther in his chair and briefly stared at the ceiling of his office before closing his eyes.

"Any other suggestions?" D.S. asked.

"Yeah, just beat me with a stick—a big, red stick."

CHAPTER 9

Armed Forces DNA Identification Laboratory, Maryland
MONDAY, AUGUST 15, 2005

Thomas Pierce was the first civilian director of the AFDIL—the Armed Forces DNA Identification Laboratory in Rockville, Maryland. He'd started there almost ten years earlier, first as an active-duty air force lieutenant colonel, then as a colonel, and now as a civilian. By anyone's yardstick he had done a remarkable job, which is why when his retirement date had rolled around he'd simply left work on a Friday, hung his uniform in the back closet, and returned in civilian clothes on Monday. The conversion to a civilian directorship had been handled so smoothly that no one really noticed a change except for the fact that the few military personnel around the Lab had taken to calling him *Tom* rather than *Sir*.

Pierce was remarkably even-tempered for a man his age, a trait that made him easy to respect and almost impossible not to like—unless you really worked at it. But most people regarded his greatest skill as his ability to broker agreements, and not just to simply broker them, but to do so with so little visible effort that you didn't realize that you'd gone and signed up to something you'd vowed never to even consider—until you were at home taking a shower. Not big agreements like SALT treaties or Mideast peace accords; his gift was in crafting the small interpersonel and interoffice ceasefires that made the gears of government mesh quietly.

It was, in fact, largely his reputation as one of the last honest men in Washington, a man devoid of any fractious personal agenda, that had recently ended the CILHI-AFDIL turf battle that had been raging like a miniature Civil War for as long as anyone in either organization could remember.

People knew his strengths. More important, he knew his strengths—and he didn't undervalue them.

Ironically, at the same time as the CILHI and the AFDIL had set aside their differences and agreed to share the playground toys, the AFDIL and the FBI had renewed a protracted internecine war over the proprietary responsibility of the mtDNA reference database. At issue was the fact that the two DNA labs shared some of the same sequence reference data.

If the shared maternal lineage is mtDNA's forensic strength, it also presents the biggest problem. How to gauge the strength of a mitochondrial match? If mtDNA is not unique to individuals, what is the probability that two individuals may match by mere chance alone? The solution is to estimate the commonality of a given sequence and then calculate the probability of that sequence occurring in the context in question, and the way to estimate commonality is to create an immense database of mtDNA sequences from around the world, and then to compare the mtDNA sequence obtained from a test sample to the database—something like calculating the commonality of the last name "Smith" by counting the number of occurrences in a phone book and then dividing by the total number of names in that phone book.

But in science, data are currency, and currency is not generally shared easily. Which is how a simple database had managed to become a major point of contention between the two organizations.

Actually, the AFDIL had begun the database project in large measure to support the CILHI's identification mission, the CILHI being the largest user of mtDNA testing for identification purposes. Over the years, however, the FBI had assumed a greater and greater involvement as the use of mtDNA increased in traditional forensic cases, and the Bureau had taken over the responsibility of ensuring that proper database protocols were being followed. To no one's real surprise, eventual data discrepancies arose, fingers were pointed, and the rift between the AFDIL and the FBI developed and widened. For a while the gap had become so great that the two organizations ran separate, but parallel, databases, neither one able to access the other's data. Recently, however, the two labs had agreed to attempt reconciliation and return to joint administration.

But cracks were again beginning to develop, and it came as no surprise to Pierce when he got a call from James Scott, from the FBI, requesting a meeting. Apparently it was time to doctor some sores.

"You've moved up in the world, got yourself a window, I see," James Scott said as he walked into Pierce's office. Thomas Pierce had recently shuffled some staff around and had moved his own office in the process. Previously he'd had a spacious, but windowless, cell deeper in the bowels of the building. Now he had a corner office with a view of the busy interstate.

"Yeah, 'bout time." Pierce smiled. He rose from his chair and extended his hand. "You know government workers, we're required to stare blindly off into the distance most of the day. I'm important enough now that they've given me more distance to stare into. Sit down, Jim, sit down. How's it going with you?"

"Oh, you know the drill. What's that they say in Asia? Same, same, only different." He took a seat across the desk from Pierce and withdrew a thin stack of computer printouts from the briefcase on his lap. He placed the papers on the edge of the desk and snapped the case shut before continuing. "You're probably wondering what I wanted to talk about."

Thomas Pierce smiled. Scott was a true Yankee from Connecticut and had never mastered the diplomacy of small talk. He was curt to the point of annoyance.

Scott continued without a break. "Truth is, there are several things, but the first one is kind of a sticky issue. Maybe we should speak in hypotheticals."

"I agree in theory," Pierce said, still smiling. Despite some professional differences, Pierce found James Scott simultaneously hard to not like and impossible to stand. Even his humorlessness had a level of efficiency that begged admiration.

Scott's eyes flicked up from the papers he was shuffling and briefly caught Pierce's own. He knew that he was often the source of other people's amusement, but he was persistently at a loss on how to tell when or why. He didn't know now. "Good," he continued. "Okay, let's just say . . ."

"Hypothetically."

"Right, hypothetically. Let's just say—hypothetically—that the Bureau's working a cold case . . ."

"So you're not really working a cold case . . . this is hypothetical."

"Yes. I mean . . . no, we are. We are working an old case, and we sequenced some mito from it. Now, here's the hypothetical part. Let's say that we got a very unusual sequence from the evidence—okay?"

"Okay. That's supposed to be good. Rare is good."

"Yeah, well . . . right. So, we got an unusual mtDNA sequence—unusual enough that it sticks in your mind, okay? Okay. And let's say that this unusual sequence also turns up in the mito database. You with me?"

"I'm with you, but I guess I'd say that if it shows up in the database, then it probably isn't too unusual. I mean, that's what the database is for—to evaluate how common a given sequence is. Or am I missing something?"

James Scott was getting increasingly nervous, and he shuffled his printouts over and over again. He chewed the inside of his cheek and blinked several times in quick succession, obviously unsure of how to best proceed. "No, you're right, but . . . but this is like a real unusual sequence. Right? And what would you say if I told you that it matched a reference sample in the database in a way it shouldn't? That there's some . . . some things in common."

"I'm not following you."

"Hypothetically, what if a reference sample from the database and the sequence from the evidence came from the same town?" He blinked rapidly again.

"Is the reference sample connected to a CILHI case?"

Scott nodded. He had stopped blinking and his eyes were now fixed on Pierce's.

"Then hypothetically, I'd say you have no business even knowing who the CILHI sample is from or where it's from. You know full well that those samples were collected to identify war dead and can't be used for criminal cases. You shouldn't know the where, when, who, or how-come about any of those samples. Did you look that information up somehow? You did, didn't you? What in the world were you thinking, Jim?"

"What I was thinking is that there was some explanation. I never thought there was a connection between the two when I started. Figured it for an error. I was reviewing the latest database additions when I saw this unusual sequence. So unusual it popped out on the page, 'cause I'd just seen the same exact sequence from a cold case we've reopened."

Thomas Pierce took a deep breath and looked out his window. He was still watching traffic on the interstate when he spoke. "Probably just a coincidence anyway. It's mitochondrial DNA, after all, and . . ."

"Oh for crying out loud, Tom. You got a calculator? Do the math." James Scott had finally stopped shuffling his papers and had arranged them neatly on the desk, turned at an angle so that they both could view them. He began jabbing a highlighted entry on a status report with his finger. "*Yes*, it's mitochondrial DNA, but *No*, it's not a very common sequence. Look at that—a C in place of a T, and right next to a G instead of an A. You ever seen that before? Not at those loci, you haven't. And look here . . . and here . . . and . . . look at this." He stabbed at each polymorphism in turn. "Get one of your analysts in here if you don't believe me, let them run the likelihood ratios," he said. He was referring to several rare base pair changes that had shown up on the two supposedly unrelated samples. "That's why at first I figured it for a data entry error."

"It probably is an error of some sort. What's the other connection—you said that there was something these two have in common—though I probably shouldn't be hearing this, should I? This is still hypothetical."

"Call it what you want. You want a connection? The fact is, both samples come from the town of Spit Wad, Arkansas, population of like a dozen. One is a CILHI case, one is our cold case, and they're separated by forty-some odd years."

"A coincidence."

"Some coincidence. Maybe to you, but to me, that's a not-very-likely occurrence, and a not-very-likely occurrence usually means a connection. And there shouldn't be a connection here."

"A connection, or more likely some sort of conversion error," Pierce quietly replied. He had stopped watching traffic and had focused his full attention on Scott's printouts. "You got to admit this smells more like a data conversion error, duplicated data, duplicated cells in the spreadsheet. This is exactly the sort of thing I've been complaining about for six months. If the database isn't reliable, what use is the database to anyone? What software version did you use to convert the data?"

"Five-point-two, but the answer is, *Nope*, I checked this case before I left my office. I even went back to the spreadsheet you guys sent—if it's an error, then the data were all cocked up before we got it."

Since the AFDIL had resumed responsibility for the initial data entry of its samples, Pierce knew that the blame had just been volleyed back to him and his people.

"Maybe," Pierce agreed calmly without conceding. He was always calm. He leaned over the table to study the figures more closely, and then rocked backward adjusting the distance. He had reached that age where he had to simultaneously get close to and move away from something in order to read it. "You're sure it isn't a repeated entry? Easiest explanation is that it occurred when the data was converted. Sequence data just slid down a row. You're sure the conversion was clean?" As the FBI was responsible for data conversion, Pierce was trying to lob it back into Scott's court.

"Positive."

"Well then, I guess the first question I'd ask is, what's the probability that it's a legit match? I wonder what the real size of this town, this . . ." he read the address on the status form, "Split Tree is?"

"Two thousand, one hundred and thirty-five—last census. Already checked."

Pierce sighed and studied the tabletop for a moment, tapping his fingers as he ran the numbers in his head. "I'll admit that that isn't a very big town, but it is Arkansas. You ever been there? Sometimes the old family tree doesn't have as many branches as it should."

"You agree that there's a connection?"

"No, but I'm not simply going to assume one of my people made an error entering the data. And you say that the conversion is clean. So we're at a standoff. I think it's worth taking another look at the raw data."

"And?"

"And?" Pierce echoed.

"And if the data check out? I still don't think it's an error. For my money, they're connected—I'm not sure how—but they are. So if the data check out, will you agree that we may have a connection?"

"We'll see."

"Okay, okay." Scott nodded quickly. "We'll see."

"I will tell you this, though," Pierce said as he leaned back in his chair, "if they are connected, you've got yourself a very big problem—hypothetically speaking, that is."

Scott hesitated as he was putting the spreadsheets back into his briefcase. He looked up at Pierce. "What's that?" he asked.

"You can't use the database to make the match in your cold case. You know the protocols better than I do. The database entries are to be anonymous."

"I know," Scott said as he stood up. "We need new evidence. That's why we have an agent down in Spit Wad right now."

CHAPTER 10

U.S. Army Central Identification Laboratory, Hawaii
Tuesday, August 16, 2005

Over the years, Kel had developed an almost Pavlovian response to the sound of a telephone ringing.

When he'd been young and courting his wife, he'd lingered for hours on the phone with her—much to the displeasure, he was sure, of his future mother-in-law and anyone else needing to use the phone in the evening. But that had been almost thirty-five years ago. Now the sound of a phone ringing made him salivate with dread. Phone calls equated to problems; some brush fire that required stomping out. He was long past appreciating any enjoyment that the adrenaline rush of crisis management used to bring.

It was his third day back at the office. His wife, recognizing the symptoms of an imminent crash and burn, had suggested that he ought to take some extra time and drop their boys off at school on his way in, and it was almost eight-fifteen when he finally eased into his desk chair.

And then the phone rang.

Whatever, whoever, it was, he knew it probably wasn't good. Phone calls first thing in the morning usually meant Washington—six hours ahead and in the middle of their crisis du jour.

And Washington meant Headquarters.

And Headquarters meant put on your fire-fighting boots and prepare to start stomping because the brush fires were about to flame up.

"Central ID Lab, McKelvey." He closed his eyes as he answered the phone, as if shutting out the light would help brace against the incoming impact.

"Well hello, Bubba." It was Washington all right, but not Headquarters. Instead Kel heard the soft, Old Dominion drawl of Thomas Pierce.

Kel smiled. Pierce was one of his favorite people in the world. They had first met years ago when they worked together at the CILHI, before Pierce had moved on to become the Director of the AFDIL, and the interfingering of their work ensured that they maintained contact, though not as much as Kel would have liked. No matter what the topic, he enjoyed talking to Pierce.

"Hey, Doctor, what's shakin' with you?"

"What isn't? I need to start exercising again."

"Yeah. Tell me about it," Kel replied. "I'm beyond things shakin' anymore, it's more like the quiverin' ripples."

"Thanks for the image; that one will stay with me for a while. Listen, I'll only keep you a minute—I've got an out-briefing with one of our Scientific Advisory Boards in about five minutes, so I can't talk long."

"Well, in that case, I'm the one who won't keep you—I know how enjoyable those meetings can be. So what's up?"

"What's up is that you can expect a call from the FBI."

"FBI? Your clearance up for review again?—seems like we just went through that nut roll not too long ago." Kel and Pierce listed each other as references on their respective security clearance reviews and always gave each other some advance warning when they were about to be interviewed. "You still a heroin addict or did this last stint at the halfway house clean you up this time?"

"No, I'm staying clean, but I'm still beating my two lesbian wives."

"Too bad. I always kinda liked them."

"For once it's not about my clearance. Scott's going to be calling about a CILHI case."

"Jim Scott? Why would he be callin'?" Kel asked. "We don't have anythin' out with them right now, and they don't have anythin' here that we're lookin' at for them."

"Don't be so sure," Pierce said.

"As usual, you seem to know somethin' I don't."

"As usual," Pierce acknowledged. "It's case number . . . let's see . . ." Kel could hear him shuffling through some papers. He knew from frequent visits to Washington that Pierce's desk was only marginally cleaner than his own. Much more organized, but only marginally cleaner. Pierce was one of those types that could keep a box of squirrels well organized. ". . . it's case AFDIL05-084—of course that's our case number, I don't have the CILHI accession number at hand."

"I may," Kel said. "Hold on, I think I've got a status report right here." He briefly surveyed the strata on his desk before plucking a thin, stapled report from a layer about an inch down from the top. It was the most recent CILHI case status printout, and it had several different colors of highlighting making it easy to spot amid the clutter. He had made significant progress the day before in bringing a semblance of order to the accumulated work on his desk—he'd even picked the files up off the floor. He hadn't done anything with them, but he'd at least gotten them off the floor. "Here we go . . . let's see, zero-five-dash-oh-eight-four . . . oh-eight-four . . . oh-eight-four, let's see," he leafed through the first two pages. "Ahh. That would be, let's see, that would be CILHI . . ." It took another moment to cross-reference the AFDIL and CILHI case numbers. He looked again. "That would be . . . no . . . huh uh, can't be . . . read me that number again."

Pierce repeated the case number and Kel grabbed a ruler from his drawer and held it under the case number on his report printout to make sure that he was reading across the line correctly.

"Nope, it can't be," he finally responded. "That's a Vietnam War case—there's no FBI connection at all." He thought back to his conversation with D.S. the previous day about the ID tag and the mismatched DNA and the possible explanations. "We got a few bugs we're workin' out, but there's no FBI involvement. None at all."

"Well," Pierce cut in, "the FBI disagrees. In fact, I spent an hour in a meeting yesterday with Scott, mostly because of this case."

"If I know Jim, it probably only seemed like an hour."

"No, it actually seemed like four. And this case was the main topic."

"You're jokin', right?"

"I wish. Seems they're working on some forty-year-old civil rights murder and the blood sample from their evidence matches the DNA from CILHI's reference sample."

"Civil rights? No way." Kel remembered from reading the personnel folder that Chester Evans was black; he'd also had a checkered past with regard to the law but he recalled nothing that even vaguely seemed associated to civil rights or anything that the FBI should be interested in.

"Way."

"No way."

"Way."

"This is the Trimble and Evans case. You know it? Trimble was awarded the Navy Cross, for God's sake. Civil rights? How can he be connected? You remember that case? Quang Nam Province. He called in a napalm run on his own ass. Saved a whole slew of folks."

"I hear you, but the FBI thinks that there's a link."

"I don't see how."

"Well, here's how Jim explained their reasoning to me. First, Trimble's reference DNA sequence is unique to the database . . ." Pierce began.

"Okay. That's a good thing."

"Right, that's ordinarily a good thing, but it also matches the DNA from this forty-year-old murder case."

"Yeah," Kel countered, "but it's still mitochondrial DNA,

it could match any number of people even if it's unique in the database. The database is just a statistical sample used to evaluate the weight of the evidence . . ."

"Thanks for the biology lecture, Doctor, now I'm qualified to run my own lab. Believe it or not, however, I said the same thing to Scott."

"Okay, okay, sorry," Kel said. "And second? If that was first, what's the second point?"

"And second is the fact that—and I admit this is a little harder to understand—his second point is that the murder sample and your reference sample for Trimble—from his mother, in fact—not only match, but both come from the same little town."

"How does he know that? I thought the database was supposed to be anonymous—at least with regard to criminal cases?"

"Long story, and, yeah, you're right, it is. But let's speak hypothetically, shall we?"

"But . . ."

"But just do me a favor, okay?"

"Okay, we'll save that one for later . . . maybe over a gin and tonic. So . . . okay, so you're sayin' that hypothetically they come from the same town. So?"

"And it's a little town."

"Yeah, well . . . I'll admit that makes it a little more unlikely, but it's not impossible—improbable, maybe, but not impossible. You sure the samples didn't get mixed up somehow? How about a data entry error?"

"Give me a break, Kel. I had to listen to the FBI try to pin that tail on this donkey's ass for two hours yesterday."

"Thought it was an hour."

"An hour."

"Sorry. So where's the town—you said it was small. That's relative. What you callin' small?"

"Try about two thousand."

"Hmm, that's small. Where is it?"

"Well now, curious that you should bring that up. I thought you might be interested in that, seeing how it's your old stomping grounds and all."

"Arkansas? No way." It took Kel by surprise. He had read the Evans part of the file in depth since Evans was the individual they were trying to find and identify, but he'd never paid much attention to Trimble's file. Trimble had been identified and buried during the war, and Kel had never had any reason to find out where the Trimbles were from.

"Yes way. But it's some little place in east Arkansas, I think. Funny name Jim was saying—Hang Nail, Split Nail, Split End . . ."

"Split Tree?" Kel sat up straight in his chair.

"Yeah, that sounds right. Split Tree—you ever heard of it?"

"Yes," Kel said. "My father was born there."

CHAPTER 11

Jefferson Barracks National Cemetery, St. Louis, Missouri
FRIDAY, 4 NOVEMBER 1966

The green-and-white-striped canvas sagged low from the accumulated rainwater and threatened to collapse the pavilion
under its weight. More than one wary eye kept evaluating it,
wondering when the thin tubular metal legs would buckle and
give way. Attempts by several cemetery attendants to discreetly drain the water to the edge of the tent by poking the
underside with long poles had succeeded only in displacing
the sag to a location a little more off-center, less noticeable
but no less ominous to those gathered underneath it. It had
been raining for the last forty-eight hours and now, to add to
the misery, the temperature had sharply plummeted into the
midthirties and foreshadowed an early winter ice storm.

Welcome to St. Louis in November.

The mourners were outnumbered by those paid to be present: the cemetery workers, the honor guard, and representatives of the Navy Casualty office.

Grace Trimble had traveled all day the day before to see
her only son buried. She sat quietly in a metal folding chair in
the front row right center, her handbag balanced in her lap and
her black dress covered by a thin camel-colored overcoat that
wasn't designed to shed water. There was a dark scarf covering her head, and she looked gray and frail well beyond her
years. Jimmie Carl's father, Carl Trimble, had drunk himself
into a grave six months earlier, but it was unlikely that he
would have attended in any case. Jimmie's surrogate father,

Raymond Elmore, Sr.—Big Ray—had made the eight-hour drive up from the little Arkansas backwater of Split Tree. He'd left well before sunup and had driven nonstop. His presence was never in doubt—not by anyone who knew him. There was a smatter of other relatives—a couple of cousins and some other shirttail kin—none all that close, but feeling obviously familial enough nonetheless to stand in the elements and eye the sagging canvas overhead. There were also a few navy and Marine buddies huddled together, marking time till they could get out of the cold and light up their cigarettes and swap war stories. And of course there were representatives from the American Legion, Veterans of Foreign Wars, and half a dozen other veteran and patriotic organizations, all turned out to ensure that a Navy Cross awardee be interred properly.

Too bad the weather conspired to the contrary.

Jefferson Barracks National Cemetery is located on four hundred rolling acres overlooking the Mississippi River, about ten miles southwest of downtown St. Louis, Missouri. It is as good a place as any to rest. Peaceful. Bucolic. Quiet. Monumental. And full. Due to its geocentric location, JBNC was probably second only to Arlington in its massed grief— at least during the Vietnam War. And in 1966 the Vietnam maw was only slightly reddened. The scene being played out would be recast over and over again in the years to follow.

The gravesite was in Section 85 by the exterior rock wall in the western half of the cemetery. It was only feet from Flagstaff Drive near the circle. A sprawling pin oak shadowed the plot.

Upon a nod from the cemetery director; the eight-man honor guard slowly and ceremoniously slid the silver metal Batesville coffin from the nearby black hearse. The American flag stretched over the casket was taped unobtrusively at the corners to hold its fold against the vagrant wind. To those standing in the weather it took forever for the eight men to slowly rotate and pivot and advance, lock-step by lock-step, to the graveside.

Hut . . . hut . . . hut.

Big Ray Elmore sat beside Jimmie Carl's mother. He occasionally held her hand or placed his arm around her or patted her knee or sought to comfort her in some way. They had
known each other since first grade—she had been the first
love of his life—and they had dated steadily with the intent of
marrying until Big Ray had gone off to the Pacific during
World War II. He had returned, a wounded, decorated hero in
his own right, only to find her married to Carl Trimble. Everyone said Carl had knocked her up and felt obliged to make her
honest.

Big Ray never believed it; his Grace wasn't like that.

As Ray Elmore looked at this woman sitting next to him,
he felt completely at a loss for how to salve her sorrow—yet
desperate to do so. He understood what she was feeling, even
if no one else in attendance did. The grief was his too. Real
and raw and hot to the touch. A part of his own heart was
being buried in the cold muddy earth. He had been the father
Jimmie Carl had never had. The one who supported him and
encouraged him and always had a needed ear and a practiced
word of caution. Despite being almost four years older, Jimmie Carl and Ray's twin boys, Ray Junior and W.R., had been
inseparable—especially Jimmie Carl and Ray Junior. Jimmie
Carl's own father was not worth stomping on with a thick-
heeled boot. He drank, whipped his kid, abused his wife—by
open demeanor if not physically. Carl Trimble and Big Ray
had grown up together. Big Ray hadn't thought much of him
when they were boys and cared even less for him in manhood.
Now Carl was gone too. No loss.

But Jimmie Carl . . . that was a pain unendurable.

Big Ray listened to the rain softly pattering the canvas
awning and popping loudly against the mud that now ringed
the plywood decking and carpet that formed a floor under the
tent. It dripped noisily and rhythmically from the pin oak. The
navy chaplain spoke from practiced memory, choosing to not
expose his good Bible to the rain, his breath a cloudy veil in

front of his face, and occasionally words like "sacrifice," and "selfless," and "honor" were discernible above the other sounds.

Big Ray closed his eyes and cast his thoughts back to a long, hot Arkansas summer only a year and a lifetime ago. He was sitting on his porch swing; the chain made a comforting clink-clank and the wooden slats creaked lazily as it swayed back and forth. Back and forth. There was all the time in the world. His wife was working on dinner, and he could smell the frying okra and cornbread and simmering beans, and he could hear the tink and clatter of a tea pitcher being stirred with cracked ice. The cicadas hummed and rattled and challenged one another for space, their chatter pulsing like something electric. Big Ray's boys had just finished high school and were looking onward to uncharted manhood. Jimmie Carl had stopped by, about to burst like a ripe melon; Big Ray smiled even now when he thought of it. *"I wanted you to be the first to know, Big Ray,"* Jimmie Carl had said. *"I've done gone and joined up in the United States Navy—just like you."*

It wasn't by accident that he told Ray Elmore first. It was Big Ray's approval that carried credit with Jimmie Carl, not Carl Trimble's.

A year and a lifetime ago.

With the crack of the honor guard's first volley, bright spiders of red and blue light exploded against Ray Elmore's closed eyelids. He felt Grace Trimble stiffen. Two more volleys followed, less surprising but no less jarring. A couple of ejected cartridge casings tinged off something hard that Big Ray couldn't see but assumed to be one of the other tombstones. Big Ray reclosed his eyes and listened to the rain, and the people shifting in their seats, and the sucking mud . . . and Taps. Echo Taps from two buglers sounding in slightly offset time. He opened his eyes only when he heard a voice.

"On behalf of the president of the United States and the chief of naval operations . . ." It was a tall, thin man dressed in navy blue, his white saucer cap covered with a clear plastic

cover. The scrambled braid on the bill identified him as a rear admiral. He was bent slightly at the waist and held a triangular folded flag with the palms of his white-gloved hands. "*. . . please accept this flag as a symbol of our appreciation for your loved one's service to this country and a grateful navy.*"

Grace Trimble didn't move; she hardly even seemed to breathe. The cold appeared to have left her. She only stared, probably from her own porch, on her own summer evening a long, long time ago.

The tall man remained bent at the waist, uncertain how long to hold his position before acting on initiative.

He didn't have to.

Big Ray Elmore quietly took the flag and said, "Thank you."

CHAPTER 12

U.S. Army Central Identification Laboratory, Hawaii
WEDNESDAY, AUGUST 17, 2005

It was fifty-nine steps, give or take, from the Laboratory to the office of the CILHI's deputy commander. On an average day he figured that he made that trek somewhere on the order of a hundred times.

This was his first of the day.

Kel had gone straight out to the Lab floor this morning. Working with bones rather than paper promised to recharge his flagging morale. Usually the twenty-or-so examination tables were laid out with the remains of servicemen from World War II, the Korean War, and the countries of Southeast Asia— one here, two there. But currently nineteen of the tables held the well-preserved skeletal remains of nineteen Marines lost on the Pacific island of Makin in 1942—the famed Carlson's Raiders. The originators of *Gung-Ho*. It had taken three recovery attempts to locate the mass grave on the island, and now a year's worth of laboratory analysis was coming to fruition. There would be nineteen identifications. There would be nineteen burials. There would be nineteen men going home after all these years. But it wasn't coming easily. Several of the men had incomplete or inaccurate medical and dental records and the last few pieces of the puzzle were requiring intensive hands-on attention.

Kel's involvement on the Lab floor wasn't required. It was gratuitous. The staff patiently stood aside and allowed their boss to move some bones around on the tables when he felt the need to—like today. He pulled a stool up to table 6 and the skeleton of a young twenty- to twenty-five-year-old caucasoid male with multiple, large-caliber gunshot wounds to the chest and head. At the foot end of the table were several clear plastic petri dishes containing small bone fragments yet to be identified and reconstructed. They wouldn't affect the final identification, but were one of the loose ends that needed mending. Kel was looking forward to spending the early morning working with the small brown jigsaw pieces—it was therapeutic in its own way—and he figured he'd have an hour or so before the rush of the day started. That's when the secretary buzzed him on the intercom and said that the deputy commander needed him ASAP. He was in extra early as well.

Fifty-nine steps later, Kel entered the deputy's office without knocking. He raided the candy dish on Leslie Neep's desk before taking one of the institutional chairs that kept Les's desk surrounded like a band of hostile Indians. As with many federal agencies, the CILHI was required by army regulations to purchase its furniture from a government-sponsored work program for gentlemen obligated to repay a debt to society. Their particular contribution, as far as Kel could fathom, was to ensure that as many federal employees as possible had as many uncomfortable chairs as they could possibly manufacture. Face it, it's hard to motivate cons to believe that quality is job one—especially if they think they're making chairs for fat-assed prosecutors and other government hacks who might have been the ones who'd sent them up the river.

"You really have got to get some better candy," Kel started the conversation. "These taste like aquarium rocks."

Les Neep looked up from his computer where he spent the better part of his day deleting e-mails. "You ass. I certainly hope you choke."

"Thanks." He crunched the hard candy loudly and reached for another. "I'm told you wanted to see me, *wiki-wiki*. You're in early for a federal employee."

"Yeah. It's the only way to get through all these damn

e-mails," he replied, swinging his chair to face the front before leaning back with his hands behind his head. He looked like a hostage being held at gunpoint. "So, what in the hell did you do to get us involved with the FBI this time?"

"I'm guessin' you got a call."

"You're guessing right. I did. And I'm guessing that you aren't as surprised as I was."

Kel realized that he also was leaning back with his hands behind his head and figured it must look pretty stupid to a bystander for the two of them to mirror each other. Probably looked like a liquor store holdup was in progress. He leaned forward and folded his arms across his chest in an effort to change his posture. "I'm only surprised how quickly you got the call. Thomas Pierce gave me a heads-up yesterday mornin', told me to expect a call, but he didn't say when. Meant to tell you, but I figured we'd have a couple-three days."

"Well you figured wrong." Les wasn't angry but he did want to make sure that the message was received that he didn't like being surprised, at least when it could be helped. He was a Texan by birth and certainly by attitude; a large black man who eschewed the tag African-American for Texan-American. He did everything big. Kel tried hard not to hold his origin against him. Don't kick cripples, his father had taught him, and Texans came close in his book.

Les had been the person who had hired Kel fifteen years earlier and was one of the few people in the organization whose tenure exceeded his own. He was a survivor, and Kel had learned a lot from him over the last decade or so on how to navigate the myriad political snares and deadfalls that populated the POW/MIA mission.

"So I reckon," Kel replied. "Am I supposed to guess, or are you goin' to share the news with me? Kind of a you-show-me-yours-and-I'll-show-you-mine."

"I don't want to see yours."

"In that case, how 'bout you-tell-me-yours-and-I-tell-you-mine? And, oh, by the way, for the record, I have not involved us with the FBI, and I have no intention of involvin' us with those pricks."

"Not yet you haven't. But, why don't you go first, Dr. McKelvey, tell me what you know."

"Sure, though I don't have all that much. From what Tom told me yesterday, some cold case—an old civil rights murder—is bein' reinvestigated by the good folks at the Hoover buildin'. A DNA fishin' expedition from the way it sounds, but somehow the FBI managed to hook a CILHI fish. Remember the Evans-Trimble case?" Kel waited for an affirming nod before continuing, "Well goddamn if the Trimble family sequence doesn't match this old FBI case."

"Trimble? How the hell? When did the FBI case happen?" He squinted as he calculated. "It'd have to be early, mid-sixties I'd guess."

"Nineteen sixty-five, I think he said."

"And Evans and Trimble were killed in . . . ?"

"Year later; in 1966."

"So what's the connection? DNA match? It's mitochondrial DNA, isn't it? Could match any number of people, right? That's what you're always telling me, anyway."

"Preachin' to the choir, and I'm the choir director in this particular church," Kel said. "The match may just be a coincidence, but here's the strange thing: The Trimble family happens to live in the same small town as the murder occurred and I do mean small town. Split Tree, Arkansas, to be exact. Population, oh, I don't know, maybe three or four good ol' bubbas on a busy Saturday night."

"With a name like Split Tree it has to be in Arkansas."

"Yeah, yeah, yeah, you know we can't all come from Mineral Build-Up, Texas," Kel replied, referring to Les Neep's hometown.

"You ass. I believe the sign reads *Mineral Wells*."

"Yeah, like I believe anyone there can read it. Anyhow, you got to admit that the chances of the DNA matchin' *and* the two samples comin' from such a small town are pretty damn slim."

"Unless they're connected."

"Right."

"Which explains why the FBI wants to know if we can send an anthropologist to their Memphis office for a short detail."

"Anthropologist?"

"Anthropologist. I'm assuming Split Tree is close to Memphis."

"Yeah, hour or so south maybe—I think. It's been a long time since I was over that way. But what do they want with an anthropologist? I admit the odds are impressive, but I'm still not convinced of a connection between these cases. I think there's a good chance somebody tanked a DNA sample, us, FBI, AFDIL. All it takes is a stray skin cell or a mixed-up sample label or a stray spark of static electricity in the computer database. Even just a fat-fingered clerk enterin' the data, and God knows the FBI has lots of fat fingers."

"AFDIL double-check everything?"

"Tom says they did. FBI claims they're clean, too, for what that's worth. Still . . ."

"Still, they want some assistance, and Colonel Boschet wants to support them. He thinks things have been strained between us and the FBI recently, and he wants to start mending fences. So check out a tack hammer and get someone on a plane to Memphis."

"Strained? That's an understatement."

"Maybe, but he thinks this is a good way to make amends."

"Wait, wait, wait. What do we have to make amends for? They're the sons-of-bitches that screwed the Gonsalves case. Not us." Kei's voice was beginning to rise, and he forced it back down.

"That's not how the FBI sees it."

"Well, if I'd gotten a serial murder case thrown out on a technicality, I might see it differently too. Our analysis was good. They're the ones that couldn't fill out a damn chain of custody form properly."

"I seem to have struck a nerve."

"Yeah, you did. I'm fed up with bein' blamed for other people's screw-ups—especially theirs."

"Calm down. I hear you, but the colonel—"

"Screw the colonel. He's a moron. We aren't makin' amends to those bastards."

"No one's saying to make amends."

"You just did."

"Ahh, okay. I did. How about just accepting the fact that we need to rebuild a relationship? Can we agree on that?"

Kel looked out the window momentarily and then nodded slowly. "What is it they want with us? *Exactly.*"

"Exactly, I don't know, and I don't think even they know for sure. The guy I talked to sounds like he's being left out to dry on this one and wants some company. He seems to have lots of responsibility but no support."

"Sounds familiar."

"Give me a break. Anyhow, from what I can gather, he'll take what he can get. Bottom line, Doctor, get somebody on an airplane. Who's available?"

Kel was quiet for a moment as he thought. "We'll do it on one condition."

"Shoot."

"I go. Me."

"Oh, no. No, no, no," Les said, sitting forward in his chair. "You just got back from North Korea. One third-world back-water is enough—we're not sending you to another."

"We have flush toilets in Arkansas now."

"Congratulations. Volunteer someone else."

"Like who? Have you been back in the Lab recently? It's like the Lost City of Gog, back there. There's a couple of dentists and a new kid whose name I don't even know, but who looks like he might be about ready to start shavin'. Shit, you wouldn't run into an anthropologist if you were paradin' around in your wife's underwear." He realized that they both were in hostage mode again with their hands behind their heads. *His turn to cross his arms,* Kel thought. *I'm not budg-*

in' until the SWAT team arrives. "Besides, I've got other reasons."

"Ahhh, I thought so. What's that old saying? You can take the boy out of Arkansas . . . But isn't your family on the other side of the state? Aren't you almost Oklahomans or something?"

"Nope. In fact, my daddy always told me to pity lame yellow dogs, Okies, and Texans—but he also said make sure not to pet 'em. Actually, believe it or not, my father and grandparents were from Split Tree—before the war, anyhow. Then they moved to the hill country on the other side of the state. I remember my parents took me there, to Split Tree, almost forty years ago, now—I'd kind of like to see the place as an adult. Besides, if we need to rebuild some bridges with the FBI, I'm the designated bridge builder around here."

"No way. We don't build bridges with a shotgun, and from where I'm sitting, you look loaded for bear."

"I'll be good. Besides . . ."

"Besides what?"

Kel hesitated. "I'm burned to an ember, Les. I mean it. I've got to get away for a while before we all end up regrettin' it."

"You were just in North Korea."

"Right. Nothin' like a trip to a totalitarian country to help you shake off work-related stress. C'mon, Les. Besides, this'll give me a good excuse to miss the SecDef's visit."

Les rocked gently in his chair staring quietly at Kel for a moment before responding. "Well, if you're going, I suspect you'll need these." He reached under some papers on his desk and extracted a green airline envelope. "I had the travel section get the tickets. They aren't happy about having to come in so early, by the way. You leave in about"—he looked at his watch—"an hour and a half. Your orders are being cut."

Kel peered inside the envelope and saw tickets. "You bastard," he said, looking at Les. "These are in my name. You knew I'd go all along."

"Didn't have a doubt. Can you be ready?"

"I guess . . . an hour and a half . . ."

"Yeah. You're going to have to get a move on. I already called your wife, she's on her way here, and she's bringing a suitcase for you."

Kel started for the door.

"And Kel," Les said. "Try checking in with Headquarters once and a while. You know, like with a telephone."

"I always do."

"You never do. That's the problem. Start. You call in this time."

"I call in when there's a situation I can't handle. Can I help it if that's never happened?"

"You ass. You call in this time, you hear? I won't cover for you when Colonel Botch . . . when Colonel Boschet starts asking how things are going and nobody's heard from you."

Kel smiled and tipped an imaginary hat.

"I mean it. Oh, and another thing. Here's the guy you need to link up with in Memphis." Les stood up and handed him a yellow sticky note. "You've got a week. Do what you can to mend fences and then we need you back here—finished or not. You better get moving."

Kel read the name written on the piece of paper. "Who's Michael Levine?"

CHAPTER 13

Memphis, Tennessee
THURSDAY, AUGUST 18, 2005

The flight from Honolulu took him nonstop to Toronto, then Detroit, and finally into Memphis International Airport. It had been one mad dash after another to make the gates. Another interesting fact about the federal government, aside from its belief that prison convicts make quality office furniture, is that it willingly aids and abets the airline industry in one of the most Byzantine forms of pseudosadism in the Western world—the capricious shunting of hapless passengers between random ports of call under the guise of procuring the cheapest ticket. This particular itinerary really was so masterful, however, that Kel had a hard time being too upset—you had to appreciate the artistry of a government travel office that could manage to find a way to route you through a foreign country for what was technically an interstate flight.

The last instruction that he'd gotten from Les Neep, shortly before he embarked on his Homeric odyssey, was that he was to rent a car in Memphis, find a hotel, and meet with FBI Special Agent Michael Levine at his office the following morning. That sounded like a plan, and Kel had been somewhat relieved to know that he could count on getting at least a partial night's sleep after being routed through the frozen north. Fortunately, his wife knew him well enough that she'd taken it upon herself to cram a week's worth of clothing into a single carry-on bag.

As he stepped out of the Memphis terminal, Kel looked

around as he stood waiting on the sidewalk for the rental car shuttle.

"You by any chance Dr. McKelvey?" a voice said.

A tall man wearing a light-blue, short-sleeved oxford cloth shirt and a red-striped regimental tie and slinging a blue sport coat over his shoulder approached to within an arm's length. His eyes were flecked gray and so was his black hair. He was thin and projected an air of hard angles and straight thinking. The evening air was still and very warm and humid, and the man was sweating noticeably.

"Excuse me?" Kel said. "Y'all say somethin'?"

"Are you by any chance Dr. Robert McKelvey?"

"Why yes sir, by chance I am."

"Mike Levine, special agent for the FBI. I believe we're going to be working together."

So much for finding the nearest motel. Kel shook his hand. "Special agent, huh? You must be special; otherwise how'd you know who I was?"

"Your boss, Mr. Neep. I called him back this afternoon to find out who he was sending, and he described you. You'd already left. He said to keep my eyes open for someone who looked like an anthropologist. I must admit that I didn't know what he meant at the time."

Kel looked down at his chest and feet, taking stock of what he looked like, and then at Levine. "Anthropologist, huh? Good guess on your part—me bein' caught out here without my pith helmet and shovel."

"He also said you had a beard and that you always wear long-sleeved shirts." He nodded at Kel's rolled-up shirt-sleeves. "You're the only one I saw getting off the plane with long sleeves."

"Anyone ever tell you that you ought to be a special agent?" Kel didn't mean to be a smart-ass but he really, really, really had been looking forward to getting a motel room and a bed before anything happened to derail that plan, and Agent Levine looked like a certain train wreck.

"Actually, your plane was a couple of minutes early, and I thought I was going to miss you. I was about to have you paged when I saw the beard and the shirtsleeves. Took a chance." Levine bobbed his head at Kel's suitcase. "Carry that?"

"I can manage. It's light."

"Okay then."

"Okay then." Kel reached down and picked up his small suitcase. The two men stood looking at each other. Each sizing the other up. Kel made the first stab at small talk. "Ya know, Agent Levine, the FBI agents in Honolulu wear aloha shirts."

"Is that so?" Levine stated without much of an attempt to show interest and even less attempt to continue the topic.

"Yup." Kel shrugged. "Thought you might find that interestin'."

Levine continued looking at Kel. After a moment he stretched his lips into something that would resemble a smile if it were backed up by any humor. The awkwardness continued for another thirty seconds, and then Agent Levine stepped off the curb and headed for the parking stall. He was in charge and he took charge. He didn't wait for Kel, but he did apply some body English to indicate that he was to follow.

"There's been a change of plans since you left Hawaii, Dr. McKelvey. Come on, I'll tell you about it in the car, we've got quite a drive ahead of us," he said over his shoulder.

Oh, great, Kel thought, feeling the kink in his leg from the long plane ride, *I get another opportunity to sit down.*

Neither man spoke as they walked, until Levine nodded in a general way at Kel's rolled-up shirtsleeves. "Hope you brought some other clothes with you. Don't know what it's like in Hawaii this time of year, but the heat down here is brutal. You dress like that and you'll be dead in an hour."

I'm not the one carrying a wool sport coat over my shoulder, Kel thought.

"I'm serious," Levine responded to Kel's silence.

"Please Bre'r Fox, don't throw me in that briar patch."

Levine's eyes choked down partway in confused suspicion, and he politely smiled again. Again without humor. "Say again?"

"You know . . . Bre'r Rabbit . . . Bre'r Fox . . . Uncle Remus . . . I was born here in Arkansas, Mr. Levine; I love this weather. Bre'r Rabbit was born in the briar patch and the thorns didn't give him no never mind. Same for me and this weather."

Levine continued smiling but said nothing. *Another damn nut case,* he thought.

Levine nosed his car onto Interstate 40 and headed west across the long, illuminated Hernando de Soto Bridge that spanned the Mississippi River into Arkansas. The river looked like a broad, flat ribbon of dull lead in the reflected light. The plan was to make for Forrest City where they would strike Highway 1; from there they would ease their way south across the floodplain toward the old river town of Helena, Arkansas. Finally, they would angle slightly farther south to the even older small town of Split Tree, governmental seat for Locust County.

The number of visible lights winking in the evening haze diminished geometrically as West Memphis receded in the car's rearview mirror. For a while, Kel managed to break his share of the silence by answering questions about the quality of the airplane food, the courtesy of Canadian immigration officials, and what living in Hawaii was really like, but slowly the talk stalled out, and he allowed himself to slump against his chest belt and doze.

"Doctor," Levine said. He paused. He kept looking over at his passenger, unsure what to do. "Doctor," he repeated, louder this time.

Kel's head snapped forward, and he felt a thin smear of drool beside his mouth now chilled by the air Levine had blasting from the air-conditioning vents. His brain was in a landing pattern somewhere over Toronto, and it was a second or two before he squared himself with his actual surroundings. He blinked his eyes in Levine's direction.

"Asleep?" Levine asked.

"No thanks, never touch the stuff."

"You mind if I call you Robert, or Bob, or Doc? This could be a long week if I have to keep saying 'Dr. McKelvey.'"

"Agent Levine, I reckon this is goin' to be a long week no matter what you call me." He put his palms on the seat and pushed himself erect against the seat back. He sucked in a long lungful of chilled air and rotated his head slowly, stretching his neck muscles. A couple of bones popped. "Most people call me Kel—as in short for McKelvey."

Levine seemed to consider that before asking, "How about Mac?"

"How about not. Kel's fine—unless you prefer Dr. McKelvey. I don't."

"Okay, ahhh . . . listen—Kel—what do you know about why you're here—aside from the fact that I requested some assistance?"

"Almost nothin'. I know that y'all got an unsolved murder case that you think is somehow connected to a case my Lab's workin' on, but other than that, I'm waitin' for you to educate me."

"It's not simply any murder case, Doc . . ."

"We agreed on *Kel*."

"Okay. Kel." He said the name slowly and enunciated like he was in a beginning language class. "I suspect not, but have you ever heard of the Leon Jackson murder?"

"Sure. Sort of." Kel paused and blinked hard while he thought back. "Don't remember many details. Seems to me . . . ahhh, let's see . . . it seems to me, he was a small-time civil rights leader. Kind of a wannabe who was killed in the early sixties, ahhh, midsixties—1965." He paused while he took in another deep breath and let it out slowly. He was trying to recall the details that Pierce had given him over the phone, and the ones he recalled from his youth. "Everyone thought it was somehow linked to the killin' of those three kids in 1963, '64, whenever—Goodman, Cheney, and Schwimmer—Schwimmer? Swimmer? That's not right, is it? . . ."

"Schwerner. The MIBURN file. It's the *Mississippi Burning* case."

"Right, Schwerner. The Goodman, Cheney, Schwerner murders over near Philadelphia, Mississippi. Neshoba County, I think it was. Always liked to say that—Neshoba—Knee-Show-Bah—makes me feel like Tonto, or somethin'. Knee-Show-Bah, Kemosabe." Kel smiled, realizing that the jet lag was having an undesirable effect on him. He collected himself. "Sorry. Ahh, other than that . . . They ever catch the bad guys? I mean in the Jackson case. I don't think they did . . . did they? I guess that's the cold part of your cold case."

Levine looked long at Kel before responding. "No, we didn't, but I'm impressed with what you know about the case—it's more than the local sheriff seems to remember."

"Well, like I told you, I was born in Arkansas. Actually, my father and grandparents were from Split Tree originally, so we paid more attention to it at the time than a lotta folks probably did—but I was pretty young at the time, and definitely pretty stupid."

That gave Levine cause for concern. His first impression of Kel was that he was somewhat dim-witted, but given the fact that he'd just stepped off a long airplane flight, Levine had been willing to grant him the benefit of the doubt. But now, after finding out that Kel had ancestral connections to the same town that produced Booger Red, Jimbo Bevins, and three generations of Donnie Hawks, he was sure he was dealing with a congenital half-wit.

"If you have ties to Split Tree, then you have my sympathies," he said cautiously.

Kel looked out the window and then back at Levine. He shrugged. "It takes some gettin' used to, that's for sure. My folks moved away from here before World War II and resettled on the other side of the state, but we stopped here a couple-three times when I was real little—on our way to visit my mom's people down in Mississippi. I remember my folks talkin' about the Jackson murder, but to be honest, what I just told you is about all that I remember without benefit of hypnosis . . . or drugs."

"That's a good start. We can get into the details tomorrow, but basically here's the skinny: The Bureau thinks that the Jackson case is worth taking a fresh look at; it's been open all these years—inactive but open—and what with the recent developments in DNA analysis and the recent conviction in the Goodman, Cheney, Schwerner ease, and so on, it warrants a relook." Levine saw no reason to surface the snipe-hunt aspect of his own involvement. "There's another aspect to the case too, though you may not remember it. There's a John Doe that was found with Jackson. Young white kid—hence one of the similarities to the Mississippi case—white kid, black guy, levee, rednecks—you can connect the dots. Anyway, I was sent down here, among other reasons, to see if we could piece together the identity of the John Doe. The basic idea is that . . . are you following?"

"Um humm."

"Well, as I was saying, the idea is that maybe if we know who he was, we might be able to figure out who did it. That's the theory anyhow, and that's why I requested an anthropologist a couple of weeks ago—to help examine the skeletal remains."

He paused again and looked at Kel momentarily before continuing. "I'll be honest with you, I'd thought I was getting one from the Smithsonian, but then I'm told that this case may be related to something that army CID is handling, and that they're sending one of their people in to assist me instead."

"Hold on, partner, how about backin' the truck up. D'you say C-I-D or C-I-L? C-I-D is the Criminal Investigation Division—the cops; I'm C-I-L—the Central Identification Laboratory—the docs. We're the ones who identify U.S. war dead."

"Yeah, well, that's what I learned yesterday when I was given a contact number in Hawaii. You're the guys that screwed the pooch in the Gonsalves case, right?"

"Oh goddamn. That was an FBI fuck-up from the start. One of your evidence techs filled out the wrong chain-of-custody forms. We linked one of the victims to Gonsalves, but the evidence was bounced because of the screwed-up paperwork. We had nothin' to do with that."

"Anyhow," Levine continued, as if Kel had said nothing. "By the time I realized what was happening, it was too late to stop you. You were already somewhere over the Pacific. Your boss . . . Mr. Neep? . . . he's a very funny man, by the way—he just kept chuckling all through our conversation. He thought you'd find all this pretty amusing. Anyway, the newest wrinkle in the case is that no one seems to be able to find the John Doe's remains, not the coroner, not the sheriff, not even the Boy Scouts . . ." Levine saw Kel about to question that last one and quickly added, "I'll tell you that whole story when we have about six hours and a large dry-erase board."

"Maybe I'm missin' somethin', Special Agent Mike; let me clarify this in my own mind since it seems to be makin' sense in yours. First, you're sayin' that you didn't request me." Kel kept count with his fingers. "Next, you thought army CID was comin', and now that I'm here, you're tellin' me that y'all don't have any remains for me to examine? Does that about bring me up to cruisin' speed on this one?"

"I think that's a fairly accurate summary."

"Aw shit." Kel closed his eyes and tilted his head back so that it pressed against the headrest. "Were you ever in the army, Mike? Do you know what a 'cluster fuck' is? This one has CLUSTER stenciled all over it in shiny bright red paint."

"Yes, I was in the army, and I couldn't agree more."

Kel took several breaths and lifted his head. He stared into the dark floodplain for several minutes. Finally he spoke. "Did I mention that I flew all the way to Toronto—that's in Canada, you know?"

"Why yes, I think you may have made some mention of that—several times, actually. And did I mention that your boss thought all this was pretty funny?"

"Yeah you did—several times, actually. Remind me to key the side of his car when I get back—he'll get a real kick out of that."

After a few minutes, Levine spoke. There was an awkward tone to his voice. "We might as well get some cards out on the table right up front. I'm here to do a job, that job happens to be the investigation of a forty-year-old double homicide. Understand? This is not my first choice of assignments and you're not my first choice of partners either—no offense."

"None taken."

"Definitely not my first choice of locations. Fucking Bible Belt." He paused. "You're not a religious nut, are you? You a Baptist?"

"Hmm. My mother's people were Methodists."

"Methodists, huh? You handle snakes and shit?"

"Right. Snakes. But only when we're not lynchin' East Coast Jew boys." A combination of jet lag and pent-up frustration at work was not helping Kel's already abraded patience.

Levine didn't take his eyes off the road. "I hate this shit hole. I hate the people. I hate the place. I hate this goddamn weather. But I follow orders. I'm here until I get this case solved or until it's clear that it can't be solved. Get this solved and I can go home—it's that simple—and I don't intend to let anything—or anybody—get in the way of that. I'm running this investigation, and I'm going to be watching you. You put any problems you got with that Gonsalves case on the shelf for now, understand? You fuck with me, your organization screws with me, and I'll rip your head off and piss down your throat. We clear?"

"I think that's pretty clear."

"As long as that's understood. Questions?"

"Yeah, one. You always been an asshole or d'you have to take lessons in school?"

"I taught the lessons."

"Good, as long as that's understood." Kel filed away his real response for another occasion and reminded himself that he'd promised to be good and mend fences—without the use of a shotgun. He waited for the air to clear and then asked, "So, what's your revised plan? Since there are no remains. Special agents must get issued a Plan B, I assume."

"Well, don't know if I'd call it a Plan B," Levine replied calmly, as if he hadn't just promised to piss down Kel's head-less throat, "but I'm hoping to finally get to meet with the Split Tree chief of police tomorrow—seems he's been out of town at some meeting. That activity should take all of about fifteen minutes, I'm guessing, and I doubt that it will be very illuminating, if the county sheriff is any indication of the qual-ity of law enforcement around here. Other than that, I'm winging this as I go, and I'm open to any suggestions that you might have as to where to go from here."

"Yeah, back to the goddamn airport."

"Not an option, Doc. Remember that river we crossed back there? We just entered the Twilight Zone. So start thinking."

"No, no—oh, no. You seem to have confused me with some-one who has any business bein' here, *Fed*. This is your forty-year-old bucket of worms; I'm not at all convinced that the case my Lab's workin' on has any connection here whatsoever. In fact, I find it almost impossible to believe that it does."

"Me either, but that doesn't matter."

"But you say goin' back to the airport is out?"

"'Fraid so."

"Uh huh . . . so . . . other than what you anticipate will be a fifteen-minute fruitless meetin' with the police chief tomor-row, what are we goin' to do for the next oh, I don't know, the next week?"

"Dunno, but we'll think of something by morning." He looked at his watch in the soft glow of the dashboard lights. "And that would be in a couple of hours from now."

CHAPTER 14

Split Tree, Arkansas
THURSDAY, AUGUST 18, 2005

Kel and Levine arrived in Split Tree about four o'clock in the morning. Levine went straight to the town's only motel, where he'd had a room for the last week. Fortunately he'd made a reservation for Kel, for as they pulled into the parking lot of the Sleep-Mor Motor Lodge on the corner of Magnolia Street and Tupelo, their car lights illuminated an armada of aluminum and fiberglass fishing boats. It was the final day of the two-day Third Annual Locust County Catfish Master's Invitational Tournament, and all of the motel's rooms had been let out to men with a singular purpose.

The motel's night clerk was also its owner; an enthusiastic Pakistani who had solved the problem of syrup-mouthed Arkansans wrapping their tongues around his unpronounceable last name by simply calling himself "Sam, Your Congenial Host." So the sign by the street read. So did his business cards. The office smelled of curry, as did the parking lot, the linens, the carpet, and everything else within a quarter-mile radius.

Despite the hour, Sam welcomed them enthusiastically and checked Kel in with a minimum of trouble and paperwork. They'd walked to their rooms past underpowered air-conditioners that ground and rattled and leaked rusty condensation onto the sidewalk. Undraped windows revealed overweight men, sometimes three and four to a room, already awake, sitting on the twin beds in their underwear and Rebel Lure hats, dry casting against the wall and hooting loudly—either in admiration or in derision for the effort—neither Levine nor Kel could really tell which.

In room 12A, Kel didn't undress. He lay in bed, eyes closed, listening to his pulse and to the sounds of summer: buzzing cicadas and fat, glossy-brown June bugs that swarmed and ticked against the windows. He listened and tried to fall asleep.

For what remained of the short night there was the irregular pop, pop, pop of plastic lures striking the adjoining walls.

And then it was morning.

Daybreak on the Mississippi floodplain erupts with heat and light that make late slumber impossible.

They had arranged to meet at eight-thirty for breakfast at the Albert Pike Café across the street from the Sleep-Mor; Sam the Congenial Host had recommended it the night before. He said it served American food. Levine arrived early. Kel was a few minutes late; he had needed to make a couple of phone calls first thing, and had to wait for some offices to open. He hadn't anticipated that this would engender much of a delay, but it did, for it seemed that Sam, to economize, had not equipped the Sleep-Mor with telephones in any of the rooms. Instead, he would carry his cordless phone to your room and then stand patiently outside your door while you completed your call.

When Kel finally located the FBI agent, he was on his second go-round of coffee and toast and what appeared to be the first go-round of a bad mood. Settling into the booth across from him, Kel flagged over a large-boned waitress who was dressed in Wrangler blue jeans that he wished were a couple of sizes larger and a once-white T-shirt that exhibited so much food residue that it could be used as a spare menu in a pinch. She was as pleasant as she was wide, and she smiled easily and called him "Sugar," as he ordered biscuits and gravy and black coffee.

The diner was filled with locals, mostly farmers in sweat-stained gim'me hats that advertised Round-Up herbicide, or Big Foot Lorsban, or Pioneer Seeds, or simply directed the onlooker to ask them some question such as "Do you give a shit?" It was a little before nine, and their day was already half over. There were a few other round-bellied men, their short-sleeved shirts so taut across the middles that they looked like late-summer melons about to burst. They had colorful, wide ties and dark socks that suggested they were probably managers at the Piggly Wiggly or the Wal-Mart or the Farmer's Bank.

"Sleep well?" Levine asked.

"Well, I didn't catch any catfish, if that's what you mean."

Levine managed a small, fleeting wisp of a smile and took another quiet sip of coffee. "So what's your game plan?"

"My game plan? I believe we chewed this piece of gristle last night. This is your game, I'm an anthropologist, remember? I'm just excess baggage until you find a skeleton. And if I recall where we left off the conversation last night—make that this mornin'—you were the one designated to think of somethin'. Remember?"

The waitress returned and smiled broadly at Kel. She called him "Sugar" again as she placed a cup of black coffee and a large platter of biscuits blanketed with a thick, lumpy gray liquid in front of him, telling him that she'd given him an extra ladle of gravy. She lingered longer than necessary and made sure that he understood that all he had to do was give a holler if he wanted anything else.

Kel thanked her.

Levine watched with amused interest, his attitude slowly improving. "Sugar?"

"You're obviously not from around here, are you, son? Everybody's 'Sugar' down here, at least when orderin' food and doin' business—you just wait till they start blessin' your heart. She's got the look of a genuine heart-blesser to her."

"All I know is that I didn't get a 'Sugar' when I ordered. In fact, I thought she was going to spit on me when I first sat down. But then, I was never much of a magnet for fat women."

"And I am?" Kel frowned, trying to figure where that comment had originated.

"No offense intended . . . Sugar." The second cup of coffee was definitely having a notable effect on Levine's mood.

Kel took another bite of biscuits and extra gravy and chewed, looking at the man across the booth from him rather than at Levine. *Definitely Piggly Wiggly manager material,* he decided. Finally he swallowed and turned his attention back to the special agent. "Now it's my turn. I'm the one who flew around the world to assist you, remember? And let's put some emphasis on the word *assist*—as in, this is not my case to figure out."

"Believe me, Doc, no one is more pissed off than I am that there seems to be somewhat of a shortage of John Doe skeletons around here. Believe me. And as I told you last night, I asked for someone from the Smithsonian three weeks ago, count 'em—three weeks ago," he emphasized the number three by tapping the butt of his coffee spoon against the wood-grained laminate tabletop, "back when I thought I was coming down here to take custody of some DNA samples. And let's also remember for the record that I didn't ask for you. I wanted some help, that's true, but not from the C-I-Sonofabitching-L."

"Well, the C-I-Sonofabitchin'-L is what you got. I'm here, remember?"

"Well, so am I, Doc, so am I—and the answer to your question is that I have nothing planned until this afternoon when I finally get to meet with the chief of police. You're more than welcome to tag along, but until then, rather than being pissed off that your boss and my boss sent us out here to the fifth ring of Dante's Inferno, why don't we shelve the I-can-be-madder-than-you-can attitude and try and get along." He finished off his coffee and replaced the cup on the table, and then met Kel's eyes, waiting for the next jab and parry.

"My wife's not fat," Kel fired back a salvo of reconciliation.

Levine replayed that response a couple of times before answering. "Glad to hear it, Doc. Neither is mine, but I'm not sure . . ."

"Just clarifyin' for the record that business about bein' a magnet for fat women."

Levine hesitated momentarily before smiling. "Consider it clarified . . . Sugar."

Kel quickly finished his breakfast and took another sip of coffee before pushing his plate back from the edge of the table. "Hey, you have a cell phone, by any chance?"

"No. Don't you? Would have thought a big-shot lab director would have one."

Kel shrugged off what he assumed was an unintentional insult. "In the rush to get here, must have left it in my wife's car."

Levine looked around for a pay phone, then back at Kel. "Sorry. You need to make a call right now?"

"Thinkin' about it. My boss doesn't think I check in often enough when I'm on the road. Thought I might give him a call at home. Just to let him know I arrived."

Levine looked confused. He glanced at his watch. "What the hell time is it in Hawaii?"

Kel smiled. "About three-thirty in the mornin'."

"You pretty popular with the front office, are you?"

"I try."

Levine wiped his mouth with a napkin. He took a breath to ease the transition. "So, do we have a plan for this morning?"

"Hmmm. Well, for starters, why don't we go talk to Jimmie Trimble's mother? Her son is one of the men involved in my end of this case, and it's her mitochondrial DNA that doesn't match. Probably a dead end, but we might as well see if she knows anythin' that could help. I truly doubt it, but if nothin' else, I'd like to verify that Jimmie Trimble wasn't adopted."

"Sure," Levine replied. "You think he was adopted?"

"Probably not, but that'd explain the DNA mismatch. Won't fix your problem, though, either way. But while we're

here I might as well tie up that loose end. Assumin' I can figure a way to ask that sort of question without gettin' us kicked
out of her house. It may be a sensitive area with her—adoptions sometimes are, especially with older women."

"Fine. She shouldn't be too difficult to locate—this isn't
the biggest city. Maybe someone in here knows her address."

"It's 504 West Boulevard North," Kel replied as he held up
a slip of paper between his fore and index fingers. "Shouldn't
be too difficult."

"Hmm, I was right, that didn't take long at all."

"That's why I was late. I called Navy Casualty up in
Millington, Tennessee, this mornin'. Talked to the rep han-
dlin' her case for us, his secretary really, to see if there was
anythin' about Mrs. Trimble that I needed to know before
goin' to see her—she have a glass eye I shouldn't stare at? She
hear voices? Carry a loaded gun? That sort of thing. Also got
an address for her."

"Current?"

"I guess you can call it current; fact is, she's had the same
one since 1945, apparently."

"You suppose she's home now?"

Kel looked at his watch. "I certainly hope so. She's ex-
pectin' us in about ten minutes."

They paid the waitress. Her name was Joletta, and she
signed the back of their bill "Thanks, Jo" and drew a small
happy face with a blue ballpoint pen. As they were leaving
she called out for them to "come on back, now." Levine kept
walking but Kel paused, nodded, and waved, sure that they
would. It always paid to leave a good impression.

Levine was unlocking the car when Kel caught up to him.
The boat trailers from the previous night were gone, and their
car now looked ridiculous parked all by itself a football field
away from their rooms. Levine paused before getting in, his
arm on the warm roof as he looked across to Kel and said,
"Something I forgot to mention. The local sheriff here and I
didn't hit it off so well the other day."

"And?"

"And he's sort of assigned me a keeper—Deputy Sheriff Jimbo Bevins." Levine got into the car and closed his door.

Kel did likewise. "And?"

"And, I'm happy to not have him shadowing us right now, and since he doesn't know I'm back in town, why don't we try and keep it that way as long as we can." He started up the car and slipped it into reverse.

In a town as small as Split Tree you don't have to drive in too many circles before finding your way. Had they not made the big-city mistake of looking for a street that seemed to fit the traditional definition of a boulevard, they could have found it much sooner. As it turned out, it was a pleasant little street lined with root-cracked cement sidewalks and heat-stunted trees. On the corner, two young boys were surveying a large nest of bagworms hanging from the branch of a sorrowful persimmon tree. The leaves around the bag were yellowed and sickly, and the boys had an old red mop handle, its end wrapped with a cotton rag soaked in kerosene, that they were fixing to light on fire and use on the worms.

The houses on the street were older than some they had passed, pre–World War II by a generation—and the better part of a generation at that. Most were wood, painted white with colorful shutters and dark asphalt shingle roofs and red-brick chimneys. Each house had a railed porch, and the number of chairs visible on them suggested a considerable amount of evening gossip still took place. The grass was parched and brittle and had been since June and would be until next March when the rain would soften it up.

The white clapboard southern bungalow at 504 West Boulevard North had nothing to recommend it over its neighbors, except perhaps for an excess of tidiness. Like its neighbors, it had a gray enameled porch with white posts. There was a glossy magnolia tree standing sentry at each corner of the house, the roots having long ago cracked the foundation

wall. They were still covered in fragrant, showy white flowers despite the late summer heat. The yard was probably quite
bucolic in the spring; there were neatly trimmed azalea and
crepe myrtle bushes and marigolds in the flowerbed—the last
gone dormant—and end-of-summer honeysuckle vining
around the base of the gaslight by the sidewalk.

They parked on the street, killed the engine, and got out of
the car.

Only then did they see her.

"Miss Trimble." Kel added an extra dollop of syrup to the
accent of his childhood as he mounted the three concrete steps
leading to Grace Trimble's house. He walked quickly, and
Levine trailed in his wake. Despite the morning heat, which
already was approaching the low nineties, the elderly woman
was seated on a green tubular-metal glider on the front porch.
She probably had been there all morning—people of her generation tended to eschew air-conditioning—and for that matter she had probably been there for most of the last four
decades. She had watched them walk up the sidewalk in front
of her house without a trace of curiosity shadowing her face.
"I'm Robert McKelvey—we spoke a little while ago on the
phone."

She smiled and nodded. The glider clicked rhythmically.
Almost hypnotically.

"And this here's Michael Levine," he said, with a sideward
bob of his head in Levine's direction. The air had that thick,
wet quality of summer in the South, and the sweet smell of the
magnolias and honeysuckle mingled with the dusty odor of
dry plantain and nutgrass pollen.

Grace Trimble kept her eyes on Kel throughout the introductions. She motioned them to two wood-and-wicker rocking chairs and as they took a seat she cocked her head slightly,
smiled, and asked, "You Robert McKelvey's little boy?"

"Yes, ma'am, I sure am. Don't know how little, anymore,"
he said as he patted his stomach as a visual aid. "You knew
my father?" The McKelveys had once been serious landown-

ers in the area, helping to found the Farmer's Bank of Locust County. But that was before the Depression and the wave of land speculators who'd offered pennies to the dollar for drought-cracked acres of Mississippi River floodplain. Still, the unexpected familiarity took Kel by surprise.

She nodded slowly before responding. "I certainly did. He was a couple of years ahead of me in school. He was about the handsomest young man—just purdy—he looked so much like a young Errol Flynn."

Kel could feel the earth shudder faintly as his father rotated in his grave—he had always thought Errol Flynn was something of a fairy. "Yes, ma'am, he was some kind of handsome. Sure was. I appreciate you sayin' that."

"You're not from around here, are you, Mr. Levine?" she asked, shifting her attention from Kel's face for the first time. Levine was already badly used by the heat, and it wasn't even noon.

"No, Mrs. Trimble. I'm from New York."

"What Mike's not saying, Miss Grace, is that he's now livin' in Memphis," Kel added quickly before the words "New York" had an opportunity to imprint negatively on her brain. He also adopted the formal informality of using her first name. He checked her eyes for any sign of offense and saw none. He crossed his legs and rocked gently, phasing his movement to that of her glider.

Grace Trimble looked rather blankly at Levine momentarily before turning her face to the street. "No McKelveys around here anymore. They all moved away some while ago. Was a time when they were purdy thick around here. There's still a lake named for them to the south of town." Her glider clicked pleasantly amid the sound of the midmorning cicadas, which throbbed and pulsed like chains being pulled across gravel. There was the faint sound of a lawnmower in the distance, and down the street the boys had finally begun torching the bagworms and were whooping and dancing about the tree trunk. She returned her attention to Kel. "How's your daddy?

Your momma's from Mississippi, isn't she? Met her once when they were passin' by on their way somewhere. Quite some time ago, now."

Almost forty years, Kel thought, *at least the last time.* Out of the corner of his eye, he saw Levine shifting his weight in his chair. Not rocking, but shifting from one hip to another like he had piles. Kel could tell that the heat was getting the better of him, but more important, he sensed that Levine was growing impatient with these conversational formalities, not appreciating the function that they played in southern culture. You don't simply go from point A to point B down here, not with strangers anyhow. And right now they were definitely strangers. If you want cooperation, you take the time to establish some common landmarks to use in navigating the way. It was the same in Vietnam or North Korea. "No, ma'am, I'm afraid he died a few years back. My mother's doin' well, though, and yes, ma'am, you've got a fair good memory; she's from Biloxi originally. My parents met down in Mobile durin' the war."

That seemed to satisfy the initial background check. There was a short pause before Grace Trimble asked, "What can I do for y'all, Mr. McKelvey? You sure have come a long way. I believe you said on the phone that I might be able to help you." There was tenseness in her voice that hadn't been there a moment ago.

"Yes, ma'am, I'm hopin' you just might. As I mentioned briefly when we spoke, I'd like to talk to you for a minute or so about . . . umm . . . your son, if you don't mind. You see, my job is to try to identify U.S. soldiers who never came home from the Vietnam War, and I have a situation now that is causin' me some fair measure of confusion."

"Are y'all the folks that identified my son, Jimmie Carl?"

The reality was that Jimmie Carl Trimble had been identified through the Ton Son Nhut Mortuary in Vietnam during the war and not by the CILHI, but Kel suspected that any attempt to clarify the two systems now in her mind would only have the opposite effect. A better course of action was to do as a British military officer had once recommended to him on another case and "exercise an economy of truth."

"Yes, ma'am. Not me personally, of course, but the army, that's right."

Grace Trimble leaned forward, steadying her hand on the arm of the glider as she slowly rose—her knees issuing soft reports like distant gunfire. "Can I offer you boys somethin' cool to drink? I made some tea a little while ago after you called." Having stood, she paused, swaying ever so slightly, while her limbs synchronized, and then she began walking to the screen door. "Y'all best come inside now."

Kel had stood when she did and gently touched her elbow, offering support. "Yes, ma'am, Miss Grace, I think we both could go for some iced tea. I know I could." He stepped forward and opened the screen door, holding it while the elderly woman negotiated the opening.

Kel looked around the front room as Grace Trimble busied herself in the kitchen. The interior reminded him of his grandparents' home. Colorless but not characterless. The furniture looked as old and brittle and thread-worn as its owner. It smelled like an old woman too—dust and camphor and lilac soap all stewed together with kitchen spice. Several old black-metal oscillating fans slowly swept the floor. The room felt dark despite the thin, white lace curtains that covered the front and side windows. But what caught Kel's attention were the photographs. Dozens and dozens of photographs. Hung on the wall and free-standing on tables and bureaus. Anywhere there had been an open space. Two had been in color once, now blue-washed by years of sunlight, but the rest were black and white and gray and yellowed with time.

But the content was all the same.

A few showed a striking young dark-haired woman holding a young boy. The boy's age varied from photograph to photograph but the look of joyous ownership on the young mother's face never failed. The other photos showed only the child, taken at various waypoints in his life. One of the largest was a black-and-white portrait shot of a sad-looking young man in a narrow-lapeled suit and thin dark tie. His hair was short and sharply parted and had a Vitalis shine. It was a year-book photo. Beside it was a photo taken at about the same age, and it appeared to be among the last made. It showed the same young, awkward-looking young man wearing a black high-school graduation robe and a somber expression. The mortarboard accentuated the angle of his ears and the tassel hung ridiculously over the corner of his left eye. Beside him in what appeared to be a dark-gray suit was a tall, handsome, big-shouldered man, beaming like an early August sun.

Also framed and hung on the wall were a series of military decorations. There was a Purple Heart and the Vietnam Service medal, but the one that caught Kel's attention was at the top. It was a bronze cross patée with a navy-blue-and-white-striped ribbon—the Navy Cross.

Levine walked over to Kel and leaned into his space. "You were killing me out there, Doc," he hushed at Kel. "You forget what you came here to ask or are you courting this woman?"

"You ever pull up kudzu, *Fed*?"

"Spare me the Huck Finn shit, will you?"

"I'm serious."

"In that case, Doc, no. Can't say I have."

"Funny thing about kudzu, you try and pull it up too fast and you break the stem right off at the root."

"Say it ain't so. Damn, the things I missed growing up in the city."

"Point is, you need to cultivate some patience, *Fed*. It doesn't pay to rush. Pull too fast and you won't get all you're after," Kel responded, turning away from the photographs on the wall and casting an eye toward the doorway to the kitchen. He could hear the lever of a metal ice-cube tray cracking and the clatter of cubes being dropped into glasses. "Can I help you with anythin', Miss Grace?" he called out as loudly as he reasoned to be polite. He received no response and was preparing to call out again when Grace Trimble reappeared carrying a tray with three tall, slender glasses of pale-brown iced tea.

Levine took the tray from her unsteady hands, setting it on a sturdy, low-slung coffee table in the center of the room. They waited for their host to settle into the flowered sofa and then took seats themselves.

There was a long silence during which Kel caught Levine's eye and smiled as if to say, "Remember—*cultivate some patience*."

They waited for Mrs. Trimble to take a glass of tea before picking one up themselves.

"Thank you, ma'am," Kel said after taking a long sip, the ice clinking pleasantly in the glass, "tastes like the tea my mother used to make for my father—don't get iced tea like this in Hawaii. They seem to think you gotta put fruit juice in it." He looked up to see Levine pressing his chilled glass to his forehead. The heat was killing this guy. *It'd kill me too if I was wearing a dark, worsted wool sport coat all the time. Why don't you take that sonofabitchin' thing off?* he wondered.

"I was noticin' your photographs. Are those all your son? Jimmie Trimble? He was quite a good-lookin' young man." Kel made a show of looking around the room at all the photographs. "He looks so solemn, though."

That was putting it politely.

"Oh, mercy no, Mr. McKelvey," Grace Trimble said as she too surveyed the wall—her eyes seeing what Kel's could not. The topic energized her. "Jimmie Carl was quite the scamp, always laughin' and playin' jokes on his friends, always makin' other people laugh. Very popular. He was a good son. But he didn't like to smile for photographs none at all. Somethin' happened . . . he had an accident when he was a boy, you see, and he never liked his smile after that." She paused and then abruptly renewed their porch conversation. "My son was buried a long time ago, Mr. McKelvey; I'm not sure what problem you think I can help you with."

"I'm not either, Miss Grace, I'm not at all sure myself. The situation is that I have the remains of a young soldier that I'm tryin' to identify and return to his mother. Initially we thought that it might be the young Marine that died with your son . . ."

"The colored boy? Chester Orel Evans?"

"Yes, ma'am. You know his name . . ."

"Of course. My son was awarded the Navy Cross for tryin' to save him." She glanced at the framed medals and then at the graduation photograph that Kel had been looking at moments before.

"Yes, ma'am."

"Is that why you needed some of my blood? For the colored boy? I don't really understand." Her eyes didn't leave the photograph.

"No . . . well, yes, ma'am, sort of. Truth is we were usin' DNA to try and identify some remains." He watched her face closely as he said "DNA," checking for signs of recognition. He had prepared a watered-down explanation of DNA testing if it was necessary but decided that maybe it wasn't going to be needed. "And our results showed that the remains were not those of Private Evans. The next step—even though your son was identified back in 1966—was to see if any of the remains could be his. Want to make sure that we had covered all possibilities. Just for the record." This was the really tricky part, since Kel had no idea what Mrs. Trimble had been told back in 1966, and the news that her son was not recovered and buried "intact" might not be well taken.

"And were they? I don't see how."

"No, ma'am, you're right, they weren't, at least the DNA doesn't match yours."

"I still don't know what you want me to help you with." Grace Trimble's voice expressed more curiosity than confusion, but the tension was there.

"Well, ma'am, ummm . . . now this is just for the

record . . . ummm . . . I need to verify that Jimmie Carl Trimble was your birth son, that he wasn't adopted, in other words. Umm, it would certainly be all right if he were, we'd just need to know it when we're checkin' the blood sample is all." Kel cringed inside, if not outside, as he asked the question.

Grace Trimble looked at Kel, her gray-blue eyes fixing on his. There was no hesitation. "No, Mr. McKelvey, my son was not adopted. He was my flesh and blood. He was the center of my world. My only child. He was a hero. He was *my* hero. He died tryin' to save a Negro boy that he didn't even know."

Kel briefly inspected his glass of tea, noting the thick slurry of sugar at the bottom, and wondered whether there was room to slither under the sofa. He felt as if he only needed an inch or so of clearance. "Yes, ma'am. I knew the answer to that question, Mrs. Trimble, but you understand that I had to establish it for the record. No offense intended." There was a silence. Offense had clearly been taken. Kel looked at Levine for some support, but he simply rocked back in his chair, quietly cracked his knuckles, and smiled back at Kel as if to say, *"Cultivate some patience."*

Out of awkwardness as much as curiosity Kel motioned to the graduation photo on the wall. "Is that Mr. Trimble with your son? I can see the resemblance."

Mrs. Trimble didn't respond. It was her turn to examine her tea glass; her eyes fogging and misting up with a pain undiminished by forty years. Tears welled up thickly. Finally she answered, and her soft voice cracked. "No, Mr. McKelvey . . . Carl was at . . ." She took a stuttering breath. "You see, Mr. Trimble had to . . . work that day and couldn't be there for Jimmie Carl." She lifted her chin and looked at the photograph and then directly into Kel's eyes. "That's Big Ray Elmore."

CHAPTER 15

Split Tree, Arkansas
THURSDAY, AUGUST 18, 2005

"Remind me to take notes next time," Levine said as he fished his keys out of his pants pocket and began unlocking the car door. Despite Kel's telling him that they were in the bosom of honesty and that he didn't need to keep locking the car, the paranoia bred by growing up in New York or from years working for the FBI held too much sway. He opened the door to let the hot air vent. "Yes sir, that was about as slick as I've ever seen; the Bureau may have an opening for someone with your satin tongue. Maybe you could negotiate hostage releases."

Kel glared across the roof of the car. "Tell me, Agent Levine, did you get the snot beat out of you a lot when you were young?"

"Yes sir, that was some masterful shit. How'd you do that again?" he said as he got into the car. He waited for Kel to get in and start fastening his seat belt before continuing. "Let's see, how'd that work? Walk me through it again, will you, Doc? Step by step. You set her up for thirty minutes talking about your father being Errol Flynn or some shit like that and how she makes tea exactly like your mother, and then, just when she starts to relax her guard—*pow*—you sucker punch her with the old 'And by the way, Gracie, is that kid you've made your living room into a shrine for really yours?' Masterful." He chuckled as he started the car and shot a look at Kel, who was still glaring. "But the best part, oh yeah—the *best* part, mind you, was when you told her that her son resembled the friggin' police chief. Quick Granny, grab the heart pills. Too bad she didn't have another son, you could have said he looked like the milkman."

"Yeah, yeah, yeah, you sure are some kinda funny, and oh, by the way, did I thank you for all your help in there?" Kel finally responded, reaching over and aiming the air-conditioning vents at himself and away from Levine. "And I appreciate you not succumbin' to heatstroke on her floor. She'll be boraxin' your sweat stains out of her furniture doilies for the next two months."

"No need to thank me, Doc," Levine continued without a pause, "for a dumb city kid like me, it was a pleasure simply watching a professional like you work."

"Well, speakin' of professionals—*Fed*—where are we headed now? You're drivin' like you have somewhere to go. Don't tell me you've finally formulated a plan in that little special agent's brain of yours?"

"Nope, no plan, really. It's too early to meet with the chief, but I thought in the meantime you might like a history lesson—you being from around here and everything."

They drove east out of town and soon left the hardball county road, turning south onto farm roads that led between fields of dry cotton and stunted sorghum. It had been a drought year, and the crops were showing the effects. The roads had long ago powdered and now resembled lanes of light buff-colored talc two inches thick that drove like an inch of wet snow. The plume that roostered behind their car lingered in the still hot air for half an hour after their passing.

Levine finally pulled the car onto what passed for a shoulder and parked it. He said nothing but left the air-conditioning running while he waited for the cloud of dust to settle. Then he opened his door.

"We're here," he finally announced.

Kel followed him. It didn't take much to figure out where they were, but what impressed Kel was how Levine knew where the "here" was. Levine must have been here before to be able to drive right to the spot. Together they stood and slowly took in the vast flatness that is the Mississippi River floodplain. Nothing, or almost nothing. Acres of cracked clay covered with thousands of foot-high crawdad chimneys looking like melted centerpiece candles. A few trees were visible, usually isolated and lonely, and Kel knew from his graduate student days doing archaeology in the region that most of them were associated with houses—past and present. Fifty feet in front of them was a low, second-tier levee, only a few feet in height, running almost due north to south; the main levee was located a couple of miles farther east, and this one was placed as a backup against the hundred-year flood. A football field or so to their right were a half-dozen needy plank-and-pole buildings, probably long abandoned by the general looks of them. In the silence they could hear the cotton growing in the nearby field crackle in the heat like a bowl of cereal.

Levine had been rehearsing his presentation in his head, mindful to not expose his inexperience working homicide cases. It wasn't that he mistrusted this anthropologist from Hawaii any more than he mistrusted everyone, it was just that the Bureau was hoping he'd step on his dick, and he wasn't about to have anyone else help him out by unzipping his pants. He looked at Kel long enough to capture his eye and then he looked forward, while seeing into the past. "August fifteenth, 1965, wettest August in anyone's living memory, Denton Deane, a young man on his way back from town— probably driving too fast the way young men tend to do— bogs his vehicle down in the mud, about a quarter-mile up the road . . . right about . . . about there." Levine pointed to his left, past his own car. "It's buried up to the axle and not coming out without some help, so he comes walking this way, probably looking for some rocks or something to wedge under his tire. Who knows? Not much luck out here, though, so he keeps walking and looking; no rocks but he does spy something sticking out of that low ridge of dirt—about there." He looked to the levee, marking another spot with a nod of his head and then following up with an outstretched arm. "Turns out to be the fairly decomposed body of one Leonidas Stephen Jackson, a-k-a Leon Jackson, of Natchez, Mississippi. Civil rights leader 'wannabe,' as you called him last night, who got his wish for notoriety by way of a rather unplanned martyrdom. He'd last been seen two and a half weeks earlier speaking to an assembled—and from all reports somewhat apathetic—group of socially downtrodden at an African Episcopal Methodist church over near the town of West Helena. Autopsy established blunt-force trauma to the head, including what they call a Le Forte fracture, I believe." He looked at Kel, who nodded his acceptance of the term. "Also some broken ribs, fractured hand bones, some other trauma. It all added up to a terrific beating."

Levine had gone over much of the same territory during the drive down from the Memphis airport, but now, standing in the quivering heat of the parched-clay floodplain, the story took on a raw sense of sadness.

"Guess I didn't fully appreciate how extensive the beatin' part was. So his body's found and identified, and then what?" Kel asked.

Levine took a handkerchief out of his pocket and blotted his face and neck. Before continuing, he removed his jacket and draped it over his left forearm. "Yeah, he was identified and buried. There was a big funeral up at Arlington—seems that Leon Jackson was a Korean War vet or some such thing. All sorts of important people who probably wouldn't have let ol' Leon in their front door were in attendance. Meanwhile, LBJ sent some specialists down from the Armed Forces Institute of Pathology, and of course the Bureau had everyone from Memphis and Little Rock, even some from the Jackson field office, out here mucking around, turning over rocks and dirt clods. Lot of money, lot of overtime; not a lot of results but a whole lot of visible effort."

"And the John Doe? When does he turn up?"

Levine started walking up the road to his right and motioned with his head for Kel to follow. They went perhaps fifty yards farther and stopped again. Walking a step or two behind, Kel had noticed the black semiautomatic tucked into a polished leather holster at the small of Levine's back. He hadn't noticed it the other night at the airport and wondered where it had been stashed. Its presence partially explained Levine's keeping his jacket on in spite of the heat that was obviously affecting him adversely. FBI tradition explained the rest.

"No one knew about a second body. Unlike over near Philadelphia where Goodman, Cheney, and Schwerner were last seen together—known to be together—our buddy Leon was last seen alone, so no one was looking for any more bodies. No reason to, right?"

Kel hunkered down in the dust, sitting on his right heel. No one stopped to talk in fields anymore. When he was younger, Kel could hunker for hours listening to his father and uncles talk; now his knees were beginning to complain after only a few minutes. He lowered his head and let a foamy ball of spit drop and ball up in the powdery dirt between his feet. He paused and then let a second ball drop. "Right," he acknowledged.

"By mid-September, the rain had stopped and the muck had dried up enough that the Bureau was able to start digging up the whole field looking for additional evidence. Not bodies, mind you, no reason to assume that, but evidence. Everyone figured a possible murder weapon—tire iron, baseball bat, whatever—might have been tossed away in the field or something. They even had the Arkansas National Guard out here tromping through everything. Certainly looked good for the media and the voters. But, like I said, no one was looking for another body, just for any clues relating to Jackson's death."

Levine again indicated a third spot on the levee with a nod.

Kel dropped his head and spat again and then looked up.

There was a new wire fence around the field, its posts a

bright red in the dusty field. In spots the weathered, split, gray wooden posts of an older, long-forgotten fence still stood. A curious bluejay had decided to perch atop the one closest to the two men. It kept turning its head sideways in hopes of better understanding what was being said.

"Right about there. Afternoon of September twenty-third. One of the National Guardsmen smells something rather unpleasant—unpleasant even for normal river muck. According to the report, it didn't take much digging; the rain had already exposed most of it. Young, white, John Doe, single contact gunshot wound to head; badly decomposed, almost a skeleton by the time they got it out of the ground. There was a fragment of a man's torn shirt wrapped around the head and neck, also a pair of pants, shoes, underwear, etc. Appeared to be bloody. No wallet or keys, but his watch and pocket money were there—no reason to think it was a robbery. Anyhow, down come all the pros from Dover, but no ID—try as they might, the remains don't match anyone reported missing from a five-hundred-mile radius. Nobody. Kids, runaways, nobody. Of course, the Head-Busters don't know what to think. Maybe they've got a whole mess of bodies out here—like one of those killing fields in Cambodia. So, the Feds bulldoze up the whole sonofabitching field looking for more skeletons; find none. Nothing. Case stalls, until . . ."

"Until?"

"Until the Bureau needs to create a gulag. Along comes Special Agent Michael Levine. I put a sharp stick up the wrong person's ass, twist it twice, and the next thing I know, some of the current powers that be decide that I need to spend a summer regretting the content of some memos that I wrote. This case happens to fill the bill."

He paused as if his life was flashing across the field in front of him. Finally he said, "And so here I am." He paused again. "And," he turned and looked down at Kel still hunkering on the ground, "here you are, my friend."

CHAPTER 16

Split Tree, Arkansas
THURSDAY, AUGUST 18, 2005

Levine spent most of the short ride back into town adjusting and readjusting the air-conditioning vents and thinking about what he was going to ask the police chief when he met with him in a few hours, and what the next step on this seemingly dead-ended case could possibly be.

Kel sat and stared out at the fields, thinking about growing up in Arkansas in the fifties and sixties. He remembered the summer his older brother had patiently explained to him how the water in the Colored Water fountains wasn't really colored, and he remembered how unfair it had seemed to him as a child that the Negroes got to sit up in the balcony at the movie theater while he and his friends had to sit below. And he thought about 1965 and Leon Jackson and about who could possess enough hate to have beaten a man that badly.

Something didn't fit but he couldn't get a handle on it. It was like the forgotten name of an old acquaintance that lingered annoyingly on the front of his brain but refused to solidify on his tongue.

It was almost noon when they hit the town limits. They passed the sign that read *Welcome to Split Tree, Home of Friendly People*, its lettering starting to flake away around all the rusty shotgun-pellet holes punched through it. Levine announced he was hungry and steered a course for the Albert Pike. It was on the western edge of town, not far from the Pacific Funeral Home, and it took a few more minutes to get there. They parked and Levine again locked the car.

"You don't have to keep doin' that, you know?" Kel said over the top of the car.

"Doing what?"

"Keep lockin' everythin' up. This isn't the big city."

"Maybe so, but shitbirds are shitbirds everywhere," Levine responded as he pocketed his keys and loosened his tie.

"Not a very Christian attitude," Kel joked.

"No shit." Levine stopped walking and faced Kel. He raised a finger. Suddenly serious. "Look, you ever been shot?"

Kel shrugged. "No."

"No? Well, let me educate you, Doctor. In 1967, when I was nineteen years old, a little kid who couldn't have been much over eleven, twelve, a goddamn little kid in cotton pajamas blew a hole through my shoulder with an AK-47. I didn't know that kid, and he didn't know me. But he shot me, and I never saw it coming." Levine's eyes seemed to dare Kel to respond. "Kind of changes your whole outlook on human beings."

Kel nodded slowly. "Fair enough, Mike. Fair enough." He paused and they resumed walking. "So what happened to the kid?" he asked.

"I killed his ass," Levine responded quietly.

They walked across the parking lot in silence and entered the diner.

"I guess that explains a lot." Kel broke the silence as they took a seat at the same booth they'd had earlier that morning. He began looking at one of the menus, as much to project a casual air as to avoid making unnecessary eye contact with Levine.

"Explains what?"

"That you don't particularly like humans."

"You got that right."

McKelvey shrugged and looked at his menu. "It shows is all."

"I'm a firm believer that the world would be a decent place if it weren't for all the goddamn people."

"No argument. That why you don't have a phone?"

"What?" Levine tugged his lapels to adjust the fit of his jacket.

"A cell phone. You're an FBI agent. In this day and all, how come you don't have a cell phone?"

"You still thinking about calling your boss?" Levine seemed willing to play along.

"Naw. He'd be awake by now. I'll wait. Truth is, I hate phones. Just surprised that you don't have one."

Levine thought a moment before answering. Finally he said, "No need. I have a phone on my desk and one in my apartment. You pegged me right. Don't have many people that I need to talk to, and even fewer that I want to talk to."

"I hear ya," Kel responded. "Me either, but I would have assumed the FBI would have issued you one, though. For this case, if nothin' else. Made you bring one."

"Shit. Like I told you, Doc, the Bureau would like to forget I even exist. They'd make me pay for my badge if they could. In case you haven't realized it, this case is not very high on their priority list. Neither am I, for that matter." He paused and looked at Kel before picking up a menu. "So if you're here to take notes and dime me out, get in line."

Kel smiled. "Your paranoia's misplaced, Fed. I'm all outta dimes."

Levine studied his menu and Kel looked around. Jo was still working, and the same shriveled little man was still cooking. The same men, in the same hats, were sitting in the same places, conducting what sounded to be the same conversations. Only now they were eating cornmeal-fried catfish and chicken-fried steak. Jo smiled at her new customers as soon as she saw them and hurried over.

"I figured I'd be seein' y'all again," she said as she took out a small pad of paper and readied her pen. Their return had proven to be the high point of her day. "Now, what can I get y'all?"

Levine flipped the laminated sheet over and back several

times before finally realizing that one side was the breakfast menu. Little things like that seemed to annoy him. He sighed loudly, and then began working the lunch side over as if it were written in hieroglyphs. "I'll have a cheeseburger and a Pepsi," he announced as he replaced the menu in the shiny wire holder that also corralled the salt and pepper and near-empty bottle of pepper sauce.

"Shiloh Burger?"

He nodded, seemingly unwilling to call a simple cheese-burger anything but that. "And a Pepsi."

"Coke Cola okay?"

He sighed and nodded again.

"And you, Sugar, what can I get y'all today?" She'd been looking at Kel most of the time.

Kel snapped a quick glance at Levine as if to say *not a goddamn word out of you*, and then looked at Joletta, smiled, and said, "Ahhh . . . can't say I'm really hungry after that extra gravy this mornin', darlin', how about just some iced tea and a slice of Karo nut pie."

"Comin' right up, Sugar. I think I got an extra-thick wedge with your name on it." This time she actually winked.

"Say there, Sugar," Levine leaned back against his booth cushion and dipped his head down as if he were winding up for a fastball, "you all sure were quiet in the car. What's you all thinking, Sugar?"

"In the first place, it's 'y'all,' not 'you all,' and secondly, jealousy doesn't become a grown man like you." Kel turned sideways in his seat and scooted toward the wall so that he could stretch his legs out on the booth cushion. "As to what I was thinkin' . . ." He took a deep breath, held it momentarily until the mood had sobered a little, and then slowly exhaled. "Somethin' about the Jackson case doesn't sit well with me, and I can't quite figure out what it is, but that dog just ain't pointin' true, as I believe they say around here."

"You sure it's not the extra gravy from this morning that's not sitting well?"

"Well, that could be. Food around here can do that sometimes."

"Don't talk until you've eaten my mother's cooking. Ever had rendered chicken fat on bread?"

"I'll take the extra gravy. But that's not the problem. There's somethin' else." He paused again. "This is probably a small thing, but how'd you know where to stop the car when we were out at the levee? There're no landmarks out there to speak of, not that I saw anyway, and one patch of a dusty cotton field has a way of lookin' like any other—especially to an outsider like you."

"Really not brain surgery, Doc. I'd already been out there the other day. It wasn't my first visit."

"Even so . . . you had to find it the first time. How? Someone show you?"

"I've got the '65 case report, remember? It has a couple of dozen black-and-white scene photos in it taken from all different angles."

"But there's still no landmarks."

"Well, that's not quite true. Remember those run-down sheds near where the John Doe was found? On past where we were standing? In the '65 photos people are living in those things, though to be honest, they didn't look much better then. But they're still recognizable even today. There's also a clump of trees off near the horizon that are visible in the photos, and you can kind of line up on those."

Jo returned with Levine's Shiloh Burger—a cheeseburger covered with chili—and Kel's slice of pecan pie, an extra-thick slice, as she'd promised.

Levine looked at the slather of chili and started to comment. He'd wanted a simple cheeseburger. Instead, he held his tongue.

"You know, maybe it's those houses that are botherin' me. Why there?" Kel retrieved their conversation once the waitress was gone.

Levine was still glaring at the food on his plate as he answered. "Why where? Why what?"

"Why there? You said Jackson was last seen at a church over near West Helena—that's a three-quarter-, half-hour drive away, easy, just to the outskirts. What was he doin' in a lonely field outside Split Tree?"

"If I'm not mistaken, he was getting his head bashed in with a blunt object."

"Ahh, well now that answers all my questions, doesn't it? . . . except . . . why was he there? You can get your head bashed in just about anywhere. Why there? One of two reasons come to mind: Either he went there for a reason and met up with someone he wished he hadn't, or, he was taken there—dead or alive—to be disposed of. In either case, the question I'd be askin' is 'Why?' "

"All right, I'll ask. 'Why?' " After a few tentative bites, Levine began shoveling in large forkfuls of chili and burger.

Kel rolled his eyes and exhaled some frustration. "Don't ask me, you're the damn special agent, remember?" He was quiet for a moment while he ate a couple of bites of pie, shaking his head as he did. "Those houses we saw out there, near where the bodies were found, you said folks were livin' in them at the time? How many were there—we saw a half-dozen or so, didn't we? The people livin' there . . . did any of those FBI reports you read mention who they were? They interview them?"

"Farmers. Migrants. There are maybe eight, nine buildings. I'm guessing they went to bed early; you know . . . see no evil, hear no evil . . . speak no evil . . . get no involved."

Kel figure-skated some sticky pie crumbs around on his plate with a tine of his fork and thought. Finally he answered. "Bullshit. When'd you last see farmers livin' in gang houses like that? Depression time, maybe, but not by 1965—not even in hardscrabble east Arkansas. I got a problem believin' those were farmers—migrants, maybe, but even then I don't think so." He looked up and caught the eye of the waitress. That was all that was required.

"What can I get y'all?" she asked as she approached their booth at a quick step.

"I'm fine," Levine replied, "but I think Sugar here may want something."

She did look like she wanted to spit on him.

"Miss Joletta." Kel smiled up at her. "D'you make that nut pie? That was some of the best I've had in long whiles. How about another slice?"

"Well, bless your heart, comin' right up, Sugar. And call me Jo."

Kel stalled the conversation while they waited. When Joletta returned with an even larger slice of pecan pie, Kel again smiled broadly and shifted gears. "You from around here, Miss Jo?"

"Depends what you mean by from around here. I was born up in Marked Tree, but I've lived here 'most all my life."

Marked Tree was maybe an hour up the road on a windy day. Kel reckoned the waitress at about his age, give or take a few hard-earned years. "Most of your life? What would that be, Miss Jo—about twenty years?"

Joletta colored slightly and smoothed her apron and hair.

Kel continued before she had a chance to reply. "My friend and I were just wonderin' somethin' and we realized that someone knowledgeable about Split Tree, like yourself, might be able to help us. You know them buildin's out south of town, right as you cross the railroad tracks and turn onto . . . ahhh . . . what is it? Route 3? Then you go about a quarter-mile, there by the stand-back levee?"

"The Rumsey property? Ain't no houses out that way," Jo replied, scrunching her face into a tight little knot amid trying to fix the location in her mind.

"Maybe houses isn't the best description; they're in pretty sorry condition, that's a fact. But there's maybe a half-dozen or so, unpainted, leanin' over like they's in a strong wind, straight out Route 3. We were wonderin' who lived there."

Jo smiled in slow recognition. "I know what you mean, Sugar. Them's houses all right, least theys used to be, but not the sort of houses that a man like you would need to be a-botherin' with."

"Not farmers?" Levine interjected into the conversation.

Joletta looked at him as if he was on display in a store window. "There was plenty of oats sowed out there, lots of other things as well, but they weren't no farmers doin' the sowin'." She paused to make sure that they were receiving the message on a single wavelength. "When I was growin' up, that was a little colored village out there. Few Mexicans and some white trash as well. Women set up near the railroad tracks. But it weren't only railroad men that kept them in business." She smiled at the information she was revealing to outsiders. "Plenty of good Split Tree citizens knew the way there without a flashlight. You hear me?"

"And this was goin' on . . . when . . . in the sixties, seventies?" Kel asked in between bites of syrupy pie.

"Oh my, started in the thirties or forties, I suspect—well before the war. But yes, they was still active in the early to midsixties, don't think it continued much into the late sixties though, if at all. Big Ray shut it down 'bout then. Course the railroad was about dead already so it probably wouldn't have lasted much longer anyhow. Cotton business was startin' to die too."

"Ray Elmore?" Levine again interrupted. "You said Big Ray? You mean Ray Elmore?"

"One and the same. Only one Big Ray. Story is he went out there one weekend and persuaded all them women to move their business elsewhere. You know—move, take it elsewhere, as in, anywhere but in Locust County."

Levine looked at her with new interest. "I don't understand," he said. "Wasn't that outside his jurisdiction? He was city police, that's county land, isn't it?"

"Honey, back then there wasn't nothin' that was outside Big Ray's business."

CHAPTER 17

Vietnam War Memorial, The Wall, Washington, D.C.
FRIDAY, JUNE 13, 1986

Big Ray Elmore had traveled the Pacific for almost three years. He'd been wounded twice, the last time by a kamikaze at Iwo Jima, and he'd spent almost a year in a string of navy hospitals, ending up in one in Pensacola where they rebuilt his hip with metal plates and screws. He'd emerged a better man from the crucible of war—a slight limp notwithstanding—and like Dorothy, Big Ray Elmore had discovered what only someone lost far from his roots could ever really understand; there's no place like home.

He had returned from the war to find much of his world changed. Not the town of Split Tree. Split Tree was inert. It was his world that was different. The one true love of his life was married to another; she had a child and a life free from his involvement; his father had died; his mother had aged and been broken by world events beyond her control; his younger brother, Ruell, was buried in a small town in Belgium whose name he couldn't pronounce. But Split Tree was eternal. It was a pole star to his heart. And it was at that moment—at the moment when he first returned home—that he vowed never to stray from its easy borders again.

In the almost forty years since then, he had come very close to keeping that vow. Aside from an occasional, short, day journey to Memphis or Little Rock, Big Ray Elmore had left Split Tree only twice; once, to St. Louis, in 1966, and now, twenty-one years later, to Washington, D.C.

Big Ray Elmore was not alone among his generation in his dislike of the Vietnam Memorial Wall. Like Split Tree, he was a simple man of great complexity. To him, monumental architecture meant rearing horses, and grim-faced men, their eyes ablaze with righteous determination and gritty resolve. He could not fathom an abstract shape memorializing anything as frankly pragmatic as young men dying horrible, painful, lonely deaths far from home and family.

Yet he had to come.

Jimmie Carl Trimble was gone. So was young Ray Junior. Not gone the way they should have, but gone nonetheless, and it was a blister on his soul that had not healed in two decades. It festered and boiled and galled. It was rubbed raw and painful every morning when he awoke. And so he had come, one more futile attempt to salve the wound.

He had asked Grace Trimble to accompany him. She hadn't. He had known that she wouldn't, but he had asked her anyway. To her, the loss of Jimmie Carl Trimble was every bit as fresh and open and just as resistant to healing as the loss of young Ray Junior was to him. And it would be every bit as fresh and just as sore and just as unhealed tomorrow and the next day, and the next one after that.

No visit to an abstract block of inscribed granite would change that.

An hour or so before he left for Memphis to catch his plane to Washington, she had called him, though. "No," she told him, she would not go with him, but could he do her a favor? A friend had told her of the practice of making a rubbing of the engraved names on The Wall. Would he do that for her? Would he make a rubbing of Jimmie Carl's name?

He agreed.

Big Ray Elmore was a practical man prone to solving problems by sheer force of will. Certainly he could manage a rubbing by himself, but for some reason he found himself wanting to watch others make rubbings before attempting it himself. He watched for over an hour. Long after he knew the

procedure. There was some sense of finality that he was re-
luctant to confront. He stalled.

He also took his time locating Jimmie Carl's name; second
panel right of center, 2E, eighth row, third entry. It was high
up, but Big Ray Elmore was a tall man, and he reached it easily enough. The rubbing was managed quickly.

Afterward, Big Ray Elmore walked slowly up the small,
grassy berm behind The Wall. It was warm and the air was
close and the atmosphere noisy, and he needed shade, and
space, and silence. He paused at the top, as much from exhaustion as from a profound sense of emptiness that robbed
him of direction, before continuing down the backside, where
he found a bench. He sat, melted in his sorrow and exhaustion, and looked at the sooty rubbing in his hands, the one
bearing the imprint of *Jimmie C. Trimble*. He thought of his
son, young Ray Junior. He thought of the last letter that he had
received from Vietnam. Ray Junior had apologized for letting
him down, for not being there, for leaving his mother and
brother, for everything and anything and all things. It was the
only letter Big Ray Elmore had saved. The rest he had thrown
away—not even something as symbolic as burning—simply
thrown them away.

All except the last letter; he had kept that one.

Big Ray Elmore was not a religious man, but the letter was
there, at home in Split Tree where young Ray Junior should
be. It was beside his bed where he could look at it, not daily,
but often enough. He didn't need to read it, just touch it, rub
his hand over it. Reassure his heart that it was there.

It was tucked in his Bible.

CHAPTER 18

Split Tree, Arkansas
THURSDAY, AUGUST 18, 2005

Kel paid their bill at the restaurant, being sure to leave Joletta a memorable tip, and joined his now-partner in the car.

As he started the engine, Levine began anew to pick at the scab of their conversation.

"I'm not sure I'm fully getting the significance of what you were asking the waitress back there," Levine said. He had become sufficiently familiar with the town that he now drove quickly and with confidence.

Kel screwed his face into a concerted frown and stared at Levine. "I want to see some ID . . . are you sure you're in the FBI?"

"Depends if you're asking me or the Bureau."

"Look, farmers are one thing. But the people who were livin' in those houses weren't farmers. They were workin' girls. Follow? Different groups, farmers and prostitutes, definitely different work habits."

"I'm still not fully tracking. You thinking witnesses?"

"Think about your files. Farmers get up early, work hard, and, yes, go to bed early—like your reports said. If they were farmers, maybe they don't see any shit that happens late at night. Though try tippin' one of their cows once and see how good their hearin' is. But these weren't farmers, were they? Do I need to remind you how hot it is durin' the summer down here? I didn't see any air-conditionin' on those buildings, did you? It has to be over a hundred in those shacks durin' the day. More. So where do you suppose those women were?"

Levine diverted his eyes from the road long enough to look at Kel. He said nothing.

"Not workin', that's for damn sure. They were out swimmin' or shoppin' or workin' off hangovers or sleepin' in the shade, but they definitely weren't on the meter durin' the day in those sweatboxes, and if they're not there durin' the day then that means work, work, work at night, and that means they weren't asleep."

"You're right. So they should have seen something."

"What'd the waitress say? 'Lots of folk knew their way out there without a flashlight.' No shit. It's not the sort of place good Split Tree citizens would announce their arrival at by honkin' their horns and flashin' their car lights, and that means the girls would be on the lookout. Hell, they probably knew you were there before you did."

"Which means they saw something, but told the agents they didn't."

"Maybe they saw somethin', maybe they didn't," Kel replied. "If they did see somethin', they probably weren't real anxious to talk to cops, especially federal agents. This was small-town nowhere and it was 1965. Then again, maybe I don't have a clue what I'm talkin' about. Maybe they really didn't see anythin'. Sounds like those bodies were buried pretty shallow out in that field; that means it was probably done quick. Maybe someone was discreet." He shrugged.

"Yeah, and maybe not."

Kel shrugged again.

"And then of course, there's another possibility."

"What's that?" Kel asked.

"That maybe they did see someone—someone they knew they weren't supposed to see."

The police chief's office was located, as one of the customers in the diner had informed them, in the "new" city hall, diagonally across the square from the courthouse. It was singularly unspectacular in appearance, a flat, featureless, one-story, taffy-colored concrete box—with all the charm and character of a roach motel. Blooms on the azalea bushes on either side of the entrance had long burned off.

Levine parked the car in a diagonal space in front of the courthouse. He got out, shut the door, and locked it.

"You sure you want me along?" Kel asked as they started across the street. He had dealt with enough FBI agents in the past to know that they typically have a very low opinion of non-FBI personnel being involved in anything, let alone one of their cases. Yet here he was, following behind Levine on a leash.

"Sure. Why, you got something better you need to be doing?"

If he were playing along, Kel could list a good dozen or so things he'd rather be doing, but what would be the point. He opened the glass door of the new city hall and held it open for Levine.

The inside of the building was as uniformly unspectacular as the outside. There was a small common room with a couple of low wooden desks, state surplus by the looks of them, and a row of filing cabinets covered with refrigerator magnets—all cats, Levine noted; somebody liked cats. Several of the acoustic tiles in the suspended ceiling looked as if someone had somehow spilled coffee on them. The walls of the room were paneled with the sort of cheap, wood-finished pasteboard paneling that one normally expects to find in mobile homes. In fact, the room gave the impression of a trailer except for its square configuration.

"Come on in; you Mr. Levine?" A young man, maybe twenty-five years Levine's junior, wearing a black, pleated police officer's uniform shirt, was poking his head around the door opening off to the far right corner, the one next to a calendar that extolled Arkansas as "The Natural State." He was medium height but clearly spent time with weights, and his high-and-tight haircut hinted at prior military service, or at least a desire to have served. "Edd Forrest, chief of police for Split Tree. Come on, come on, take a seat." He motioned them into his office and pointed at two padded metal folding chairs in front of his desk. On the wall behind his desk was a framed diploma from Southeast Missouri State University in Cape Girardeau.

"Mike Levine, FBI," Levine said. He took a seat, introducing Kel as he sat down. "Thanks for meeting with us. This is Dr. Robert McKelvey of the Army Central ID Lab."

"Glad to meet you, Mr. Levine. Doctor. CID?"

"No, no," Kel quickly corrected. "C-I-L. The Central Identification Laboratory."

"The fellas that identify the MIAs?"

"That's right," Kel acknowledged.

Chief Forrest nodded as he took his seat behind his desk. "I read about y'all in the papers. Well, what can I do for you boys?"

"Chief, I know you're a busy man, so I'll get to business. What do you know about the murder of Leonidas Jackson? Ring a bell?"

Chief Edd Forrest looked at Levine for several seconds while he reached forward and removed a pen from a large coffee mug on his desk that doubled as a pencil holder. "Not much, really," he finally replied as he rocked back into his chair. He commenced tapping the ballpoint pen on a report lying on his desk, and he watched the point intently while he accessed his memory. "Let me see, summer of 1965, I think. Black civil rights activist from . . . Mississippi—Jackson or Natchez—got the ACLU snoopin' around down here for a while. Last seen at a church rally over in Helena, West Helena, maybe. Local kid finds his body washin' out of a fallow field. Clear homicide. Your office implicated the Klan, but no indictments were ever handed down, and no one was ever convicted, as I recall. Body of a white kid found nearby a couple of months later. Other than that, don't remember much, I'm afraid."

Levine was surprised that he had remembered that much. He hadn't even been born when the murder had occurred. "That's more than anyone else around here seems to remember, Chief; I'm impressed."

Edd Forrest smiled and took these two men in. "Not everyone sees the virtue in rememberin' the past, Mr. Levine."

"So I gather."

"I also have a bit of an advantage. To be honest, we read about that case in a criminal justice class I had in college. Bein' from here and all, I took notes."

Levine nodded. "Chief, the reason we're here is that the Bureau has decided to reopen the investigation. Where it will lead, if anywhere, is anybody's guess right now. My interest is in what your office might be able to contribute."

The chief laid his pen down and leaned farther backward in his chair, tipping it onto its hind legs, propping his brown, alligator-grained cowboy boots onto his desk. "Hate to disappoint you, Mr. Levine, but that occurred in Locust County, not in Split Tree. I'm afraid that's outside my jurisdiction. You need to talk to the sheriff."

"Understood, Chief. But to be honest, Sheriff Elmore doesn't seem to be a great deal of help in this matter."

"As I said, Agent Levine, not everyone sees the virtue in rememberin' the past. You'd really do well to remember that. But now let me ask you a question." He shifted his focus to Kel. "What's this case got to do with Ray Elmore?"

"Ray Elmore?" Kel had been daydreaming and wasn't running at full speed with regard to the conversation. "I'm not sure I understand your question."

"Well," Chief Forrest replied, cocking his head to one side. The expression reminded Kel of a bird dog he'd had when he was growing up that used to give him that same look when he was pondering something important. "I assume that if the CIL is involved, it must have somethin' to do with Ray Elmore. I mean, the sheriff's brother is still missin' in Vietnam. Correct? Two of our boys died over there. The VFW hall is named after one of them—Jimmie Trimble—he's the big-time hero around these parts, Navy Cross and all. His body came home, but Ray Elmore never returned. Not sure of the details. He was in the navy, I know, but the Elmores were always kinda quiet about the matter. All I know is that he got killed and didn't come back. They say Big Ray took the loss real hard. Ray Junior was his absolute pride, you know? Idolized that boy. His wife never did recover, kind of stove her up permanent. Mental case."

"When'd it happen? You remember?" Kel asked.

"You mean when'd he die?" Edd Forrest took a deep breath as if it would help clear the cobwebs from his memory. He slowly exhaled and stared closely at his folded hands resting on his belt buckle. "Don't know. Maybe six months, year after Jimmie Carl Trimble's death. Truth is, don't really know. Before my time. Probably not too long after that Jackson fella's death."

Levine wanted to get the conversation back on track. "This visit doesn't involve the sheriff's brother. Dr. McKelvey is here to support the Bureau, not as a representative of the army's lab. My intent, once we locate the remains of the John Doe—the white kid—found with Mr. Jackson, is to reanalyze them and possibly do some DNA work. That's the game plan, anyway. The Bureau requested Dr. McKelvey's assistance in taking a fresh look at the remains. That's all."

Edd Forrest nodded and smiled. "Guess I jumped to a conclusion."

"The Trimbles and Elmores close?" Kel broke in. He didn't intend to sidetrack the conversation any more than it had already strayed, but the memory of their meeting with Grace Trimble and the photographic shrine in her living room pricked his train of thought. "We visited Mrs. Trimble and saw a photograph of her son and Big Ray Elmore on the wall," he added as if by way of explanation.

The chief stretched out his arms and then clasped his hands behind his neck; he tilted his head slightly back so that he was sighting down the length of his long nose at Kel. "You want facts or gossip?"

"Either. Both," Levine now picked up the question.

"Can't say I know the facts. But gossip always held that Big Ray and Miss Grace was to be married. High-school sweethearts and all. Then he went off to the Pacific during the war and she apparently couldn't wait. He got wounded and spent some time healin' up in a hospital in Florida or somewhere like that. When he got back here to Split Tree, Miss Grace was married to that fat-assed Carl Trimble. No offense to the dead, but Carl Trimble wasn't worth much."

"Why'd she marry him then?" Kel asked.

"There were rumors, of course. Carl had the good fortune to have flat feet and managed to serve out the war comfortin' the women on the home front. Miss Grace was one of them, I guess. In any case, she gets herself married and has a son— Jimmie Carl. Everyone calls him 'short-stack,' 'cause his birth date and Mr. and Mrs. Trimble's first weddin' anniversary don't quite have the spread as you might like. He hated it—Jimmie Carl that is. I remember my older brother called him that once after a football game, and Jimmie Carl 'bout beat the thick snot out of him. He wasn't big, but he was pretty good with his fists. Have to be with his upbringin'."

The chief paused and nodded slightly to his two listeners to verify that they were still interested. When they nodded back, he continued. "Back then there wasn't anythin' to do but get on with gettin' on. Big Ray and Miss Grace lived their separate lives. Big Ray came home from the war and got married and had his own kids—Ray Junior and Waymond Ray— W.R.—you've met him, you say. Big Ray and Carl had to get along too, they were in the same . . . clubs . . . but they clearly didn't have much to do with one another. Shit, Big Ray wasn't called Big Ray only 'cause he was tall; like him or not, he was one helluva drink of water. He projected power, you know? And Carl was a fat little piece of shit. Big Ray was everythin' Carl wasn't, includin' bein' a man."

The chief paused and stared at the acoustic tile ceiling for a few breaths. "Carl took to drinkin', and when he'd been a-drinkin' he took to beatin' on Jimmie Carl, maybe on Miss Grace too, I don't know, you hear all sorts of things. Anyhow, Big Ray catches hold of him after a meetin' one night and parts his hair with a pick handle. Damn near killed him, they say. Course Carl wasn't goin' to admit it was Big Ray that did it, so he says it was a bunch of niggers that jumped him out by the levee. Excuse the expression."

Edd Forrest waited for his guests to process that information, but got blank expressions in return. "Maybe y'all not from around here but that story don't wash. Not in 1965, anyways. No respectable white man, especially one as insecure as Carl Trimble, was going to admit that he let some colored boys whup his ass—even if it was true. That was the tip-off. Shows how much he hated Big Ray that he'd rather folks think that some blacks whupped him rather than Big Ray Elmore. Sure, some of the local boys around here used that as a convenient excuse to raise hell with the blacks; knock out some windows, disturb some sleep, but the reality was that everyone knew who'd done it. And it weren't the blacks. Grace Trimble knew as well; story was that she supposedly talked to Big Ray and told him no more. Never happened again, but Carl Trimble never touched his family again, either. After that, Big Ray just sort of moved in, at least figuratively, and acted like a father to Jimmie Carl, and Carl Trimble done stayed functionally drunk.

"So, to answer your question, Trimbles and Elmores close? Depends who you're talkin' about. Not Carl and Big Ray, that's for damn sure."

There followed a long silence. Levine could hear the soft, rhythmic click of his watch. He waited for someone to pick up the conversation, but both Kel and Chief Forrest seemed content to sit in silence. Finally he cleared his throat and shifted his weight in the metal chair so that he was leaning slightly forward. It creaked under his weight. "Thanks,

Chief, didn't mean to get so far off target but that helps put some things into perspective. But about the Jackson case . . . as I said, I'm here to see what can be done to jump-start the investigation."

Chief Forrest removed his feet to the floor and slid up under his desk. His look conveyed little. "Well, Agent Levine, as I said, that's outside my jurisdiction. This office will support you in any way we can, but I don't see much of a role for us."

"You mentioned the ACLU, you know what that was all about? I've read the Bureau's take on the matter, but I'd be interested in your version." Truth was, Levine had read something in the FBI case file about ACLU involvement, but it hadn't seemed particularly pertinent, and he'd glossed it more than he should have. Now he was mildly curious but didn't want to admit to this sharp, young kid that a special agent for the FBI hadn't done his homework.

"Don't know much. Jackson claimed his rights were bein' violated by local Jim Crow officials; the official police version said he was drunk and disorderly. Don't think much ever came of it one way or t'other, but I'll also admit to not knowin' much about it."

Levine nodded as if in agreement. "Thanks, that pretty well jibes with what I have in the case file." Now he shifted gears. "Mainly I was hoping that you might have some records or files on the case that aren't in the Bureau's folder. Understand that it was out of this jurisdiction, but thought you might have something."

"No sir, not to my knowledge. Course I've only been in this job a few years, but I don't have any historical records like that. They'd be county records if there are any." He smiled. "You'd have to ask the sheriff."

"Well, as I said earlier, the sheriff doesn't seem too motivated to assist." Levine tapped his fingers on his thigh and looked at the chief, who returned his stare. "By any chance, you wouldn't know where this town might keep some skeletal remains, would you? Specifically those of the John Doe."

"The Leon Jackson John Doe? No, sir. Might check with Donnie Hawk, he's the Locust County coroner."

"I did. He told me to ask the Boy Scouts."

Edd Forrest smiled. "Welcome to Split Tree, Mr. Levine."

CHAPTER 19

Split Tree, Arkansas
THURSDAY, AUGUST 18, 2005

They emerged from the refrigerated air of the new city hall into the soggy heat of midday. The overhead sun shut down their eyes, and Kel shuddered involuntarily from the change of temperature. *Rabbits,* he thought. His grandmother had always said that a surprise shudder was the result of rabbits running over your grave. It hadn't made any sense to him as a child, and it didn't make any more sense to him as an adult.

Levine was standing on the sidewalk in front of the building, not moving. He had a look on his face as if he was scouting out a hard surface to bang his head against.

"Don't tell me you honestly thought you were goin' to learn somethin' from this meetin'," Kel said, watching Levine's curious expression. "You said yourself that it was goin' to be a waste of time."

"Maybe I was wrong. Did you catch that part about Big Ray taking Trimble apart after a meeting? What the hell kind of meeting, do you suppose?"

Maybe he wasn't looking for a hard surface, after all. Maybe he was just focusing on a hard nut to crack.

"A staff meeting at CILHI, maybe. God knows they make me want to club people."

Levine's expression wasn't amused.

"Ahh, okay. I guess I don't know," Kel atoned. "I'm sure they have all sorts of clubs down here. Little towns can be very social."

"Maybe. That's the second time I've heard the expression, though."

Kel noticed that Levine's look had suddenly changed. So had his voice.

"And here comes the man I first heard it from," Levine said, his eyes focused on someone over Kel's shoulder.

Jimbo Bevins was walking up the sidewalk toward the two men. He was wearing his hard straw cowboy hat and its glossy waxed surface glinted in the light. He also was smiling broadly, but his eyes had a sharp sliver to them.

"You sure can be a hard man to track down, Mr. Levine, that's for dang sure," he said as he drew up close. The smile was still broad and the sliver sharp. He adjusted his pistol belt and put his hands in his hip pockets as he looked at Kel, taking his measure.

"Didn't know anyone was tracking me down, Deputy. Long time no see." Levine saw that Jimbo wasn't taking his eyes off Kel. "Deputy Bevins, this is Dr. Robert McKelvey; Doc, this is my trusty keeper, Deputy James Bevins of the Locust County Sheriff's Department."

"How y'all are, Mr. McKelvey." Jimbo kept his hands in his pockets but offered a calculated nod in Kel's direction.

"Fair to middlin', Deputy, and yourself?" Kel replied.

"Same. What brings you here to Split Tree; you workin' with Mr. Levine?"

"Yes and no—mostly no. I work for the army. I'm tryin' to identify the remains of a young man who died in Vietnam thirty-some years ago—that's my job—and I simply needed to talk to some folks."

"Like Miss Grace?"

"Mrs. Trimble, that's right. Needed to clear up a few things. Case just happens to overlap with Special Agent Levine here." Kel didn't necessarily want to distance himself from Levine, but saw no obvious reason to risk being collateral damage in a pissing contest either.

"So, Deputy, I take it you're still assigned to watchdog me?" Levine resumed control of the conversation.

"Sheriff still thinks y'all might still need some assistance, is all."

"Probably do, Deputy Bevins, no doubt I do. In fact, right this moment I need some assistance getting something cool to drink. Kel and I were heading for the Albert Pike Café. Care to join us?" As was his practice, Levine had already started walking across the street to his car and left both Kel and Jimbo to catch up.

By the time Jimbo Bevins had pulled his Sheriff's Department cruiser into the Albert Pike's parking lot, Levine had locked his car and started to walk inside. Jimbo hurried and the three of them entered more or less knotted together. The usual crowd was assembled—at least they all looked the same, even if they weren't—but the booth that Levine and Kel had staked out earlier was now occupied by two heavy-set middle-aged men in short-sleeved dress shirts and shiny brown cowboy boots. They were eating breaded catfish and big, crumbly cubes of buttered yellow cornbread. Levine still had a hard time adjusting to the early dinner times that everyone here seemed to schedule.

They took an adjoining booth, Jimbo Bevins pulling up a chair from a nearby table and sitting at the end rather than next to either man. He adjusted his pistol belt so that it didn't bind him as he sat, and the leather creaked softly. His attention was focused now on Levine, and he had a look that made it appear as if he were trying to memorize the federal agent's face in case there was a quiz later. Jimbo had never been too quick at quizzes, and this man was stacking up to be one of those puzzles with lots of little pieces.

"Sorry you had such a hard time finding us, Deputy," Levine said as a waitress dealt out menus. Joletta had been replaced by a skinny, blue-skinned old woman with thinning

hair and a smoker's cough that racked her whole body peri-
odically. It was the fruity sort of cough that made anyone
within earshot cough in sympathy. "Did you have to look
long? To find me, that is."

Jimbo smiled and shuttered his eyes partway as he continued looking at Levine. "No sir, Split Tree ain't a big place;
that's one advantage to it." He eyed Levine a moment longer.
His eyes flashed feral and then softened. He looked up at the
waitress and ordered some iced tea and some peach cobbler.

Kel ordered tea and another slice of pecan pie. Levine, apparently adjusting to the heat somewhat, or perhaps conceding to a chemical habit, ordered coffee.

"Well," Levine continued, "if a place has to have an advantage, finding wayward FBI agents easily would be a good
one to have. But tell me, how'd the sheriff know I was back
in town?" Levine suspected he knew the answer but hoped he
could tease the information out of Jimbo. "Not from recognizing my car; the motor pool gave me a different vehicle
when I was back in Memphis." That was true, but only because Levine had requested it.

"Mr. Levine, I ain't nothin' but a Locust County deputy
sheriff. How W.R. knows things ain't but none of my good
business. He tells; I do; that's the way it works 'round here."

The waitress had delivered their orders, and Levine waited
for her to move on to the catfish-and-cornbread men, checking their status, before he continued.

"Sorry to have upset Mrs. Trimble. That certainly was
never anyone's intent." Levine was trolling his baited hook
and waited for Jimbo to rise to the surface.

He bit. "Yes sir. You got to understand that she's terrible
sensitive about Jimmie Carl; even after all these years.
Strange people askin' questions and all. Sheriff knows how
she is, and he just don't want her upset none. He's got a special place for her, you understand?"

As Levine had suspected. They probably had no sooner
left her house than Grace Trimble had called Sheriff Elmore.

Levine took a sip of coffee, replaced his mug on the table, and smiled. "Seems like a nice lady." He flashed a look at Kel who had been quietly watching the dynamic between the two, trying to figure out the game rules before joining in.

"Yes sir," Jimbo replied between bites of cobbler. "She's a mighty nice lady. We believe in showin' proper respect 'round here. Maintainin' order."

"Of course you do. That's your job, isn't it?" Levine prodded and poked. "You and the sheriff maintain order and keep everything orderly. What is it that you people call her—'Miss Grace'?"

Jimbo's eyes began to flash again. "Your people probably do things different, but around here, callin' her Miss Grace is just a sign of respect."

Levine started to respond but Kel interjected quietly. "Around here, anyway." He wasn't sure what was happening but both men looked like they were about to eat each other. "Go some other places in the South—across the river into Mississippi, I suspect, and some people might call that nigger talk."

Jimbo broke stares with Levine and eyed Kel. Dismissal was replaced with curiosity.

"That so?" Levine asked. He still wanted to take a bite out of Jimbo's ass with a dull spoon, but he recognized Kel's attempt to defuse a tightening situation.

"That's the way house slaves used to address the masters. Mr. or Miss and the first name. There was a time in certain areas of the South when no respectable white folk would talk like that to other white folk. It was thought to be demeanin' to them; to the speaker, that is. Other places, here in Arkansas, for example, I don't think that was ever really the case. More a sign of respect, like Deputy Bevins says. Maybe 'cause Arkansas was never as much of a slave-ownin' state as were the likes of Mississippi or Alabama." He shrugged as if to say, *So now you know.*

"Y'all from around here then?" Jimbo's interest in Kel had

sharpened somewhat over the last few minutes and he finally put voice to it.

"Naw. Not really. Other side of the state."

"McKelvey, you say? Used to be a mess of McKelveys in these parts. You any kin to them?"

Kel smiled. "You're right, Deputy. There used to be McKelveys here, but not in a long time. Now let me ask you somethin'." He deflected Jimbo's question. "Chief Forrest mentioned that your boss lost a brother in Vietnam, is that right?"

Jimbo hesitated. No doubt he was uneasy about supplying too much information to two men he was supposed to be bird-dogging. "Yes sir," he finally responded, his IQ outweighing his judgment. "His twin. Ray Junior. They was the kind that looked exactly alike, and I mean exactly alike. Didn't act nothin' at all the same though—unless they was tryin' to. They were both a few years older than me so I never knew him. Heard of him, though. Ray Junior was an All-State Honorable Mention halfback for the high-school football team—big-time athletic scholarship over at Tech; W.R.—the sheriff—he played too, but not nearly as good. He was a wingback. *Delta Devils*. State Triple-A champs three years in a row."

"No shit? That's somethin'," Kel said by way of starting to shift conversational gears. Now he paused. "He didn't come back, though, is that right? I mean, they never did recover his body from Vietnam, did I understand that correctly?"

"Ray Junior?"

"Uh hmm."

"Naw, they never did find him. Surprised everyone. Enlisted right after graduation, shipped off instead of goin' to college, and never came home. His daddy took that piece of sorrow to his dug grave."

"How many men from Split Tree died in Vietnam?" Kel asked. The martial dedication of small southern towns is a historical fact, but two from a town the size of Split Tree was an impressive statistic.

"Not but two. Dozen or so served over there, but only two got killed: Jimmie Carl Trimble and Ray Junior. Their names are on the monument over there at the courthouse."

Jimbo Bevins shoveled another bite of cobbler.

Levine had allowed conversation to drift somewhat, to calm, and now he wanted to pull it back to the matter of concern to him. "Jimbo"—he waited for the deputy to swing his face around and fix his eyes—"you said the sheriff didn't want us upsetting Mrs. Trimble—Miss Grace—is that what he thinks we were doing?"

"Yes sir. That's how we, that's how he sees it."

"Well, shit, Jimbo, I'm certainly sorry to get you caught up in all this. I really am. I can see why the sheriff told you to get a handle on us. Two strangers arrive in town and start kicking up all sorts of bad memories that everyone else wishes would stay forgotten. I certainly can understand his being upset."

"Yes sir, you know, he's just kind of funny about Miss Grace."

"I certainly can understand that. I imagine he probably gets pretty pissed when someone starts messing around with her, asking about her son, and all."

"You got that right," Jimbo confirmed.

"You do me a favor. You make sure you report back to him that we are very, very sorry and that no offense was meant. You'll do that, won't you?" Levine lifted his eyebrows to make sure that Jimbo understood a response was in order.

Jimbo nodded.

"I certainly don't want the sheriff coming after me all pissed off," Levine continued.

"No sir, you don't. That's for damn sure, you don't."

CHAPTER 20

Split Tree, Arkansas
THURSDAY, AUGUST 18, 2005

The rest of the day went quietly.

Levine and Kel retired to the Sleep-Mor early, after convincing Deputy Bevins that they would involve themselves in no further mischief for the remainder of the evening. Levine had announced his intention of driving back to Memphis in the morning to get a leg up on some administrative matters and, no doubt, to get out of Split Tree for the weekend. For his part, Kel wasn't happy with flying a quarter of the way around the world to support the FBI only to have the FBI abandon him for the weekend. He'd decided to ride along with Levine as far as the Memphis airport, where he could rent a car—the prospect of being a pedestrian in Split Tree for an entire weekend was more than even Bre'r Rabbit wanted to bear.

The motel was busy again. Not as chaotic as the first night when the fishing tournament had been in midangle, but busy nonetheless. The temperature had moderated some from the heat blister of the afternoon. A front had moved in from the southwest and teased of rain. None fell, but the temperature cooled noticeably, or at least everyone convinced themselves that it had.

Kel was flagged out but knew that if he took a nap early he'd be awake all night. Every day at about this time the cost of jet travel caught up with him. The problem, he reasoned, was that he hadn't been back in Hawaii long enough to adjust his clock from North Korean time before flying another quarter of the way around the world. *What time was it in North Korea anyway? Hell, I think they're on about June 4, 1000 A.D., or something. No wonder I'm tired.*

He booted up his laptop computer and took out some files that he'd brought with him. The one on top of the stack was a thick brown folder labeled *TRIMBLE, Jimmie C., HM.* He sat at the desk and began reading it. There was a copy of the wartime Tan Son Nhut mortuary file with a body diagram shaded to show what parts had been present and what was missing. The paper was marked and stained with time and mortality. There also was a report from one of CILHI's teams that documented the recent recovery efforts, but what caught Kel's attention was a copy of a Marine Corps After Action Report dated 14 October 1966. It appeared innocuous, but to someone inoculated against the boilerplate of military memoranda, this AAR was a smoker. Its author, a Marine lieutenant named Dwayne Crockett, had either an excess of balls or a paucity of brains, but in either case it was clear to Kel that the young officer's military career had effectively ended with this report. Phrases such as "inept intelligence gathering," "incompetent leadership," and "a tragic waste of brave men's lives" were guaranteed to rattle the wrong cages. Kel smiled as he reread the report. It mostly addressed the shortcomings of what clearly had been a botched military action and didn't offer any great insight into whose remains were on a shelf at the CILHI, but it did get Kel's mind headed in a different direction. An idea began to percolate, and he closed his eyes to help it gel. Jet lag took over from there, and he found himself doing less thinking and more nodding off. Eventually he gave in, kicked off his shoes, and lay down on the bed.

He'd simply intended to rest a few minutes. He'd lain there staring at the acoustic panels overhead. Above each of the two beds were a series of concentric depressions. Kel puzzled over them for several minutes until he realized that they were the imprints of heads. Kids, he assumed, jumping on the beds, seeing who could put their heads through the ceiling panels. *How funny,* he thought, *how funny,* and then he was out.

When Kel awoke the room was dark, only a faint yellow glow from the bug light outside his room providing a sense of depth to the shadows. He looked at the window and saw a black sky. He fumbled for the little button that would light up his watch: eleven-eighteen; six-eighteen in Hawaii. *Crap.* Something had been nagging at him like a little itch for the last couple of hours, and as much as he hated it, he needed to make a call to the Lab in Hawaii. And now he'd missed his opportunity. It was probably too late to get hold of anyone there who could answer his questions.

Crap, crap, crap.

He sat up and shook the silt and mud out of his head. Maybe it was worth a shot. With him gone, D.S. might be working later, and then, of course, Les Neep often put in long days. He slipped his shoes on and ventured outside.

The cool breeze that had come wafting ahead of the front earlier had passed with nothing more than a lingering promise, and although it was now nearing midnight, the temperature had begun to rise again, and the air had a thick, fecund, muddy smell tinged with . . . tinged with what? Curry. Of course. Everything smelled of curry. Kel briefly closed his eyes and stood on the sidewalk. He heard a lone whippoorwill and wondered where on the floodplain it had managed to find anything to nest in. As he looked off into the darkness he saw the dim silhouette of a car parked on the fringe of the lot. A man in a cowboy hat was leaning against the hood, and Kel could see the small red starlight of a cigarette. Another fisherman probably. Or not.

The Albert Pike had once been an all-night diner, but then traffic patterns changed and the cotton gin had scaled back its operations and people all acquired home air-conditioners— that was the main thing. Air-conditioning meant people stayed home. In the end, the owner had bowed to fiscal reality, and the diner was now open from 5:00 A.M. to midnight. In a small place like Split Tree that was still something unusual.

It was cool and brightly lit, and empty. Almost. Two over-weight, middle-aged men sat in a corner booth drinking coffee, no doubt on their way home from a night shift of some sort—maybe the Wal-Mart Supercenter over near Helena. They both wore Dickie slacks held up by clip-on suspenders. Kel walked over to a booth near them and took a seat. Joletta was still nowhere in sight, probably home in bed. In fact the only staff who appeared to be around was the same skinny, weathered stick of wood whom Kel had seen working the grill that morning. The same one that Levine had thought might be Albert Pike, at least until Kel had told him that Pike was a local Confederate Civil War figure. Kel looked at his watch, eleven-twenty-five—this guy had been cooking for at least sixteen hours, probably more.

It took a few moments, but the old man—his name was Lee Boy Spencer, though he hadn't been a boy in a good many years—finally noticed his new customer and made his way out to the dining floor. He walked as if he were Nordic skiing, with a shuffle that did not require his feet to leave the linoleum and an exaggerated swing of his arms. Kel smiled. Neither he nor his waiter was in any particular hurry, though Kel did have a call to make before it got any later. The waiter paused as he passed the two overweight men, bobbing his head as he checked on the status of their coffee cups, and find-ing them satisfactory. Something was mumbled back and forth. When he finally arrived, Kel waved off his offer of a menu and ordered scrambled eggs, hash browns, and toast. The old man nodded, committing the order to memory, and began to retrace his steps, stopping again to mumble to the two overweight men before steering a more direct downhill course to the grill.

The pay phone was near the street side wall, next to the display that held tourist brochures for Silver Dollar City, Branson, Blanchard Springs, and some floating casinos out-side Tupelo.

He listened as the phone rang. After the second ring he

knew there'd be no answer. The CILHI voice-mail system finally kicked in and Kel left D.S. a message saying that he'd try to catch him tomorrow; that it was nothing crucial. Then he dialed again, trying Les Neep's number. Again he waited. The CILHI had recently installed a new phone system that ensured that no one could get through to anyone without thrashing through a half-dozen menus and listening to more *aloha*s and *mahalo*s than a Hawaiian wedding reception. He suspected the same convicts that designed his office furniture were behind the phone software. Neep's voice mail finally rang on, and Kel left a similar message, saying that he'd check in tomorrow. He hung up.

He glanced at his booth, saw that there was no food waiting for him yet, and took another look at his watch: eleven-forty-five—six-forty-five in Hawaii. He pulled out his credit card again and dialed home.

"Hello." It was the soft accent of his wife. She was from the hills of northwest Arkansas and had more of a lilt to her speech than the slow, thick-tongued syrup that he was encountering here on the lowland floodplain.

"Hey, hon, interruptin' anythin'?"

"Hey, yourself. No, I was just cleanin' up after dinner, and thinkin' about you, of course."

"Glad to hear that. Thinkin' about you too. Thought I'd call before it got any later."

"The boys are going to be so sorry, they just went for a walk up to the park. Your office called here, by the way. Said they hadn't heard from you, and wanted you to check in."

"Hmmm."

"Hmmm yourself. Which reminds me, how'd you go and manage to leave your cell phone in my car, you suppose?"

"All the rush to get to the airport, I guess."

"Funny thing is," his wife said, "it got wedged way down behind the seat. I'd like to never have found it."

"That is funny."

"I'll laugh later. Anyhow, how's it goin' there? Accomplishin' what you need to? Enjoyin' the countryside, I bet."

Kel debated briefly whether to start unraveling the whole sweater of the last twenty-four hours and decided against it. "Well, that depends on how you define accomplish. I've eaten lots of Karo nut pie, if that counts; butted heads with one of Mr. Hoover's G-men; insulted an old woman who worships her dead son; and caught the eye of a very attractive young waitress—I think she's kinda sweet on me."

"Well bless her heart—the old woman, that is. How'd you insult her?" Mary Louise was another honor graduate of the bless-your-heart school of southern manners.

"Oh, the usual, you know, suggested she wasn't his real mother, that sort of thing."

"Why Robert McKelvey—do you have nothin' better to do with your time? You'd be better off flirtin' with that waitress."

"I tell you what, that's the problem. I don't have anythin' better to do. This has been three miles of goat rope, and I haven't even seen the goat yet."

"Then come on home. I miss you. Plus, I could use your help drownin' the boys in the bathtub—they're gettin' so big it's hard to hold them both under water at the same time."

Kel smiled and closed his eyes. "What this time?"

"What do you think?"

"It's an engineering problem, hon. God gave teenage boys brains and penises but only enough blood to operate one at a time."

"I'd settle for their brains operatin' at all."

"Bad?"

"You want the whole list or just the highlights?"

"Highlights."

"Another call from school. It's so much fun to switch identities and confuse the teachers, you know. For the life of me I will never understand why twins find that so amusin'."

"We're not twins; I don't reckon we can understand."

"Suspect you're right. But that's not why you called."

"Hmmm. Wanted to check in; hear your voice, mainly. Goin' to get somethin' to eat and then go to bed; it's almost midnight. I'm catchin' a ride up to Memphis tomorrow to get a rental car. I may try and do some sightseein' this weekend."

"That'll be fun."

"Maybe."

"It will. Just be careful. Get some sleep now. Come home soon. We miss you."

"Miss y'all. Be home in a couple of days. Love you."

"Love you . . . 'night."

"Goodnight, hon."

Kel returned to his booth to find his food ready. As he sat down and began eating, the old man began a slow shuffle out to the dining floor. The overweight men were still there, still drinking coffee.

"Getcha anythin' else? Gonna be shuttin' down the kitchen in a few minutes," he asked when he finally reached the booth. He had skied right past the coffee drinkers without a mumble this time. His tone suggested that the correct answer to his question was "No."

"No sir. This here's fine," Kel replied correctly.

The old man lingered. His expression looked like cement getting ready to set up. Kel took a couple of bites and looked at his plate, thinking that the old man was trying to coordinate his limbs for the trek back to the kitchen. But he wasn't.

"You mind I ask y'all a question?"

"No sir, what's on your mind?" Kel answered. He put his fork down.

"Why you here? Where y'all from?"

"Hmmm," Kel considered. "Well, that's a good question. This is kind of a vacation for me. I'm from the other side of the state originally, live in Hawaii now, but I used to have kin hereabouts—thought I might do some genealogy."

The old man leaned forward and placed his knuckles on

the end of the table like an ape. He looked directly at Kel. "You always have FBI men help you shake your family tree?"

My, it is a small town, Kel thought. He smiled. "No sir. That there FBI man is here all on his own. I was just asked along in case he needed any help—which it doesn't look like he does. So I'll be leavin' shortly. I do want to study up on my family tree while I'm here, though. No point wastin' a trip. Like I said, sort of a vacation."

Now it was the old man's turn to smile. "Never been to your side of the state. Been to Jackson, though." He paused and Kel was reasonably sure that the old man knew that Jackson was in Mississippi and not in western Arkansas. His little sortie into regional geography was merely to establish his bona fides as a man of the world and thus add some import to his words. "Saw you talkin' to Jimbo Bevins. You'd be smart to steer clear of that boy."

"Deputy Bevins? He seems like a good old boy. Good kid," Kel responded. He thought about the way Jimbo's eyes flashed hot and cold.

"Maybe, but I'd keep my distance."

"Well, I'll, ahh, I'll try and do that. Anythin' else I should know?"

"Yup. He'd be the least of your problems."

Kel smiled, unsure where the conversation was headed. "Huh. I wasn't aware I had any problems. I'm not here to bother anybody, so I don't see anybody botherin' me."

"Don't know about where y'all come from, but 'round here we don't step on a cottonmouth lest we 'tend to be killin' it. And if we do, we make for damn sure that our boots is big enough."

Kel made a note to remember that one. "I'm not sure what I'm 'sposed to say. I don't—"

"You don't needs to say nothin'. Fact of the matter is, you needs to be askin' not sayin'; askin' yourself if your boots is big enough. W.R. Elmore's your problem. No sir, don't do no good for nobody to be botherin' Grace Trimble . . . and you sure don't want to get crosstways with Sheriff Elmore, no sir, you don't. He's one big, ugly cottonmouth, that boy is. That's guaranteed."

Kel finished his meal as quickly as he could. The old man had gone about his business of shutting down the diner. He spent a good ten minutes stacking chairs onto the tables—a remarkable expenditure of energy given that he would be back in less than five hours to unstack them and start up again. The two overweight men were still at their booth when Kel left, seemingly oblivious to the dimmed lights and stacked chairs.

Heat lightning popped and shot erratically across the western sky as Kel made his way back to his room at the Sleep-Mor. There would be no rain. The whippoorwill was still awake, but most of the motel's windows were dark.

He unlocked the door to room 12A and entered, shutting and locking the door behind him. He pushed the power button on the television and steadied himself against it, reaching down to untie his shoes as CNN flickered on. They were covering a train wreck in Bangladesh that had killed hundreds. "I wonder if Sam's watching this," he said to the room. "Might be kin."

He had decided during his short walk back from the Albert Pike that he could shower in the morning before they left for Memphis. His full stomach had brought on a fresh wave of fatigue, and all he really desired at the moment was to crawl into bed and die a quick, painless death. As he lowered himself into the well of his bed, he looked at his watch: twelve-thirty-five. He had to be up in seven hours.

Normally he brought a travel alarm on trips but that had been another victim of the hurried departure. Kel sighed deeply as he summoned up the energy necessary to crawl out of his bed and walk to the window to open the drapery. The morning light, he figured, would be sufficient to wake him.

Shit.
The curtains.

The curtains were closed.

They hadn't been.

Had they?

No. He remembered now. When he woke up earlier, before going to make his telephone calls, he'd noticed the sky was black and he remembered thinking it had only minutes ago been blue. No, the curtains had been open when he left for dinner, he'd seen the glow of the yellow bug lights, and now they were closed.

Shit.

He snapped on the light, all fatigue gone. Was anything missing? Suitcase was there, clothes, laptop computer was still there—still on, the green sleep-mode light blinking rhythmically, the CILHI case files he had brought along to work on were still there next to the computer, and yet . . .

The file folders were neatly stacked.

They hadn't been, Kel was sure of it. If he had any good qualities, neatness and organization were not to be counted among them. He examined the folders. Everything appeared to be there, but they clearly were more neatly stacked than he had left them.

Shit. Shit. Shit.

"The maid?" he questioned the room. "At midnight? At this motel? I don't think so."

He replayed it all in his head, over and over. He'd dozed off, with the curtains open, he was sure of that, and then he woke up, with the curtains open, he was sure of that. Had he closed them before going across the street? He didn't think so. He thought back. He'd slipped his shoes on, tied them, taken his wallet and key from the dresser, and . . . and then he'd walked out the friggin' door. He hadn't closed the curtains. And if he hadn't, then someone else had.

Kel sat back onto the bed and tightly closed his eyes, willing a plausible explanation to the surface. It had to be the maid.

Kel slipped his shoes back on. He opened his door and

looked out. He saw more heat lightning and heard a thousand crickets arguing against the waning night. It had warmed up since he returned from dinner, or was it he that had warmed up? He walked quickly to the main lobby, his untied shoes clumping and scuffing on the cement. It was open and the lights and television were on. A young Bob Eubanks was asking four newlyweds, "Ladies, will your husband say he has a whoopee cushion?"

"Hello?" Kel called out. There was a dim light on in the small office behind the counter. No answer. One of the newlyweds was giggling.

"Hello?" He called louder. He was preparing to try again when Sam came bustling out wearing a long-tailed lilac-colored shirt and dark-green shorts.

"Yes sir, yes sir," he said quickly, and then, recognizing Kel, he asked, "Yes sir, Mr. 12A, what can I do for you, sir?"

"I hate to bother you at this hour . . . Sam," Kel replied, not really sure how to best angle his question, "but by any chance did the maid clean my room a little while ago? Maybe an hour ago?"

Sam looked at him strangely, as if he'd just pulled a hard word at a spelling bee. "No sir, my wife, she is asleep, sir. She will be cleaning your room in the morning, sir. Can I be of help to you with something now, sir?"

"You're sure she hasn't been in my room recently? It's okay, I simply need to know."

"No sir. I am certain, sir. You are having a problem?"

"Anybody been by to ask for me? Or Mr. Levine? Maybe someone lookin' for Levine got my room by mistake. Anybody been by that you are aware of?"

"Only Mr. Levine, sir."

It took Kel a moment to digest the answer. "What do you mean, only Mr. Levine?"

"Mr. Levine, sir, he was here asking about you, sir. Wanted to know if I knew where you were or when you were coming back."

Kel pinned Sam to the wall with his look. "When was Mr. Levine so interested in my whereabouts?"

"Sir?"

"When was Mr. Levine askin' about me?"

"About an hour ago, sir."

"Thank you, Sam."

"Open up, you sonofabitch." Kel was prepared to kick the door in if necessary.

"Hold on. Hold on. Doc? Is that you?"

Kel was pounding so loudly on Levine's door that he almost didn't hear him. Almost. "Yeah, *Fed*, it's me all right. Open up this goddamn door."

"A minute, a minute."

Kel could hear the chain being removed and the latch thrown. When the door finally opened, Levine stood there in a New York Knicks T-shirt and boxer underwear. The light on the stand beside his bed was on. The television was off.

"What the hell's the matter? You okay?"

Kel pushed passed him into the room. "You bastard, you paranoid fuckin' New York prick."

"Glad to see you too, Doc," he said, rubbing his face. As he did so, his T-shirt rode up on his right arm exposing the pale curdled skin of an old scar on his shoulder. "Mind telling me what this is all about? I was getting ready to have an erotic dream, and you don't exactly figure prominently in it."

"Were you in my room?"

Levine squinted hard and turned his head slightly to the side. "Say again."

"Were you in my goddamn room?"

"When? . . . No. I haven't been in your room at all."

"No?"

"No—unlike you—I might point out—who happens to be standing in *my* room. You want to clue me in, Dr. McKelvey? Or is this going to be twenty questions?" The early effects of a shallow sleep had worn off and been replaced by a growing ire as Levine realized he was being blamed for something. He simply didn't know what it was.

"Somebody's been in my room. What do you know about it?"

"No shit."

"Shit."

"Anything missing? What'd I tell you about shitbirds? They steal anything?"

Kel's feet were separated and his hands were on his hips. The body language was unmistakable; he was spoiling for a fight. "No, nothin' was stolen—best as I can tell. Just looked at. Examined. *Investigated* is probably a more appropriate description. Some case files, maybe my computer, don't know what else—why don't you tell me."

"Whoa. Time-out, time-out, Gomer. You think I did it?" Levine moved to close his door, looking out to make sure there was no one else outside his room. He locked and chained the door.

"Who else? Who the hell else would have any interest in some files in my room?"

"Not me, that's for damn sure. Maybe someone interested in this case?" He seemed to notice Kel's stance for the first time. "And I suggest you back your attitude down a notch before I forget my New York manners and kick your hillbilly ass out to the curb."

"Someone interested in this case? What case? Do you hear yourself? There is no case, haven't you figured that out? Certainly not as far as I'm involved. All I've done since I got here is eat nut pie and insult old women. There is no case. I'm an anthropologist, I look at human remains—you see any remains? I don't see any remains. You see remains? No, of course not. You have no human remains, remember? None, zip." He hadn't completely backed down, but he softened both his tone and features somewhat—enough. Not that he was afraid of Levine, but he also didn't relish the idea of being punched out by a guy in his underwear. And Levine looked as if he might be quickly getting to the punch-out stage. "Face it, Special Agent Levine, there isn't anyone in this town that gives a shit about what I'm doin' here. They don't know what I'm doin' here. Hell, *I* don't know what I'm doin' here. In fact, the only reason I'm still here is that I needed to get out of my office before I had a meltdown and because my commander wants to mend fences with the FBI for somethin' we didn't do. I'm here because you can't keep your alphabet straight and requested help from the C-I-L rather than the C-I-D or the C-I-A or the Kiss-My-Ass."

"Sit down," Levine instructed as much as offered. Kel hesitated. He compromised by leaning against the dresser while Levine sat on the end of his bed. Levine rubbed his face again and took a deep breath. "Are you sure someone was in your room?"

"Positive."

"Did you consider the maid?"

"This is the Sleep-Mor, Levine, not the Hilton. Sam's congeniality does not extend to midnight maid service. No turn-down service; no mints on the pillow; that includes no snoopin' through files. But yes, for the record, I checked with Sam. The maid's been asleep for hours."

Levine seemed to consider the response. "Well then who?"

"Well ding-dong, Elliot Ness. I believe that's what I want to know. The only person who might, just might, give a flyin' rat's ass about what I may be writin' down in a report would be someone paranoid enough to not want the truth of this investigation to get out."

Levine looked genuinely puzzled. "You thinking Sheriff Elmore?"

"Elmore? Are you out of your goddamn government-issued mind?"

"Who else has a reason to keep a lid on this case?"

"Well, not Elmore. Not anybody here. There is no case, there is no lid, no case, no lid—can't you get that through your head? Who? You want to know who? I was thinkin'

about someone who may not want his boss to know what a
goat rope this whole investigation is turnin' out to be. Someone in hot water with his boss to begin with. Someone that
might be worried that I'll write an After Action Report saying
that the FBI has way too much time on their hands and way
too little brains in their goddamn skulls. Someone who
couldn't wait for me to get off the plane so they could tongue
whip me and tell me they were goin' to piss down my throat.
Someone who said they were in charge and that they'd be
watchin' me. Remember that? That's who."

"That's not what I meant."

"Yeah? And just what did you mean?"

"I meant I was going to cover my ass. C'mon, McKelvey,
put yourself in my place."

"What place might that be?"

"Here in Crackerland, U.S.A. In case you haven't figured
it out, *Doctor*, the Bureau would like nothing better than to
bury me here. It's a no-win situation for me. I crack the case
and you know what they'll say? They'll say I was doing my
job. Period. But if I fail, if I fail they'll drive another nail into
my coffin. So put yourself in my place. I ask for someone
from the Smithsonian and I get you. What would you assume?"

"I'd assume you're better off. We're the Pros from Dover.
Not the Smithsonian."

"So you say. From where I sit, the Bureau's covering their
bet and making sure I fail by sending me the same Gomer that
screwed the pooch in that Gonsalves case."

"Aw goddamn. I'm so goddamn tired of hearin' that shit.
It's you boys that screwed that case to the wall, not us."

"So you say."

"Yeah, so I say."

"All I know is that I don't want to get hung out to dry in
the process."

"Shit, G-man. If I wanted to hang you out to dry, you'd be
a goddamn strip of jerky by now."

Levine's eyes narrowed to slits and he glared at Kel for a moment as he measured his response. His voiced dropped a couple of degrees in temperature. "I'll say this once, Dr. McKelvey. Once. I didn't go into your room, I won't go into your room without an invitation—or a warrant, I don't care what you have in your room. You can be writing letters to *Penthouse* magazine for all I care. Yeah, maybe my career is in the tank already, but I've got less than two years till retirement, and while I'm holding on by my fingernails, I'm still holding on. I'll leave when I hang it up—and not a minute sooner—unless you screw this up for me. What that adds up to, in case you don't have a calculator, is that I don't give a shit about any *report* you might write—as long as it's accurate."

"Screw you, Levine."

"No, screw you, McKelvey."

Kel grabbed the sides of his head as if his skull was about to explode. "I don't believe this," he said, as much to himself as to Levine. "I don't have to put up with this shit."

"You do until you earn my respect."

"Respect?" Kel almost shouted. He squared his shoulders. "Your respect? That's a two-way street, cowboy. When are you goin' to show me a little respect? Respect, such as not searchin' my room. Why don't we start there?"

"I believe we settled that."

"So you weren't in the lobby askin' Sam where I was and how long I'd be out of my room?"

"What? No."

"No?"

"Look," Levine replied, taken slightly off-guard. He exhaled deeply and tried to calm his voice. "Look, Doc, yeah, I was asking where you were. I was going to suggest that we leave here tomorrow morning at eight-thirty rather than nine o'clock, and I couldn't call you since neither of us have phones. So I went to your room, and there wasn't any answer. I thought you might be at the office getting some ice or something so I went down there. When I saw you weren't there, I asked Sam if he'd seen you, I knew you didn't have a car and I figured you were around somewhere; took a walk or something you enjoy this freakin' weather so much. I told him that if you came by in the next thirty minutes to tell you to stop by my room. But I did not ask him how long you were going to be gone. If he told you so, he's mistaken."

"Then who was in my room?"

"Beats me, Doc. Not me."

He certainly seemed sincere. Maybe Kel had imagined it all.

No, he hadn't. Someone had been in his room.

The two men faced each other, both breathing deeply. Both struggling for calm.

Levine finally broke the silence. "And Doc, let's have another understanding. You ever come beating on my door again, you ever accuse me of something like this again, and I'll feed you your nuts on a slice of toast. We clear?"

Kel paused long enough to save some semblance of face. "Perfectly," he said.

CHAPTER 21

They left at eight-thirty the next morning. Not surprisingly, the conversation was strained and limited to essentials, at first. Kel had lain awake most of the night thinking and re-thinking the evidence of someone having been in his room. Try as he might, he couldn't convince himself that it hadn't happened. He thought of the fisherman he'd seen smoking out in the parking lot when he'd walked over to the diner, but that theory gained no traction. He thought again of Levine and his paranoia and disdain for anything bipedal, but while he didn't completely trust Levine, he also found it hard to believe that he had nothing better to do than break into his motel room. Levine, more than anyone else, knew that there wasn't a case, no evidence, nothing to see, nothing to snoop around for. And he couldn't really believe that Levine might be concerned with something Kel might write home in a memo—no matter how much of a waste of time this trip was turning out to be. By his own admission, Levine was a pariah at the FBI, and pariahs typically don't give a damn; or worse, give a damn about the wrong sorts of things. But in any case, it didn't add up to Levine being the culprit. It had been a long and unpro-ductive rest of the night.

Despite rationalizing away any involvement Levine might have had, or not had, Kel wasn't about to swallow a large enough bolus of pride to apologize for the chest-beating be-havior of the night before. So the car ride started quietly.

The plan was to take the same route they had taken the other night when Levine had picked Kel up at the airport—only in reverse; north on Highway 1 until they reached Forrest City and then catch Interstate 40 over to Memphis.

Kel looked out his passenger window as they drove, as much to avoid Levine as to marvel at the undisturbed floodplain, so flat that a marble dropped out the window wouldn't be able to decide which direction to roll. Unlike Locust County, which was still dominated by cotton, most of northeast Arkansas was acres and miles of flat lowland fields of deep-green rice and sun-crisped soybeans all badly in need of rain.

Although still early in the morning, it was already in the lower nineties and a blue-brown haze of hot, saturated air and powder-fine dust obscured the horizon. Levine had turned the radio on to disrupt the silence, and one of the Memphis stations was matter-of-factly reporting the number of heat fatalities from the previous day: four in the metropolitan area alone.

Kel made the first move at serious reconciliation by asking about Levine's family and background. The agent's responses were short and obligatory at first. Enough to establish that he'd grown up in Brooklyn, in an apartment above his father's grocery store. That he'd served with the Twenty-fifth Infantry Division in Vietnam. That he had a wife and two high-school-aged daughters who played lacrosse and stayed on the phone. With time and distance, the details were caulked into the cracks: an epileptic Irish Setter named Gretchen, a split-level house in Ijamsville in Frederick County, Maryland, how the house had been the absolute right place to buy when he thought he would finish out his career at the Hoover Building. Two-story neo-Colonial with a finished basement. One and a half acres. Lots of trees. Good schools. How he was now renting a small apartment in Memphis, and his family was functioning smoothly without him. How it was no use making the children change schools because their dad couldn't keep his mouth shut—or more accurately, couldn't keep his fingers off the e-mail send button. How he had hopes of getting back there soon to visit. Had hopes of getting back there soon, permanently, if he could simply crack the code on the Jackson case and stay out of the line of fire.

The conversation continued to warm along with the morning, and the more vivid aspects of the previous night faded into a dull sensitivity. Still a sore spot, but it could be worked around, provided neither one of them brought the matter up. Both men forced civility.

"You going straight back to Splitsville after you pick up a car? Or are you going to take in the big city of Memphis—do the tourist thing and see the Peabody ducks, have some barbeque at the Rendezvous? I'll deny ever having said this, but this town does have a few nice features." Levine's eyes didn't leave the road.

"Not sure. I was halfway thinkin' about runnin' over to the Navy Casualty office in Millington."

"Sounds fun."

"Yeah. I've got a couple of things I want to check on. You? What's your plan?"

Levine was silent for a while. His mouth was a tight line but the gristle behind his jaw was working and pulsing as he thought. Finally he glanced at Kel and then back to the road. "Couple of things I need to check."

Kel didn't ask.

Kel thought they made good time, but he'd also dozed off somewhere around Forrest City and that helped the miles go by. Levine had the air-conditioner running full blast but with the morning sun in the southeast, and them headed northeast, Kel took its drowsy brunt from his seat on the passenger's side. That, combined with the pleasant white roar of the tires, had been a powerful sedative.

He'd been dreaming. It had been a funny dream. Even funnier because he could recall it so clearly later. He'd been standing in a field of waist-high elephant grass; wet and slick from a morning rain. The sky was hazy and thick and smelled of freshly mown hay, but also of smoke and kerosene. He felt that he was in Hawaii, but he wasn't, and he seemed to know that. The mountains lacked the dramatic pleated folds of the Waianaes or Koolaus; they were round and soft, more like the Ouachitas of his youth—or the backbone of Vietnam's Central Highlands. Wherever he was, his wife was there too, young and pretty and looking like she had in high school. She had on a thin yellow sundress. His boys were there as well, except they had grown to recognizable manhood. They had their backs to him, but he knew it was them. His wife was mad and saying something, and she held something in her hands that Kel couldn't see at first. He'd had to move and rise up on his toes to see past his sons. It was a bird. She was holding a large black-and-white mockingbird cupped in her hands, and he could hear his wife now, she was scolding the men, her sons—his sons—for killing the bird. And they were protesting and kept saying it wasn't dead. Kel moved toward her and reached between the two men to touch the bird. None of them paid him any attention. It was soft, and when his fingers touched it, it sprang up and began singing. First it was the meadowlark, then a chickadee, then the troublesome jay. It sang and sang, using every voice but its own.

Levine cussed softly to himself and Kel stirred.

When Levine looked over, he noticed Kel blinking and shifting his weight in his seat. "Have a nice nap?" he asked. "We're here, except I missed the exit for the rental car place. Got to swing back around." They were approaching the terminal building.

Kel sat up fully and shook his head like a wet dog, trying to clear his thoughts. He rubbed his eyes and took stock of where they were. Not in a field surrounded by wet grass and singing birds. "That's okay. You can drop me off here at the terminal, and I'll catch the shuttle," he said.

"You sure?"

"Yeah. Fact, you can let me off right here."

Levine responded quickly and pulled to the curb in front of the terminal, breaking only long enough for Kel to climb out. They agreed to meet at the Sleep-Mor Sunday night. They nodded at each other as if to acknowledge that the trouble between them was resolved.

Thirty minutes later Kel was behind the wheel of a rented Ford Taurus bound for Millington, Tennessee.

CHAPTER 22

Kel called and e-mailed the navy's Casualty Assistance and
Retired Activities Branch frequently to discuss matters relating to CILHI identifications, but he'd only visited their office
a couple of times before. New security measures had been put
in place since his last visit, and he had a little difficulty navigating from the front gate. Millington is a large base, relatively flat and devoid of memorable landmarks, and easy to
get lost on.

It took him a while, and a couple of loops around the same
block, but he finally found what he was looking for on In-
tegrity Drive. It was a red-brick building, not old, but not new
either. The interior had been recently renovated.

On the second floor, Kel passed large, four-color posters
for Papa Franco's Pizza and King Midas sub sandwiches. It
had surprised him on his first visit, and even now it took a
minute before he remembered that Navy Casualty shared office space with the section that governed the food franchises
that operated on navy bases. No one else seemed to appreciate the incongruity of grieving families and extra pepperoni.

McCann's office was near the end of the long hallway in a
corner suite. The door was open. So far, so good. He poked
his head in. The secretary was at her desk typing on a computer, her nose six inches from the screen as if she had for-

gotten her glasses. Kel tried to recall her name. *Marge?
Mary?*

"Yes sir." She smiled when she saw Kel's head appear.
"Can I help you?" She had that west Tennessee cross between
a twang and a drawl, and even to Kel's usually sympathetic
ear it sounded more like "Kin ah heap yew?" She was a local
hire.

"Yes ma'am. I hope so. By any chance, is Gary in? Tell
him Kel's here. It'll only take up a few minutes of his time—
I promise." Kel smiled back. He wished he could remember
her name. *Martha?*

"Oh, my breath and soul, Dr. McKelvey, now I didn't recognize you. I'm so used to talking to you on the phone that it's
odd to see you here in the office. I'm Maggie. How's that
weather in Hawaii?"

Maggie, that was it. "Oh hey, Maggie, I should have recognized the voice. Weather's gorgeous, same as always—tell
your boss that you need to come out to the Lab to discuss
business—we'll show you all around. Speakin' of your boss,
is Gary here? This really will just take a couple-three minutes."

"Sure is. I think he's on the phone, but you just go right on
in. Can I get you some coffee or something?"

"No ma'am, thank you though." Kel stepped past Maggie's desk and tentatively peered around the doorjamb of the
adjoining office. Gary McCann was sitting at his desk, feet
up, carrying on such an animated telephone conversation that
the file on his lap kept slipping off, only to be retrieved every
few seconds. He was an older man, wiry and spare, with an
avuncular nest of silvery white hair. He was well suited to the
job of soothing grieving next of kin. He smiled through his
conversation and motioned Kel into a chair with several rapid
flicks of his wrist. Kel nodded his acknowledgment, but opted
to continue standing, walking over to the window to look out
at the grassy lot next door. He was still looking out when he
heard the phone rattle home into its cradle.

"Well, the famous Dr. Robert McKelvey. Come on in and sit down, sit down . . . Sorry, that was some chucklehead from Fort Sill. Get this, we're trying to get a navy funeral scheduled on an army base, and on short notice too—long story . . . the hoops we have to jump through, right?" he half-winked and gestured toward the telephone that he'd hung up as if the chucklehead was stuck inside it and might be listening. He released a long, though not unpleasant, sigh. "Anyway, what brings the globe-trotting Dr. Kel here? I had a message that you called yesterday. D'you get taken care of all right?"

"Sure did. Actually, I was down in Split Tree, Arkansas, when I called—ever heard of it?"

He cocked his head. "You bet. Mrs. Grace Ellen Trimble, resides at something, something, something West Boulevard North. Mother of Jimmie Trimble, Navy Cross awardee. I had to go get a blood sample for DNA testing from her, remember?"

Kel smiled. He knew that the casualty reps hated having to contact the next of kin of resolved cases, years after the fact, to get blood samples. Nothing like knocking a thirty-year-old scab off. "I remember. Sorry."

"Should be. Which reminds me," McCann said as he searched through a stack of e-mail messages, finally pulling one to the surface and holding it up. "Tell me, what's all this crap about Mrs. Trimble not being the birth momma? Got a message here from your office that y'all want us to go and ask her whether her son was adopted. Why in hell do we need to go and do that? He's identified and buried—ain't he?"

"Yeah, he is. And the answer is, you don't. Cancel that request. Bad idea. Bad, bad, bad idea. Believe me. Super bad idea."

"Bad idea, huh? I take it you've already asked her."

"Bad, bad, bad idea."

McCann's eyes showed a great deal of amusement as he deciphered the look on Kel's face. "She throw you out of her house, or'd she have the sheriff do it."

"Didn't have to. I sort of slunk outta there on my own

belly. But I gather you've had some dealings with the sheriff down there. I've heard about him."

"You got that about right. She had him there when I went down for the DNA blood draw. Edmund, Eldon, Etkin—something like that. Big guy with a bad attitude. He's very, and I mean very, protective of Mrs. Trimble. So what's going on down there anyway? What would make you fly halfway around the world to little old Millington? Can you talk about it?"

"I could if there was anythin' to talk about," Kel answered. "It's like jugglin' a bunch of canaries. FBI is investigatin' an old civil rights case and somehow managed to get it into their collective brainpans that it may somehow be linked to Trimble's loss—I'm sure it isn't, but Colonel Botch-It wants us to be a team player and rebuild some broken fences between the CIL and the FBI . . ."

"That Gonzalez case you all messed up?"

"Screw you, Gary. The FBI botched that one, not us. And it's Gonsalves."

"Okay, okay." McCann raised his hands in mock surrender. "If you say so."

Kel took a breath to regroup. "Anyhow, here I am, spendin' my time imaginin' the pile of work that's accumulatin' for me at home, and I'm stuck workin' with this paranoid FBI nutball who's all wrapped around the axle because it's a big-time case and his job's on the line. The Leon Jackson murder—ring a bell?"

"No. Should it?" McCann was from West Texas originally, and even though he was certainly the right generation, the Jackson case probably had received very little print space in his neck of the woods.

Kel shrugged and shot his eyebrows. "Not necessarily. It attracted a fair share of attention forty years ago. Anyhow, that's not why I'm here. What I could use some help with is runnin' a check on a couple of names."

"Sure."

Kel pulled a small piece of paper from his shirt pocket and

looked at the name he'd written on it. "You got access to the VA's files, right?"

"Not supposed to."

"C'mon."

McCann swung his feet off his desk and jiggled his computer mouse to rouse it. He pecked at a few keys in what appeared to Kel to be a totally random sequence, and then asked, "What's the name and what do you need to know?"

"First. Dwayne Crockett—last name as in Davy. Marine."

"He alive or dead?"

Kel shrugged. "Alive, I hope."

McCann pecked a few more keys. "Got two showing. Desert Storm and one from Vietnam. Both alive as of last month."

"Gimme the Vietnam one. Phone number?"

"Coming up." McCann clicked a mouse button and his printer engaged. "Next."

"Next one is a Vietnam case, so call up your MIA file." Technically, there were no more MIAs from Vietnam. In the late 1970s and early 1980s, military review boards had amended the status of all the missing servicemen to presumed Killed In Action, but the term MIA continued to be used informally.

Gary clicked and pecked. "Go."

Kel leaned forward, placing his elbows on the desk. McCann turned the monitor slightly to an angle where Kel could see it more clearly. "I'm interested in a guy named Elmore, E-L-M-O-R-E, Raymond, or Ray, some combination like that. I think he's navy, but I'm not sure. I may be mixin' him up with Trimble. I'm curious as to when and how he went missin'."

"Shit. That's the name. Elmore. Sheriff Elmore—the big guy. Don't tell me this is the same Elmore . . ."

"Same family, anyhow . . . a brother."

"Did I just say don't tell me? Don't tell me. Shit. What's this about anyhow? Never mind. Nope. I don't know nothing, and I don't want to know nothing." McCann shook his head while he pecked away at the keyboard like a trained rooster and then clicked his mouse. He read silently for a moment before looking over at Kel. "E-L-M-O-R-E? One L, right?"

"Pretty sure."

"Nope. No Ray or Raymond Elmore listed as missing." Spelling it with two Ls was no more productive.

"Well now, isn't that curious." Kel knit his brows and squinted at the computer monitor. "None, huh? Try resolved cases. Maybe he was identified. Though if he was, the sheriff and the rest of the town don't seem to know it."

A few more key pecks and McCann said, "No luck. Nine Elmores are listed as resolved casualties—all in South Vietnam, but none are named Ray or Raymond or anything at all like that. There're five in the Army, four Marine Corps, no Navy, no Air Force. I didn't think that name rang any bells for me. He's not a navy casualty that I know of."

"Any on that list happen to be from Arkansas?"

"Let's see." McCann ran his finger along the names on the screen as he read. "California, Oklahoma, Arizona, hmmm . . . nope, no Arkansas. There's one from Missouri— Kansas City, but that's it. When'd he supposedly die?"

"In 1966, I think. Give or take a year max."

McCann returned his finger to the screen. "You're in luck there. Two of 'em bought the farm in 1966, three died in 1967, couple in '68 . . . a '65 and a '69—but none of them are named anything like Ray or Raymond, not even any middle names that are close. And they're all resolved. All identified."

Kel stared at the screen.

"You sure this Ray Elmore fella died in Vietnam?"

Kel thought about sleeping mockingbirds. "No," he said softly, "I'm not."

CHAPTER 23

Navy Casualty Assistance Office, Millington Naval Base, Millington, Tennessee
FRIDAY, AUGUST 19, 2005

Gary McCann went outside to smoke a cigarette while Kel used his telephone. It took three calls to track down Dwayne Crockett; first to his home, then his office, and finally his cell phone.

"Mr. Crockett," Kel began. "Sorry to bother you, sir. Your wife said it was all right to use this number. My name's Robert McKelvey, and I'm with the army. I was wonderin' if I might ask you a few questions. It'll just take a minute. Is this a good time?"

Dwayne Crockett had returned from the Vietnam War to Oak Ridge, Tennessee, in 1969. He'd taken over the management of his father-in-law's drive-through car wash and, with a work ethic tempered by a vision of his own thin mortality, had built it into a successful chain that now was washing cars in over twenty-six locations. For the last thirty-seven years his routine hadn't varied; every Friday he visited a different location and sat in his vehicle while the spray and the soap did their job.

"Sure thing. You'll have to speak up, though. It's kinda noisy where I am. What's the name again?" Dwayne Crockett spoke above the roar of the water blasting his windshield.

"McKelvey. Robert McKelvey."

"What can I do for you, Mr. . . . . You're in the army, you say?"

"No, sir. Work for the army. I'm a civilian."

"So what can I do for you, Mr. McKelvey?"

Kel hesitated, not sure how to proceed. His father had always told him, when in doubt, put your head down and bull through it. Kel put his head down and bulled. "Mr. Crockett, did you serve in Vietnam with a navy corpsman by the name of Jimmie Trimble?"

There was noisy silence on the other end.

"Mr. Crockett?" Kel said, not sure if he'd lost his connection.

"You'll have to excuse me. I haven't heard that name spoken in a long time, Mr. McKelvey," Dwayne Crockett replied slowly, his voice barely audible over a roaring in the background.

"So you knew Jimmie Trimble?"

"Yes, sir, I did. I did. Why do you need to know this, Mr. McKelvey? No offense, but that's a part of my life that I don't discuss freely. And here you are calling me out of the bright blue, and all."

"I understand," Kel offered up. "You see, I work for the lab that recovers and identifies the remains of missin' U.S. servicemen, and I'm workin' a case right now that kinda involves Jimmie Trimble."

"Jimmie Carl."

"Sir?"

"Jimmie Carl. He always went by Jimmie Carl."

"Yes, sir. This case involves Jimmie Carl Trimble."

"How so?" Dwayne Crockett cut Kel off. "Can't say I understand. Jimmie Carl was recovered and identified. I recovered him."

Kel thought about the case file he'd read the night before. He'd read Crockett's name on the recovery report. "That's right. Yes, sir, I read your report. It's the young Marine that died with him . . ."

"Evans."

"Chester Evans. He wasn't recovered. That's who we're

lookin' for really. The problem is that we've recovered some remains from the site that don't match either Trimble or Evans."

"Lot of good men were killed that day. Thirty-two, in fact."

Kel was nodding as he strained to hear Crockett. "That's correct, but not from where we did our recovery. Only two that should be there at that location—Evans and Trimble."

"If you read my report, Mr. McKelvey, then you know that . . . well, we didn't recover all of Jimmie Carl. His remains weren't intact." Dwayne Crockett paused and nursed a ragged thought. "I always knew there could be more of him out there somewhere, but the area was so hot with VC that we couldn't search everywhere."

"Yes, sir. I've seen the identification file that they did at the mortuary in Tan Son Nhut. Your recovery was more than adequate given the conditions. The real problem is that what we found recently doesn't match him. Doesn't match his DNA."

Crockett was quiet for a moment and then he spoke. "So what do you want from me?"

Kel hesitated. "Don't really know, Mr. Crockett. I was hopin' that maybe you could tell me somethin' that might make sense of it."

Crockett laughed. "You weren't in Vietnam, were you, son? No offense, Mr. McKelvey, but, make sense of it? That's what you want? You want sense. Nothing over there made any sense. What could I possibly tell you that would make any sense? Maybe you want me to tell you that Jimmie Carl's death made any sense? That it? That he died for a good cause. How 'bout you want me to say he was a hero?"

"No, sir," Kel tried to interrupt. "I—"

"I did three tours in Vietnam. Three. You think I'm a hero, Mr. McKelvey?"

Kel started to respond, then realized that no response was expected. He unconsciously hunched his shoulders as if bracing for a storm. He hated telephones.

"You hear that word used a lot nowadays. Hero. Shit. I weren't no hero. I did what I was asked to do; what my country asked me to do; what I had to do. My family's been in the Marines since before the Spanish-American War. Crocketts bleed red and gold. You understand me? I volunteered and I didn't have a choice. Few of us did, really. That's the ugly little secret. You do what you have to for whatever reason. Most of us were there because we didn't have any choice. You understand? Too afraid not to go. But heroes, heroes have options. Heroes are the ones that make the hard decisions."

Kel didn't know what to say. He'd obviously chafed open a wound and ended up in the path of an emotional buzz saw as a result. "I reckon you're right," he responded weakly. As soon as he heard it he knew how weak it was. "Jimmie Carl Trimble was a hero in anyone's book."

"You weren't in Vietnam, you say, but were you ever in a war? Or what passes for wars nowadays. Grenada, maybe? Panama? Desert Storm?" Crockett's car had emerged from the car wash and the roar of the high-pressure jets had subsided. The volume of his voice had not.

"No, sir," Kel answered.

"They gave Jimmie Carl the Navy Cross. Second highest decoration a man can get. He deserved the damn Medal of Honor, if you ask me. That's what I nominated him for." Crockett finally adjusted his volume. He slowed slightly. "Know what it takes to get the Navy Cross? No offense, but it takes something you and I don't have. Jimmie Carl did. Jimmie Carl had it. You think he was a hero?"

"I, ahh, of course," Kel stumbled. He was trying to find an opportunity to get his foot into the conversational door long enough to thank Crockett and hang up. He'd hoped that there'd be a shred of information that hadn't been in the written file; something that would help explain away the rogue DNA sequence.

"Jimmie Carl didn't have no choice either," Crockett answered his own question. "Don't know why, but he didn't.

What he did, calling in that napalm strike on himself and saving the platoon's ass—my ass—he had to do. I didn't realize it at the time, but I do now. Still don't know why, but he had to do it. No choice."

"I don't understand," Kel's interest in the conversation re-warmed.

"Like I said, nothing that happened over there makes sense. I told you I hadn't heard his name spoken in a long time. That's not really true, though. Truth is, I hear that name just about every day. I hear my voice calling it. Mr. McKelvey, I knew him as well as anyone, I guess, and I didn't understand him. But when I think back now, I can see that he was the same as most of us. He never had a choice."

"Mr. Crockett, you say he didn't have a choice, just what do you mean?"

"It was there all along. In his eyes. His look. He was a dead man long before he got to Quang Nam Province." The wild urgency to tell his story had left Crockett's voice. Where there had been a rush there was now a tired trickle.

"How so?"

"I don't know. All I know is that he never intended to go home. He had a one-way ticket; it was just a matter of how he got it punched."

Kel thought about Grace Trimble's shrine to her son and of Edd Forrest's description of Carl Trimble's relationship with his son. "He ever say anythin' about his family back home?"

Dwayne Crockett was quiet for a moment, though it wasn't clear whether he was thinking about Kel's question or simply lost in the past. "Not really," he replied. "The usual, I guess. How good a cook his mother was, that sort of thing. Not much else. Wrote home a lot, though. At least every week. Some days he'd write two letters; one after the other."

"To his mother?"

"No," Crockett replied, surprised by his own realization. "No, come to think of it, I believe they were to his father."

CHAPTER 24

Memphis and Shelby County Library, Memphis, Tennessee
FRIDAY, AUGUST 19, 2005

Levine decided to go into the office later. After dropping Kel off at the airport he drove into downtown Memphis, but not to the office. If he went by work, he'd very likely have to explain to some ass-kissing jerk-off with half his time in grade what he was doing back in town when he was supposed to be working off his purgatory in his east Arkansas gulag. He didn't have the patience to answer anyone, nor did he have the inclination to try to muster any up. Besides, he had copied almost the entire Jackson-Doe case file and had everything he needed at home, and he'd be there soon enough. And other than checking mail and a few other administrative dust motes to sweep up, he really had no reason to venture anywhere near the office.

Instead he had a notion to go to the library.

There was something that Chief Forrest and Deputy Bevins had said that kept percolating through the finer sand in his head. It probably was a dead end, but he was desperate enough that dead ends were starting to look promising. How had Chief Forrest put it? *He got the ACLU snooping around here*—or something like that. Leonidas Jackson, ACLU, Split Tree—there was some sort of pattern there if he could figure out how to connect the dots. The Bureau had dismissed the ACLU's involvement forty years ago as a dead lead. Was it? Perhaps, but given how far he'd driven up the dead-end cul-de-sac, it was worth taking a second look at.

The American Civil Liberties Union seldom did things in the dark—not today and certainly not in 1965. Their currency was publicity. Publicity meant donations and volunteerism and activism and support. Publicity also meant records—newspaper accounts if nothing else—if only he could locate them. For that, he was at the right place, the Memphis and Shelby County Library at 3030 Poplar Avenue.

Levine didn't know exactly where to start, but he was an accountant by training and mindset, and he knew that there was always a trail of paper. Could be any type of records, any kind of paper, and he figured the local Memphis newspaper files were as good a place as any to start the hunt. He remembered from the Bureau's file that Leon Jackson's short-lived efforts in eastern Arkansas began in November or December 1964, right around Christmas. By late summer 1965 he was Tango Uniform—tits up—in an earthen levee in hardscrabble Locust County. That meant that if he was involved with the ACLU in this area, if he'd gotten them "snooping around," it had to have been between early November when he arrived and late July when he was last seen. Probably the earlier. It was reasonable that if his trouble with the Split Tree police had occurred right before he died, it wouldn't have been so quickly dismissed by the Bureau as a dead lead.

Levine went to the microfilm room and searched through the chocolate-colored metal cabinets. He opened each of the shallow drawers and scanned the dates written on the small yellow and gray boxes within. He quickly found what he was looking for.

Sitting at a microfilm reader, Michael Levine spooled up the first roll. November 1 through November 14, 1964, *Memphis Commercial Beacon*. The take-up spool squeaked and complained, but forty-five minutes and a splitting headache later, he had finished the first roll. Only fifteen more to go. He threaded the film leader and began winding the take-up reel. The black-and-white microfilm strip streaked by and his headache intensified, but with practice, his scanning abilities improved markedly, and he was able to complete the second roll in under thirty minutes. Roll three. Roll four. Roll five. Midway through roll six he found what he was after.

The first article he found was really the third. The first two had been so small and buried that they had zipped past him in a gray-and-white blur. The last one was really not an article but rather was an editorial. In a column headlined "Whither a New South?" and dated January 23, 1965, the editor of the *Beacon* had applauded the ACLU's involvement in what they were calling a rash of civil rights abuses in Arkansas and Mississippi. *Big talk coming from Memphis,* Levine thought. The reality was that the editorial was nothing more than an excuse to chunk rocks at two glass houses across the river: Mississippi and Arkansas. But what Levine found interesting was the reference to one of "last month's" alleged abuses. It took a minute to backtrack to roll four, but there they were, thirty-five and thirty-seven days before the editorial. The first was buried toward the bottom of page 3 in the December 17 edition; a short article captioned, "Negro Leader Arrested, Drunk and Disorderly, Police Charge."

Levine read, and reread, the short article. *Shit, was this in my file?* he wondered. He read it again.

Helena, Ark. Split Tree mayor Sammy Allen yesterday defended the actions of his Chief of Police, Raymond Elmore, Sr., in last week's arrest of Negro voter registration activist Leon Jackson. Jackson, 52, of Natchez, Mississippi, was arrested December 12, on charges of public drunkenness and disorderly conduct. . . .

The article went on to explain that Jackson had alleged that he was the victim of a harassment campaign on account of his work to register voters in the predominantly black sections of Locust County, and that he was loudly seeking Elmore's dismissal. In response to his clamor, the American Civil Liberties Union had announced their intent to dispatch some headhunters from the Memphis and Little Rock offices to investigate. In reflex, the Split Tree City Council had publicly avowed to support their local police.

The second article was even smaller and harder to find. It was dated two days later, its small san serif headline announcing, "Charges Dropped, Jackson Vows to Continue Registration Efforts." It didn't really say much more, other than that the drunk and disorderly charges were being dropped. Nothing more was said. Jackson loudly voiced his resolve to continue the fight, but avoided any more allegations of harassment. Particularly notable was that the ACLU was not trumpeting a victory. They were, in fact, conspicuously quiet. And within days, conspicuously gone.

But what Levine kept going over and over again in his head was his recent conversation with Sheriff Elmore and how he didn't, or couldn't, recall any details about the case. Elmore had been in high school, he'd said. He didn't recall any details. It wasn't of concern to him.

Levine reread the first article.

Split Tree Mayor Sammy Allen yesterday defended the actions of his Chief of Police, Raymond Elmore, Sr. . . .

"That son of a bitch, that lying son of a bitch."

CHAPTER 25

Split Tree, Arkansas
FRIDAY, AUGUST 19, 2005

Kel drove back to Memphis and then headed west into Arkansas. As he crossed the bridge over the Mississippi River he recalled a joke he'd heard growing up in the western part of the state. Folk would say that if you could get everyone living in West Memphis to move across the river into Tennessee, it'd raise the average IQ in both states. He always thought that was funny, but he also always suspected that the folks in West Memphis probably told similar versions about Texarkana and Fort Smith.

It was just past one o'clock when Kel cleared the state line headed west on Interstate 40. A throbbing summer sun was straight overhead, and he caught himself going snake-eyed against the afternoon glare. The air-conditioner was blasting at high but was barely holding its own against the dark-blue Ford greenhouse he had rented. The radio said it'd be over a hundred degrees again. It was probably close to that already. He needed something to drink; he'd forgo eating until he could return to the comfortable confines of the Albert Pike, but he did need some liquid.

He stopped at a convenience store before continuing down the interstate another five minutes and turning off at the next marked rest stop. At the edge of the property was a large sweetgum surrounded by newly mown grass. It looked particularly inviting with its large, dappled oval of blue-green shade, and he walked over to it and took a seat, leaning back against the trunk and letting his legs stretch out in front of him. He sat for a moment before fishing into his paper sack and extracting a sweating twenty-ounce plastic bottle of Coca Cola and a small, cellophaned package of Tom's salted peanuts. Kel opened the bottle and poured the peanuts into the bottle. The Coke foamed up the neck but stopped short of overflowing. He eyed the potion suspiciously. He hadn't had a peanut Coke since he was a young kid, but for some reason that he couldn't explain, he needed one now.

His visit to Navy Casualty and his phone call to Dwayne Crockett had given him a great deal to rattle around the inside of his head. The Jimmie Carl Trimble case was more of a mystery now than when he'd started, and the Elmore case was totally unfathomable. If young Ray Elmore hadn't died in Vietnam, then why was his family promoting that idea that he had? Under what circumstances is it better to let people think your son, your brother, died halfway around the world and was never recovered? What would be worse? What could be worse? He thought of Grace Trimble's shrine and the pride heaped upon the ghost of Jimmie Carl Trimble. Maybe there was one thing worse. One thing unimaginable in a small town founded on long memory—desertion.

Could Ray Elmore be a deserter? Kel could verify it with a phone call to Les Neep. The CILHI kept a list of the Vietnam War deserters to crosscheck against their identifications. Navy Mortuary had access to the same list, of course, but the news that Ray Elmore wasn't a casualty had so caught him off-balance that he hadn't thought to ask—until now, that is, and now was too late and he wasn't about to turn around and backtrack through Memphis traffic. Telephone or no telephone, he'd call the CILHI later.

He took a final swallow of his drink, tipping the bottle back so that the last few peanuts sluiced their way out and into his mouth. He sat there for a few moments, quietly chewing the peanuts and listening to the throb and pulse of a thousand unseen insects. He tilted his head back, looking up into the still branches of the sweetgum tree. It caught his eye. On the trunk of the tree, right above his head, was the discarded, hollow, translucent-brown shell of a cicada; its one-time owner now singing from a new body out on some other tree.

Kel looked at it.

"A deserter," he said out loud. "A deserter."

CHAPTER 26

Memphis, Tennessee
FRIDAY, AUGUST 19, 2005

Levine had stopped by a Krystal's on Poplar Avenue on his way home from the Memphis and Shelby County Library. He hadn't eaten all day, and it was about to catch up with him. He'd picked up a dozen little mush-meat belly bombers and a soft drink to go from the drive-through window and headed home. He was anxious to check something that he vaguely remembered from the Xeroxed Jackson-Doe file, an itch that he couldn't quite find the source of to scratch. With the midafternoon Friday traffic, he'd reach his apartment by four o'clock, four-thirty at the latest. Much too late to turn around and go back to the office, he reasoned, and all the more reason to go in tomorrow—Saturday—when all the big-snots would be playing golf or scratching their marbles while they sat around someone's pool discussing how they wanted to bang each other's young trophy wives.

When he'd gotten to Memphis six months ago, he'd signed a short-term lease on a small apartment in what he quickly learned was a less-than-desirable part of town. In the beginning it hadn't really mattered as he'd hoped that Memphis was a temporary posting, a few months, maybe a year, on the outside, and then back to the familiar comfort of the eastern seaboard. Sure, he'd made some enemies, perhaps a lot of enemies, but he figured that he also still had some old friends in the Bureau who retained enough juice that they could intercede on his behalf to make things right.

But then he learned one of life's richer lessons. Old friends sometimes turn out to be simply old and not friends. It was now looking more and more like he was to be here in Memphis for the duration—whatever that might be. Six hundred and sixty-two days until retirement, not counting holidays and vacation time. Six hundred and sixty-two days more in the Big Muddy. He might need to think about getting another place. At least not a third-floor walkup. The liquid air in this river town made him wheeze like the Little Engine That Could every time he had to climb the stairs.

Levine opened his apartment door and took note of the hot, stale air that had worked its way up through years of dust from the lower two floors. He had only been gone a week but closed up in the August heat the place smelled like his grandparents' attic when he had been a boy—pine knots and limestone mortar and old newspaper bound with thick, white twine. Other than the pent-up smells, the apartment appeared the same as he'd left it a week earlier. There was still a pair of dark-blue socks casually discarded at the foot of the couch, and he noticed a half-empty water glass that he'd left on the end table. *Or is it half-full?* he thought, which made him smile.

He closed and locked the door, and then put down his food and flipped the switch on the window unit to max cool.

The copied case file folders were still on the small dinner table where he had been reading them last weekend, minus a few specific folders that he had taken with him to Split Tree. Those were mostly the ones that detailed the information concerning the John Doe—the autopsy report, the initial blood work, the trace evidence write-ups, a recently authored DNA report that made absolutely no sense to him. He sat down, took up the Krystal bag, and spilled the contents onto the table. He unwrapped a burger, pushed the whole thing into his mouth in one bite, sluiced it down with a swallow of watered-down Pepsi, slipped on his glasses, and opened up the topmost folder.

It was almost five o'clock.

When Levine closed the last folder, it was almost eight-thirty. He sat back and stretched and popped his knuckles. The room had cooled perceptibly. It was almost pleasant. There was still another half-hour of daylight, but the northern orientation of his windows did a poor job of capturing the light. He'd found nothing, and yet something kept tickling the roof of his brain, and he was sure it was in the case folder.

He'd have to read through the folders again.

Levine got up, stretched more fully, and retrieved a cold Pepsi from the refrigerator. He really wished he had a beer, but not badly enough to venture out at this hour. Then he sat down, turned the light on over the table, and opened the first folder again.

It was almost midnight when he finished the second read. Still nothing. There was a third folder, a bunch of Bureau hot wash: After Action Reports, lessons learned, cover-your-ass memos. He put his glasses back on and sat staring at the folder for several minutes. He sighed several times. It wasn't like he had much of a life in Memphis. Not with his family in Maryland. He sighed and opened the cover and started reading.

It was unbelievably dry, even for someone used to authoring and reading government sandpaper, but he finally found it. It was an obscure LHM—Letterhead Memorandum—for the deputy assistant director of the FBI, dated September 12, 1968. It had been routed through the SAC, or special agent in charge, of the Memphis Field Office. The author was B. Carlton Smith, head of the FBI's "Task Force on Organized Racial Violence: South"—probably some forgotten spinoff of the Bureau's WHITE HATE COINTELPRO, the Counterintelligence Program, directed against the KKK from 1964 to 1971. Levine remembered reading the memo a month earlier when he'd first begun chasing his tail. He remembered it for its absolutely arid style of prose and for the fact that he'd never heard of the Task Force on Organized Racial Violence before, nor of B. Carlton Smith. The latter wasn't all that surprising.

If Agent Smith, or Dr. Smith, or Professor Smith was heading a major task force back in the mid-1960s, then he must have had some seniority, and that was thirty-five, forty years ago. He certainly was retired now and maybe even dead.

The couple of sentences that Levine had been looking for hadn't meant anything a month ago in the abstract sterility of his Memphis office, and they really only acquired meaning in light of what Jimbo Bevins and Edd Forrest had said to him about gentlemen's clubs and social clubs. Chief Forrest had said that Big Ray was a member of some "social clubs." Jimbo had said almost the same thing. And there it was: Page 14 of 35, Section 2, Paragraph C, under the section entitled Historical Background. Carlton Smith had written:

> The Bureau, indeed many others in the varied judiciary and law enforcement agencies dealing with the thorny issue of organized racial violence, have but a poor understanding of the myriad native culture(s) in what is too often termed "The South," as if it were a monolith lacking internal variation. The New South, in fact, is a broad, vastly complex region, and it is critical to understand that in isolated pockets, many southerners view organizations such as the disparate chapters of the Klu Klux Klan not as organs of violence but rather as sodalities serving an important social function; a necessary membership ticket for career advancement in business and politics, indeed, in society in general.

Career advancement, such as making chief of police, Levine thought.

CHAPTER 27

Split Tree, Arkansas
MONDAY, MAY 25, 1987, MEMORIAL DAY

It should have been a day of immense pride. A day to swell one's chest and pop some buttons.

Instead Big Ray Elmore felt—what?—what did he feel?—not humiliation . . . that wasn't quite right. Shame? That was probably closer to the mark. It was a bright, late spring morning. Cool and blue and green and yellow and red. Big open sky. The air smelled of impending summer vacation and long days swimming and fishing and playing baseball until late into the evening. You could smell hot dogs and hamburgers and crinkly paper bags of pork rinds and hear the buzzing insects, and dogs barking, and children laughing. It should have been a time of joy, a time to drop a young, sweet melon and enjoy the long-lit day. It was all there: the sights, the smells, the hopes. Big Ray was newly retired as police chief, and his grandson—W.R.'s oldest boy, Jimmie Ray Elmore, had recently gotten a football scholarship to Arkansas Tech.

Just like Ray Junior had, so many years ago.

Big Ray had to smile when he looked at him. Big and strong and so absolutely full of himself. The young women flocked around him; so did the other young men, jostling one another like young rams butting heads; reveling in their proximity to him. Every time Big Ray looked up, his grandson had some other boy in a good-natured headlock, holding it just long enough to register currency in some pretty young girl's eye. He'd be leaving in a couple of months for school, but right now, on this day, young Jimmie Ray was the hottest young stud in Split Tree.

Just like Ray Junior had been.

Memorial Days in small southern towns are special times; big-time events. There are parades and picnics and Air National Guard flyovers. The school bands are at their best after a long year's practice. The girls are the prettiest in their cotton sundresses and straw hats. It is a time when old men dust off the dreams of their youth, and young men imagine a wide-open world.

But not for Big Ray and the ghost that kept close to his side. The one that chafed his soul daily.

Grace Trimble was there, in a place of honor on the reviewing stand. She was the mother of the town's Navy Cross awardee. The town's hero. She had on a blue dress with small white speckles and a large, flat-brimmed white hat with a band of tiny yellow-white flowers. Big Ray's wife, Ella Mae, was there, too, next to Grace, one chair off from the center. Her son might not have been awarded a Navy Cross, but Ray Junior's loss affirmed her status on the stage. Twenty years later, she still grieved pitifully, and it was only on rare occasions, like today, that she would tentatively emerge from her protective shell. She smiled and chatted politely with Grace, but she might as well have been sitting on the shaded side of the moon. She was fragile, and Big Ray could see the cracks widening each day.

Big Ray had been asked to be the grand marshal of the parade. A decorated veteran of World War II, Purple Heart club, and the father of one of the fifty-eight thousand young men who never came home from Vietnam. He'd declined.

How could he marshal a parade? Did he not wear the mark on his forehead? He saw it in the mirror every morning. Saw it every night. Didn't everyone else? He'd wondered, ever since he visited that memorial in Washington last year, how long it would be before someone checked the record and uncovered the shameful truth. That would be the final hammer blow. His wife would shatter into so many slivers of delicate glass that there would be no mending.

How did he live with himself?

How did his other son, W.R.?

He had never confronted W.R. about it; he didn't have to. He knew. He'd known. He'd figured it out. W.R. had covered for his brother, had wickered the lie, and Big Ray had willingly gone along with it, to his everlasting shame. Why? He told himself that it was to protect his fragile wife. But had it been? Was it that, or was it to protect his own image, the reputation that he had crafted in this small community over a lifetime? He didn't think so, but the question gnawed on him daily like a growing cancer.

In the end, it didn't matter "Why?" All that mattered was that he'd gone along with a lie and a deception because he couldn't change what had happened. It was done and had no undoing. And it was only a matter of time before the truth would be flushed out into the light and then it would all be for nothing.

He looked at his wife sitting next to Grace.

Soon it would all be for nothing.

Ironically, declining the position of grand marshal had only raised Big Ray's esteem in the minds of Split Tree's citizenry. They attributed it to the self-effacement of a humble man rather than the shame of a man eating himself up from the inside out. He hadn't been able to avoid the other request, however. Split Tree's fathers had decided that the time had arrived to dedicate a memorial of their own; to honor and record for posterity the valor and sacrifice of its Vietnam generation. Big Ray, as the father of the town's only MIA, was asked to read the benediction. He couldn't refuse. This was not a matter of humility. To refuse would be to dishonor them all, not only Ray Junior but Jimmie Carl Trimble and the other eleven men whose names appeared on the tablet—many of whom were here today, bearded and long-haired and dressed in old military fatigues or leather motorcycle vests covered with patches.

The Reverend Johnie Webb, Jr., of the Oak Glen Baptist congregation had given him the intended passage last weekend to practice: Isaiah 13: 2–3:

Raise a banner on a bare hilltop,
shout to them;
beckon to them
to enter the gates of the nobles.
I have commanded my holy ones;
I have summoned my warriors to carry out my
    wrath—
those who rejoice in my triumph.

The mayor of Split Tree had been speaking for quite some time. He was talking of sacrifice and healing. Big Ray hadn't heard any of it. Just a soft buzz not unlike that of the cicadas that filled the trees. His mind was on the state football championship in 1965. The one still talked about at barbershops and at the diners and at the feed mill. Folk around here still talked of Ray Junior's performance that evening—so long ago when the world seemed open and good and neverending.

It was only the silence that had finally grabbed his attention. Even the insects seemed to have hushed on cue.

The mayor had finished. Big Ray looked up and around. How long had everyone been staring at him? He glanced from one face to another; the faces he'd known all his life, now looking so utterly foreign.

He stood up slowly, his bad leg unwilling. He buttoned and smoothed the front of his suit coat as he glanced to his wife and to Grace Trimble. One looked at him with pride, the other with the delicate vacancy of a life cashed out of purpose. He wanted to smile but nothing would come. He walked to a small podium set in front of a bigger-than-life-sized bronzed statue of a Vietnam-era soldier.

Big Ray Elmore looked at the plaque at the foot of the figure; thirteen names in alphabetical order. The fifth from the top bore a small cross beside it indicating Killed In Action: Raymond Sallis Elmore, Jr.

He closed his eyes and thought of the reverend's chosen passage. He'd memorized it easily over the last week, never intending to have to read it, but now his memory failed him. It wouldn't come. Not a line, not a word. Instead, all he could picture was a page in his Bible, a particular passage, not the one that Reverend Webb had assigned him, but another. It was in his Bible, the one by his bed at home. He saw it with absolute clarity. It was the page where he kept his son's last letter.

He swallowed.

Then he began softly,

> *"Your wound is incurable,*
> *your injury beyond healing.*
> *There is no one to plead your cause,*
> *no remedy for your sore,*
> *no healing for you.*
> *All your allies have forgotten you;*
> *they care nothing for you.*
> *I have struck you as an enemy would*
> *and punished you as would the cruel,*
> *because your guilt is so great*
> *and your sins so many.*
> *Why do you cry out over your wound,*
> *your pain that has no cure?*
> *Because of your great guilt and many sins*
> *I have done these things to you."*

When he opened his eyes he saw that everyone was still staring at him.

CHAPTER 28

Split Tree, Arkansas
FRIDAY, AUGUST 19, 2005

Kel made good time after leaving the rest stop. Before long he reached Forrest City where he left Interstate 40 for Highway 1 headed south.

Out here in rural east Arkansas, there was something dead on the road every mile or so. Except for the unmistakable gray armored plates of an armadillo, usually it was nothing but a collection of dull feathers or tufts of dark fur and a little clump of reddish meat, with the occasional chemical smell of skunk. He'd forgotten what driving these roads was like, but it was coming back to him.

Near Forrest City he had seen a brown highway sign for Parkin State Park, a seventeen-acre American Indian mound complex on the St. Francis River that dated from around A.D. 1300. Kel had trained as an archaeologist and had done his dissertation on a related site in Missouri, but he had never visited Parkin; now he thought about detouring over there for a few minutes before heading back down to Split Tree. He reconsidered. The weekend promised to be particularly slow in Split Tree, and he might need the diversion more on Saturday or Sunday than he did right now.

Nevertheless, his memories of youthful field work in the lower Mississippi River Valley had been rekindled. When he first took the job at the CILHI it had been a departure; a shift from the abstract academic world of archaeology to the pragmatic, fact-filled world of forensics. Archaeology had begun to seem too much like building a house of cards. Grand speculation and extrapolation that could never be proven, just argued over endlessly. How many Indians could dance on the head of a pin? Forensics, on the other hand, was proved daily. The identities matched or they didn't. You were right or you were wrong—little room for debate. But lately he had begun feeling doubts where there had been none before. Not doubts about the quality of the work that his laboratory did—that was not a concern. Kel took great pride in the fact that the CILHI had achieved a hard-won reputation as the best skeletal identification laboratory in the world. He believed that, certainly. The doubt was something else. Medical doctors relish playing God; Kel didn't. Who gave him the right, who gave the U.S. government the right, to wade waist-deep into people's grief, grief that they have walled off for a quarter-century or more. The majority of the families affected by the identification of war dead were grateful. Closure was the byword of the day.

But not everyone.

Increasingly Kel encountered families—women like Grace Trimble—who had managed to knit over an open wound only by sheer daily effort; wounds that the government, that the CILHI, would scrape bloody with their analytical reports and photos. *Who gave us that right?* He found himself asking that question more and more frequently, and he never heard an answer. And so, even if for a short ride, it was pleasant to relive the days of academic pursuits. Pointless, perhaps, but it had never made an old woman cry.

The vast Mississippi River floodplain swept by, stretching as far as Kel could see, like a gentle undulating ocean of buff and gray, colored with patches of green soybeans and thick rice and white cotton. At one time, barely a thousand years after Christ, the middle and lower Mississippi River Valley had been the center of one of the most advanced civilizations in the North American continent. Veritable cities and centers of trade and art and culture. He smiled at the irony of it. Here he was, a thousand years later, and the same region boasted one of the lowest standards of living in America.

You could still see the remnants of those great centers of civilization. Parkin with its ceremonial mounds was one of the more conspicuous satellites, but plenty of others were here and there, less awesome perhaps, but still discernible to anyone asking the right questions. Small mounds still occasionally dot either side of the road. Once upon a not-too-distant time there had been even more, but the popularity of land planes (large earthmovers that use lasers to control the depths of their cuts—capable of leveling a field almost perfectly flat) in the eighties had resculpted the valley. For the most part, only those mounds with trees growing on them that were large enough to present more headaches to remove than was worth, still remained.

As he drove he noted the presence of trees in fields. Trees were rare in Locust County, at least outside corporate limits, and usually denoted some vestige of antiquity. Occasionally coffin trees could be seen, usually pines, planted in pairs at the birth of a child to mature and provide wood for their coffins when the time warranted. Some lined the fringe of a meandering stream.

Why hadn't Jimmie Carl Trimble had a choice? The question kept intruding on Kel's thoughts as he drove, and he couldn't shake it loose. Dwayne Crockett had said that Trimble was dead before he even got to Vietnam. *Why? What could so kill a young man that it showed on his face? In his eyes?* As he looked out into the field, at the mounds and headstones and tufts of grass and trees that represented the final family reunion, Kel couldn't help but think of Jimmie Carl Trimble. He couldn't help but think of all the young men who died so far from home and the ones they loved. He thought of the almost two thousand from the Vietnam War whose remains were still scattered and buried in unmarked graves so far from home and family.

Buried.

It was the cluster of trees that finally made Kel realize what was wrong.

All wrong.

He cussed himself for not seeing it sooner. It hadn't made sense at the time, but that was because he hadn't really stopped to think about it. He'd been enjoying Levine's obvious frustration adapting to Split Tree's pace and character so much that he hadn't done his own job. It hadn't made sense, until now. Now it did—because of the trees; the trees made sense.

Donnie Hawk had been bullshitting Levine, jerking this New York wise-ass's chain, and neither Levine nor Kel had gotten a whiff of it. You don't give bodies to Boy Scout troops or high-school chess clubs or anyone else. Not in New York, not in Little Rock, and not in Locust County, Arkansas. That's a fact, and it doesn't matter if you're a medical examiner or the town barber elected coroner. Kel knew that; he worked for a government agency dedicated to bringing men home for burial. Burial. Levine should have known it, but he let his preconceptions blind him. Levine had treated these people like inbred rubes from the beginning, and they, in turn, had played him for the fool.

And the answer was there all the time; you only had to look at the trees.

No medical examiner, no coroner, anywhere, had unlimited space—certainly not in a small-town county coroner's office in one of the poorest counties in the United States. Open case or not, at some time the decision has to be made to dispose of the remains, to get them off the shelf. In a case like this one, the most likely option would be burial.

The trees.

Burials.

Cemeteries.

John Doe's remains had been buried, Kel was sure of it. Levine had been so absolutely spun out of control that he couldn't think straight, and Kel had been so amused watching him that he hadn't thought straight either. Now he was thinking. They were buried; he knew it. He was also equally sure that the coroner knew where they were, or at least knew how to go about finding that information. But Donnie Hawk wouldn't tell Levine now, and the chances weren't good that he'd be any more forthcoming with another outsider, whether the outsider had roots in Split Tree or not.

But there were other ways. There was sure to be a document trail; it was only a matter of sniffing it out.

Kel stopped by his room at the Sleep-Mor long enough to use the toilet, splash some cold water on his face, and take a wet washcloth to the grime that had accumulated on his neck. He looked closely in the mirror, noting the reddish cast to his eyes, the result of dust and sun and lack of honest sleep. He scanned the room for evidence of any disturbance. He didn't see anything, but it was hard to tell since the maid had been in. Then he got back into his car and headed for the courthouse. What he was counting on was bureaucracy. For better or worse, he was now a bureaucrat. He spent most of his time analyzing memos and spreadsheets and trends and policy.

Frightening.

But he could use it now. He ran the process over and over in his head. In the United States, when someone dies, a death certificate is required for the collection of insurance, remarriage, probating the estate, sale of property, and perhaps most important, disposal of the body. The law wants some proof that a person really is dead before people get the green light to start disposing of the body. Death can be handled with three basic types of death certificates: natural deaths, which can be signed by an attending doctor, or in some cases a licensed nurse, police officer, ambulance driver, even a ship's captain; same for stillbirths and fetal deaths; and then there are suspicious deaths—medicolegal deaths they're called—those that have to be signed by coroners or medical examiners.

But the bureaucratic gears aren't finished grinding with the completion of a death certificate. Death certificates certify death, but another document—a certificate of disposition of remains—is required to physically do something with the remains. Rules are rules and even unidentified homicide victims have to follow them. Someone—in this case the Locust County coroner—would have had to certify the John Doe's death. And that certificate would be on file somewhere, certainly at the Bureau of Vital Statistics in Little Rock, but sometimes small counties like Locust County kept copies as well. Made things easier in prefax days, when travel to and from Little Rock was more time-consuming. But more important, if the remains were buried—and Kel now was sure they had been—then there should be some sort of certificate of disposition of remains on file. A burial permit or a cremation permit. Given that this was an open homicide, it was unlikely that the coroner would have agreed to a cremation. Burials are exhumable, but cremations are like diamonds—forever. And if the remains were buried, probably by a licensed mortician, it had to have been in a state-approved cemetery. Once again, most likely somewhere in Locust County.

The key was to find the burial permit. The original would have been forwarded to the state registrar in Little Rock. Kel could drive there on Monday, but the Locust County clerk might have indexed a copy for the county ledger. Kel was banking on the county courthouse again. Locust County was poor, and poor people have poor ways. Travel to the state capital involved an expense. Records, at least copies or voucher entries, would be retained locally, at the clerk's office. The trick would be to get in there and out without attracting too much attention.

Cecil Berle kept checking his watch; it was almost three o'clock on a long Friday afternoon, and he was looking toward shutting down early and going home. His boss, Emery Jane Hennig, the county clerk, had already left early, and there was very little keeping the spindle-thin fence post of a man at his desk other than the slow progress of the clock hands. Hardly anyone had been in all day. No one was likely to come in now, not late on a Friday afternoon. He wanted badly to take to the new hammock his wife had given him for their anniversary.

He was looking out the second-floor window overlooking Tupelo and Main streets when the door to room 202 opened. The jamb was swollen from the humidity and it stuck and rattled when it was opened. He turned at the sound and saw someone he'd never seen in Split Tree before puppet his head around the door. So much for going home early.

"Yes sir, can I hep you?" Cecil's voice betrayed no desire to be of service. It was said in the same manner he might have said "bless you" if he'd heard someone sneeze.

Kel walked into the office and closed the door behind him. "Well, I sure do hope so," he said as he walked up to the counter. The room was floored with a short-napped industrial-grade carpet that was supposed to be a mottled blue-gray but looked an off-plum color in the buzzing fluorescent light. The old hardwood boards underneath could still be heard creaking under each step. "I'm looking to find some records."

Cecil Berle looked at him as if he was a talking goat with a necktie. "Then I reckon you're in the right spot. This being County Records and all. It's pretty late in the day; can I be of any hep?"

Kel placed both palms flat on the counter as if he were about to order a drink. He looked at the man. *How much honesty is called for in a situation like this?* he wondered. "Hmmm, well sir, I'm doin' a piece of research, and I was interested in some old . . . I guess old isn't quite right, you might say, older, county records. I was hopin' you could save me a trip to Little Rock." He smiled. It wasn't returned.

"You be a lawyer?" Cecil squinted.

"No sir. I may be a whole bunch of things, but a lawyer I ain't."

Kel couldn't tell if that was the right answer or not.

"What kind of records? Exactly," Cecil asked.

"I'm interested in . . . ahh . . . well, I guess they're vital statistics. Death certificates, burial permits, location of local cemeteries, that sort of thing."

"Next of kin, are you? You be next of kin? Of the folks' records your aimin' to look up, that is."

"Well . . . ahhh . . . naw, sir, not exactly."

"What part is *not?* . . . exactly, that is."

"Oh," Kel smiled again, wider this time, "the kin part. No, I'm not kin—not that I know of, that is. Just doin' some research, mostly for an acquaintance in Memphis."

Kel watched as Cecil ruminated. Kel didn't know it, but Cecil Berle was calculating the time investment on his part and how that was going to affect his getting home, rather than the propriety of the request. He sighed deeply, and his dark-blue bow tie cocked to starboard slightly as he exhaled. The lifetime civil servant won out in the end.

"When'd these deaths occur—approximately? We store the records in different places dependin' on when they occurred."

"Somewhere 'bout forty years ago—here in Locust County."

"Got a name?"

He reminded Kel of a mud dobber; brown, spindly legs, belt cinched up too tight. Kel wasn't entirely sure if he was asking whether he, Kel, had a name or if he meant the name of the dead person he was looking for. He hesitated, then gave the latter a shot. "Naw, he doesn't have a name, least none that anybody around here knows. He died as an unknown. John Doe, would be my guess." Kel noticed that he had involuntarily slipped deeper into his boyhood accent. *Hey, when in Split Tree* . . . he thought.

The thin man nodded as if he understood all, or understood nothing. Then, without a word, he turned his back on Kel and slowly returned to his desk. He had a slight hitch in his step, as if he had a small rock in one shoe. Kel watched, afraid that his final answer had so driven the man over the bureaucratic frustration ledge that he was simply going to be ignored.

Instead, Cecil Berle reached slowly under his desk and extracted a two-foot-long wooden pole with a single key attached to the end with a loop of cord. He walked back to the counter and slapped the instrument down in front of Kel.

"Third floor, room 304, on the right. Y'all on your own, though. If I'm not here when you come back, leave the key outside the door." He gave a nod in the general direction of the office door to indicate that he meant for Kel to leave the key by the door here and not the door on the third floor. It was clear that the little man had no intention of going upstairs unless he had a gun to his head, and even then it might be open to debate.

Kel smiled and took the stick. It looked better suited to clubbing a washtub full of monkeys than being a key holder, but it no doubt was effective in keeping people from inadvertently pocketing the key. "Yes sir, surely will. And I thank you. Third floor, room . . ." He arched his eyebrows to indicate that he needed a little refreshing with regard to the number.

"Three-oh-four," Cecil replied as he turned and headed once again for his desk. He wanted to clear the last few papers off it and head home, and he'd already spent too much time dealing with this stranger.

Kel didn't hang around. He walked into the hallway and looked in both directions, trying to remember which way the stairway was located. He turned right, found the stairs, and took them two at a time to the third floor. It was unbelievably hot. So hot that, from what he could tell, no living being had an office on the third floor. All the doors were closed and the entire floor had the feel of having been shut down for a long vacation. He quickly found room 304 and swung the key up to unlock the door, rapping his shins with the baseball bat attached to it. He cussed and decided that he was going to go ahead and steal the key if only as a public service.

Kel only thought the third-floor hallway was hot. When the door to room 304 swung open, he understood what "understatement" meant. It was easily 120 degrees inside the room, and Kel was literally forced to stagger a step back. The air smelled old; a heady mixture of dust and cracked yellow varnish and dry rot slow-stewed in 90 percent humidity. He took a breath and stepped back into the doorway. The room was filled with lidded brown cardboard boxes stacked almost to the ceiling. There was a narrow pathway that snaked through the approximate center. Kel thought of Howard Carter cracking the seal on King Tut's tomb. "Wonderful things," he said to himself.

From what he could tell, the accumulated Locust County records for the better part of the 1900s were here. They appeared to have been filed by whim and windstorm, certainly not by year or type or any other conventional element of organization. Kel was already dripping wet and was feeling lightheaded. Sweat stung his eyes and cut thick, salty rivulets down his face and into the corners of his mouth.

Now he understood why the friendly neighborhood mud dobber downstairs hadn't volunteered to escort him up here.

The older boxes were easy to spot, as each had an acid-brittle, yellowed, hand-written label taped on the end; the inked letters in that flowery script that was once taught in precomputer, pretypewriter grade schools. The more recent boxes—those from about 1960 onward—had the contents labeled directly on the cardboard with what appeared to be black permanent marker. The lettering was simple and blocky and devoid of character or self-discipline. He blinked several drops of sweat from his eyes and wiped his hair away from his forehead with the crook of his left arm. His hands were already grayish black from accumulated time and insect droppings. As best he could tell, most of the records nearest the door were from the seventies and eighties. Farther back in the room, closest to the wall and the rippled-glass window, were boxes from the forties, fifties, and sixties. This semblance of organization resulted not from planning or ad hoc design but from a reluctance on any-one's part to venture farther into the interior of the sweatbox than necessary. It was always easier to simply deposit the most recent boxes in the doorway and push—especially since there was hardly ever any call to access them later.

It took the better part of a half-hour to find the boxes dating from the mid-1960s. Part of the delay was the result of his having to step into the relative oasis of the ninety-degree hallway every few minutes to revive. There had also been a short delay caused by the need to move many of the later boxes out of the room to clear some work space.

There were five boxes that looked promising. Kel pulled them closer to the window for better light since the overhead bulb appeared to have long ago burned out. The window was painted shut with a hundred years' worth of maintenance, and the dried husks of dozens of dead flies littered the windowsill where they'd battered their brains out against the glass. He sat cross-legged on a small clearing he'd made on the floor and opened the first box, removing a stack of bound ledgers. The covers were burgundy-colored fake leather and they smelled of paper mold and animal glue. Birth records. So was box two.

Box three was what he was after. Five thin binders.

He sorted them into order and opened the one labeled *Vital Statistics Jan. '65—Dec. 1966 County Deaths*. The dry cover made quiet cracking and snapping sounds as it was opened. Inside were ledger pages listing Locust County coroner's findings of death, now browned and brittle like ancient parchment. Each entry was spread across two pages, thin blue ink lines ruling it into ten columns. Only the first couple of dozen pages were filled in with neat script. As he turned the leaves, several edges broke free in thumb-sized crescents of the acidic paper. Unlike the boxes, the pages and entries were ordered chronologically. He leafed quickly through the pages, scanning the left margin until he found an entry dated June 4. He began scanning slower, running his finger down the red line separating the first and second columns. Levine had said that Jackson's body was found in mid-August sometime.

He soon found it. A faded, blue, fountain-pen ledger entry dated August 16, 1965. The handwriting was small and precise and spoke of a uniform mind. *Decedent's Name: Jackson, Leonidas S.; Address: Natchez, Miss.; Sex: M; Race: Colored; Age at Last Birthday: 52; Cause of Death: Injuries resulting from blunt force trauma; Manner of Death: Homicide; DOD: On or about August 15, 1965. Death certified by: Granville Begley, M.D., Coroner, Locust County, Arkansas.*

Thank God for bureaucrats, Kel thought. *Now to find Mr. John Doe's.*

Levine had said that the second body had been found in September. Locust County wasn't big and there weren't many deaths between August 1 and October 1. He found it easily. Another faded entry, this one dated September 24, 1965, but in a different hand, one more casual, loopy and less efficient. The writing was larger and extended beyond the ruled columns. *Decedent's Name: Unknown; Address: Unknown; Sex: M; Race: White; Age at Last Birthday: Unknown; Cause of Death: GSW to the head; Manner of Death: Homicide; DOD: O/A August 1965.* It, too, had been certified by Granville Begley, M.D.

That had to be it. Gunshot wound to the head, date of death on or about August 1965, unknown identity.

Kel stepped out into the hallway and bent over, hands on his knees, trying to shake off the heat. His head was pounding in sync with his pulse. His nose had plugged up with heat and dust, and sweat pooled at his feet. So far, so good, but also, so far, so what? An hour in the sauna and he had proven what everyone already knew to begin with: Leon Jackson and some unknown white boy were murdered in 1965. The only promising aspect was that Locust County seemed to have a hard time disposing of paper.

The actual certificates of death were in two boxes near the floor, but they required moving a dozen others to reach them.

As with the ledger books, the death certificate for Leon Jackson proved the easier of the two to find. Arkansas didn't use a separate disposition form. Rather, the top section of the death certificate contained the body release information, and the certificates were filed by release date instead of the date of death. In Jackson's case, his remains were released to a representative of the Jefferson Funeral Home in Natchez, Mississippi, a week and a half after being identified. From there they were signed over to a military escort for transfer to Arlington National Cemetery.

The John Doe's record, however, was not there. In fact, Kel searched through the 1965 binder twice from September on. No release of an unknown body for burial. He started on 1966. He slowly checked each page.

He found it about the same time that he had decided to give up. The afternoon heat and lack of fresh air had sucked him dry like one of the dead flies on the hot windowsill. *One more page,* he'd thought, *at least I'll have given it a good shot.* That's when he found it.

It was dated September 25, 1966—a year and a day after the death had been certified. "Of course," Kel said out loud, "just like the old Missing Persons Act." He read the top of the form: *Death Certificate and Release of Body for Disposition Permit. Decedent's Name: John Doe; Address: Unknown; Sex: M; Color: White; Age at Last Birthday: Unknown (Adult); Place of Death: Vicinity Split Tree, Locust Co.; Date of Death: O/A August 1965; Means of Disposition: Burial.* But it was the other name on the form that caught his attention: *Released to: Mr. D. Hawk, Funeral Director's License No. 471102, Hawk Funeral Home, 113 Price Avenue, Split Tree, Arkansas.* And then, *Location of Burial: Wallace Cemetery, Locust County, Arkansas.*

"I'll be damned," Kel said.

CHAPTER 29

Split Tree, Arkansas
FRIDAY, AUGUST 19, 2005

Fitting all the boxes back into the room was like repacking a suitcase in the middle of a crowded airport—the volume of what had to go in well exceeded the space into which it had to go. It took a while. Kel muscled the last stack of boxes through the entryway with his hip and was backing out of the room, pulling the door shut, when he bumped into a mass.

"Boo."

"Holy shit," Kel exclaimed. He physically jumped.

"Scare you?" Jimbo Bevins asked. His smile indicated real enjoyment.

"Scared the piss out of me. Yeah. Goddamn, Sheriff." Kel took a deep breath to steady himself. His heart thumped in his throat.

Jimbo smiled even bigger. "Deputy. I'm not Sheriff yet. Gimme some time, though." He winked and took a long drag on a cigarette. He blew the smoke out the side of his mouth. "You're that McKelvey fella, right? We met yesterday over at the Albert Pike. You're Mr. Levine's buddy."

Kel nodded. "Robert McKelvey. Yeah, we met. Good to see you again, Deputy Bevins. Kinda surprised me. So quiet up here and all. Figured I was all alone."

"So I gathered. You jumped like a goosed cat." Jimbo paused. He smiled again. "How's the room at the Sleep-Mor? Sam treatin' you okay?"

Kel looked at Bevins. It was an odd segue. He thought about the intruder in his room.

"Where's your buddy?" Jimbo Bevins continued.

"Levine?" Kel shrugged. He still hadn't figured out where the conversation was headed but decided that he needed to offer some sort of response. "Out doin' special agent things, I reckon. He doesn't check in with me."

Jimbo Bevins kept his eyes locked on Kel's. "S'pose he's still chasin' down his Klansmen? Hey, you ever hear the one about the two good-ol'-boy genies?"

"Can't say that I have, Deputy."

"Well, you bein' from Arkansas and all, you'll appreciate this. See, there's this New York fella, sorta like Mr. Levine, and he's drivin' acrosst the country and he stops here in Arkansas. Needs to take a leak, right? So he gets out and un-limbers and he's pissin' into a ditch and all when he sees somethin' shiny. He goes and picks it up and it's an old Lone Star beer can. You remember Lone Star?"

Kel nodded.

"So he rubs this can and out pops two good-ol'-boy genies. Now this New York fella, this one sorta like Mr. Levine, he doesn't believe that they're genies 'cause he's from the city and doesn't believe in shit like that, but what the hell, right? So, he goes ahead and closes his eyes and makes three wishes. And when he opens his eyes, damn if he's not standin' in the middle of a mansion full, and I mean slam full, of beautiful women. Each of them buck naked. And when he looks down, damn if the floor isn't just covered with hundred-dollar bills. Like ankle deep and all. And just when this fella is sayin' to himself, 'Well shit, them boys must have been real genies,' the doorbell rings. So this New York fella opens the door, and there are these two Klansmen standin' there—just like the ones that your buddy Levine's lookin' high and low for—and these two Klansmen grab this fella and drag him out into the front yard and string him up on a tree limb." Bevins paused.

"That's pretty funny, Deputy Bevins. You got a real flair

for stories," Kel responded. The door frame was to his back and he couldn't move.

Jimbo Bevins took another drag on his cigarette and blew out the smoke before continuing. "Ain't got to the funny part yet. See, as this New York fella is hangin' there, these two Klansmen pull off their hoods, and damn if it's not these two genie bubbas. And they're lookin' at this fella and one of them says to the other, he says, 'Now, I understand that house full of naked women, and I understand all that money, but why anyone would want to be hung like a black man is beyond me.'" Jimbo Bevins flashed an enormous grin, but his eyes were cold.

"You're right," Kel nodded slowly. "That sure was the funny part. Glad I waited. Do me a favor, will you? Make sure you tell that to Mr. Levine next time you see him. I think he'll get a kick out of that one."

"I plan on it, Mr. McKelvey. I definitely will do that. But now tell me, what's y'all doin' up here anyway?"

Kel paused. Jimbo Bevins had a different tone to his voice. There was an edge to his good-old-boy words, like a glass shard hidden in amongst newly mown grass. "Ahh, well, Deputy, I wasn't quite honest with you yesterday there at the diner. You asked me about bein' from around here and havin' kin here and all, and I didn't really give you a good answer. Truth is, my people used to be from Split Tree, and, well hell, you know how it is. You get cut loose from your roots as a kid and you get all curious. Thought I'd do some genealogy while I'm in town."

"That right? Can understand that all right. They tell me the library's got all sorts of good records for stuff like that. Family tree and all."

"Fixin' to go there next," Kel said.

The two men stood close to each other. Too close in the heat. Their shirt buttons were almost touching.

"So tell me, Deputy, you doin' some genealogy as well? Your office is downstairs somewhere, isn't it?" Kel made a conscious effort to stand straight, squaring his shoulders and slowly drawing in his belly.

Jimbo Bevins took another long draw on his cigarette. A wisp of smoke curled across his eyes causing him to squint as he did so. He sniffed and smiled again. "Caught me, Mr. McKelvey," he said, holding up his cigarette but keeping his eyes on Kel. "All them damn rules nowadays. Can't smoke in the buildin' unless of course you sneak away."

"Of course. And you're a sneak?"

"Don't you know it now."

It was Kel's turn to smile. He was coming off the defensive, and he tilted his head upward so that his jaw jutted forward. "Tell you what, Deputy. If I was goin' to sneak off for a smoke, I reckon I'd go outside. If it was me, that is. Must be a hundred-and-ten, hundred-and-twenty degrees up here."

Jimbo Bevins hesitated, but he didn't blink. "Caught me again, Mr. McKelvey. Smoke's just a bonus. I was comin' up here anyway."

Kel's back was still pressed to the door, and he began to shift to the side to break contact with the deputy. "That right? Doesn't look to me that there's much activity up here."

"Now, you know, that's about right. Matter of fact, that's why the sheriff sent me up here." Jimbo shifted sideways in sync with Kel, keeping him pinned against the door frame.

"Sheriff Elmore?"

"He'd be the sheriff, yessir. His office is right . . . down . . . there." Jimbo nodded at the floor. "These old floors is so loose they creak like Grandma's knees. He heard a noise up here. Sent me up to check on it. Afraid it might be a damn rat."

"Rat?"

"Yessir. Or some other pest."

Kel shifted some more. He shook his head. "Didn't see any signs of rats. Mice neither. You got rats here in the buildin', do you?"

"Nope," Jimbo Bevins replied. He took a final draw on his cigarette and dropped the butt to the floor. He broke eye contact as he scrubbed it out with the toe of his boot. "If we did, we'd eliminate the little suckers."

Kel used the opportunity to maneuver away from the door. With his back to the empty hallway he was again in control of his personal space and was able to begin backing away from Jimbo Bevins. The temperature seemed ten degrees cooler. "It must be shit to be a rat," he said.

"You got that right, Mr. McKelvey. It's the shit."

CHAPTER 30

Lady of Mercy Hospital, Helena, Arkansas
THURSDAY, NOVEMBER 12, 1987

As one of the more junior Locust County sheriff's deputies, W. R. Elmore often pulled the river run, and spent his shift driving the one-lane dusty ribbons that paralleled the river. He could drive back and forth for hours and not pass another car. Usually he hated it, accepting it quietly as the dues that must be paid, but today it had worked in his favor. He was close to the county line when the call came in.

"Unit Four, Base, over." The radio mounted on the transmission hump of his cruiser squawked alive. "Unit Four, Base. You there, W.R.? Over."

W.R. keyed the mic. He recognized the dispatcher's voice. Tubby Boil. They'd been friends since Miss Butler's second-grade class. Tubby was well suited to his nickname. He was large and seldom got excited, but his voice now, even distorted as it was by the radio acoustics, had a measured fever to it. "Base, this is Four. What's up, Tub? Over."

"What's your location, Four? Over."

Elmore looked outside. In the hypnotism of the drive he'd lost awareness of where he was and needed to acquire his bearings. He keyed the mic again. "Base, this is Four. Ahhh, Tub, I'm on the River Road, 'bout two miles south of the county line. You sound all exercised, son. What's the problem? Over."

"W.R., it's your father, man. It's Big Ray."

"Whoa, whoa. Calm down, Tub. What's my father? What's Big Ray? Over."

"It's Big Ray," Tubby Boil repeated. In the agitation he'd forgotten departmental radio etiquette. "He's been hurt, W.R. Big Ray's been hurt. Bad."

W.R. squinted and looked at the radio, as if the machine itself held the answer. When the dispatcher didn't say anything else, W.R. keyed the mic. "Say again? Base. Tub. Say again? Over."

The radio hissed and skipped. "To the hospital. Hurry," broke through the static.

"Roger, Base. Hospital. Say again. Which hospital? Over."

The reception was better now and Tubby Boil's voice was loud. "Takin' him to Lady in Helena. It's bad, W.R. You better hurry, man. You better hurry."

W.R. didn't respond. He threw the mic onto the floor and pressed the accelerator. On the nearly abandoned county road there was no advantage to the lights and siren, but it made him feel better, and he hit the switch. He made good time and arrived at the emergency room within minutes of the ambulance.

He stopped in front of the door to the emergency room and ran in, not sure of where to go.

"W.R.," someone called.

W.R. looked up and saw a nurse at the admissions desk. It was Murleen Connor. They'd dated briefly in high school before her parents had moved into Helena. He went up to the counter, his eyes speaking for him.

"It's your daddy, W.R. It's Big Ray. They just brought him in. He's in room 200. Over there. There." She pointed to a curtained doorway as she came out from behind the desk and began leading the way.

W.R. passed her in two steps and shoved past the curtain. His father lay on an examination table. Big Ray Elmore's eyes were open but heavy-lidded and unresponsive. His breathing was wet and labored and had the thick sound of close mortality. The right side of his face was swollen and what could be seen of his right eye was blood red, the color of a late-season

Indian peach. The ambulance attendants had swaddled his head in layer upon layer of gauze that had to be cut away and now lay piled on the floor, stained red and yellow. The attending doctor had inserted a shunt in the gaping wound near Elmore's right temple in an attempt to relieve the mounting pressure on his brain. It was cosmetic. The hospital had no trauma surgeon on duty, and it was taking time to find one who could deal with a massive brain injury.

In the meantime, Big Ray Elmore lay dying.

The attending physician straightened up when he saw the uniformed deputy push aside the curtain. He looked at Murleen, coming up behind.

"This is his son," she said quickly.

The doctor's first inclination was to keep W.R. out. The patient was critical, and the ER was no place for relatives. The second inclination was to let him in. The patient was beyond critical; he was dying, and no one should die alone. He stepped aside and let W.R. enter.

"Dad. Dad." W.R. positioned his face in front of his father's unresponsive eyes. He spoke quietly but directly. "Big Ray, it's me. It's your son—W.R. Big Ray? Dad?"

Big Ray Elmore's eyes fluttered slightly, but the pupils remained unresponsive.

"Big Ray, it's goin' be all right. Momma's comin'. Miss Ella Mae's comin'. I arranged for another deputy to drive her up here. Hang on, Dad. You hang on. You can. You can do it . . . you're Big Ray."

The eyes twitched again, and there was a soft sound, like a short, moist sigh, that left his lips.

"Tha's right, Big Ray. It's me. It's W.R. You recognize me, Big Ray?"

"Ray . . ." It was said so softly that W.R. doubted that he'd heard it at all. The eyes didn't change. The lips didn't move. The sound seemed to come from deep within.

"You'll be all right, Dad. Hang on."

"Ray." It was unmistakable this time.

CHAPTER 31

Jimbo Bevins watched Kel disappear into the stairwell but made no discernible effort to follow. Kel forced himself to walk slowly, conscious of the adrenaline hammering his heart. He measured his breathing, listening for footfalls behind him.

The second floor seemed deserted. With the office doors all closed the only light came from a few small, dim light fixtures hanging from the high ceiling. The whole floor had the sound of empty, and the boards in the floor popped and complained from under the thin carpet. Kel's uneasiness was turning to annoyance with each step. "Jackass," he muttered. "Prick." By the time he reached room 202 he was mad at himself for letting the likes of Jimbo Bevins get the better of him. Between the heat and the surprise, he'd been thrown off-balance and hadn't recovered. "What a jerk," he muttered again, this time referring to himself. He shook his head like a wet dog, clearing his head of the memory.

He tried the door and found it locked. It surprised him. Not so much because the county clerk had entrusted him with the key to a century's worth of county records, but more because Cecil Berle had looked to Kel as if he lived there, and Kel had assumed that he probably slept cocooned-up in one of his desk drawers. True, he had told Kel that he might not be there when he finished in the storage room, but after Kel got up to the third-floor death oven, he'd assumed that the old man simply was counting on him to pass out from the heat and not come to until sometime in mid-November when the temperature finally moderated. Or maybe the old man was counting on Deputy Bevins to rid the building of pests. Kel rattled the knob again, then looked around. He glanced at the stairwell and at the closed door of the sheriff's office, saw nothing and nobody, and propped the key holder against the door frame.

The first floor was even cooler than the second, all the conditioned air sinking to the lobby. His clothes were wet with perspiration, in part because of the heat, in part because of the encounter with Jimbo Bevins, and Kel physically shuddered. He blew his nose and looked for the public restrooms. They were off to the side of the lobby, beside a blind vendor's snack shop, now closed. He looked at his watch, almost five o'clock, and he realized that with the exception of the rat catcher on the third floor, he was alone in the building. He smiled at the thought. Only in small-town America would everyone go off and leave a stranger in the courthouse all by himself. He went into the bathroom and washed his face and arms. He dried them with a wad of paper towels and blew his nose a final time. By the time he left the building, he was feeling better.

Outside, it took a moment to get his bearings. He glanced up at the third floor, half-expecting to see a face watching him from one of the windows. All he saw was glare. The sun was still high, with almost another four hours of late-summer light. Somewhere out of sight, a mockingbird was patiently trilling through his repertoire. Kel was in the front of the courthouse, and his car was at the street off to the right. Otherwise, the square was deserted. He had seen the library the other day when Levine was driving, but he hadn't paid much attention to where it was in relation to the courthouse. It was close by, he knew that. He suspected he could probably hit it with a small cat if he'd had the wind to his back and knew where to throw it. He started walking, intending to circle the courthouse. He got as far as the northeast corner.

There, tucked under a mature magnolia tree, was a larger-than-life-sized bronze statue of what appeared from a distance to be a Vietnam soldier, his M-16 gripped tightly in his right hand, his left hand slightly raised for balance, as he turned a determined eye to some unseen event on his horizon. Below it was a small plaque bolted to the granite base. Kel walked over to it. It read, *"Dedicated To Those Locust County Sons Who Served In Vietnam, 1965–1972 Dulce et decorum est pro patria mori."* Below that were thirteen names in alphabetical order. Two of them had small, simple crosses beside them: *Raymond Sallis Elmore, Jr., USN* and *Jimmie Carl Trimble, USN.* A footnote explained the crosses—*Killed In Action.* Kel stood, staring at the plaque and the statue for a long time.

"Dulce et decorum est pro patria mori," he said to the bronze figure, pronouncing the words slowly. It had been the motto of confederate General A. P. Hill. *"It is pleasant and fitting to die for one's country."* He stepped back and looked into the determined eyes of the statue, his thoughts returning to Ray Elmore and the possibility that he might have been a deserter. "Was it, Ray? Did you die for your country?" he said softly.

When he finally moved on, he continued working his way clockwise around the courthouse, occasionally glancing up to the third-floor windows. He hadn't gone far, less than a quarter-turn, when he spied the library; on the east side, directly across the street.

The building was set a couple of feet up above street level on what amounted to a significant rise for Split Tree, and it required mounting two steps. Kel walked up the short cement sidewalk past the sign that identified the building as the Split Tree Community Library and Meeting Center. *Must be small meetings,* Kel thought as he read the sign. The whole one-story cement-block building was the size of a small two-car garage. He pressed his face to the glass door and peered in. It was dark inside. He glanced again at his watch—five-ten—and then at the lettering on the door:

**8:00 A.M. till 5:00 P.M. Mon–Fri
9:00 A.M. till 12:00 P.M. Sat
Closed Sundays and Holidays**

"Aw, crap," Kel said as he tugged at the handle. He looked back inside and saw shelves of books. Off to one side was a door with a sign beside it that read: FAMILY TREE CENTER. *There we go,* he thought, *cemetery records.* Kel knew from his own experience that most small-town libraries had a genealogy room, and most genealogy rooms have books and lists of family cemeteries within the county. This one obviously was no different. If only it wasn't closed.

"Nine o'clock," Kel said, looking at the door again. "Okay. Tomorrow mornin'."

CHAPTER 32

Split Tree, Arkansas
SATURDAY, AUGUST 20, 2005

Kel awoke early. He lay in bed for some time, staring at the half-moon dents in the ceiling tiles and reviewing the previous day. Finally there was a ray of promise. Levine's long-lost John Doe was buried at Wallace Cemetery—wherever that was located. Kel only hoped it was in Locust County and that he could find directions to it. He checked the time: seven-forty-five. He'd know in a little over an hour.

But it was yesterday's other development that filled his thoughts. Sheriff Elmore's twin brother Ray Junior—contrary to Locust County lore—was not missing in Vietnam. In fact, as unbelievable as it might seem, Ray Elmore, Jr., might be a deserter.

Aw, damn, Kel suddenly remembered. *I was going to call CILHI and check the deserter list.* Now it was Saturday and no one was at work, and it certainly wasn't worth making someone run back into the office to check. He didn't know what he would do with the information anyway. It didn't appear to have any direct bearing on the Trimble case, and even if it was true, it was none of his business. That was the Elmores' shame to bear and not his to expose. Who was he to argue with a bronze statue?

He stretched and closed his eyes again for a moment. He took a deep breath and then quickly rolled out of the bed and dressed, more casually than before, since it was Saturday. He stepped into faded blue jeans, put on an oversized white cotton shirt, and washed his face and teeth, and ran a hand through his hair, riling his cowlick even more than the pillow had managed. He wasn't hungry; he didn't normally eat breakfast, plus he'd been in Split Tree long enough now that his stomach had finally caught up to Central Daylight Savings Time, so it shouldn't have been expecting anything at this hour. Still, he had over an hour to kill before the library opened. He pulled his curtains apart and looked out. The Albert Pike was up and running and the lot was filled with shiny new American-made pickup trucks and SUVs. Kel decided that he'd make his way across the street for something to drink while he waited.

It was a mistake, and he knew it as soon as he walked in the door. No sooner had he taken a booth than Jo was there with a large platter of biscuits and gravy. She had on a clean shirt and new jeans, the latter stretched more tautly across her ample hips than was comfortable to look at, and as she squared her body to him, her chest imposed into the neutral zone. "The usual," she said with a too-friendly smile. Kel had eaten breakfast there once, two days ago, and that day's selection now constituted his "usual."

He smiled and thanked her. *Glad Levine didn't see that,* he thought.

Despite a lack of any conscious hunger, he found that he was enjoying his breakfast. The sight of sunburned farmers in their gim'me caps, the sounds of pleasant conversations and the tink and rattle of china being served on hard-topped tables, the smell of bacon and ham and grits; it all evoked a sense of belonging that Hawaii would never be able to produce. He caught himself thinking about his sitting in his car in front of the Lab, and how each day he sat there a little longer than the day before, taking a little longer to find the resolve to continue. He chewed, and he thought.

"You doin' just all right, Sugar?"

Kel opened the car door of his thoughts and looked up into Joletta's face. "Excuse me?"

"Bless your heart. Did I disturb you?"

"No ma'am." Kel smiled. "Just thinkin'."

"A penny, then. What can I get for y'all? Need anythin' else, or are you doin' just fine?"

Kel shook his head. "No ma'am, doin' just fine, thank you."

"Well, y'all call me if you change your mind, hear me?" She turned and started to go.

"You know, Miss Joletta, you gotta minute?"

Joletta beamed. "Sure do, Sugar, and it's Jo. No need to be such a gentleman. Now, what do y'all need?"

"I don't recall if I mentioned to you, but my people were from around here years ago. McKelveys. Used to be quite a slew of them hereabouts. Anyway, since I've got the weekend free, I reckoned I'd try and do some work on the old family tree—you know? Visit my granddaddy's property, see where my daddy grew up, hunt up some of the old cemeteries and see where some of the kin are buried, you know?"

"Sure do." She was smiling but wasn't sure whether Kel was asking her to accompany him or not and wasn't quite sure how she was going to answer.

"Anyhow, I got some information that I may have some kin buried in the Wallace Cemetery—by any chance, you know where that might be?" He figured that this was one of those occasions where a little crimping of the truth didn't cause any lasting harm. Besides, who was to say he didn't have kin buried there?

Joletta looked somewhat disappointed and relieved at the same time that Kel hadn't been leading up to a marriage proposition. "Now Sugar, don't you know that I am the wrong woman to be askin'. Like I said, my family's from Marked Tree originally. Can't say I've heard of the Wallace Cemetery. Might be a small one. You sure it's in Locust County?"

"No ma'am, can't say that I am," Kel replied. He looked at his watch. "I'm really kinda killin' some time until the library opens. I figure they must have some kind of listin' of local cemeteries. Sign on their door says they'll be open in about fifteen minutes . . . and speakin' of which, I reckon I'd better be gettin' my bill."

Jo picked up his empty breakfast platter and balanced it on her left forearm while she wiped her free hand on her thigh. She smiled and said, "Let me go and get that rung up for y'all." She returned in a few minutes with the check and a handful of red-and-white peppermints that she broadcast on the table like bird seed.

Kel counted out his bill and added a tip, and then, waving across the room at Jo, he left, returning to the Sleep-Mor's parking lot to get his car. He rolled down the window and allowed the warm air to vent before getting in. A few minutes later he was parked in front of the Split Tree Library. It was already open.

The room smelled of little cloth-wrapped sachets of dried flowers and fresh tea. Old-woman hot tea rather than iced. In addition to him, there was only one other soul in the library, a tiny, heart-shaped woman in a bright green dress that made her look like a springtime redbud leaf. She was sitting behind a desk that doubled as the checkout counter and library office, drinking her tea very precisely from a thin, white china cup. She smiled as Kel walked in the front door, setting a pair of small brass bells to ringing as he did so. He estimated her age at somewhere in the broad vicinity of eighty. Her hair was silver white and her face was a cobweb of intersecting lines etched into a skin the soft, cream color of handmade paper.

"Good morning," she said. "How are you this morning?"

"Fair to middlin', ma'am, and how are you today?" Kel replied.

"I'm doing but real fine. Is there anything I can help you with? You're certainly free to go and look yourself around, but if I can help you with anything . . ."

"Thank you, ma'am. If you don't mind, I'd like to use your genealogy room, if I might. Is that it yonder?" he replied as he pointed at the room labeled FAMILY TREE CENTER.

"Why yes, sir, it is. Be free to help yourself." Her diction was conscious, and she tended to it as precisely as she drank her tea. She seemed focused on finishing off her words properly rather than following the east Arkansas habit of dropping the final Gs and Rs—the way Kel habitually did.

He smiled and thanked her as he walked past her desk and through the doorway into the small room that held the library's genealogy records. He paused and signed in at a guest book on a small table near the door; smiling as he wrote his address as *Honolulu*, knowing that it would provide a source of endless speculation for the room's usual patrons. The room wasn't much larger than the desk and two chairs that occupied the center, and there wasn't much in the way of records. He quickly spotted what he was after. Along the back wall were two old red-oak bookcases, their shelves drooping with exhaustion, or perhaps boredom. The one on the right, nearest the window, had a small hand-printed sign that identified it as the location of "County Vital Statistics." The shelves contained several dozen books bound in blue and red and green, all vanity press from what he could tell. Some were family histories with self-possessed titles like *A Noble Breed: The Rumseys in America* or *The Kings of Cotton: The Pate Family Tree*, but what caught his attention were several multicolored books stacked alone on the third shelf and entitled such things as *A Gazetteer of Locust County Cemeteries* and *Let the Dead Bury the Dead: A History of Local Cemeteries.*

Kel emptied the shelf and found a small table where he could sit and review the books. It was time-consuming. Most of them were set in large print, but they were poorly indexed, requiring Kel to go through each one, page by page by page. It took the better part of two hours. None of them mentioned a Wallace Cemetery, though he did run across a McKelvey Cemetery that distracted him for the better part of almost thirty minutes. He made a note to visit it before he left the area.

But no Wallace.

Kel leaned back in his chair, tipping it onto two legs. He closed his eyes and arched the muscles of his back and thought. The Wallace Cemetery didn't appear to be located in Locust County. Plan B would require going through similar books for nearby Lee, Phillips, and Monroe counties—to start with. Fortunately, the library seemed to have copies of all the materials he would need. He was about to sit up and get started when he heard a voice.

"Didn't your mamma ever tell you that you'll bust your noggin leaning back like that in your chair?" It was the old woman. She was standing in the door looking at Kel. When he opened his eyes he saw that she was smiling broadly and had meant her comment as a joke rather than a scold.

Kel laughed and assured her that his mother indeed had raised him better, and that he did in fact know better. He returned his chair squarely back onto its four legs.

"You look right stumped. Anything that I can help you with? Lived here my whole life, not much that I haven't seen . . . problem is, there's not much that my poor old brain can remember, either." She was joking again, but as Kel sized her up, he realized that there was, in fact, probably very little that she *didn't* remember.

"Yes, ma'am, you just might." Under normal circumstances, he would avoid asking directions or asking anything, for that matter, until he had completely exhausted his attempts to solve the problem on his own. In this case, he was not stumped to that level of desperation yet, but his watch told him the library would be closing soon and it wouldn't be open tomorrow. "I'm lookin' for a grave. A burial. From what I've read, it's located in the Wallace Cemetery, but I can't find any mention of it in any of the Locust County books. By any chance, do you know of a Wallace Cemetery? Is it in this county?"

The old woman looked at him for a long time. So long, in fact, that Kel began to reassess his opinion of her brainworthiness. Finally she spoke. "You got kin buried in that cemetery?"

"No ma'am, not directly. I'm sorta doin' some research for a friend."

She studied him at great depth again, then she slowly nodded her head. "Yes, sir, it's in Locust County. But, Lord of mercy, I haven't heard it called the Wallace Cemetery for"— she paused as if adding up some great number—"well, for probably close to seventy years." She smiled at Kel but didn't elaborate, simply looked at him with a strange smile.

"It's still around, though?"

She nodded again. Slowly. "Cemeteries don't usually move around too much."

Kel smiled at her again. "True," he said, "but sometimes the land-graders don't give them much choice. I gather you know where it is? I can't seem to find it in any of these." He closed the last book and added it to a stack that he had searched.

"No, I suspect not. Not under that name, anyhow. You'd have to be a very old resident of this county to call it by that name. Fortunately for you, I happen to be a very, very old resident of this county."

"What name would I be likely to find it under . . . if I was to start all over again in these here books?"

"Elmore," she said.

"Elmore?" Kel now straightened up in his chair. "Elmore? As in your current Sheriff Elmore? That kind of Elmore . . . the same kind of Elmore?"

"That'd be the name I'd look up . . . if I was you—or if I was your friend." She smiled again and turned, walking back to her desk and teacup.

Kel sat, staring at the empty doorway for a moment, thinking that she had simply gone to retrieve something. She hadn't, and when he finally realized it, he hurriedly turned his attention to the stack of books in front of him. He remembered seeing an Elmore Cemetery in one of the books—but which one? It had caught his eye because of all the talk about Big Ray and of course the discovery that Ray Junior wasn't

missing in Vietnam. He'd looked at it briefly—hunting up Big
Ray's listing—but otherwise had passed it by. It accounted for
a good four or five pages worth—but in which book? He
fanned them out on the tabletop as if they were giant playing
cards. Which one was it in? Which one? He looked at his
watch again; five minutes until closing, assuming they closed
on time. He looked at the books. He'd been about midway
through his reading when he'd seen it, so he could probably
rule out the first two books. He picked up the third one, the
blue-covered one entitled simply *Locust County's Historical
Cemeteries*, and began quickly thumbing through it. No
luck—or at least he didn't see it as the pages flickered past.
He cracked the fourth book, *Comprehensive List of East
Arkansas Tombstone Inscriptions: Lee, Locust, Monroe, and
Phillips Counties.* There it was. The Elmore Cemetery, Locust
County. It covered several pages, 27–32, and there were a
good three dozen entries by quick count.

   Kel scanned the pages in frustration. There was no apparent organization to the names; not alphabetically, not chronologically. It read as if someone had simply driven out to the
cemetery and written down the tombstone inscriptions as he
encountered them—which, of course, was most likely what
had happened. He ran his finger down the listings. Not all
were Elmores; there were a fair number of Wallaces, a couple
of Rumseys and Davidsons, even a "Loving Son and Devoted
Father, Pleasant R. McKelvey." He saw Big Ray's epitaph
again: *Raymond Sallis Elmore, Sr.; July 4, 1916–November
12, 1987, U.S. Navy, World War II, Shriner, "Correct me,
Lord, but only with justice—not in your anger, lest you reduce
me to nothing."* A page later he found one for *Ella Mae Elmore, Loving Wife of R. S. Elmore, Sr., Aug 31, 1917–Aug 12,
1989, "She Rests With The Angels."*

   Kel looked at his watch and then back to the page. It was
twelve-fifteen, already past closing time. He read on. There
were a number of tombstones that apparently had been too
weathered to be legible and were listed as a mixture of letters

and question marks; an author's notation following each entry provided an estimate of the burial year. Some must have been so water-worn that none of the inscription remained readable; these were entered as simply "Grave Marker, date unknown."

His finger passed over it the first time, but luckily his eye was lagging behind and caught hold of it. It was on the third page, sandwiched between two Wallaces whose markers dated to the late 1800s. The entry read: *Luke 15:31*, but the compiler's note indicated that this stone was set "probably sometime after August 1966 and before June 1967." How the author came to that temporal estimate, Kel didn't have a clue, but John Doe's burial permit was signed on September 25, 1966. So far, Luke 15:31 was the only entry in the right time frame. He continued scanning the pages but found no others that fit a late September to early October 1966 burial date.

"Well, Luke, how do you do?" he said.

Kel quickly searched the room, tracking down a scrap of jotting paper from a small cardboard box on one of the shelves. There also was a small, stubby yellow pencil like the ones used at miniature golf courses. He was beginning to write the entry down, verbatim, when he heard her voice from the other room.

"I'm so sorry, but I'm afraid it's time to close up for the weekend. Are you about finished?" He could tell by the volume of her voice that she was walking toward the Family Tree Center. She soon appeared in the doorway, smiling as before. "Find what you were after? Was I right about the Elmores?"

"Yes ma'am, you sure were. Got it right here." He stood up and waved the little fragment of paper. "Now all I've got to do is find the cemetery—the book here," he nodded to the one still open on the desk, "seems to assume that the reader knows his way around these parts."

The old woman canted her head to the side. "And you're not from around here?"

He smiled and paused, considering his answer. "No ma'am . . . I'm not from around here."

"Now, young McKelvey . . . what would your daddy think about you saying that sort of thing?"

"McKelvey?" he asked. Then a smile broke. "You know who I am? How?"

"Of course I know. You're Robert McKelvey's youngest boy, aren't you? Atlas McKelvey's grandson? This is Split Tree, Mr. McKelvey, Split Tree can be a very small place at times." She turned and started to walk away. "My own grandson will be here any minute . . . if you'd like, I can show you the Wallace Cemetery."

Kel quickly reshelved the books and followed her into the library. "Yes ma'am, that'd be wonderful . . . I mean . . . if you've got the time. I hate to take up your afternoon."

The old woman had walked to the window and was leaning forward, peering out to the street in front of the library. She seemed to not hear Kel. "Here he is now," she said.

A minute later, the front door of the library was opened by a tall, whip-thin young man in his early twenties. The small brass bells jingled. He wore an Arkansas Travelers baseball cap over his sandy crew-cut, and he grinned lopsidedly at the old woman. "Hello, Gran'ma . . . you ready to git?"

The old woman turned to Kel. "Mr. McKelvey, this is my daughter's youngest son, Bradford Wayne." She looked at her grandson. "Bradford, this is Mr. Robert McKelvey. His folks used to live around here. Long time ago now."

"Drink," the boy said, stepping forward and taking Kel's hand. It was a make-um-squeal-type grip. Kel didn't, but it took biting his tongue to avoid it.

"Drink?" Kel said.

"Yup. People here call me Drink—most people, that is. Not all." He gave a quick nod to his grandmother. "Good to meet you, Mr. McKelvey."

"It's Kel . . . Drink . . . people call me Kel—most people, that is. Good to meet you too."

"We're going to take Mr. McKelvey to the old Wallace-Elmore Cemetery," the old woman said as she bent down to the base of her desk and retrieved her handbag. "Ready, Mr. McKelvey?"

Gladys Hayden was her name. She had never introduced herself, but when Kel finally ran out of polite ways to address her without knowing her name—*Ma'am* would only work so long—he'd simply come out and asked. She hadn't taken offense. She didn't seem to be the type to take offense easily.

Quiet grace.

She was distant kin to both the Wallaces and the Elmores, she'd told him as she was locking the door to the library. As it turned out, she also had known Kel's father and grandparents, and she too had reckoned his father to be about the most handsome man she had ever known. Kel often heard that, and certainly it was true, his father had been incredibly good looking both as a young man and when mature. Kel also was aware that no one ever seemed compelled, even by politeness, to complete the statement with "and you look just like him."

As they left the library, Gladys tried to convince Kel to ride in the front seat next to young Drink while she sat in the rear. "So you can see better," she said. He declined. Drink's car was a semirestored 1968 green Pontiac Le Mans with a peeling cream-colored vinyl top, and the rear seat was a bit of a squeeze. He couldn't imagine the old woman being accordioned into it without the use of a good lubricant, a sturdy shoehorn, and an appalling lack of manners on his part.

The sun was almost straight up and had a mean late-summer glower to it. As they headed south out of town, they passed the light-blue, spider-legged water tower that proclaimed Split Tree to be the "Home of the Delta Devils." Assorted colors of spray paint also documented various affairs of the heart amidst the signatures of a half-dozen recent senior classes. Kel leaned forward between the two bucket seats, as much to talk as to wring the most out of Drink's weak air-conditioning system. He was just about to inquire about the

Wallace-Elmore Cemetery when Drink abruptly hit the brakes to slow the car.

"Shit," Drink said, his eyes focused on something in his rearview mirror.

"Bradford Wayne," Gladys scolded. "Language."

"Yes ma'am," Drink responded habitually. His eyes stayed on his mirror. "It's just that son of a . . . that fat little Jimbo Bevins and his radar gun."

Kel swung around in his seat and looked out the back window. He could see a Locust County sheriff's car swing in behind Drink's Le Mans. "How fast were you goin'?"

"Not too, but that don't matter with that little bastard."

"Bradford Wayne," Gladys reasserted patiently. "Tend to your driving and leave Deputy Bevins alone." She touched her grandson's thigh gently as punctuation.

Drink looked at the old woman and then back at the reflection in his mirror. "Yes ma'am. Let's just hope he's not in one of his moods."

Kel watched the sheriff's cruiser slow and turn off onto a side street. He swung back to the front and leaned forward between the seats. "He turned off. I suspect you're okay."

"Hope so," Drink replied.

Kel thought about his encounter with Jimbo at the courthouse. "The deputy have *moods*? What kind of moods?"

"He can be a goddamn psycho," Drink replied. "That's what kind of moods."

"Bradford Wayne," Gladys cautioned once more, then she took a breath and conceded the point. "Jimbo Bevins was always a bit . . . complicated. Even as a little boy."

Drink laughed. "Complicated, Grandma?" He looked into the rearview mirror and caught Kel's eyes. "That boy can go from zero to asshole like that," he said as he snapped his fingers.

"Complicated," Gladys repeated in a tone that suggested the topic should be changed.

The three rode in silence for a few minutes. Kel thought

about the almost goofy Jimbo that Levine had introduced him
to and the menacing Deputy Bevins that had pinned him to the
door frame in the courthouse and how his eyes flashed hot and
cold. From zero to asshole.

Gladys Hayden was the first to break the silence. She half-
turned in her seat and caught Kel's attention, and then began,
as if there had been no interruption, to explain that the cemetery they were headed toward was on land that once belonged
to the Wallace family—one of the first to settle Locust County
in the early nineteenth century. Hard-bent Scotch-Irish who'd
moved west from the Duck Hills of Tennessee to the flatlands
of eastern Arkansas. Early on, however, the Wallaces had bent
to the habit of having an unusually high number of girl children, many of whom married into another old Locust family,
the Elmores, who sired more than the usual quota of sons. The
result was mathematically predictable, and over the years the
number of Wallace surnames showing up on tombstones declined in favor of Elmore markers, and the cemetery, which
had first been known as Wallace, became Wallace-Elmore,
and finally, by the early 1900s, was known simply as the Elmore Cemetery.

It wasn't a long drive. Maybe ten miles due south of town
along a shimmering dark-gray ribbon of asphalt. The road—
like most in the county—didn't have much call to deviate
from straight, and clumps of hot-weather wildflowers like
yarrow and black-eyed Susans were crowding the shoulder
like children waiting for a parade. Kel spotted it through the
windshield while they were still several miles out; a small,
raised spit of tall grass and a couple of mature trees surrounded by a glass-flat sea of green and gray-brown cotton
plants; a few early bolls starting to crack open. It was exactly
like the little, half-forgotten cemeteries he'd passed on the
drive down from Memphis.

Drink braked to a stop alongside the road. They all waited
while the trailing brown dust cloud drove on past them and
started to settle before opening the car doors. The cemetery

was about seventy-five yards into the field, and Kel squinted into the southern sun in hopes of spotting a road or path leading out to it. There was none, but as he turned to speak to Gladys, he saw that Drink was threading his way down the furrows with his grandmother locked in close tow. Kel shrugged and followed.

From the road, the cemetery looked overgrown and unkempt, covered with ragweed and Johnson grass and poke, but as he got closer he saw that the tall grass and weeds ringed the island like the rough around a putting green, but on the interior, on the slight mound, the grass was recently mown and the weeds were well-controlled. Kel eyed the tall weeds warily, trying to gauge the magnitude of the dose of chiggers that he was about to inoculate himself with. Drink and Gladys seemed unconcerned as they charged through, parting the tall grass with their forearms as if they were wading into the surf. Kel did likewise.

There were at least three dozen gravestones visible and no discernible organization. Headstones were clumped into little pockets of three or four. None were standing up straight; all were canted to one side or another, resembling teenagers hanging out at the mall. Kel, lacking a better plan, started with the clump nearest to him. The markers were old and weathered almost slick—Matilda Wallace and Captain Wallace and two smaller unreadable markers, all four seeming to date to the 1840s and 1850s. He walked to the next cluster, and the next, and the next. Elmores, a scatter of Wallaces, a Davidson, a couple of Rumseys. Some were surnames he'd heard his grandparents and father mention as a child. He noticed that Gladys was on her hands and knees weeding around a large limestone marker for Peter Elmore. Drink was leaning against a shagbark hickory tree, patiently watching his grandmother work but careful not to disclose any inclination to assist her.

Kel continued looking. Two more Elmores, another Wallace next to the lone McKelvey whose entry he'd seen in the book, the one that Gladys had told him on the drive down was no discernible relation to him but represented another sprig of the McKelvey tree out of North Carolina. He remembered hearing of them as well. The Bogus McKelveys, his grandfather had always called them, as if their claim on the name was somehow invalid.

He took out a handkerchief and was blotting the sweat off his nose and eyes when he noticed an area to the side that seemed to have received less attention recently. As he walked over to it, he saw that the weeds were thicker and wickered and laced with briars and step-lightlies. There were at least three stones amid the overgrowth, at least three that were still semiupright and visible; two were older—from the late 1800s—and he could make out the name Wallace on both of them from where he stood. The third marker was younger in appearance and cleaner and cut more like a military stone. A large shaft of poke was growing at the base of the marker, its stem the thickness of Kel's wrist, and its glossy leaves partially obscured the chiseled face. Kel high-stepped into the growth and pulled the leaves back.

Luke 15:31.

It was midafternoon when Drink and Gladys dropped him off back at the library where he retrieved his rental car. He thanked them profusely, Gladys in particular, and she responded by sending her regards to his mother. She'd also smiled strangely and wished him luck in his research for his friend. The whole ride back into town he'd been aching to ask her what Luke 15:31 referred to, but successfully bit back the urge. He figured she might interpret his lack of Bible learning as a deficiency in his parental upbringing and decided for the sake of his father's lingering reputation to defer his curiosity.

As he entered his room at the Sleep-Mor he paused only long enough to verify that his air-conditioner was set on high and to close the blinds against the throbbing sun before diving for the bedside stand. He was counting on the frugality of his congenial host, Sam—the man who was too cheap to put telephones in his rooms—to recognize a good deal when he saw it.

He wasn't disappointed.

Sam had accepted the Gideon's free Bibles.

The pages were tissue thin and had stuck together in the humid air; nevertheless, he found the chapter and verse easily. Luke 15:31, page 1392:

"My son," the father said, "you are always with me,
and everything I have is yours.
But we had to celebrate and be glad,
because this brother of yours was dead and is alive
    again;
he was lost and is found."

CHAPTER 33

Split Tree, Arkansas
SUNDAY, AUGUST 21, 2005

Kel had been exhausted, and it wasn't just the residual effects of jet lag. He wasn't seventeen years old and running wind sprints during two-a-days or earning spare money by detasseling an acre of corn. He'd loved the hot summers then, but the afternoon spent under the sun at the cemetery had siphoned away his energy like an opened vein. He'd taken an early dinner at the Albert Pike, drinking almost two pitchers of iced tea in the process, and once again retired to watch television and drift off to an early sleep.

He awoke about two o'clock having clawed his ankles bloody raw in his sleep. The Arkansas State Insect—the chigger—had welcomed him back to the Natural State. His ankles, waist, armpits, and of course, his testicles were swollen and inflamed and beyond help until morning when he could get to a drugstore. It had taken the next hour or so to fall back asleep—and that had been fitful.

Sunday proved uneventful. Kel had nothing planned other than to meet Levine for dinner that evening when he returned from Memphis. In the meantime, he'd napped, scratched, worked on the computer, scratched some more, tried calling his wife, and took several short drives around the county. The driving provided another opportunity to think and sort through the last few days. He was still working on young Ray Elmore's Vietnam status and now, in an unrelated but equally confusing case, he had the cryptic Prodigal Son tombstone that he firmly believed was the murdered John Doe. Fortunately, it was all just a brain twister, a crossword puzzle; neither matter was within his governmental jurisdiction and at the end of the day he could shrug and forget it all. Levine, on the other hand, now had what he'd been wanting—the location of the John Doe and an even bigger puzzle.

What was it the Greeks used to say? When the gods want to punish you they grant your wishes.

The knock on the door came at 6:20 P.M. Kel opened it to find a smiling Levine.

"I'm starved, let's go across to the . . . what do you people call it . . . the Zebulon Pike or whatever and get something to eat." He had the largest smile that Kel had seen him manage over the course of their short, stressed working relationship. "Have I got shit to tell you."

Kel left him standing in the door frame while he turned and stepped into his shoes, lifting each foot in turn to the dressertop for tying. He paused to scratch both ankles. "It's Albert Pike—not Zebulon Pike—different guys. One has a mountain named after him, the other . . . well . . . the other has a diner named after him."

"Yeah, yeah, yeah, I don't give a shit if it's Prince Albert in a can, let's go."

Kel grabbed his wallet from the dresser, slipped it into the hip pocket of his jeans, and pulled the room door shut behind him as he hurriedly joined Levine, who was already headed off across the parking lot.

"I've got some interestin' news, myself," Kel teased, the tension from their encounter the other night seemingly forgotten. "Been doing some research . . ."

Levine set a pace that kept him about two steps ahead of Kel, and he kept looking back over his left shoulder to talk. "I'm sure you have, Doc . . . but it's not like mine, not like mine. Guaranteed."

Kel took a couple of jog steps to catch up. "Don't be so sure there—Fed."

Levine reached the door to the diner first and pulled it back, holding it for his trailing companion. "Tell me yours first," he said as he swept in behind Kel. They paused inside the door, and Levine pointed to a booth near the back, away from other customers. "Best save mine for dessert."

There were a half dozen customers in residence, some of whom they now recognized as regulars—mostly thick-waisted guys in slacks and shirts that had started the day pressed and had ended the day looking like a bag of rocks. The Wellington boots and straw cowboy hats and scabbed knuckles from the afternoon were gone. Kel had noticed, over the few days he'd been in Split Tree, that the restaurant guard changed at about four o'clock in the afternoon. The early morning hours into the early afternoon were the farm shift, mostly, and the talk was of rain—or its lack—and crop futures and who was going bust; afterward, shift workers and assistant managers filtered in and the conversation followed a different tack. Noon was everyone's turf and they intermingled easily and talked SEC football and minor league baseball—and the Delta Devils, of course. Tonight was church night and the crowd would be light for another hour or so as the faithful got themselves square with the Lord for the rest of the week.

They each took a seat and Levine motioned to the waiter, a skinny, long-boned boy whom they hadn't seen before. Maybe eighteen years old; maybe not. The boy took notice of their arrival but seemed almost painfully incapable of purposeful movement. Instead of actually moving, he slouched slowly toward their booth and winced as if he were dragging a two-ton anchor chain by his testicles. Levine watched him with great amusement. The special agent's newly found good mood was not lost on Kel.

"So . . ." Levine finally turned his attention back to their interrupted conversation. He had decided that he had a good forty-five minutes before the boy waiter arrived and would occupy the vacuum by listening to whatever the doc had been anxious to tell. "You've been doing some interesting research, you say. Discover the elusive six-finger gene? Hate to tell you this, Dr. Livingston, but it ain't too elusive here in Baked-Brain, Arkansas." He checked on the status of the waiter and saw that he had demonstrably picked up his pace and was actually making good time. In fact, he was about to reach their table.

Kel also noted the proximity of the waiter and decided to hold on to his news a moment longer. He wiggled in his seat to better scratch some chigger bites that required public discretion. Levine ordered another Shiloh Burger with onion rings; Kel opted for chicken-fried steak and breaded okra. Their waiter began a slow, looping turnaround back to the kitchen.

"Okay, we're alone now, Sugar; you all going to tell me you all missed me?" Levine's whole face was lit up like he'd been drinking. Kel decided that he was about to like Special Agent Crusty better.

"No. But remind me later to tell you about your buddy Deputy Bevins."

"Jimbo?"

"Yup, Jimbo. That bubba's got a side to him that I don't think you've seen."

Levine laughed. "Jimbo Bevins?"

Kel nodded. "That boy's got a streak to him."

"Well then he may have just gone up a notch in my book. What kind of streak?"

"Mean. But I'll fill you in later," Kel said. "It can wait. That's not what I wanted to tell you."

"Can hardly wait. So what d'you have?"

"Two things," Kel said as he held up two fingers. "First, there's somethin' screwy with Ray Elmore."

"No shit. He had a prick for a brother."

"Hmm. Not quite what I meant. What's screwy is that this town has a statue to him for gettin' killed in Vietnam, but I can't find any record that he was ever in Vietnam—let alone died there."

Levine squinted. "What are you saying?"

Kel shrugged. "Don't know, but I keep tryin' to think of what could be worse than gettin' killed. What's so much worse that you can't come home and your family can't talk about you? You tell me. What's so much worse that it's better for a whole town to think you're dead?"

Levine didn't respond.

"I don't know," Kel continued. "But I've been thinkin'."

"And?"

"And what if young Elmore, Ray Junior, what if he was a deserter?"

Levine's eyes painted every corner of Kel's face, then he applied a second coat. "Holy shit. You sure?"

"No. Not at all. I can check on it tomorrow, but until then . . ."

"That sanctimonious bastard sheriff. What a piece of . . ." Levine erupted.

"Hold on," Kel cautioned. "Hold on. There may be some other explanation. Fact, most likely is."

"Like?"

"Like maybe a record fell through a computer crack or somethin'. Best not say anythin' that you'll have to eat later."

Levine nodded as if he was in agreement, but his mind continued to chew on the idea of Ray Junior being a deserter.

"Besides," Kel continued, "that isn't the really big news. You ready for this?"

Levine continued nodding, his mind elsewhere. "Yeah," he responded. "Yeah, sure."

Kel took a long sip of water, making Levine wait a little longer. Then he slowly set the glass down, registering it with the water ring it'd left on the tabletop. He looked up. Without a smile, and in as smooth a voice as he could muster, he said, "I found y'all's body."

"Glad to hear it. Super." Levine smiled.

"No. No, you're not listenin', are you? I said, I found your body. Your John Doe's."

The meaning finally soaked through, and when it did, Levine looked as if he had been whacked on the back of the head with something solid. His eyes bulged, and he turned his head slightly to the side and adopted a look that clearly conveyed to Kel that he had better repeat and elaborate. Quickly.

Now it was Kel's opportunity to grin, his eyebrows shooting a high arc. "I said, I found Mr. Doe's long-lost body . . . it's a-molderin' in the grave, sure as ol' John Brown's."

"You're shitting me . . . don't shit me, Doc. You're shitting me, right? Don't."

"No shit," Kel said.

"How? Where?"

"Right where you'd expect it to be—sort of. I'm still kickin' myself for takin' so long to figure it out. Where do you normally find bodies?"

"Hell, I don't . . . ask the friggin' Boy Scouts, how the hell should I . . ."

"In graves . . . right? In cemeteries."

Levine squinted and nodded, slowly at first and then faster as the obviousness crystallized.

"You handle many murder cases, Mike?"

Levine shook his head. "Good God, no. I'm an MBA . . . Fordham University, magna cum laude . . . bank fraud, embezzlement, check kiting . . . never worked a homicide in my life—until now."

"Ahh," Kel said in his most all-knowing tone. A great deal now made sense. "Okay, here's how it works—and again I apologize for bein' so slow to figure this out—coroners, or medical examiners, whatever, in this ease a coroner—they don't have unlimited space . . . small budgets, especially in small jurisdictions like this one, and especially when the remains are unpleasant to keep around. As in, they smell. So, what do you do with them?" He shifted again in his seat. "Two choices really—if no one claims them—bury them or burn them. That's it, really. In an open case, like this one, where you may need to reexamine the evidence at some future

time, you'd best bury them. Can always dig 'em up, right?"
He paused and took another sip of water.

Levine continued nodding as if the scales were sloughing
off his eyes.

"Now, in the United States, you have to have a permit to
bury someone, even in a family plot. You need a death certificate and a burial permit. Cremations are a little different—
set those aside for the minute—but burials require these two
documents. In Arkansas, it turns out, at least from what I can
best figure, these are one and the same—sort of. Top and bottom of the same form anyhow. Top's the death certificate;
bottom's the disposition permit—column A and column B,
kinda like a Chinese menu. These are legal documents, and
since it's a legal matter, copies have to be kept."

"Go on."

"Well, in this case, I'm guessin' that the originals would be
at Vital Statistics in Little Rock, but a lot of smaller counties
keep copies—makes it easier for people around here if they
need a copy for some reason—and this is a small county. It
took me a few minutes—and cost me a couple of pounds of
sweat, which I'll admit I could afford—but I found a copy of
the burial permit for a John Doe, signed out a year and a day
after the body was found at the levee. Young, white male,
gunshot wound to the head. Date of death matches. All
matches."

"Shit," Levine said. "I'll be goddamned."

"Gets better. The body was signed over to a Mr. D. Hawk
from Hawk's Mortuary—isn't that the place you visited?"

Levine simply stared at Kel. His thoughts flashed back to
Donnie Hawk, and his "Aw shucks, Mr. Levine, why don't
you check with the Boy Scouts" act.

"And . . . and this is the part you're not goin' to believe . . .
it seems the burial took place in the Wallace Cemetery."

"Wallace Cemetery? Is that supposed to mean something?
I'm not in a mood to fish. Is that here . . . local? You mean it's
around here after all? You know where it is?"

Kel leaned forward and took Levine's eye intently, pulling it in close. "I do . . . and this is the cork in the bottle: It seems that only old-timers from around here call it Wallace—and I mean real old-timers. No one else has called it that for almost a hundred years. Everyone else knows it as . . . the Elmore Cemetery."

"Elmore?" Levine almost shouted, then there was a pause, like thunder following a distant lightning strike. "Why that sonofabitch. Elmore? As in Sheriff I-don't-have-a-friggin'-clue Elmore? That's twice that bastard has lied to me."

Kel nodded. He looked around to see if anyone was watching them. Fortunately, the conversational pitch was loud enough that Levine's outburst had gone unnoticed.

"That sonofabitch." Levine's good mood seemed to have rapidly melted away. "Do you know where it is? This Elmore Cemetery? D'you look for it? D'you find it?"

Kel sat back against the cushion of the booth before nodding again. "South of town. Scouted it out yesterday. The grave's there—I'm sure of it—and it's got a funny tombstone: Luke 15:31."

Levine frowned. "I told you I'm not in the mood to fish. Luke?"

"Chapter and verse. Don't tell me you don't know your Bible, Mr. Levine?" It was, of course, a joke, since Kel wasn't any more familiar with the Bible than Levine probably was.

"Wrong testament, Doc. What's it mean? You figure that out?"

"Now what it means, I don't know. It's the parable of the prodigal son, though—I can tell you that. It's about a man with two sons, one of whom strayed . . ."

"I know that much, Reverend, thank you for the service." Levine, too, sat back and stared out into the diner. A few more customers had drifted in. "But I don't understand what it means . . . the prodigal son . . . What's it mean?"

"Beats the crap outta me, and I've been woolin' it about for the better part of a day now."

Levine suddenly leaned forward and looked intently at Kel. "Help me out here, Doc. What's the procedure for digging this guy up? This Luke guy. I mean, what do we have to do next?"

Kel wiped his hand across his face and mouth and pinched his nose while he collected his thoughts. "I've been thinkin' about that as well. Unfortunately, bein' the weekend, everythin's closed. Process varies from state to state, but for sure you'll need an exhumation permit—a disinterment permit. The family can request it—but unless you know where to find Mr. and Mrs. Doe—there is no family in this case." He touched the tip of his left index finger as if he were ticking off the start of a long list, then his middle finger. "Or, the coroner can order it, especially in this case, since it's still an open homicide—I assume that's your best course of action."

"And if he won't? That fat little piece of sausage wasn't the most cooperative public servant the other day."

"Then a judge." He tallied the third option onto his ring finger. "District or circuit, I think. I'm not sure how Arkansas divvies up its jurisdiction. This may be outside a district judge's power, but in any case, a judge can do it. You'd just need to figure out who's got jurisdiction and present some evidence."

"Okay, okay." Levine's eyes began darting around quickly as his brain revved up. "That's easy. I'll check into this exhumation permit . . . can you put together a list of what you'd need, I mean, shovels, shit like that . . . whatever it is you bone-diggers use?"

"You're talkin' about physically exhumin' this grave?"

"Fucking-A, I am. This is my ticket out of here. Yours too."

"Well, ahhh, in that case . . . a funeral home or crypt company would probably do the actual backhoe work, but, yeah, I can get a list of a few items that I'd need if I was goin' to be involved. Camera, trowel. You want any analysis and I'll need some other stuff. Cheap set of calipers, tape measure . . . I won't need much. Bone-diggin'—as you so reverently described my profession—is a simple sport."

"Good. Do that. Elmore Cemetery, south of town, Locust County. That lying sonofabitch." Levine stood and fished a twenty-dollar bill out of his pocket, tossing it on the table. "Dinner's on me—if it ever arrives." He cast a glance toward the kitchen as he started to the door. "Be ready to roll in the morning. Early."

"Whoa, time out there, partner. You were goin' to tell me somethin', remember?" Kel called after him.

"What?"

"Your news. You said you had some news to tell me. We were savin' it for dessert."

"Shit, it can wait. Just some research I did. More of Elmore's goddamn lies. This is more important right now." Levine resumed walking toward the door.

"Hey. Where you headed off to?" Kel shouted.

Levine didn't even slow long enough to look back. "To lance a boil, Doc. A fat boil."

CHAPTER 34

Split Tree, Arkansas
MONDAY, AUGUST 22, 2005

Kel didn't see Levine the rest of the evening. The glacier posing as a waiter had finally delivered Kel's dinner, along with Levine's, and Kel had eaten his silently. Chewing his thoughts as thoroughly as his food, and scratching as little as he could.

Levine had run out of the diner so fast that they hadn't coordinated when they were leaving in the morning. He'd said early, and Kel guessed that the earliest Levine could get an exhumation order signed by a judge—assuming he could find one willing to act on such scant evidence as an obscure biblical passage, which would be an achievement in its own right—would be sometime late in the day. Kel really didn't know what kind of paperwork was required in this jurisdiction, but he doubted that Levine could arrange it in anything less than a week. And Kel wasn't staying another week, no matter how interesting the case might become.

One of Sam's other pieces of creative economizing involved not investing in an ice machine. Instead, every afternoon about three o'clock, Sam or his wife would venture over to the Pic-n-Tote, a rock's throw down the road, and return with a five-pound bag of Handy Dan's Crystal Clear Ice that he would then dole out to his guests upon request, a half-dozen cubes at a time, in sandwich-size Ziploc Baggies. At this time of year, that usually meant that by the time you arrived at your room, you were carrying four or five small, rounded marbles of ice adrift in a bag of water. Kel had made at least three trips to the office for ice to put on his raw ankles, and each time he rapped at Levine's door on the way back to his room and scanned the lot for his car. At half-past-eleven, he lowered himself into the center of his sagging bed and went to sleep.

He'd only been asleep for a few minutes when Levine began pounding on his door. Or maybe it wasn't only a few minutes. He hit the button lighting up his watch—almost 10:00 A.M. *Jesus,* he thought, *I just slept ten hours.*

Kel leaned over and looked at the crack between his curtains as he worked the latches on the door. He could see a hot, white sliver of day, like a shard of splintered glass and twice as painful, working its way through the drapes, confirming the time on his watch.

He groaned like something about to painfully expire.

Levine was standing a foot or two back from the door, near the edge of the sidewalk, his back to the room. He was talking on a cell phone and didn't break conversational stride but used expressive body English to convey that Kel had better get dressed, and do it quickly, for the game was afoot.

Kel blinked, trying to coax his pupils to relax from the pinholes they'd shrunk to, and then realized he was standing in the open doorway in his underwear. Reflexively, he retreated into the waning darkness of his room and pulled on a pair of khaki military-style cargo pants and a light blue cotton shirt. He had at least had enough sense to lay them aside before going to bed last night and they were ready to go—even if he wasn't. He carefully worked a pair of socks on, careful not to start an argument with the chiggers that he was unlikely to win. That done, he stepped into the bathroom and held his head under the faucet and took a swallow to rinse his breath. He dried off as he was stepping into his boots.

Two minutes after opening his door to Levine he was on the sidewalk.

Levine didn't wait. He stepped off the concrete walk and headed for his car, talking forcefully to someone on his cell phone while motioning for Kel to follow. He was saying things like "Hey, ask me if I give a shit?" and "Tell me something I don't know." Kel braved the glare of the sunlight bouncing off the black asphalt long enough to sight-in the car and then navigated the short distance with his eyes shuttered closed. He felt for the car handle as Levine cranked the engine over, and had barely gotten in when, with a jolt, the car backed and then shot forward, turning right on Magnolia and then right again onto Tupelo.

Kel looked over at Levine, who was still instructing someone on the other end of the phone on some finer point of doing his job properly. He looked at Kel out of the corner of his eye and said to the phone, "Yeah, yeah, I hear you . . . Look, you let me know as soon as you get a name—understand? . . . Good . . . Yeah, yeah, out." He closed his cell phone and looked full-face at Kel. "Sorry to wake you so early, Dr. McKelvey—but I didn't want you to miss lunch."

"Yeah, hate to do that," Kel replied. "Nice phone—steal that from Sam?"

Levine held up the cell phone as if he'd never seen it before. "Like it? Drove over to Helena last night and found a twenty-four-hour Wal-Mart Super-Duper Center that sells cell phones with next-day activation. Thank God for government credit cards, right?"

Kel rubbed both eyes with his fingertips and then brushed his wet hair back from his forehead. His pupils were fully functioning now, and he could see that they were nearing the town square. "Thought you didn't like phones."

"Never said that, Doc. It's people I don't like. There's a difference. Phones sometimes come in handy."

"Hmmm, if you say so," Kel mumbled. "So, where we headed?"

"You get that list together like I asked? Stuff for an exhumation."

"Yeah," he replied. "Bone diggin'. That where we're headed?"

"I'm going to hit an ATM machine and get you some money. Will two hundred do it or d'you need more?"

"Thought you said the FBI wouldn't give you any money for this case?"

"I didn't say they were going to reimburse me, did I? Just answer the question. Two hundred enough?"

"For bone-diggin' equipment, or are we hittin' the casino over in Tupelo?"

Levine shot him a look.

Kel smiled in response. "I guess you mean equipment. Sure. Easy. I was thinkin' maybe twenty."

"I'll give you two hundred . . . to be sure. Get what you need. Save the receipts just in case. Right now, we're headed—" The phone rang and Levine picked it up. "Yeah, Levine . . . No . . . No . . . did I say that? No, the answer is, No, I did not say that. I'd rather it be Little Rock . . . All you got to do is call me when you get a name. Yeah. Out." He closed the phone and set it down firmly on the seat between his legs. "Goddamn moron." He looked at Kel and exhaled loudly through his nose. "How many employees work in your organization, Doc?"

"About a third of them," Kel replied, looking out the window.

Levine smiled. "If I didn't know better, I'd say you worked for the federal government."

"If I knew better, I wouldn't."

"You sound like me."

"Hey, don't get me wrong. I'm proud of my folks. Good lab, good mission; it's the damn bureaucracy that's beatin' me down."

"As I said, you sound like me." They drove in silence for a moment and then Levine cleared his throat and spoke. "Tell me something?"

"Sure."

"Tell me your version of what happened in that Gonsalves case."

Kel snorted. "My version? You mean the truth?"

Levine smiled and shrugged.

Kel rubbed his eyes again before answering. "Pretty simple. Eddie Gonsalves was a thirty-two-year-old drugstore clerk in Poughkeepsie, New York. He ran the sixty-minute photo machine. He also abducted, killed, and dismembered nine prostitutes over an eighteen-month period. Made the mistake of disposin' of the remains in garbage bags along interstates, includin' some in New Jersey—across the state line. That's what got you Feds involved. Good investigation, actually. Y'all narrowed it down to Gonsalves on some circumstantial evidence pretty quickly; you just needed the last nail to hammer the coffin shut."

"That's where your lab came in?"

"Yup. We matched cut marks on some of the dismembered bones to a hacksaw found in Gonsalves's basement workshop."

"So what happened?"

"What happened is that we got the bone samples, matched them up, wrote a report—bang, bang, bang. Great case. Problem was that your evidence tech transposed a number on the chain-of-custody document. That's the number we used in our report, so when the case goes to trial, guess what? Our guy goes to testify and—"

"And the defense counsel points out that the case number doesn't match."

"You got it. Nobody caught it until too late. Our analysis gets bounced and so does the case."

Levine seemed to consider Kel's version as they neared the front of the courthouse. "If that's what happened, why's the Bureau trying to point the finger at you?"

"You got a fever or somethin'?" Kel asked in mock concern. "Do I really have to explain this to you? The Bureau's been takin' body shots right and left: Ruby Ridge, Waco. And now they go and flush a serial killer case down the crapper because someone has dyslexia. I have to explain this to a man who's convinced the Bureau's tryin' to bury him down here?"

"Not really," Levine sighed. "Not really. So if it's true, why'd you agree to come?"

Kel was looking out the window, but his thoughts were drifting elsewhere. "Don't know, really. To be honest, if an FBI agent had walked into the Lab two weeks ago on fire, I wouldn't have taken the time to piss on him."

"So why?"

"Why?" Kel repeated. He thought for a moment. "Because if I'm honest, I was about to melt down. I'm burned out, Mike. Burned flat out."

Levine took his eyes off the road and looked at his passenger. His defensive skin softened momentarily. "You're too young for that," he said.

"Gettin' older by the minute."

Levine understood. He stopped the car and killed the motor. As he did so, he nodded at the courthouse and shifted mental gears. "Look, Doc, if you don't want to come in, I understand. This is my case, my fight. Understand? I'd like you there." He opened the door and got out. Kel did the same. "If for no other reason, I'd like someone else there to make sure I don't strangle that lying sonofabitch Elmore."

"I'll come."

"Good. But if you come, there are rules. I just want you to sit and watch."

"Unless you start to strangle him."

Levine smiled. "I'm serious. Understand? You don't talk. Don't interfere. Just watch. This is a Bureau matter. Shit, this is beyond the Bureau; this is a Michael Levine matter now . . . it's up close and goddamn personal. You're to be a bump on a log. We square?"

He was almost running up the sidewalk as he issued his directions and Kel again had trouble keeping up.

"Understood; fortunately for you, I'm feelin' quite bumpy this mornin' anyhow."

Levine took the stairs to the second floor two and three at a time. At the top of the landing he pivoted left and headed for the second door, the one marked *Locust County Sheriff's Department*. Levine was already through it by the time Kel made the landing, and he had to stop and look both directions to figure out where he'd gone. He saw the sheriff's office to the left, diagonally across the hall from the records room he'd visited a few days earlier.

Inside room 204, to the right of the door, was a large laminate desk similar to the one in the sheriff's office. Deputy Sheriff Jimbo Bevins had planted his rear on the corner, his left leg dangling free. He was eating a banana moon pie and chasing it with coffee from a thirty-two-ounce red-and-white plastic mug that read Java Jokers. He muscled up when Levine walked in.

"Mornin' there, Agent Levine," he said. A few stray, dry moon pie crumbs flew as he did so.

"Good morning, Deputy Bevins," Levine replied as he walked past him, headed for the sheriff's office like a man about to put his head through a brick wall. He waved him down with his hand. "No need to get up. Sit."

Jimbo was caught completely flat-footed and full-mouthed, and Levine had opened W. R. Elmore's office door before he could swallow his bite of moon pie and rise to follow.

Sheriff Elmore was sitting behind his desk with his back to the door, his boots propped on the windowsill beside the air-conditioner. They were expensive boots but ill-kept of late, scuffed and badly in need of polish. "Come in, Special Agent Levine . . . I saw you drive up. Not alone, are you? Lose your shadow on the stairs?"

"Good morning, Sheriff Elmore."

"I didn't know you were back in Split Tree. Deputy Bevins informed me that you were last seen drivin' in the direction of Memphis a couple-three days ago. Guess we both thought that maybe you'd finished your . . . your F-B-I investigation . . .

and had gone on back where y'all are from." He was chewing on his thumb, his eyes focused on something outside the window that no one else was likely to see. His hair mirrored his boots. Once black and shiny but now dull and scuffed and in need of a brush.

"I'm afraid I've got a few loose ends to knot up before I can close this investigation," Levine replied, taking a seat in front of the sheriff's desk.

Kel had finally made it to the room, wheezing and out of breath from the run up the stairs. He walked past Jimbo Bevins without making eye contact. He found Levine conversing with the back of another man's head. He assumed it to be the sheriff's. He quietly took a seat in the remaining chair and assumed his designated status as a bump. He exchanged a quick look with Levine. For the first time since they'd met, Kel sensed that the FBI agent was securely within his comfort zone.

"Sorry to hear that, Mr. Levine. I'd hoped you were back in your big, fancy F-B-I office, writin' up some big, final report on some big, fancy letterhead." The sheriff still hadn't turned around. Had Levine been able to see his eyes, he would have recognized the look. It was not far different from what Levine had seen in the eyes of some of his buddies in Vietnam. Kind of a purposeful vacancy. A detachment from the unpleasantness of sunlit reality.

"Soon, I think. Very soon. Like I said, couple of loose ends before I get the fancy letterhead out. That's why I'm here, Sheriff. I thought you might be interested in a couple of recent developments." He paused but W.R. showed no inclination to move or respond. He quietly kept staring out the window. "Probably the most interesting of the developments is that we've finally managed to locate the remains of that John Doe—remember him? The white boy found with Mr. Jackson's body . . . we couldn't find his body for a while, remember? Oh, that's right, Sheriff Elmore, you don't remember much about this case . . ."

That got a response.

W.R. dropped his boots to the floor and swiveled his chair around so that he was facing Levine. He looked likely to spit clotted blood any moment, but he said nothing.

"Yeah, damnedest thing," Levine continued. His voice was honed. "The body was buried. Can you imagine that? A body being buried in a cemetery. Course I'm sure you can imagine how foolish I felt when I found that fact out. Goddamn big-city rube, and all. Kinda ironic, though. I mean, when you think about it, where else would a body be? It's not like the Boy Scouts would borrow it or anything." He smiled slowly.

The sheriff continued to look at Levine but still said nothing.

"Want to know where he's buried?" Levine's voice took on a slight twang, as if he were trying to imitate Elmore's accent. "Here's the real can-kicker; he's buried right here in little ole lonesome Locust County—right under our very noses . . . can you imagine that? Just a couple of miles from this very office, in fact. Yeah, Sheriff, he's buried in the Wallace Cemetery. Don't suppose you've ever heard of that either?"

No answer.

"No? I'm not surprised." Levine's voice resumed its Brooklyn tone. "Maybe that's because they tell me only old-timers call it that—old-timers and of course people with a reason to confuse the record of where he's buried. Now, everyone else calls it . . . oh, damn . . . what do they call it again?" He made a show of snapping his fingers as if trying to recall. "Oh yeah, the Elmore Cemetery. That's what everyone calls it. Elmore, as in Sheriff W. R. Elmore, as in Chief of Police Big Ray Elmore, as in . . . Hey, that would be your name, wouldn't it?"

"Mr. Levine," there it was again, pronounced slow like LEE-Vine, "I'm a busy man, I'm sheriff of Locust County, Arkansas, and the good folks of this county pay me to do *real* work. I'm sure you can understand how that is. Or maybe not. Now, what is it that I can hep you with? Or is this another so-cial call?"

"No, no . . . I'm afraid this is quite official. I'm a busy man too, Sheriff Elmore, and as much as I'd like to hump your leg all morning, I've got some other things to attend to myself." He pulled a trifolded piece of paper from the pocket of his blue sport coat and opened it before placing it on Elmore's desk. "One of which is exhuming a body."

The sheriff took his eyes off Levine's only long enough to flick a quick look at Kel. Kel thought it was odd that the sheriff hadn't questioned who he was, or what he was doing in his office. It was clear that he already knew.

"That's a permit to exhume, Sheriff," Levine said. He pointed to the paper with a nod of his head. "About halfway down the page is a place for you to sign—I checked with the county clerk this morning, seems you're the official owner of that property—but I suspect you may have already known that, don't you? Your permission would make things a lot easier . . . Take as long as you need to read it."

Sheriff Elmore slowly and deliberately pushed the exhumation form back toward Levine, never looking at it, his fingertips barely touching it. "I told you the first day we met, Mr. Levine, let dead men sleep."

Levine reached out and took the form, refolding it as he did. "Sorry you won't sign, Sheriff. But it doesn't really matter. We're exhuming that grave at two o'clock. You're welcome to attend if you like . . . or not. I know how busy you are. Your choice."

Sheriff Elmore drew himself up several inches, his back bowed-up into a tight spring, and his voice took on a tone that would make most men flinch. Not Levine. Kel was glad he was nothing but a bump on this log. "This is still Locust County, and this is still the sovereign state of Arkansas, Mr. Levine. FBI got no right to exhume nothin' at that cemetery if I don't sign. And I believe I didn't sign that paper."

Now Levine drew himself up, canting in toward the sheriff as he removed a second piece of paper from his coat. He didn't open it, just held it up beside his face. "Your turn for a civics lesson, Sheriff. This is still the United States of America, and I'm still representing the *Federal* Bureau of Investigation, and this," he looked at the paper and then back to the sheriff, "is an exhumation permit, signed by Mr. Hawk, duly elected coroner of this county." Levine now stood and leaned forward with his knuckles on the sheriff's desk. "As I said, you can be there or not, Sheriff, no skin off any part of my body . . . but that casket, and whatever's in it, is coming out of the ground at two o'clock."

Sheriff Elmore and Levine stared at each other for several moments, neither man blinking or talking.

Finally, the sheriff looked past Levine to the door and called out, "Deputy Bevins."

Jimbo appeared in the doorway. He did so quickly, and it was obvious that he had been hovering right outside. "Yes sir."

"Deputy Bevins." Sheriff Elmore shifted his look back to Levine's eyes. There was fire where earlier there had been glaze. "There's a dark-blue Caprice illegally parked outside. Outta-state plates, I think. Illegally parked right in front of the courthouse too. You know how I feel about folk disrespectin' the local law around here. If it isn't gone in five minutes, call Tubb's and have the sumbitch towed off."

Jimbo looked at the sheriff, then at Levine, and finally at Kel. His indecision was palpable but fleeting. He looked back at the sheriff, and his eyes began to flash hot.

"Yes sir," he said.

As they walked back down the stairs to their car, Kel asked Levine if he could see the exhumation permit. Levine smiled as he produced it, and Kel held it up to the light. It certainly looked legit, and appeared to be properly filled out and signed. For a minute he thought maybe Levine was running a bluff and had managed to get himself called on it.

"How'd you get the coroner to sign it?" he asked. "From what you told me about your first visit, he wasn't much more cooperative than your best bubba up there."

CHAPTER 35

Lady of Mercy Hospital, Helena, Arkansas
THURSDAY, NOVEMBER 12, 1987

"Ray . . . home . . . finally," Big Ray Elmore repeated.

"No, Dad. It's . . ." W.R. paused. Big Ray had always seemed to blame him for what Ray Junior had done. Seemed to place the pent-up family shame on his shoulders; the good and faithful son who stayed home. His only crime was covering for his brother. Shading the truth and concealing where he'd gone; cleaning up the mess. His father had never asked him about it directly; had never even raised the topic in discussion; had just apportioned blame. Had erected a wall between them. W.R. had grown to resent his brother; to resent his father's love that seemed so disproportionate, to resent the silence. In the end, it was W.R. who had proven his loyalty, who had lived in the shadow, who had worked his whole adult life to gain his father's respect. And in the end, it was Ray Junior that his father saw in his last minutes—not W.R. In the end, it was Ray Junior—it was always Ray Junior.

And in the end, W.R. loved his father so much that he accepted the reality of it all.

"That's right, Dad," W.R. said quietly. He sought out his father's hand and gripped it. "Ray Junior's home. I'm home, Big Ray, I'm home. Your son, Ray Junior, is home, and I'm goin' to make everythin' right. I'm sorry for everythin' that I did. I'm sorry for runnin' scared. I'm sorry for the years—for all the time that I wasn't there for Momma and you. I'm sorry. I'm not like you, Big Ray, I got scared. I had to run, Dad. But

I'm home now. I'm home now. Dad, I . . ." Waymond Elmore realized that his father couldn't hear; that he'd passed beyond all hearing.

He hadn't said it in time. Hadn't gotten the words out. Hadn't been able to say "I love you" in time. As the doctor and Murleen moved him aside, he realized that he'd never said it. Had never told his father that he cared.

Neither had Ray Junior.

And now it was too late.

CHAPTER 36

Split Tree, Arkansas
MONDAY, AUGUST 22, 2005

Levine spent the rest of the morning talking on his new cell phone, always very animatedly, arms swinging like a marionette with an excited puppeteer; Kel went from store to store buying a few materials he needed for the exhumation—and scratching—and Deputy Bevins kept watch, from a distance this time, the facade of down-home familiarity of the previous week now gone.

They headed back to the Albert Pike for lunch. It was packed full, and they had to wait and then settle for a table in the middle, surrounded by hard-baked men with reddened necks and flaking ears and work-faded overalls. Levine and Kel kept their conversation in low tones, though they knew that soon the whole town would be up to gossip speed on the morning's events. Still, there was no point in advertising their intentions any more than they had to.

Jimbo Bevins sat at the counter drinking a glass of Coke through a red plastic straw and watching them with hard eyes bent on currying his boss's favor.

Kel decided on sweet iced tea and another wedge of pecan pie; Levine ordered another Shiloh Burger from Jo, who was back on the job with a fresh smile and thick, colorful eye makeup. Levine was the sort who didn't vary his habits much when on the road. Find something—stick to it. Kel recognized the pattern of repeating the comfortable. He did the same. He thought of his mother and how she used to comment on her in-laws. "Those damn McKelveys," she'd say, "if they thought one can of beans was good, then fifty must be better."

"Okay. All right . . . tell me again how this exhumation works," Levine said after ordering. It was the third time he'd asked Kel this question, and now he was about to hear the same description for the third time in less than an hour.

"I don't usually chew my tobacco twice, Mike, but here goes. A funeral home representative—that would be your newly found friend, Donnie Hawk—will be there, so will the coroner—that would be the same Donnie Hawk. Convenient, isn't it? I suspect there'll be a crypt company to do most of the actual diggin', dunno, I'm not sure in a small town like this what they have. May be one-stop shoppin' with your Mr. Hawk. Anyway, they'll probably be a backhoe and a couple of big-muscled bubbas with shovels—there's always need for shovel work, even with a backhoe."

Jo was back with the food and after sugaring Kel and blessing his heart a couple of times, she drifted off to tend to other customers.

Kel unconsciously scratched an ankle and continued. "I'll take some pictures as soon as we get there. General shots to record the settin', one of the grave and tombstone before diggin', and so on. Got this expensive piece of Swiss optics here," he said, holding up the cheap cardboard point-and-shoot camera that he'd purchased earlier. "Then they'll remove the top couple of feet of overburden, down to the top of the crypt. More photos. Pop the top on the crypt—assumin' there is one. I'll take some more pictures. The rest will be dug out by hand until they can slip some chains under the actual casket, then the backhoe will lift it out. We inspect it, hopefully it won't be in too bad a shape, not caved in, take some more pictures, and then Mr. Hawk can take it back to his funeral home where the analysis will take place."

"Yeah . . . yeah . . . okay." He had been nodding throughout Kel's explanation. It was tracking with the first two versions he'd heard. "Right. What else do we need?"

"I tell you what, if I were you, I'd still look to get a foren-sic pathologist in here. For the analysis part, anyhow. Don't know if there'll be any soft tissue. I haven't seen the original autopsy so I can't comment on it, but you really should con-sider havin' a pathologist take a look . . . a second autopsy. Always good in these old cases—especially if it has to go to court."

"Taken care of. I called Washington after you mentioned that this morning, and they're sending some big-shot out of New York that they consult with. Supposed to be the best. Be here midday tomorrow."

"New York? They're not gettin' someone from AFIP?" Kel knew the Armed Forces Institute of Pathology had assisted in the original 1965 autopsy.

"Guess not. They tell me New York. State police. I ask, they send, I don't question. I'm lucky to get any support. Any-thing else?"

Kel paused while he measured his words. "Yeah, there is. The Gonsalves case, I . . . thing is, Mike . . . thing is I'm goin' out on a limb for you. We're goin' be doin' this work under some piss-poor conditions. I'm not sure why I'm even agreein' to do this except . . ."

Levine held up a hand. "I've got a lot of faults, Doc . . . Kel. Too many. But one thing that I won't do is burn people who've been square with me. What I said the other night about you earning my respect—that was out of line. Anything goes to shit, it's on my head, not yours. Mine."

"Thanks."

Levine nodded an acknowledgment. "So, anything else?"

"Not that I can think of. Got everythin' that I need . . . which reminds me," Kel removed a wad of money from his pocket and pushed it across the table to Levine, "here's your money . . . and the receipts."

Levine suddenly stiffened as if he'd dropped an ice cube down his pants. His phone had been ringing so frequently that he'd flipped it to vibrate mode before going to visit the sheriff. He hadn't gotten used to it sneaking up on him in his pocket, and apparently it just had. He groped it out and answered it.

"Yeah, Levine here." He listened closely, squinting as he did so, then he looked at his watch. "Right. Fifteen minutes." He snapped the phone shut without saying good-bye. If Levine's calling plan charged by the spoken word, he'd gotten a good deal. "They're ready, Igor. Let's go get us a body."

Levine took the roll of money from the table and extracted a ten-dollar bill and some ones that he left to cover their meal. Then he stood. Kel did the same, catching the eye of Jo and the little man behind the grill, the one he'd talked to the other night. He waved to them both and then followed Levine out to the car. It was almost one-thirty and with the sun again standing straight overhead, they cast almost no shadow, and the black asphalt parking lot was turning soft in the heat. He waited, watching the heat waves ripple the air above the hood of the car while Levine worked the locks. Soon they were seated with a blast of air-conditioning directed at their faces, heading south of town at a high rate of speed. When they left the hardball, they roostered a tall plume of fine brown dust in their wake. If Jimbo was following, he'd better know the way by feel.

Kel had purchased a bottle of calamine lotion that morning and had brought it along in a small paper sack. He took the opportunity to dab the pink liquid on his inflamed ankles with a cotton ball. He had to synchronize his movements with the bouncing of the car as it took the rough road. The lotion stung when it hit his raw skin. He sucked a short breath of air in between clenched teeth.

Levine kept casting quick glances at him. He wasn't at all sure what Kel was doing, but he disapproved on some general principle. When it looked as if Kel was about finished, he asked, "You do remember how to get there, I assume?" He'd slipped on a pair of dark sunglasses that Kel hadn't seen before, and he looked so much like a G-man that Kel had to smile.

Kel arched his brow, placed the soggy pink cotton in the ashtray, and reached up to drop the sun visor to block the glare. "Think so. Just head south and look for a clump of trees off to the right. Aren't many around once you leave town."

It was a short ride. As he had earlier, Kel saw it from a distance, a clot of trees and tall grass about seventy-five yards off the road in a sea of heat-stunted cotton. A big John Deere 510 backhoe and three cars were at the edge of the field. One of them was a dark hearse, and there was a shiny white pickup truck there as well; their occupants standing out on the mound looking at the tombstones and pawing the ground like young horses. About fifty feet behind the backhoe, a sheriff's cruiser was parked, engine and air-conditioner running, driver inside.

It wasn't Jimbo Bevins.

Levine slipped to a stop, whipping the dust into cloud that took almost fifteen minutes to completely settle, and when it did, it covered everything. He got out and flashed a look at the sheriff's car. As soon as Kel had gotten out and retrieved his bag of supplies, Levine locked the vehicle and started off across the field, trampling cotton plants in his way. Kel paused long enough to soak his pant legs and shoes with bug repellent and then followed, threading his path carefully so as to not damage any more plants than he had to.

Levine reached the mound first, thrusting the tall grass aside before Kel could issue a chigger warning. Donnie Hawk came walking over to greet him, hand outstretched.

"Mr. Levine," he said, smiling, "we're almost ready to go here. Just tryin' to figure out the best way to get that there backhoe out here." He nodded to the green earthmover parked at the edge of the field as if there might be two backhoes present, and he didn't want Levine to be mistaken as to which one was under discussion.

Levine looked first at Donnie and then at the backhoe and then back at Donnie. "Is this some sort of IQ test?" he said slowly, as if proposing something quite radical. "Why don't you have the driver start the goddamned thing up and drive the sonofabitch over here."

Donnie was forced back a step. "Ahhh . . . the problem is, you see, there ain't no road, and if we go and drive it over here . . . well, we're gonna tear up some o' that cotton sure as shit. Now, that may not bother you, Mr. Levine, but it sure does bother that man standin' right over yonder, yes sir," he employed a discreet jerk of his thumb to indicate a tall, thin man in overalls standing at the edge of the cemetery with Skeeter Boy and two others. "It's his crop, don't you see, and I ain't nothin' but an elected county official with no money to pay for miscellaneous expenses like crop damage this close to harvest time. Mercy."

Kel had walked up in time to eavesdrop on the conversation.

"Oh, goddammit," Levine said, starting toward the man in overalls. "I'll pay for his friggin' cotton. How much does this schmuck want?"

Kel caught him by the arm and pulled him back. "Hold up there, partner. I can see this gettin' hosed slam up. Gimme that wad of money of yours and cool your afterburner," he said. "I used to have to negotiate crop damage all the time when I was doin' archaeology in these parts . . . I'll do it."

Levine paused and considered but handed over the money, and Kel slipped it into his pocket along with both hands. He started walking over to the men, but paused and looked out into the field, surveying the knee-high cotton plants.

"It's been a while since I negotiated cotton damage. What is that . . . is that El Dorado?" he asked, nodding in the direction of the cotton plants. "Been too damn long. What is that, Mr. Hawk? El Dorado Acala . . . is that it?"

"Ahh, El Dorado?" Hawk answered.

"Seed. You know what seed that is?" He shifted his look to Donnie Hawk.

"If you're askin' me, your guess is as good as mine. All I do with cotton is stick it in people's cheeks . . . and other places," Donnie replied with a slight grin. "I don't plant it, don't harvest it. But I think that sounds about right."

Kel shrugged and then slowly walked over to the group of men and shook hands all around. It took a while. In fact, Levine thought it was taking forever. From where he stood, they seemed to be talking about everything but crop damage. They were laughing and pointing in all different directions. Kel was scratching. At one point three of them were squatting down, chewing on blades of grass and spitting excessively. *What was it with these toothpick-chewers that they were always spitting?* Levine thought. Before too long, however, Kel and the man in overalls stood up and shook hands again. They laughed a couple more times for good measure, and then the man waded out through the tall grass and headed for the white truck; Kel walked leisurely back over to Levine and handed him the wad of money.

"Remind me to have you negotiate my next raise," Levine said with a measure of respect as he repocketed the money. "I take it we're good to go."

"Yup. Good to go. Turns out we're kin, sort of. Plus, he remembers my father. No charge—for me." He looked over at Donnie Hawk. "And, by the way, it's Diva seed—not Acala."

"Talk about your faux pas. There goes your chance of being elected King of the Cotton Festival," Levine responded, amazed that people could even care about such things. He then turned to Donnie Hawk with a look that conveyed surprise he was still standing there. "Well . . . saddle up."

Donnie sprang into high gear as if Levine had goosed him with a wet stick and hustled over to Skeeter Boy and the other two men. One of them nodded twice and then slowly walked to his backhoe. Shortly it had ground a path straight across the field and up onto the mound.

The exhumation progressed fairly much in the manner that Kel had outlined. He'd taken some photographs of the grave as it was. He also took a sample of the topsoil. When Levine asked him why, he'd said it was to cover their ass. "Just to be safe," he'd replied. "You never know when somethin' may become an issue—poisonin', for example—and a sample of the surroundin' soil may be necessary as a control. Unlikely, but better safe than lookin' foolish later in front of a jury." *Better than getting blamed for something later,* he thought.

The backhoe operator was quite skilled, and the top of the casket was soon exposed. That accomplished, he backed the machine off a few feet and shut it down. Kel took some more photographs, and then Skeeter Boy and a man who'd introduced himself as Hump took turns climbing into and out of the hole with their shovels. Hump presumably was so called because he had a rather large irregular lump over his left shoulder. It made one think that a small animal was curled up asleep under his shirt. Despite that, at one point Skeeter Boy had pulled Kel aside and whispered that he shouldn't take obvious notice of it, "'Cause he's kinda hinky about it, you know?" Kel had assured him that he understood, though he wondered why any man "hinky" about a deformed back would introduce himself to people as "Hump."

Donnie Hawk spent most of the time orbiting around Levine like a small satellite. In the afternoon heat, his cinnamon-roll hairdo had started to unwind, and several long strands were cascading wetly over his right ear like an oily brown graduation tassel.

"Mr. Levine," Donnie Hawk finally said, "I sure am sorry about that misunderstandin' the other day. You remember, though, I told you I didn't think them Boy Scouts had your skeleton—I told you that—I said, 'I don't think that's the one you're after.' Course, after you reminded me about the Elmore Cemetery, then I remembered this here place here. We're goin' to get this straightened all out here shortly, though. No harm, no foul. Right?"

Levine pinned him to the tree with a look. "That's right, Mr. Hawk, we're going to straighten this whole thing out once and for all. I'm simply glad that the phone call from Judge Clifford was able to refresh your memory last night."

Donnie Hawk looked over to the ongoing excavation, not so much to check the status as to avoid further eye contact with Levine. "I was just a boy when all this took place here," he said softly. "That was a long time ago, Mr. Levine."

Skeeter Boy saved his father from Levine's answer by a sharp whistle. He and Hump had gotten the grave dug out to a point where some lifting chains could be snaked under the ends of the casket. He was motioning for his father to come advise and approve. As Levine watched him walk away, a motion took his eye. Off to the side, partially obscured by the ragweed and tall Johnson grass, stood Sheriff W. R. Elmore, the sun glinting off his hard-cane cowboy hat. He'd gotten out of his car and was standing on the fringe, watching. The two men stared at each other but made no movement. Levine looked away only when he heard the backhoe start up.

Kel had taken advantage of Skeeter Boy and Hump being out of the hole to take more photos and inspect the condition of the coffin. It looked like a Batesville glass-sealer. The top was bowed in from the weight of the soil, but otherwise it looked intact. There was no crypt, and it was likely that some groundwater had gotten in. The bottom of the grave pit was beginning to muddy up badly just in the short while Kel had been in the hole, and this was the driest part of a particularly dry year. He'd also taken the trowel he'd purchased earlier and used it to scrape two more soil samples, one from each end of the casket, into separate Ziploc baggies. Then he hefted himself out and let Skeeter Boy back in to secure the hoist chains.

Hump fastened the free end of the chains to the backhoe, and at Donnie's signal, the operator slowly began raising the bucket arm. The chains popped and thumped as they cinched up, and there was a wet sucking sound as the coffin began to pull free from the muck. Skeeter Boy halted the operator a couple of times to skinny into the hole for some adjustments to the chains or to remove some hindering dirt. Within a few minutes the casket was swung up and over the hole. Water streamed out the bottom, confirming Kel's concern. Hump and Skeeter Boy took hold of opposite corners and steadied the coffin as the backhoe moved it over to firm ground. Then they freed the chains and the backhoe withdrew.

While the casket was being lifted, Donnie had walked over to the hearse and had backed it slowly over the furrows, careful to keep in the tracks made by the backhoe to minimize crop damage. Hanging half out of the driver-side window to better see, he eased it through the gap in the surrounding weeds made by the big John Deere and drew up alongside the coffin and opened the back. The interior was spread over with clear plastic sheeting, which Donnie double-checked to ensure it was smoothed out and covering the floor. Kel took additional photos as Donnie, Skeeter Boy, Hump, and the backhoe operator lifted the muddy coffin and slid it into the hearse.

"Well, Mr. Levine, if y'all will follow us back to the funeral home, the boys will tidy up this here mess here," Donnie said as he walked up to Levine, bending over to wipe his muddy hands on the dry grass.

Levine suddenly remembered Sheriff Elmore and turned to rejoin his earlier stare. But Elmore was gone, having driven away sometime while the casket was being raised.

"Mr. Levine . . ." Donnie Hawk repeated. "Mr. Levine—you all right?"

Levine turned back.

Everyone, including Kel, was looking at him.

Kel opted to ride back to the Pacific Funeral Home with Skeeter Boy in the hearse. It was good evidence-handling practice to have someone stay in sight of the casket at all times, and while he knew this wasn't his case, at least technically, he wasn't going to have the finger pointed at his Lab if something went sour—Levine's willingness to take the heat notwithstanding. Besides, he figured that if there were to be a question about chain of custody the FBI would rather have him take the stand than Skeeter Boy. *Do you, Skeeter Boy, promise to tell the whole truth and nothing but the truth, so help you God?*

Levine drove himself. So did Donnie Hawk. Hump and the back-hoe operator stayed to fill in the hole before some old grandmother on a genealogy field trip fell into it.

Fortunately, it was a short ride back to the funeral home. Fortunate for Kel, because Skeeter Boy had turned out to be about the level of conversationalist that one would expect from someone with that name, and the silence was quite loud. For the most part, Skeeter Boy had chewed on his muddy thumb and hummed quietly, seemingly unaware of Kel's presence beside him. Behind the hearse, in his blue Caprice, Levine had spent most of the short drive working his phone like a telethon operator. Donnie Hawk, following third behind him, spent the whole time wishing he hadn't won the last election. *Should have backed out and let old Blind Boon Pugh take that one,* he thought. *Don't need this headache, mercy no.*

The rear of the Pacific Funeral Home had a large aluminum-sided add-on garage that served as the embalming and prep room. It was accessed from the outside by a double-wide garage door with a chain-drive electric opener. Less than a year old, it was a testament to the financial stability of the mortuary business. The old prep room had been converted to a showroom for caskets and cremation urns—though in Split Tree there wasn't much need for the latter. None of that odd-ball shit in Locust County; folks still expected to be buried proper.

Skeeter Boy backed the hearse into the garage, closed the door, and quickly killed the engine before the exhaust fumes built up. Donnie Hawk and Levine entered from the interior of the building. With Hump and the backhoe operator detained at the cemetery, it took Kel and Levine to help pull the muddy, wet casket from the back of the hearse, setting it down roughly onto a stainless-steel church truck.

"This here's y'all's show now," said Donnie, apparently forgetting that technically he was the only one in the room who had any actual authority in the case. "What d'y'all want to do now? You can use the embalmin' table if you've a mind . . . I think that would work, leastwise I think . . . I'm not really sure what y'all have planned."

Neither was Levine, but he wasn't about to admit that in this company. He looked at Kel for some direction—hoping that he would take the reins.

Kel caught Levine's look. "Hmmm . . . well, if you don't mind my opinion . . . you've got your pathologist due in tomorrow. I suspect he won't want us messin' with much until he gets here—I know I wouldn't." Kel sensed that he needed to fill in the vacuum without diminishing Levine's authority. He scratched several chigger bites at his armpit and waistband while he evaluated the social dynamics in the room. "I tell you what, though, I also don't think it would hurt to crack that box and get a little look-see. Hell, if they buried a sack of cement in 1966, we might be able to save your pathologist a trip. Y'all's call, though."

"No cement was buried here—not in Locust County—no sir—I can guarantee you that. My daddy buried this here coffin." Donnie stepped forward. He bowed up like a rooster.

Levine smiled. "Glad to see your memory is improving, Mr. Hawk. I mean, sonofabitch, last night you couldn't even remember that it was buried."

Donnie Hawk took a step back. Skeeter Boy looked at his father with a particularly blank look.

Kel once again filled the tense silence that was growing. "I think we best take a look. If nothin' else we can give the pathologist a heads-up as to what to expect."

Levine agreed, and Donnie Hawk shrugged. At his nod, Skeeter Boy wheeled the cart into the section of the room that had been walled off as the new embalming room.

It was well lit and tiled, for easy cleanup. Levine and Kel stepped back while Donnie and his son began backing out the screws that fastened the lid. They had to pop the screw heads with their screwdriver handles to knock off the rust.

Kel photographed the process.

Even with the screws removed, forty years of accumulated corrosion didn't want to give up easily. Donnie stepped out to the garage and quickly returned with a tire tool that he plied around the edges of the coffin, making it squeal and complain, but ultimately yield. Donnie Hawk stood back, not wanting to take the responsibility of opening what he fully equated to a Pandora's coffin.

Kel examined the lid carefully, and when satisfied that there was nothing amiss, he motioned with a nod and a look for Levine to help him lift it off.

It was a plain casket, not a glass-sealer as Kel had guessed. Inside, the satin upholstery of the coffin had long ago tattered and the cellulose padding was now scattered over the interior like damp, loose hay straw. In the center of the coffin was a bundle of yellowed plastic, like a large amniotic sack, once clear but now fogged by groundwater and time. Kel could still make out the shape and form of human bones. There appeared to be little soft tissue present, a few small clumps dusted with a white powder, but nothing of substance.

"Bricks?" Levine asked.

"Naw," Kel responded, watching a fleeting look of concern flicker across Donnie Hawk's face. "Remains all right. Skeletal."

"If you say so, Doc. Not much left, huh," Levine said, peering over the edge of the coffin. He nodded at the white powder. "What's that?"

"I'm afraid it looks like hardenin' compound," Kel said, looking up at Donnie for confirmation.

Donnie Hawk nodded.

"Supposed to be there? What is it?" Levine asked.

"I was hopin' not. It's bad stuff, that's what it is," Kel replied. "It's a powder that morticians use on soft tissue that can't be easily embalmed. It's plaster and formaldehyde."

"Sometimes sawdust," Donnie said.

"And sometimes sawdust," Kel repeated. "Y'all use it, right, Mr. Hawk?"

Donnie Hawk nodded. "Course. Daddy mostly used Seep-Tite. Mostly. I use 4-Sure."

"There you go," Kel said to Levine. "That's what it is. Daddy used SeepTite."

"But what does that mean?" asked Levine. "It won't keep you from doing your study of the bones, will it?"

"Naw. It won't keep us from doin' an anthropological workup, but it may mess your DNA analysis all the hell up. The military liked the stuff a lot. Makes it easy to ship remains around the world. They used it liberally on some of the Korean War unknowns buried at the Punchbowl National Cemetery in Hawaii. After we identified the Vietnam unknown in 1998, we decided to take a look at some of the eight-hundred-plus unknowns from Korea. Figured we could use DNA on them too. No luck. Best thing anyone can figure is that the hardenin' compound is part of the problem—makes the DNA kinda sticky and it binds up on itself somehow. AFDIL's workin' on it, but . . ."

"But we're screwed. Is that what you're saying? All this and we're screwed to the wall by some talcum powder."

"No, not at all. May not be hardenin' compound, though Mr. Hawk here seems to think it is, but even if it is, maybe all the groundwater has diluted it, who knows? I sure don't. D'you?" Kel looked at Donnie Hawk.

Donnie's eyes were wide, and he held his hands up defensively as if warding off an assault. "This here's y'all's tar baby, not mine."

"The real question," Kel looked again at Levine, "is what do you want now? I mean right now. You want me to go ahead and get started or wait on your pathologist?"

Levine took a deep breath and ran his hand through his hair several times. He looked at his shoes and then at Kel. "Better wait. We know there are remains—even if it looks like it's nothing but bones. He gets in here tomorrow about noon. Better wait. Makes it cleaner if we go to court. Right?"

"Your call."

"Tell me, Doc, now that you've seen what we have here, how much will the pathologist be able to do? I mean, where does pathology end and what you do begin?"

Kel looked back at the bundle of plastic before answering. "Case like this one, honestly it's likely all anthropology. Pathologist probably can't tell much, 'cept maybe for trauma. Really won't know until we open it up the rest of the way."

"So we don't really need a pathologist?"

"Didn't say that. If this is a murder victim, you better have a pathologist here just in case. That's my recommendation anyhow. I don't want to be blamed for screwin' up an FBI case."

"You mean, another one."

"Don't go there. Do not start."

"Joking."

"Yeah. For the record, I'm sayin' get a pathologist."

"In that case, let's wait another day. Now that we've found Mr. Doe, he isn't going anywhere." He then turned so as to face Donnie Hawk. "Right, Mr. Hawk? This is evidence in an open homicide case. Can you see to it that this room is secured overnight?"

Donnie Hawk bristled. "I am the coroner of Locust County, Mr. Levine. I know my job."

"Yeah. Glad to hear it. Problem is that while you may know it, you sometimes seem to get a little forgetful."

CHAPTER 37

Split Tree, Arkansas
TUESDAY, AUGUST 23, 2005

As was becoming the pattern, Levine was up first, knocking on Kel's door at six-fifteen. Though unspoken this time, his expression conveyed a sense of disapproving wonder that Kel was still asleep. For his part, Kel noticed with some amusement that while they stood in the doorway talking, Levine was vigorously scratching his ankles and underarms and groin.

Both men had retired early the night before, but not before locking their doors. Kel had also taken advantage of Levine's cell phone to call the CILHI. It was by far the last thing that he'd wanted to do, but it was unavoidable. He'd spoken to Les Neep and told him that he was going to be away from the office a day or two longer—but no more. He'd also taken the opportunity to warn Les that if the commander's intent was to mend fences with the FBI, this might not be the case to do that with, given that his Bureau counterpart seemed to be something that had crawled under the fence in the first place, and nobody in that organization seemed in too much of a hurry to get him back into their own yard. Before he'd gotten off the phone, he'd asked Les to have D.S. check the deserters list for Ray Elmore. Check all the lists. Les promised that one of them would get back to him with the information. Then he'd called his wife and spoken to his boys.

As Kel blinked at the early morning light, Levine told him that he was heading off for the Memphis airport and would be back with the pathologist around ten-thirty—at the latest.

Kel went back to bed.

At nine o'clock there was another knock at the door. Kel looked at his watch. *Too early for Levine to be back,* he thought. "Who is it?" he called out.

"It's Sam, sir," came the voice. "I have with me a telephone for you, sir."

Kel yawned and blinked a couple of times. "Do I need a telephone, Sam?" he called out.

"Yes. Most certainly you do, sir. You have a gentleman who must speak with you, sir."

Too early in the morning for D.S. or Les—it was four in the morning in Hawaii. "Just a second," he finally acknowledged.

He opened the door to find Sam amid the midmorning glare, dressed in white pants and a white, short-sleeved shirt, holding his cordless phone. The motel owner smiled and half-bowed as he handed the phone to Kel, saying, "Take as long as you please, sir, I only will be waiting here."

Kel thanked his host and stepped back into his room with the phone. The reception was predictably poor, the handpiece being a good two hundred feet and a dozen walls from its base. "Hello," he said. "This is McKelvey."

"Doc," it was Levine's voice. "Hit a snag. Pathologist missed his friggin' plane. They may be able to get him on a later flight, but no guarantee. I'm going to sit tight here until I know what's going on, but my thinking is that you don't wait any longer on this guy—go ahead back to the funeral home and do what you need to do. If you can hold off cutting DNA samples till Dr. Rip Van Winkle gets there, great, otherwise . . ."

"Sure, not a problem," Kel replied. He yawned again.

"You still in bed? What's with you docs and sleeping so much?"

Kel yawned again. "Talk to you later, Levine." He opened the door as he was hanging up. He blinked painfully at the sunlight. Sam bowed slightly again and took the phone, assuring his guest that he was welcome to use the phone any time.

The draped room was still dark, and Kel was tempted to crawl back into bed. Instead he took a shower, dabbed fresh calamine lotion on his chigger bites—thirty-seven as of last night's tally—and dressed, then crossed the street to the diner. He sat near a window where he could watch the sparse traffic passing by on Magnolia while he roadmapped his plans for the analysis of the remains. He nursed a couple of glasses of tea and smiled politely at Jo, who fortunately was well occupied by other customers.

At ten-thirty he paid his bill, walked back to the Sleep-Mor and picked up some materials that he would need from his room, and got into his car. Ten minutes later he pulled up in front of the Pacific Funeral Home. Donnie Hawk met him at the car and together they unlocked the door to the embalming room.

"Mr. Levine gonna come?" Donnie Hawk asked, seemingly a little unsure of the propriety of Kel being here by himself.

"Afraid he's hung up in Memphis waitin' on his New York pathologist. He missed his flight." He shrugged. "Agent Levine called to tell me to go on ahead with my analysis . . . if that's okay by you . . . but if you want to wait, that's okay too. Your call. This is your case."

"No, no, mercy no," Donnie Hawk replied quickly. He clearly was eager to not get any more crossways with Levine than he already was. "What do you need to get started here?"

"Just some table space, maybe a toothbrush and some tap water . . . roll of paper towels would be nice. And some help removin' the lid."

Together they lifted the lid off the coffin and removed the bundled remains, placing them on the white porcelain embalming table. The head end of the table had a drainage hole that was centered over a large commode. Donnie Hawk lingered long enough to determine that he was no longer needed before excusing himself to another part of his building. Kel watched him leave and took advantage of being alone to vigorously scratch the chiggers that couldn't be dealt with politely in public. He took a couple of quick photographs to document the condition of the bundle. Then he took a deep breath, stretched his back, and bent over the bundle, slowly unwrapping it. The plastic was brittle and tore easily. Immediately his eyes began to tear up and his nose burned as if he'd snorted battery acid. The white powder on the bones was hardening compound, all right. The formaldehyde was as strong now as it must have been forty years ago. It didn't look good for getting any DNA. Kel backed away from the table, blinking the water from his eyes, and looked around for a pair of rubber gloves. He was thinking latex medical exam gloves, but this was an embalming room, and instead, he located a pair of thick, blue, industrial-grade neoprene gloves. He put them on and started removing the remains from the plastic.

It took Kel almost forty-five minutes to get the skeleton laid out in approximate anatomical order. The main elements were sided and in place within a few minutes; it was the little pieces, the hands and feet and ribs, that took most of the time to side and number. His osteology skills were more than rusty, and he hadn't brought a reference text with him. Fortunately, most of the hands and feet were still lashed together by dried tendons and muscle, so Kel didn't have to identify and side every bone.

Once the remains were arrayed on the table in an order that even a layman would recognize, Kel stripped off the gloves, pulled a stool over to the foot of the table, and climbed up so that he could capture the entire layout in another photograph. Then he photographed each quadrant in detail. That done, he picked up a blue folder he'd brought from Hawaii. Inside it were blank skeletal diagrams and forms used by the Lab for analysis of remains. He looked again at the table, assessing what was present and what wasn't, and selected the appropriate sheets. One of the pages was a skeletal diagram depicting an articulated skeleton in both front and back views. With a red pen he colored in the few bones that were missing. There weren't many. A couple of fingers, couple of toes, the left kneecap; probably all overlooked and left out in the muck and mud forty years ago. Otherwise all of the skeletal elements were there.

When he'd finished, he dated and initialed the diagram. At the top he wrote, *Locust County, Arkansas—John Doe/FBI Homicide.* He'd get a local coroner's case number from Donnie later. Then he set that form aside and put the gloves back on. He stood, looking up and down the table, trying to decide where to start. He picked up the next form. He needed to know the sex, but that was easy. Very robust skeleton, the mastoids—the bumps behind the ears where the big neck muscles attach—were large and well developed. Similarly, the nuchal crest on the back of the skull where the muscles in the back of the neck are anchored was also quite well defined. The jaw was square and robust. The brow ridge well buttressed. The hips were slender but well muscled and the ear-shaped platform where the sacrum joined the pelvis was flat. Likewise, the angle below the symphysis, where the right and left halves join, was narrow—all in all, not the hips of someone adapted for childbirth. Both legs were well developed. The linea aspera running lengthwise down the posterior side of the femoral shaft was large and rugged, suggesting a well-muscled individual. The ball-shaped femoral heads were equally large— over forty-eight millimeters in diameter. Even allowing for some error with the cheap calipers he'd bought at the hardware store, they were large. Usually any measurement over forty-six indicates a male. All the other indicators were consistent with a large, robust, well-developed individual.

He filled in the blanks on his forms and then in the blank labeled SEX he wrote: *Male.*

Next was race. Almost as easy as sex in this case. The skull was narrow and round, with a large prominent nose exhibiting a sharp bony spine at the base. Big anchors for the big nose of a Caucasoid. The nasal opening was narrow and tall. The jaws featured a pronounced underbite.

He wrote on the form: *Caucasoid.*

Age would be a little more difficult, but not much given so many bones to work with. He examined the ends of each long bone—arms and legs—starting with the shoulder, then elbow, wrist, hip, knee, and ending with the ankle. The ends were fused, suggesting the person was over about twenty years of age, but the growth plates still appeared youthful. There were still remnants of the epiphyseal fusion lines showing on several of the elements. Not much over twenty. Next he looked at the pubic symphysis again. The margin where the two pubic bones joined, right behind the pants zipper, displayed the youthful pattern of furrows and billows. It would smooth out and lip-over with age, but now it suggested twenty to twenty-five years of age.

There were a few other indicators that Kel made a note to check more thoroughly later, and he wanted to get an X-ray of the teeth to look at their age-related development, but for now he wrote down: *≈20–25 yoa (tentative).*

Stature was the most straightforward determination of all. Kel had decided he'd do a more complete examination after the pathologist arrived, but for now he stretched out a measuring tape against the right femur. For an accurate measurement he'd need an osteometric board, but for an estimate, a tape measure would work. He adjusted the tape until the maximum length could be measured and double-checked the figures twice. He compared them to the stature table in his folder.

He entered: *180.3 cm +/–3.8 cm (71 inches +/–1.5 inches)—tentative.*

Kel arched his back again. It hurt from leaning over for—how long had he been at it? He looked at his watch; it was almost one o'clock. He stretched and popped some joints and took several deep breaths. His nose had adjusted, or had gone numb, and he wasn't aware of the formaldehyde smell any longer. "Now for the fun part," he said out loud. "Let's see what happened."

He started with the skull. It was hard not to notice the oblong hole on the forehead. It was shaped like a fat exclamation point. He examined the margins of the hole carefully, and then turned the skull upside down so that he could peer through the foramen magnum, the large hole at the base that the spinal cord enters through, in order to examine the inner surface of the defect. He reached for his backpack and removed a small penlight that he used to illuminate the inside of the skull. Gunshot wound, that much was clear. It had been at an acute angle rather than straight on and had partially glanced off—hence the elongated hole. There were radiating fractures from the hole, but they were short, suggesting relatively low energy.

He set the skull down and wrote: *GSW to left frontal near temporal line. Keyhole defect. 3.5 cm long x 1.0 cm wide.*

He also drew the location of the wound onto a diagram of a skull, carefully tracing the tiny cracks that spidered off in all directions. But there was more. He gingerly picked the cranium and lower jaw up and articulated them, working them back and forth assessing the correct alignment. The left side of the mouth displayed an old, healed injury. Teeth 14, 15, 16—the three upper left molars were missing. The bone was well-healed, but in a jagged manner that suggested that the teeth had been traumatically avulsed—forcibly removed—some time well before death. Similarly, tooth 13, the left upper second premolar, had been chipped and then reshaped and contoured with a dental bur so as to be smooth rather than jagged. *That must have been some big-time painful,* Kel thought. The lower jaw wasn't much better. Tooth 18, the left second molar, had also been avulsed and tooth 19, the left first molar, had been broken and reshaped like the premolar above it. "Goddamn," Kel found himself saying. "What in the hell happened to you?"

There was other old trauma present. Nothing as dramatic,

and probably not as painful, as the broken teeth. Two of the lower right ribs—probably numbers 8 and 9—had been broken and showed dense, thickened calluses where they'd healed. One left rib, it looked to be number 7, appeared to have a healed callus that overlapped an earlier one. There were a few other healed fractures, a left ring finger and possibly one of the right metatarsals of the foot. *Whoever you are, you took a beating—several beatings, most likely,* Kel thought as he filled out his forms and diagrammed what he saw.

The analytical notes and diagrams totaled up to nineteen pages. Kel labeled each page the same—*Locust County, Arkansas—John Doe/FBI Homicide*—and then initialed and dated each one. Next he sorted them into order and numbered each—1 of 19, 2 of 19 . . .

Kel was completing his preliminary notes when Donnie Hawk came back into the room.

Donnie looked at the skeleton laid out on the table and then up at Kel. He had the head-shaking look of a young child who's just watched the magician's scantily clad helper get sawn in half. "I'll be," he said. "Will y'all take a look at that? Mercy, I'll never understand how y'all can do that. Give me a body been put through a cotton gin and I'll put him back to-gether—make him look good enough to take to the Sunday dance too. But that . . . all them bones and little pieces that look like pecan shells. Mercy." He had walked up to the foot end of the embalming table at this point and was looking at the sorted skeleton, his head shaking in undisguised wonder. "That done absolutely amazes me."

"Me too, sometimes."

"So . . . what's the verdict? Y'all finished?"

"I'm finished for now. This was just a preliminary look-see. I wanted to get enough to answer the two thousand ques-tions that I'm sure Special Agent Levine will have when he gets back this afternoon. In case you haven't been payin' at-tention, he's wound up pretty tight."

"Yes sir, Mr. McKelvey. That's for damn sure he is; pretty

damn tight." Donnie Hawk seemed glad that he wasn't alone in the observation.

Kel smiled. "Anyhow, I'll go back over all this with the pathologist when he gets here. If he gets here. Make some refinements. More details. I've got some more reference materials back at the motel that I need to take a look at. Once I find out what Levine really needs from me, I'll be able to focus a little more. As to the verdict, well . . . we got us a young, white male, probably twenty to twenty-five years of age, thereabouts, somewhere around five-foot-eleven in his stockin' feet, took a glancin' gunshot wound to the head. Also has some old injuries, probably from repeated whuppin's." He pointed to the healed fractures on the ribs and hand, and then he picked up the skull and jaw. "But here's the real cork in the bottle . . . Look here." He held the bones at shoulder height and turned them at an angle so Donnie could see the healed trauma. He pointed to each missing tooth one by one. "And here, here, here . . ."

"All them teeth busted out whilst he was alive?" Donnie Hawk asked. He no longer sounded awed, just very interested.

"Yeah," Kel answered. "These have been smoothed off by a dentist, and these are all old and all healed. Same for the other fractures. Whoever this was, he had a damned rough first twenty or so years."

Donnie Hawk was quiet as he looked at the skeleton on his embalming table. He was silent for a long time before responding. "Very rough," he said softly.

It was two o'clock when Kel finally left the funeral home. He'd lingered awhile after the examination, on the off-chance that Levine might make an appearance, but when he hadn't shown by one-forty-five, Kel tidied up his notes, watched Donnie lock up the embalming room, and then left. Back at the motel, he'd showered, refreshed his calamine lotion, and transferred his notes to his computer. Then he drafted a shell report. He'd fine-tune it later.

He looked at his watch frequently. It was now almost four

o'clock; if Levine didn't get back here soon with the pathologist they'd have to put the exam off until tomorrow morning—unless Donnie Hawk and the pathologist were willing to work through the night.

He was contemplating a stroll over to the diner for another time-killing glass of tea when there was a knock on his door. He got up to answer it. *About time,* he thought. *Hope he brought the pathologist with him.* Instead of Levine, however, he again found himself looking into the smiling face of Sam.

"Begging your pardon, sir, once again I have with me the telephone for you."

"Thank you, Sam," he replied, taking the phone from his host and covering the mouthpiece. "You don't have to wait; I'll bring the phone back to your office when I'm done."

"Not to worry, sir, I am happy to be waiting."

Kel returned his smile and then stepped back into his room. *Not to worry, Sam, I am happy to be having some privacy,* Kel thought as he shut the door. Shaking his head and smiling, he put the phone to his ear and said, "McKelvey."

"Me again, Doc," Levine replied. "No show on the New York doc. They say tomorrow morning for sure, but I'm not waiting on the sonofabitch. I'll have some other poor bastard from the office drive him down if necessary. Listen, I've got some papers I need to get signed here and a couple things lined up, and then I'm heading back down to your *Land of Opportunity.* Should be there by seven, seven-thirty at the latest."

Kel looked at his watch. "Fine by me, I'm not goin' anywhere."

"Yeah—well, I'm going friggin' nuts. Got fleas or something. I itch all over. My nuts are the size of tennis balls."

"Congratulations. And thanks for that image. I'm sure you're very popular with the women."

"Well, I wish that were always the case, but no, they're all swollen up with some sort of crud. Itches like hell. Haven't had it this bad since I was in the army."

Kel smiled—and scratched. It was like watching someone

else yawn. All the talk about scratching had a sympathetic effect. "Welcome to Arkansas, Mr. Levine. They're called chiggers—red bugs—you got them from that tall grass around the
cemetery. I was goin' to warn you, but you rushed in where
fools know better than to tread. Don't fret it though, they'll be
gone in a couple of weeks."

"A couple of weeks? My Lord, isn't there anything that
can be done—I mean now? Besides scratch. There's got to be
some sort of medicine."

"Well, when I was a kid, my grandmother used to slather
us up with kerosene and sulfur."

"Sounds awful. It work?"

"Sure, it'd get rid of 'em in a couple of weeks. You want
faster results I think you got to light the kerosene. But if it
makes you feel any better, you're not alone in your misery."

"You, too? You all swollen, too?"

"Yeah, the chiggers paid the boys a visit. I tell you what,
though, it's best not to talk about them—the chiggers, that
is—they hear you talkin' about them and they get all riled up
and feel like they have to put on a show."

"Then change the subject while I've still got some skin on
my ankles," Levine said.

"Okay. Well, I finished a preliminary analysis of the skeleton. Figured I'd do a little more in-depth stuff when the
pathologist got here—if he ever gets here. Wish now I'd just
gone ahead and finished this afternoon."

"Well that's the other reason I called. What's the skinny?"

"The skinny is that I'm pretty sure it's your guy. Young
white male, twenty to twenty-five years old when he bought
it. Gunshot wound to the left forehead, temple area. Also a
mess of older injuries. Healed rib fractures, broken hand, broken foot, busted jaw—all happened long before he died.
Don't know about gettin' DNA . . . that hardenin' compound
is all over the bones—it may be a problem after all."

"Aw shit." Kel heard him exhale sharply on the other end
of the phone. "You're sure it's the same John Doe from 1965,

though? I mean, we got the right grave? Luke whatever: whatever?"

"Based on what I know, I'd say yes. You got a copy of the '65 autopsy? If so, I can compare it to the skeletal inventory and make sure. Should be relatively easy."

"Yeah, it's in my room there at Sam's curry emporium; brought it back the other night, I've been meaning to show it to you . . . Oh, Doc, one other thing. Some guy named D.S. called for you—said to tell you that he's not on the list. In fact, wasn't on any list. Wouldn't tell me any more since he didn't know who I was, but said you'd know what he was referring to." He hesitated. "Who's not on the list? That about Elmore being a deserter?"

"Yeah," Kel said. "I counted on you bein' here by now so I gave him your cell-phone number last night." He paused and sighed in thought. "So . . . apparently Ray Elmore not only is not on the deserter rolls, but you say that D.S. said that he wasn't on any lists?"

Levine made an acknowledging sound.

"Shit. That includes the service lists. That means there's no record that shows he even served—now how do you figure that? He's not KIA, not MIA, not a deserter, apparently not even in the military—yet they've got his name on a big, bronze statue in the town square."

"Look, I've got some thoughts on that, and I think we need to talk. Tonight. As soon as I get there."

"Well, I hope you can make more sense of it than I can. I can't get it to tally up at all."

"Doc," there was a long hitch in his voice. "About the John Doe . . ."

"Yeah," Kel finally responded when it seemed that Levine wasn't going to continue without a prompt.

"You said he had some injuries . . . could they be from playing football?"

"Ahhh . . . I don't . . . I mean, yeah, they certainly take their football seriously in Arkansas, but they don't generally shoot players in the head with pistols—best I recall. A few coaches might, I suppose, but . . ."

"Yeah, yeah, you're a funny man, Doc, but that isn't quite the injury I meant. The healed ones—you said he had some healed fractures. Could they be from playing football?"

Kel thought. "Sure, I suppose. Ribs easy, hand and foot too . . . maybe. Jaw would be harder, it's some serious trauma, but then they don't call it smash-mouth football for nothin'. Why? Those injuries mean somethin' to you?"

"Like I said, we need to talk, Doc; it's definitely time for us to talk."

CHAPTER 38

Split Tree, Arkansas
Tuesday, August 23, 2005

Levine must have sped the whole way down from Memphis. It was half-past six o'clock when he knocked on Kel's door. Kel had spent most of the rest of the afternoon pacing, waiting for Levine to arrive with what promised to be, if not answers, insights into the identity of John Doe.

Kel answered the door and was surprised when Levine motioned for him to get into the waiting car. A few minutes later they were heading north in the direction of West Helena.

The trip didn't take long.

Along the way, Kel recapped the results of his preliminary analysis. Levine, once again, showed a great deal of interest in the antemortem fractures, particularly when they could have occurred and what could have caused them. Kel said there was no definitive way to know with those types of injuries, and that they could have been inflicted five, ten, maybe even fifteen years before death. Radiographs might help, it was unlikely but possible, but that could wait for the pathologist, who might want X-rays for his own purpose. X-rays involved moving all or part of the skeleton to the small medical clinic on the outskirts of Split Tree, and it didn't make sense to do that twice.

Levine drove up to a small plank-and-post building with a hand-lettered sign reading *Pete's*. Few locals frequented the place any more, displaced instead by people in relaxed-fit jeans and Tony Lama boots who drove from as far away as

Little Rock to sample a Pete's Fried Burger. Levine wasn't looking for a deep-fried hamburger tonight as much as he was hoping to avoid being around anyone with Split Tree ears. Tonight he needed to talk to Kel without the risk—however remote—of a full report being telegraphed to Sheriff Elmore before midnight.

Pete's was full. Levine and Kel took one of the last available tables and ordered quickly from the limited menu—two deep-fried gut-busters with fixings. When the waitress had gone, Kel said, "Okay, we're here; no one's payin' the least amount of attention to us . . . time for you to start talkin'."

Levine tilted his head to one side as if he had water in one of his ears. He looked at Kel, validating in his own mind that he could trust him with what he was preparing to say. As much as he felt that he was beginning to grasp the threads of the case, he couldn't completely shake the vestigial fear that he was being hung out to dry. He leaned forward. "Like you told me, I'm going out on a limb here. I'm trusting you, and maybe I shouldn't, what with the Gonsalves case and the Bureau putting the squeeze on me, but dammit, Doc, none of this has been making sense to me . . . and I'm not alone there, right? Hell, I admit that I've never worked a homicide before, let alone one as cold as ice, but I am a good investigator and evidence is evidence, and this one just hasn't been adding up right." He squeezed his eyes into narrow slits and searched Kel's face for affirmation. He saw something that seemed enough to satisfy him, though Kel hadn't intended to convey anything. "Then today—while I'm sitting at the airport—I get that phone call, the one from that D.B. guy . . ."

"D.S."

"Right, that D.S. guy that was trying to reach you, and the pieces began to tumble into place. I don't have them all, but I'm starting to make out some shapes in the fog, you know?"

"Good for you, 'cause I'm still lost. Are we talkin' about your John Doe or Sheriff Elmore's brother Ray?"

"Both, maybe. Look, Doc, what do we know here?"

"Ahhh . . . that would be nothin'."

"No, not true. We know a lot." Levine held up his thumb as he began the tally of his evidence. "One. Ray Elmore goes off to Vietnam—least everyone in the whole town thinks so. Why? I mean why do they think so? Why do they have that statue with his name on it? Because his daddy, Big Bad Ray, the town chief of police, and his brother, the current county sheriff, they say he did, that's why. They also say he didn't come back. They say it, but at the same time they don't really say it, right? Remember Edd Forrest telling us that the Elmores were always tight-lipped about the matter? Everyone chalks the silence up to 'Big Ray taking it hard'; hell, the less he said, the more everyone believed it happened. Am I right? That's how that shit works. They got that statue erected to him and everything. But he didn't go to Vietnam, did he? He didn't die, didn't come up MIA . . . and he didn't desert . . . didn't even serve in the military, you're telling me."

"Go on."

"So where is he if he's not humping a ruck in Vietnam?"

"You think he's your John Doe? . . . I don't see it."

"Why not? Look, he disappears from town a couple of months before the body was found. Right? You didn't find any record that he enlisted—or at least no record that he served during that time period. Remember, Deputy Dawg told us he had some big-time athletic scholarship, but instead of going to college, he up and enlists in the navy and is never seen again." Levine had extended his index finger, keeping track of point number two.

He paused while the waitress placed their fried burgers before them, satisfied herself that her immediate duties had been completed, and moved sullenly on to another out-of-town customer in designer jeans.

When he saw that Kel didn't have a response, Levine moved on to his third finger. "Okay, now third, we have an unknown body—in a small town where no one is thought to be missing, mind you—and you tell me it's a young, white male with injuries consistent with what an All-State, Honorable Mention, Double-damn-A starting Dirt Devil halfback might have accumulated."

"Delta Devil . . . Yeah . . . but those injuries could be from any number of things—like I said, the trauma to the jaw in particular would be pretty extreme for your average football injury . . . and the age is a little off too . . ."

"But? I mean, it could be, right?"

Kel shifted in his seat and looked at the wall, picturing the skeleton at the Pacific Funeral Home in his mind. He mentally analyzed it again and then nodded slowly. "Yeah, yeah . . . could be. Still unlikely, but it's possible, I guess. I'm still listenin', anyhow."

"Fourth," Levine now tucked his thumb and held up four fingers, "and go figure this one; Big Daddy Elmore simply up and decides to bury a complete stranger, a John Doe, in the family cemetery."

"You don't know that it was Big Ray that did that."

"You're a real putz, you know it? Were you on the fuckin' debate team in college, Doc? Yeah, yeah. I don't *know*, but c'mon, you understand the nature of circumstantial evidence?"

"Go on."

"Okay. So, Big Ray buries a John Doe, and if that isn't strange enough, he makes sure that what little paperwork is required uses an old name for the cemetery that no one is familiar with. Covers the tracks. And the tombstone—he goes and puts the biblical reference to the prodigal son on it? C'mon, Doc, for cryin' out loud . . . who in their right goddamn mind goes and does something like that?"

"Yeah, I'll admit that parts of it sound good . . . except for . . ."

"Except for what?"

"Except for . . . well, except for *why*?"

"I'm not sure of the why part."

"Well, it seems to me that you've got to answer that before

passin' Go and collectin' your two hundred dollars. Why? Okay, there's somethin' funny goin' on with the Elmores, I'll give y'all that one as a free space, but why would the chief of police bury his son as an unknown homicide victim? And who killed him? From what we've heard about Big Ray, I'd expect he'd be movin' heaven and hill to find the killer, not helpin' dispose of the evidence in a levee. Same goes for the brother, W.R."

"You would, wouldn't you? Unless"—he took a sweeping glance around the restaurant and saw that everyone was properly preoccupied with their greasy burgers—"unless you— and by that, I mean you personally, Big Ray Elmore—had a damn good reason to keep a lid on it. I did some researching myself when I was in Memphis last weekend. This is what I was going to tell you the other night. The Bureau had a big COINTELPRO looking into the Klan in the middle to late sixties. Ahhh, sorry, that stands for Counterintelligence Program. It was an attempt to get inside groups like the Klan."

"I'm aware of it."

"Well, this one was code-named WHITE HATE. Most of it was focused in Mississippi and Alabama, places like that. Arkansas wasn't really on their scope—kinda on the margin—but the Klan was here, despite what Deputy Bevins and others might like to remember nowadays. Couple groups: Imperial White Knights of the Ku Klux Klan, Order of the United Knights of the Ku Klux Klan . . ."

Kel nodded weakly but otherwise listened without response.

"We know that over in Mississippi and elsewhere," he gestured in the approximate direction of east, "some police and government officials were members of one group or another—or at least very sympathetic to their goals." Now he shifted his rear back and forth, settling into his chair more firmly—either for comfort or as a way of discreetly scratching, Kel wasn't sure which. "There's been something kinda gnawing at me, and I couldn't figure it out. Both Deputy

Bevins and Chief Forrest made mention of 'social' clubs and groups. Remember, the chief told us about Big Ray catching Jimmie Trimble's father 'after a meeting' and beating the crap out of him with a pick handle? What kind of meeting was it, do you suppose? PTA? You usually take pick handles to PTA meetings in Hawaii? I know I don't."

"You're sayin' you think Ray Elmore—Big Ray, the father—was a member of the Klan?"

"Yeah—that's exactly what I'm saying. His ticket to re-election and prestige in the community."

Kel leaned back and exhaled slowly, emptying his lungs. He paused before refilling them. There was a happy tink and rattle of china and the buzz of pleasant evening conversation all about them. He took the room in. Finally he looked back at Levine and shook his head to convey that the significance wasn't clear to him. "Maybe, maybe not, but what does that change? Your son is still your son. Despite what you may have heard, Klansmen still love their kids. You don't just let his killer go scot-free to get yourself reelected. Not in New York and not down here neither."

Levine thought back to his first meeting with Sheriff Elmore. What had he said? *What makes you think a killer can ever sleep, Mr. Levine?* "No, I don't suppose you do, Doc. But then again, what if it was an accident? Suppose . . . stick with me, here . . . what if something went so wrong that there wasn't an easy way out? Nothing's going to bring your son back; the only thing you have to decide is how much more of your life is destroyed. Damage control. C-Y-A, right? Cover-Your-Ass. People do it in New York, people do it down here as well. Remember Cain trying to bullshit the Lord? Brother, what brother? I don't see a brother. Been going on for a long time."

"Thought you didn't know the Bible."

"Old Testament, Doc. Even I know the basics."

"How fortunate for Cain that Special Agent Levine wasn't assigned to his case."

"You got that right."

"Okay, so tell me what went wrong. I guess I'm still not trackin'. What is it exactly that you're sayin'?" Now it was Kel's turn to lean in close and hush his voice. "Are you sayin' that the father and son had somethin' to do with Jackson's death? The chief of the goddamn police—here in little Split Tree, Arkansas?"

Levine nodded. "Yeah. Wake up and join the real world, Professor. Shit like that happens. And here's another piece of the puzzle. Leon Jackson had been rousted by Daddy Ray a couple of months before he turns up dead. Arrested him on what appears to be some trumped-up charge of drunk and disorderly. Bullshit harassment, I'm guessing. ACLU got involved, sent some real drum-beaters down from Memphis and Little Rock to turn over some rocks. Jackson was very vocal about wanting Big Ray fired. Big stink. Capital-S type stink. The city fathers seem to have gotten a lid on it somehow, and so nothing ever happened, but there was bad blood between Big Ray and Mr. Jackson; that much is clear from the record."

"And?"

"And I think that some of that bad blood was spilled out on that levee one night. And I think Ray Junior was involved. Maybe he was avenging his father. Maybe it was the son all along. Hell, I'll even give the daddy the benefit of the doubt. Maybe Big Ray was there to try to stop Junior from doing something rash, I don't know—but I do know that when it was all over, there were two bodies out there. Jackson and young Ray Elmore, Junior. Two bodies and one big problem for one Big Ray."

Kel was vigorously shaking his head. "No, no, no, no . . . I just . . . I can't see it. Remember what Edd Forrest, the police chief, said? Remember? He says Big Ray idolized his son. Why would he . . . *how* could he let his son be buried like that—in an earthen levee, for God's sake—even if it was an accident? All the more reason if it was an accident. It just doesn't make sense."

"No, Doc, it's the only thing that does make sense. Don't think today. Put yourself in Big Ray Elmore's shoes in 1965. You lived here then, you ought to remember even if you were a kid. You harass a black civil rights leader; roust him on some trumped-up D-and-D charge; the ACLU's watching the case; all eyes are on you and Split Tree thanks to what happened over in Neshoba County; and here you are, a card-carrying member of the KKK . . ."

"You don't know that—about the KKK."

"True, but I suspect I'm right. Think about it. Who was indicted in the *Mississippi Burning* case?"

Kel shook his head. "You mean originally?"

"Yeah. Back in the sixties. Guys named Lawrence Rainey and Cecil Price—the damn sheriff and deputy sheriff of Neshoba County—that's who. And who was convicted a few months ago in the same case? Edgar Ray Killen, *The Preacher.* An unsuccessful candidate for sheriff."

"Still . . ."

"Still this. You're Big Ray Elmore. You're a member of the KKK and this same civil rights putz that's been a thorn in your side for months ends up beaten to death on the outskirts of your town—not any old town, mind you, but in your old town. The one you run. Coincidence? Maybe, but where do you think the finger's going to be pointed?"

"Yeah, but to bury your son's body in a levee? Unmarked? No way."

"Maybe he didn't do the burying."

Kel shook his head to indicate that he wasn't following the logic.

"Look, maybe he didn't bury him. Maybe someone else cleaned up the mess. His good lodge buddies, maybe. Think about it, the white boy's body wasn't buried next to Jackson's, was it? Think about it. It was some distance away, like maybe a racial thing—segregation—don't want the body buried too closely to that Negro, after all. And it was shallow, remember? Not permanent—almost as if maybe someone was intending to come back and move it to a more suitable location as soon as things had calmed down a little, and they had time to think. A more suitable location—like maybe a relatively obscure grave in the family cemetery."

Kel had continued to shake his head. As much as he didn't believe it, Levine had a way of making it seem perversely sensible. "Will no one rid me of this troublesome priest?" he said quietly, almost to himself.

"What?"

"King Henry. The Second, I think. Remember? Thomas à Beckett was a thorn in his side. Story goes that Henry is supposed to have said, 'Will no one rid me of this meddlesome priest?' or somethin' like that, and a couple of loyal Sir Bubbas took care of the problem."

"Yeah, I like that. Henry, huh? Well, maybe that's what happened here, I think. Something similar anyway. And don't forget, not long after that, what does Big Daddy Elmore do? He sends all the working girls living out near the levee packing, that's what he does—outside his jurisdiction, yet he decides the area needs cleaning up and he's a one-man scrubbing bubble."

Levine paused when he saw that Kel was working up a response. "Go on," he prompted. "But what? I know you've got a 'but what?' in you."

"Not *what*, but *why*? Why didn't he move the body? You say it was buried there temporarily, okay, so it's temporary. I can buy that, sort of. But why'd Big Ray not move it? Why'd somebody not move it?" Kel asked. "Why'd they leave it to be found?"

"Bothered me, too. I don't think he, they, whoever, got the chance, is why. I checked the records at the library and at the National Weather Bureau in Memphis. Funny thing about these rural areas—Ma and Pa Kettle don't know who the president is on any given Sunday, but they can tell you every drop of rain that fell in the last two hundred years. According to the official weather bureau records, the day after Leon Jackson was last seen, one of the worst thunderstorms of the century blew in. I mean biblical stuff. Hail, frogs and toads, almost hurricane winds. Storm lasted the better part of a day and a half, but even then the rain continued in torrents for almost a solid week. After that it rained off and on for almost another month. Very unusual for August, they say. Levees failed all the way from Alton down to Baton Rouge. More important, the fields all along here were flooded and never got a chance to dry up. Wettest August on record. Newspapers were filled with pictures of people out stacking sandbags; cows on roofs; front-page stories about whole crops being ruined. I'm betting he, they, whoever, didn't have a chance to move anything. The burial was supposed to be temporary, but then Jackson's body washes out and suddenly all eyes are on the area . . . too late then to be seen anywhere near the place. Just didn't have a chance."

Both men sat quietly, Levine watching Kel closely, Kel looking inward at his own past. He thought of his father and the last time they had visited Split Tree. He'd been younger than his two boys were now, yet parts of that trip he could remember with glasslike clarity: the strangeness of the people and the places mixed with an easy affection that his father exuded. He thought of his own two boys.

"You've got two children. Is that right, Mike? Girls, you said?"

Levine nodded. "Yeah, girls. Both of them . . . both in high school."

Kel nodded slowly. "I've got two boys—twins. They're still pretty young."

They sat silently. Kel stared at the table. Levine watched him, waiting for him to speak. Neither man touched his food.

"God. What it would take to allow your son to be buried and forgotten . . . like that," Kel said after a pause.

"Yeah," Levine said, and there was a note of understanding that surprised Kel. "Must have torn him up."

CHAPTER 39

Split Tree, Arkansas
TUESDAY, AUGUST 23, 2005

As they passed the green sign that announced the city limits, Kel asked Levine what the next step would be. Even if Levine was correct, he was a long way from proving anything, and they needed to plan the next twenty-four hours. Despite his burnout with work, Kel was missing his family and growing anxious to return home. After a moment's thought, Levine replied that nothing would happen until the pathologist had arrived and gotten a chance to analyze the remains—they hoped that would be sometime in the morning. After that, Levine indicated, it was his intention to pick Sheriff Elmore up for questioning. He admitted that W. R. Elmore might or might not have been involved in his brother's death—a speculation that for Levine had crystallized to fact—but Elmore certainly knew a great deal more than he was sharing, and it was time to shake the tree a little more vigorously than he had been doing up until now and see what sort of fruit was ripe. If this were a bank fraud case, Levine would bring charges even if he knew they wouldn't stick. It certainly had worked with the senator from Pennsylvania—at least until the Bureau had told Levine to back off the investigation and flush the files. Even the threat of charges often loosened tongues. Levine had already made tentative arrangements with a federal judge in Little Rock to issue an arrest warrant on an accessory to murder charge if necessary, but he admitted that that was probably premature. The judge's support wasn't rock solid. Ideally, they'd get some DNA from the remains and confirm Levine's suspicions about John Doe's real identity. That would be the nail he needed.

It was almost eight o'clock when they got back to their rooms at the Sleep-Mor. Levine said he wanted to go to Donnie Hawk's first thing in the morning; he was anxious to see the remains and have Kel go over his findings with him in detail. Then, with any luck, the pathologist would arrive.

They decided to shoot for seven-thirty in the morning.

Kel latched his motel-room door and booted up his computer. He opened up the shell of his report and typed for a few minutes, but his head wasn't into it. Instead he lay down on the bed and stared at the dented ceiling and imagined his children jumping up and down, popping their heads against the acoustic tiles and giggling.

But mostly he thought of Levine's vision of the world. He tried to imagine an alternative that accounted for the facts in a more parsimonious way. Occam's Razor. The simplest explanation is usually the correct one. He tried to imagine a father having to abandon his son like that. What would he feel? Would he salve his sorrow with a biblical epitaph? What would he feel?

Shame?

Fear?

Or simply some bowel-deep sense of loss?

Something wasn't right. He pictured the skeleton laid out at the funeral home. He went over it again—bone by bone, curve by curve, landmark by landmark.

What was it?

Was it the injuries? Maybe.

A thick alternative was starting to form—to carve and mold into something almost tangible. He knew he should share his thoughts with Levine, but he couldn't shake the memory of the Gonsalves case and the undue criticism that his Lab had suffered. As much as he wanted to trust Levine, he couldn't bring himself to be fully open and exposed with his suspicions. Not yet.

He put his forearm over his eyes, shutting out the light that was fueling his thoughts.

There's plenty of time, he thought, *plenty of time.*

His mind drifted laterally. He thought of growing up in Arkansas. Of the secure, calm warmth of his father's even-tempered voice. He thought of Big Ray—that raw-boned, smiling man that he'd seen in the photo in Grace Trimble's living room. That visit to her home seemed a lifetime ago.

Before long he dozed off.

The dream returned. The strange one he'd had several nights earlier. It was the same, but different. He was walking through waist-high cotton, the sharp leaves of the drying, dying plants cutting through his pant legs. Little flecks of bright-red blood flowered on his skin and blossomed on his clothes. His wife was there again, still young and pretty. The sun was behind her and the outline of her slender body was visible through her light summer dress. His boys were still there as well, grown exactly like before. They kept their backs to him the whole time as if they were hiding something. It was a hot summer day, but rain was in the air; you could smell moist earth on the breeze, and moldering pecans, and late-season honeysuckle. The rain was coming, blowing in from the southwest. Kel smiled at his wife as he walked toward her, but when she raised her eyes to his there was nothing but a weary sadness. Her hands were empty where before they'd been holding a sleeping bird. He realized that one of his sons—he wasn't sure which one—was holding the big-barreled ten-gauge shotgun that Kel's father had taught him to hunt with as a child. When Kel looked at the ground he saw the black-and-white mockingbird. His wife wasn't scolding this time; it was more of a quiet keening. He didn't understand why no one would wake the bird this time—to make it sing. He knelt and touched it. It was cold and wet, and when he looked up to his wife she had changed. It was still her—he knew that somehow—but she'd changed. Her face was old and grayed and webbed by years. It was the face of Grace Trimble.

The first two shots caught him by surprise. He jerked his head up to see which of his boys had fired the shotgun—instead he saw the brightly lit motel room and the indentations in the ceiling. His head was filled with the thick, stringy molasses of shallow sleep, and he blinked hard. He glanced at his wrist and saw that it was almost eleven-thirty.

Then he heard it again.

Bam, bam. Followed by, "Will you open the goddamn door." It was Levine's voice. He had been pounding on the door.

Kel blinked again. Not gunshots.

Bam, bam, bam. "Goddammit, Doc—wake the goddamn hell up."

He managed to clear his head and go to the door. He opened it to find Levine, shirttail untucked, about to pound his fist against the door again. He had his cell phone out and was talking animatedly to someone. He stopped himself from hitting the door and glared at Kel. To the phone he said, "I need it now . . . it'll take me two hours—I want it ready to go when I get there . . ." He grabbed Kel by the front of his shirt and pulled him roughly to the sidewalk as he talked. ". . . And I want two uniformed troopers as well . . . I don't give a flaming shit, do it . . . I don't care how . . . You're a special agent, aren't you? So do something special."

Kel watched his face and listened to his words, trying to piece together what was going on. Levine saw his look and understood his confusion. He impatiently pointed across the parking lot to the northwest as he continued speaking into the phone. Kel followed his outstretched finger. There was an orange glow to the night sky, like a great cloud of luminous dust blowing up.

"Yeah, yeah, just get it done . . . two hours." Levine snapped his phone shut and looked at Kel. "I'm going to get that cracker-ass schmuck. I'm going to chainsaw his nuts off and hang them from my rearview mirror like big fuzzy dice. Goddammit, goddammit to hell. I was right. I was right."

Kel shook his head, still not understanding. He looked at Levine and back to the glow.

"Know what the hell that is? Do you?"

"No. What's goin' on? I think . . ."

"I'll tell you what's going on." He pointed to the glowing horizon. "That's the Pacific goddamn Funeral Home—or what's left of it. Burned to the friggin' ground. That son-ofabitch. There's your friggin' evidence, Doc. Up in friggin' smoke."

"Burned? The funer . . . Holy Christ. You're shittin' me? The whole place?"

"Whole thing."

"You sure? I mean, how . . ."

"I'm sure. Went to the office to get some ice cubes about twenty minutes ago—saw the glow. Didn't think much of it for a minute until I realized what it was and where it was. Just drove over there. Dozen or so county firefighters are standing around watching, grabbing their cocks, and telling cremation jokes. Mr. Donnie the Coroner is struck friggin' dumb—standing there watching his business go up in flames."

"Christ, I knew I should have taken those DNA samples when I had the chance—I just didn't want to cut anythin' until the pathologist had seen everythin'. Now there's no chance. That heat'll destroy any DNA . . ." Kel said, more to himself than Levine.

"I'm going to nail him, Doc. Right to a tree."

"Nail him?"

"Yeah. With a big hammer."

"You're not talkin' about Mr. Hawk, are you?"

"I'm talking about Elmore."

"The sheriff? You really think he's responsible?"

"Where were you raised? You raised by blind, crippled nuns or something? Of course he's behind this. Who else would be? Who else has a reason to destroy that evidence? The whole funeral home happens to burn down the night after we exhume the body. C'mon, Doc, I spent twenty years working fraud cases, I may not know details about how medical examiners work and where bodies are stored, but I can smell when something stinks. This stinks, and it's Elmore's stink. He's marked his territory all over it."

"I . . . I don't know, it's just that . . ."

"Just nothing. I'm going to Little Rock. You sit tight. Understand?" He poked Kel in the chest with an emphatic finger. "Two hours there, two back—I'll be here by daylight, and I'll have a federal marshal and a couple of state troopers with me. And then we go find that bastard."

"What do you need from me?" Kel asked as he stared at the pulsing orange glow. Little snowflakes of drifting ash were visible under the streetlights.

"Nothing. Just make sure your notes are in order. They're all we got on the body now."

"Levine . . . Mike, about the body . . . I should have told you earlier . . . I've been thinkin', there's somethin' that's been botherin' me and I think I finally . . ."

"No time now, Doc. Tell me when I get back." He was already at his car, unlocking the door. He had his cell phone to his ear as he got in and turned the ignition.

"Mike . . ."

"Daylight," Levine shouted as he closed the door.

Kel watched him back up and pull out of the parking lot headed west. He stood silently for a moment, watching the reflection of the fire bounced back by dust and heat waves, and then turned and walked back into his room.

Unbelievable.

CHAPTER 40

Split Tree, Arkansas
TUESDAY, AUGUST 23, 2005

After Levine left, Kel undressed and took a shower. He had just gotten out and was standing in the center of the room, dripping, toweling his hair, and his air-conditioner was blowing loudly, the unbalanced fan clicking with each revolution. The television was tuned to CNN and contributed its own share of noise. He almost didn't hear the knock. He'd gotten so used to Levine's pounding that the soft rap he now heard didn't register immediately, and when it did, he recognized it as the polite knock of Sam—probably delivering the phone. No doubt Special Agent Dervish had thought of something as he went whirling up the highway on his way to Little Rock and was calling back to issue some new directive.

Kel slipped on a pair of jeans and pulled a light-green shirt over his head. The top two buttons were undone, and the thin, cotton cloth stuck to his wet skin. He was snapping his pants when he opened the door.

It was Sheriff W. R. Elmore.

Kel stared at him, unsure what to do or say. Could Levine be right about this guy? Immediately, Kel was aware of being barefoot. It made him feel vulnerable somehow. Without shoes he was slightly shorter than the man at the door; he hadn't really seen the sheriff standing before—not close up anyhow—and he looked to be about six feet tall, though at the moment he was projecting himself much taller.

Kel said nothing.

"You that little shit they call 'Kel'?"

"I'm Robert McKelvey. What can I do for you, Sheriff Elmore?" Ordinarily Kel would have unlimbered his tongue and fired away, but not this time.

Sheriff Elmore pushed past Kel into the motel room. When Kel stepped back, Elmore grabbed the door handle and shut it.

"Make yourself at home," Kel said, attempting to keep his voice even-toned. It was an effort. He swallowed audibly and began rolling up his shirtsleeves, in part to mask the fact that his hands had begun to shake.

"Don't remember me, do you? Don't expect you would." The sheriff looked around the room as if he were attending a housewarming party and was trying to think up an appropriate compliment for the hostess.

"Sure. I was in your office yesterday with Special Agent Levine. Didn't get a chance for introductions, though; you and Levine seemed to have eyes only for each other. I was the bump on the log. Over in the corner."

Elmore continued to examine the furnishings. "That's not what I mean." He walked to the window and tugged the curtains, making sure that there was no gap. "Your daddy brought you around here when you were but a little shit—called you *Kel*—I thought that was pretty funny. Still do. He took you fishin' out at McKelvey Lake. I was fishin' there that day myself. You don't remember?"

"I remember the day fishin', can't say I remember you. You were friends with my father?"

Sheriff Elmore snorted a laugh. "Not friends. Knew him. He knew my father. Your father warmed the bench for him on the football team here in Split Tree. McKelveys was always second-stringers to the Elmores—you know that? I remember my daddy sayin' that Robert McKelvey couldn't run in a lazy circle without fumblin' his own balls." He was walking about the room, touching things: lampshade, ashtray, television. He walked over to Kel's laptop computer and ran his fingers along the top of the screen. The screen saver was on, and a digital clock was rebounding about the screen. Seven-oh-eight P.M.—Hawaii time—twelve-oh-eight in the morning in Locust County.

Kel was watching the digits change when he suddenly realized that his preliminary analysis of the John Doe was detailed on the screen. A small jolt would turn the screen saver off and reveal the report, and right now, his gut was telling him that that report probably was not the best topic of discussion to be having with the sheriff. He walked, as casually as he could manage, over to the desk and pushed the top of the computer closed. It clicked shut. "What can I do for you, Sheriff? Here to relive fishin' stories or you got somethin' else on your mind?"

"Where's your boyfriend, Special Agent Levine of the F-B-I?" He drew the sentence out slowly, emphasizing each word.

"Probably in his room. We're supposed to have a meetin' in a little while. I was just getting ready to head over there. Want to accompany me?"

"Hmmm." Elmore stopped looking around the room and focused on Kel. "Meetin'? Now that's funny. Thought for sure I saw him drive away about fifteen, twenty minutes ago—looked to be headed west. Deputy Bevins—you got a chance to meet Jimbo, didn't you? Not much for brains but he does what he's told—he tells me that Mr. Levine, of the F-B-I, is headed out in the direction of Highway 49 . . . looks to be goin' to Little Rock, I'd say."

"That so?"

"That's so." He gave a short laugh. "He must have forgot all about your meetin'. Maybe he has somethin' else on that little F-B-I mind of his, you reckon?"

"Maybe."

"Well," Sheriff Elmore said with a puff of finality that sounded as if he were announcing a long-worked-at decision, "why don't we take advantage of his forgetfulness and have our own little meetin'? Just you and me. How's that sound?

Why don't you get some shoes on there, Mr. McKelvey? Hell, people see you barefoot, they'll think y'all from Arkansas. And you . . . ain't from around here, are you?"

"I got a better idea, Sheriff, seein' how it's past midnight, why don't we wait and have our meetin' in the mornin'? I'll be happy to drop by your office—with or without Levine— as you wish. Can you give me an idea of what the agenda will be?"

W. R. Elmore looked at Kel. Neither man said anything. Finally, the sheriff straightened his back, and the leather of his gun belt creaked loudly in the quiet of the room. He took a deep breath and released. "Get your shoes, Mr. McKelvey."

CHAPTER 41

Split Tree, Arkansas
TUESDAY, AUGUST 23, 2005

Levine turned right out of the Sleep-Mor's parking lot and then left on Tupelo heading west. The roads were empty, and he accelerated rapidly. The road continued, narrowing and losing its shoulder, and its name devolved into some obscure rural route number, until it hit Highway 49. He intended to follow that northwest until he hit Interstate 40, which would take him all the way into Little Rock. A total of about 120 miles, give or take a few. There were probably shorter routes, if you knew the back roads, but Levine didn't, and this way offered the least chance of getting lost. Besides, once the road straightened out a little bit, he could safely goose it up to eighty, maybe ninety, miles an hour. If a state trooper stopped him, so much the better—he could use an escort into the city.

He'd seen the Sheriff's Department cruiser parked in the Albert Pike's lot as he pulled out of the motel. He wasn't surprised. The lights were off, but he still could make out a figure behind the wheel. Watching like the good keeper he was.

"C'mon, Deputy Bevins—see if you can keep up with me," he said to himself as he watched the parked car shrink in his rearview mirror. He punched the accelerator, and his car's engine surged. Jimbo wasn't following. "You and your boss are too late anyway. It's out of your control now."

There was a bright, orange late-summer quarter moon

hanging low in the western sky. The floodplain receded behind him as he drove. He could see small hills and rises and more and more trees presented dark silhouettes as he headed west away from the river. Large bugs popped the windshield in bright, greasy smears. He had to use the wipers frequently, but that only homogenized the mess.

He kept running the events and facts over and over and over in his head. Levine knew that the chances of making anything stick against Elmore were razor slim. Conspiracy possibly. Maybe, if the DNA worked, he could get him on some after-the-fact charge, but the Doc seemed to think that the DNA evidence had gone up in smoke—literally. There were plenty of other holes—he knew that—but so much was starting to fall into place; the dominoes were lining up. Just a few nagging holes to caulk up. But they admittedly were big holes. Doc McKelvey had seen it clearly. Old man Elmore leaving his pride and joy out on that levee didn't add up like it should. Even if Big Ray was buying time, covering tracks, he was the damn chief of police—he could have staged any number of scenarios that would have worked, would have explained his son's death. Could have worked out some better solution.

Why bury him in a shallow grave out there in an empty field?

Doc McKelvey was right. That was the biggest hole of all. The big, square, fire-engine-red peg that wouldn't fit in the round hole. *But what if Daddy Elmore wasn't the one cleaning up the mess? What if he didn't know—until later?*

What if it was someone trying to protect him?

What'd Doc say about King Henry?

There was a car following him now. There hadn't been one at first, but it was there now. It had angled in from a county road off to the south. It was closing fast. Occasionally, when it crested a low hill behind him, the moonlight allowed him to make out the shiny rack of gumballs on its roof. Somehow,

Jimbo Bevins had caught up to him. Goes to show that knowing the back roads makes a difference.

Up ahead he could begin to make out the sign welcoming
him to Lee County. *Decision time, Deputy,* Levine thought as
he glanced into the mirror. *You got what it takes? Gonna cross
the county line?*

CHAPTER 42

Split Tree, Arkansas
WEDNESDAY, AUGUST 24, 2005

Kel didn't really have much of a choice.

On the one hand, Elmore was an officer of the law—by everyone's account a good one who knew his job and did it conscientiously. On the other hand, there was a teetering element of unbalance about him. He clearly seemed to be a man about to pull apart at his seams, and to cap it off, Kel thought he smelled sour mash.

But what was he to do? If the sheriff meant Kel harm, who was going to stop him? Sam? Unlikely. Levine? He was gone. Kel himself? Maybe in his younger days, but certainly not at his present level of physical conditioning. And if the sheriff intended no harm, if this was a legitimate visit, which it probably was despite the sheriff's current lack of a cordial bedside manner, what was he to do? Refuse to go? Drop to the floor and start yelling and acting like a fool? Maybe. That would be the safest course of action, even if his pride precluded it.

In the end, Kel complied against his better thinking and got into the passenger seat of the sheriff's cruiser. He buckled in for the ride—whatever that ride was about to entail. Elmore took his place behind the wheel but didn't buckle. He turned the key and the engine fired on the first crank. A blast of cold exploded out of the air-conditioner vent. Kel looked at the twelve-gauge mounted on the drive-train hump.

Sheriff Elmore jerked the transmission into reverse and backed up with a jolt; he hit the handle on the steering column again, and the car shot forward with a slight squeal of rubber on asphalt. Not even slowing to look, he turned left on Magnolia and headed south.

They weren't headed back into town. Kel knew where they were headed.

The levee.

From time to time, the radio squawked, interrupting the silence until Sheriff Elmore had finally reached down under the dash and turned it off. That only made the silence louder.

They rolled to a stop and sat in the car. The headlights illuminated the small rise that formed the levee visited by Levine and Kel a few days earlier. Sheriff Elmore looked out the windshield, not saying a word as he reached into his left shirt pocket—under the six-pointed star of his office—and pulled out a cassette tape. He looked at the handwritten label on it briefly in the light that reflected back into the car and then slipped it into the tape deck in the dashboard. Abruptly the cracked, tinny yodel of Jimmie Rogers singing "Pal of My Heart" began in midsong. It scratched and popped.

The sheriff adjusted the volume upward twice until the dashboard vibrated and the gauges rattled.

"Get out," he said above the noise. He waited a moment and then added, "Now."

Kel thought once about pretending he couldn't hear, but realized that would only delay the situation and further abrade Elmore's thin patience. He undid his lap belt.

Sheriff Elmore hesitated long enough to make sure that Kel was complying before he opened his door and stood up, a bottle of George Dickel in his hand. He'd been tugging at it for most of the ride, and from the sound of the slosh, it was near empty. Now he looked over the top of the car at Kel and motioned with a jerk of his head for him to move to the front, then he rolled down his window so that the music flowed easily across the floodplain.

It was a hot night that stuck to the skin. Sweat formed thickly and coated like heavy corn syrup. There was an earthy smell, dust with a hint of river—miles and miles of river; smells from long-off Iowa and Missouri working their way slowly down to New Orleans and beyond.

And a new smell. Sweat and fear. Kel recognized it. It was his own. He hated himself for it. He'd let Levine's paranoia, however unreasonable, smudge off on him.

The waxing moon lit up a sky of humid, yellowish haze, and the car's headlights shut down Kel's night vision, making it impossible to see anywhere but the twenty yards directly in front of the car.

Sheriff Elmore took a seat on the hood, his left leg partially blocking one of the headlamps. He seemed not to notice, or not to care.

"My father's favorite song . . . 'Pal of My Heart'—this and 'Mississippi Moon.'" He took another drink and let out a short spit of air. "Harder to find that one though. Not many folks listen to Jimmie Rogers nowadays. Shame."

Kel looked all about him. There were no lights for miles—just the yellow cone made by the car's headlights—and no sounds except for the broken yodel coming from the tape, sweeping across the cracked floodplain mud.

"Know where this is?" Elmore asked. The bourbon sloshed loudly as he took another drink.

"Yeah, it's where the bodies were found forty years ago."

"That all? Your daddy never bring you here, or you just forgot?"

Kel shook his head with small, tentative moves. His right leg had started to jackhammer with adrenaline and fear, and he couldn't stop it. He could feel a fresh rivulet of sweat working a crooked line down the center of his back.

The sheriff pointed off to his left, his hand gripping the neck of the bourbon bottle. "This here's the original Split Tree. Right over there. See that dip? That shadow above the levee wall?" He waited for a response, but when none came, he continued. "When I was a boy . . . when I was young, there was still an old stump there. When your daddy was growin' up, mine too, there was still a tree there, so they used to say. It was dead, but it was still there. A mean, old, twisted black locust—split right down the center, straight to the ground by a bolt of God's own righteous lightnin'."

He took another drink and spat. The George Dickel bottle was near empty and it sloshed again, more loudly than before.

"Kill it? . . . I mean, the tree . . . did the lightnin' kill it?" Kel's father had told him the story many times when he was growing up. How the town had originally been named Franklin, after Franklin Pierce, but how after the tree was hit no one ever called it that again. The whole town simply changed its identity one day, in the blink of an eye, like a bolt of lightning.

"No." For a long, quiet moment it seemed as if that was the extent of the answer, but then he continued. "One side of it shriveled up and died, but t'other side lived . . . almost a hundred years more, I'd guess. Just like it'd never happened." He finished the last swallow of liquor, inspected the label in the available light as if he was reading the fine print on a medicine bottle, and then flipped it—end over end—out into the field. There was a dull *clunk* as it hit the sun-hardened clay. "Split in two, yet it lived. Scarred for life but still alive. I remember seeing the trunk when I was a boy. Shit . . . and all that's left now is that." He flicked his hand weakly in the same direction. "Nothin' but a hollow spot in the ground now. A shadow in the moonlight. A dyin' memory kept in the heads of dyin' men."

While the sheriff was talking, Kel had eased over to the right fender and was now leaning hard against it, trying to steady his leg. He felt foolish for being scared, but it didn't stop the hammering of his leg.

The sheriff looked briefly at Kel in the reflected light. "You scared?"

"No," Kel answered.

"Bullshit."

"Maybe. Should I be?"

"You know where the old McKelvey place was?" the sheriff asked after what seemed like another long silence. Kel jolted at his voice.

"Not really."

"Doesn't do to forget your roots, Mr. McKelvey." He was looking at Kel again. He looked a long time, and then he pointed off to the right into the formless dark, away from the split tree. "Over there, other side of that little clump of trees . . . maybe a mile. An old oxbow lake there—McKelvey Lake—your daddy took you there. That's where you fished. Mostly silted-in now, choked and dyin' . . . just like everythin' else around here."

Kel became aware that the song on tape had changed. It was still Jimmie Rogers but he didn't recognize it—no yodeling, just slow and sad; it was quieter but it still filled the air, drowning out the other sounds of the night.

"You know that Levine's goin' to Little Rock for an arrest warrant," Kel said quietly. It was intended as a statement of mutual understanding rather than a question requiring an answer.

"Hmm. And just who does he plan on arrestin'?"

"You."

Elmore didn't respond. He stared out at the levee for a moment and then slowly let his head tilt back as he closed his eyes. He breathed deeply, taking in the fecund smells of the floodplain and the night.

"He thinks your father was responsible for what happened out here. Maybe your brother too," Kel continued.

"Maybe he hasn't heard. My daddy and brother are dead."

"Thinks maybe you were an accessory." Kel was trying to keep his voice low, trying to inject a tone of understanding or sympathy—anything but confrontation. "Thinks he can squeeze you into talkin'."

With a burdensome exhalation like a man wrapped in chains, Sheriff Elmore raised himself off the hood and walked to the side of his car, reaching through the window and killing the headlamps. He stood momentarily and then returned to the front of the car.

Despite the slivered moon, the blackness closed about them physically as their eyes were slow to adjust to the darkness.

Kel saw a quick glint in Elmore's hand and realized he'd grabbed a second bottle from inside the car.

"And tell me, what is it that Special Agent Levine thinks happened out here?"

Kel blinked hard, trying to regain his night vision. "He thinks your father killed Jackson."

"That so? And why would my father want to kill Mr. Lee-on-eye-das Jackson?" There was a touch of exhausted humor in his voice.

"Levine says your father had Klan connections, and that he had it out for Jackson after he got the ACLU on his tail. Your father had been harassin' Jackson with some trumped-up charges."

Sheriff Elmore said nothing.

Kel continued. "Your father was a decisive man. He caught up with Jackson after his meetin' over in Helena, brought him out here, and beat him—may not have intended to kill him, maybe just warn him off—but it happened. Somethin' went wrong. Lost control. Nothin' to do then but damage control. That's when he disposed of the body in the levee over yonder." Kel flicked his head to the spot in the levee that Levine had indicated was the site of the burial, but he kept his eyes on the sheriff.

Elmore sat looking into the darkness as if he wasn't involved in the conversation. Then he asked, "And the other body? There were two people killed out here, as I recall."

"Levine thinks . . ." He stopped himself.

"Yes, Mr. McKelvey, what does Mr. Levine think? He have any ideas who that second body was?"

"He thinks it's your brother's. He thinks that your brother was part of the killin', somehow. Either part of the beatin' or maybe he even tried to stop your father—got himself killed in the deal somehow. Maybe it was an accident." He paused to better catch the sheriff's reaction. He could discern no change of expression or posture in the darkness. "But whatever happened, however it happened, Levine's convinced that the other body found out here was your brother—Ray Elmore."

At that, Elmore laughed. Short and quiet and with no apparent enjoyment; perfunctorily. "And you—Dr. McKelvey— do you think that too?" He was looking at Kel now. His voice was honed and sharp. "No, you don't, do you? You know better. You know that wasn't my brother Ray Junior buried out here, don't you?"

"Yes," Kel said softly. Even though Elmore was facing him now, Kel couldn't read his expression in the dim moonlight, but he saw the flash in Elmore's hand again. His eyes had adjusted enough that he could see that it wasn't another liquor bottle.

It was his service revolver.

"How'd you know?" Elmore's voice was so quiet that Kel could hardly hear him above the music. Above the pounding of the blood in his ears.

"The teeth."

Elmore cocked his head. "Yeah?"

"When I met Mrs. Trimble the other day . . . I noticed that her son, Jimmie, he never smiled in any photographs. She had a lot of them, and he didn't smile in any of them. She said he had an accident when he was young and was ashamed of his smile. The body we exhumed had all the teeth on the left-hand side broken out . . . It was Jimmie Trimble buried out here, wasn't it?"

The sheriff didn't answer immediately. He stared out into the moonlit field. Finally, he said, "Jimmie Carl Trimble was a war hero—haven't you heard? He's buried in a big national cemetery up there in St. Louis. Flag from his casket is over at the VFW hall in town." The sharpness in his voice had given way to a strange sense of bitterness that flavored his words.

Kel just shook his head. He didn't know all the answers, but he knew the truth.

"Yes sir," Elmore continued. "Big war hero. So, why would he be here . . . in a mud levee in east-godforsaken Arkansas?"

"I don't know. Maybe because Jimmie Trimble killed Jackson . . . or tried to. I saw a photo of your father and him. They say your daddy was like a surrogate father to him . . . proud of him . . . protective of him. I think maybe Jimmie Trimble returned the feelin' . . . I think maybe he idolized your father. When Jackson went after him, tried to ruin his career after that bogus drunk charge, maybe Jimmie Trimble decided to square the ledger and make things right. He was goin' off to join the navy and decided to clean up some business before he left." Kel thought again of Henry and Thomas à Beckett. "It probably was just intended as a beatin', a get-the-message ass whuppin', but it went south somehow. Went too far."

"That doesn't explain the second body."

Kel took a deep breath and continued. "I know. There's lots I can't explain. Lots that don't add up. Maybe your father found out and tried to stop him . . ." Kel looked at Elmore and a new thought formed in his mind. "No. No, not your father. Not him at all. Maybe your brother. They were close, weren't they? Your brother and Jimmie Carl. That's it—isn't it? Maybe there was a struggle . . . hell, I don't know . . . but somethin' happened. Somethin'. All I know is that Trimble ends up dead, and someone—your brother Ray—he buries him along with Jackson. That's it, isn't it? Your brother. And then he runs. He goes off to Vietnam posin' as Jimmie Trimble . . ." He paused again while he slid some more puzzle pieces into place. Then he continued, talking almost to himself.

"That's why there's no record of your brother servin'. That's why the DNA doesn't match up. The Lab got DNA from Trimble's site in Vietnam—but it doesn't match Mrs.

Trimble's blood sample . . . because it wasn't Jimmie Trimble. Everyone thought it was, but . . ." He refocused on Elmore. "It wasn't Jimmie Trimble, was it?" More pieces tumbled into place as he spoke. His mind flashed to his conversation with Dwayne Crockett. Crockett had said that Jimmie Trimble wrote home religiously—to his father. The real Jimmie Trimble wouldn't have written letters to his father. "Your brother Ray did serve in Vietnam, didn't he, Sheriff? But not as Ray Elmore. That's it, isn't it, Sheriff?" For a moment the scientist took over. *One drop of blood, Sheriff, and I can prove it,* he thought. *A single drop of blood.*

Sheriff Elmore spat on the dust. "Shit, Mr. P-H-D. Is that the sort of expensive thinkin' they teach in college?" His words had acquired more of a slur, and when he gestured with his hand his gun flashed a dull pewter color in the moonlight. "You been hangin' around Mr. Levine too much—some of his stupids are wearin' off on you."

"Then why don't you tell me how it was, Sheriff. Explain it to me." A challenge crept into Kel's voice. "I suspect you've been wantin' to tell this story a long time, haven't you? It was your brother that was the war hero, wasn't it? Ray Junior—your twin brother—he was the real hero, 'cept everyone thought he was someone named Jimmie Trimble."

"You don't know shit about me, college boy. You want the truth, the whole goddamn truth, so help me God . . . huh?" He held up his right hand as if he was being sworn in; the gun flicked again in the blue moonlight, and Kel slipped a step back along the car's fender. Elmore noticed. He looked down at the gun as if he'd been searching for it and was surprised to find it in his hand. He cocked the hammer and slowly pointed the gun at Kel's forehead. "S'matter, Dr. McKelvey—y'all scared now?"

"No." Of course he was. Scared didn't start to accurately describe the situation. Kel had once been in a base camp in Cambodia when the Khmer Rouge dropped some rockets on it, but that was abstract, almost surreal. It was hard to be scared of something as unreal as that.

But W. R. Elmore was real. W. R. Elmore was a man unspooling before Kel's eyes.

"Still bullshit. Your nuts drawed up so far, you cough and you'll castrate yourself. Aw crap," he spat again. He motioned with the gun barrel for Kel to sit on the edge of the hood, and then dropped the gun to his lap. It remained cocked.

Kel didn't move, but his leg began to jackhammer again. It was hard to swallow; his tongue was glued to the roof of his mouth. Kel's momentary surface bravado, brought on by the intellectual bracer of fitting the puzzle pieces together, now drained quickly away.

"My father . . . my father was an honorable man. The hardest-workin', most honorable man that walked God's acres. He hated the Klan and all it stood for. Hated the small, pig-faced pieces of shit that belonged to it. Men like Carl Trimble. He didn't roust Negroes either. He wasn't like that. You after truth? You want to know the truth about Mr. Lee-on-eye-das Jackson? Do you?"

Kel moved closer to the front of the car, still not sitting, but closer so that he could quiet his thumping leg against the bumper. His heart was rattling in his chest, and the blood roared in his ears. He was sweating heavily, and a drip formed on the tip of his nose.

"Mr. Leonidas Jackson was a whorin' damn drunk . . . and that's the devil's own truth. That time my father arrested him was a righteous bust."

Kel's body language must have conveyed some level of disbelief.

"Them ACLU fellas came down here—they didn't find no substance to it. Think about that, Mr. McKelvey, it's 1965, big-city ACLU lawyers come down here to small-town Split Tree, Arkansas, lookin' to investigate a racial incident. Got the president's damn blessin' to skin my father alive, yet they up and leave a few days later, back to their big-city offices, and the matter is never mentioned again. Ask yourself why. I'll tell you why, it's because they got down here and saw what a piece of trash Jackson was. Wasn't good for *The Cause*, so they put some miles between them and him."

"Maybe so, but still . . . somebody killed him. He didn't bury himself."

There was silence. The Jimmie Rogers tape had finished and had started playing itself again from the beginning.

Finally, Sheriff Elmore said, "Yeah, you're right 'bout that. Someone did. Why don't you take a seat?" His voice had lost its drunken slur. Elmore spoke with a clarity honed by forty years of pent frustration.

Kel sat. He swallowed hard.

"July twenty-ninth. Hot sumbitch. One of the hottest summers I remember. Least it seems that way. My brother, Ray Junior, and Jimmie Carl was right about here—maybe a little off thataway some more." He pointed to his left and took a long painful breath. "Just sittin'. Dreamin'. Bein'. Ray Junior was off to college on a football scholarship in a few weeks . . . bright future. He was some big-time good too, and that's a fact." Elmore seemed to momentarily lose himself in his memory. With a jerk almost like a near-sleep startle he resumed talking. "Jimmie Carl, he was due to report for his induction into the navy the next mornin'. On his way outta town. They was always real close, those two—you were right about that. Closer in most ways than me and Ray Junior ever was—more alike certainly. It was their last night together, for a good whiles anyway. They came here for the quiet and the . . . and the refreshments." Now he pointed off to the right, where the run-down buildings were located. "That used to be a thrivin' little community of all sorts of forbidden fruits. Whores, 'shiners. Jimmie Carl used to have to come down here to get corn liquor for his father, so course they all knew him well, but that night he got some just for him and Ray Junior. They was sittin' on the hood of Ray's car—kinda like we are now—drinkin' and rememberin' and plannin' such big things. Not much moon that night. You think it's dark now, shit, forty years ago it was black as a coal miner's snot." He paused to make sure Kel was listening.

"About eleven o'clock Mr. Leon Jackson comes out of one of those shacks yonder—drunk—weavin' like a wet possum—and he stumbles up the road this here ways. Where the hell he was headed, who knows—ain't nothin' out that way. Anyhow, he's almost upon them when he finally sees 'em. He don't know Jimmie Carl from Adam's yeller cat, but he sure does recognize Ray Junior as bein' the Big Ray's son. Starts jawin' at him—sayin' how he's gonna take my father and all this redneck county down. Trash talk, you know. Trash talk from a piece of trash. Ray Junior tries to ignore him; he could too. Ray had this almost biblical sense of control over everythin'. But Jimmie Carl, he just can't turn a cheek, never. You know, Jimmie Carl had a real sensitive spot when it came to my daddy, to Big Ray. Couldn't let it be." He paused again as the scene began to spool out in front of his eyes.

"Now, Jackson just keeps at him, callin' my daddy all kinds of names—at some point he takes out a little silver .22 pistol and starts wavin' it around, sayin' the next time my father tries to lay a hand on him he's gonna regret it. Shoot his ass, he says. Shit. Wrong goddamn thing to say. Jimmie Carl, he takes about as much as he can, and then he jumps up and he starts to whuppin' up on Jackson. And I mean whup his ass but good." He looked out over the levee, his left hand waving slowly in front of him as if he were directing the ghosts playing out their roles before them.

"I don't know what happened next exactly, I wasn't here, but somehow in the scuffle Jimmie Carl ends up with a damn bullet in his head. My brother Ray . . . Ray just . . . he just flipped out. He beat that sumbitch Jackson to death with the butt of his own pistol." Sheriff Elmore was looking closely at the butt end of the nickel-plated revolver in his hand as if he half-expected to see blood and tissue there. He was silent so long that Kel assumed the story was completed.

"And then your brother Ray buried them both out here . . . in the levee."

The sheriff didn't respond.

"Why here? Forgotten and . . ."

"Shit, Mr. McKelvey. An eighteen-year-old kid with two dead bodies—that doesn't add up to the clearest thinkin'. Needed a temporary solution. Never intended to leave Jimmie Carl out here."

"Did your father know?" Kel asked.

"Naw. Not at first, he didn't. Not at first. But you're wrong. Ray Junior didn't bury nobody. Fact is, he didn't know what to do; he had the patience of Job, but he never was good at quick decisions. He could run like a damn deer." He smiled and his voice momentarily took on the warm tone of a long-forgotten amusement. "Unfortunately, he was about as smart as one sometimes. Anyway, he wanted to tell Big Ray—turn himself in, try and explain it and all. In fact, he drove back into town lookin' for Daddy. Found me instead . . . we came back out here together—the two of us. Shit, wasn't nothin' we was gonna do that could bring Jimmie Carl back to life. Nothin' at all. All we could do then was protect my father—what with them ACLU shitbags havin' just been here, and with them three boys bein' found over in Mississippi, and all. That sumbitch LBJ would have had my daddy doin' time in Tucker Prison, for sure—just to make sure he looked good to them big-money liberals in Washington.

Kel looked at Elmore's profile in the darkness. He swallowed, and it seemed as loud as a thunderclap. The final puzzle piece. "It was you. You're . . . you buried them. Wasn't your brother Ray at all."

Elmore snorted at the remembered exasperation of that long-ago night. "I finally convinced Ray Junior to just get—and get far away and get fast. Run like a deer. He did. Went home and packed. Left a note sayin' he had to leave and that he'd explain it all later. I didn't know where he'd gone; didn't know he'd taken Jimmie Carl's place in the navy, his name and all, until he wrote me a letter a couple months after. No one at the navy induction center knew what Jimmie Carl looked like—wasn't like now—no one had photo IDs then, and Ray Junior knew all about Jimmie Carl's background. Simple. He just . . . hell, he just became Jimmie Carl Trimble. Crawled into his skin."

"And Ray disappeared. What did your father think happened to him? He went and disappeared all of a sudden—your father must have wondered."

"He did, sure did, but then Ray Junior wrote my daddy too—from boot camp and then from Vietnam—long letter that said that he and Jimmie Carl had gotten all fired up with the patriotic fever and enlisted together. It was called the 'buddy system.' In 1965 people still did that sort of thing. Nobody checked. How could they really? Why should they? Letters postmarked from Vietnam were comin' in regular—some signed Ray Junior, some signed Jimmie Carl. Similar handwritin' if anybody checked, but nobody did. My daddy was proud of Ray Junior—proud of Jimmie Carl too. No one asked no questions."

"Until the second body washes out of the levee a month or so later."

"That's right, until the body washed out . . . course my father recognized it right away. He didn't have no doubt. He never said nothin' to me, but he knew . . . Fact is, he never said much to me at all after that. It was never the same. He knew somethin' had happened, and he figured that I must have been at the center of it. That's the way he always thought—Jimmie Carl and Ray Junior could do no wrong, but me . . . Shit, I could do no right."

"And then word comes from the navy that Jimmie Trimble— who's really your brother Ray—has died in Vietnam . . ."

"Yup. Brother Ray dies in Vietnam—'cept they think it's someone named Jimmie Carl Trimble. A shiny brass war hero too. Saved a whole company of Marines. Stayed behind to save a Negro boy." Elmore vented a long sigh. "In the big picture, I guess it kinda balances the scale in some way, don't it?"

"Must have been hard for your father to lose a son, but even harder to have him die such a hero and not be able to even acknowledge it publicly."

Elmore snorted another short laugh. "His son was a hero all right—just not the son everyone thought. You still don't get it do you, college boy? . . . Jimmie Carl *was* his son, mind, bone, and blood."

It took a moment for the words to seep in. When they did, Kel felt his breath leave him involuntarily. How absolutely stupid. He thought back to the photograph on Grace Trimble's wall, of the resemblance between Big Ray and Jimmie Trimble. "Trimble was your half-brother?"

Elmore could sense Kel's confusion even if he couldn't make out his expression in the dark. "You could say it was always more like I was the half-brother. Jimmie Carl was the one true son of my father's one true love. Ray Junior was a close second, but Jimmie Carl, he was the one. Grace Trimble was pregnant when my father went off to war. He didn't know. She didn't want him to worry none, so she didn't tell him. But things were different back then—women didn't have bastard children in small towns like this. She thought about leavin' and movin' to California where she had some kin—but she didn't. Don't know why she didn't, but she didn't. Guess her roots was too deep here in Locust County to get shamed off. Anyway, she didn't, and then that sumbitch Carl Trimble offered to marry her. He never did love her, just coveted what my father had. He could never be the man Big Ray was—not even close—he'd always been in his shadow, but now he could have his woman. In the beginnin' I think Carl Trimble believed that he could raise Big Ray Elmore's son right under his nose and not be bothered by it. Take some sort of sick pleasure in it. But as Jimmie Carl got older, he looked more and more like Big Ray every day, and Carl Trimble couldn't stand that. It ate him up, and he took to beatin' Jimmie Carl regular—didn't need no reason; the reason was staring back at him with my daddy's eyes."

"That what happened to his teeth? Carl Trimble knock them out?"

Elmore laughed loudly this time, and with honest enjoyment. "No, you got to blame me and Ray Junior for that one. Jimmie Carl was always afraid of lookin' weak—you could dare him into anythin'. July fourth one year—we was . . . maybe nine, he was twelve or so—Ray dared him to hold a Red Rascal firecracker in his teeth and light it. We didn't really think he'd do it. Hell, we thought it'd blowed his whole head clean off."

He had stopped laughing and was looking down, shaking his head sadly. "When we took him home, that bastard Carl Trimble said he deserved it and wouldn't take him to the doctor. All he done was pack his mouth full of Red Man to stop up the bleedin'. Got all infected and wouldn't heal right. Finally, Big Ray took him to a dentist in Forrest City and got him fixed up best he could. But there was a price; Carl beat the livin' tar out of Jimmie Carl when he found out what my daddy done." He paused while more memories percolated to the surface of his consciousness. "But Carl Trimble paid a price too. When Big Ray found out about the beatin', he damn near killed Carl with a pick handle."

They sat quietly on the hood of the car, staring ahead, the music rolling across the field. Jimmie Rogers was singing "Mississippi Delta Blues."

Kel was trying to wicker the threads together when he noticed the sheds off to the right, dark-blue specters in the moonlight. He motioned to them. "Why'd your father close those down? Was he afraid that someone had seen somethin'?"

Elmore looked up and across Kel to where the buildings stood. He knotted his face in confusion. "No. Nobody saw nothin'. But it was about what happened here that night, you're right 'bout that. Big Ray weren't no prude, but he also never did approve of that sort of behavior neither . . . prostitution, moonshinin', sins of weakness and wont. Mainly of lack of character. He never could stand that, but when it came to those sheds he'd always looked the other way and let it go since it was county business and not city. Not his jurisdiction. But after that . . . night . . . at least after Jimmie Carl's body was found here, he turned different. Somethin' soured and rankled in him. Blamed them houses and the folks in 'em for Ray Junior and Jimmie Carl bein' out here, for Jackson bein' here. He'd done had enough—jurisdiction or no."

It was time to ask the real question, though Kel wasn't sure he wanted to know the answer. "What now?" he managed to say.

"Tonight, you mean? Now, that's the Sunday mornin' question, isn't it?"

"Levine will be back in a few hours, you know that. From what you tell me, you had only a minor part in a self-defense killin'—whatever you call it. More like an accessory after the fact. And it was forty years ago. You can get a good lawyer, Sheriff. Hell, the prisons don't have room for real criminals, let alone young boys tryin' to protect their father."

There was a pause before Elmore responded. "Ain't about me."

"What?" Kel asked. The sheriff had responded so softly that Kel wasn't sure he'd really said anything.

Sheriff Elmore took a long, deep breath as if he was girding for something unpleasant. "You ain't a twin, are you, Mr. McKelvey?"

"No, but I do have two twin boys. Just turned teenagers."

"Tell 'em apart?"

"You mean . . . yeah, usually. They look alike, but usually you can tell 'em apart."

"They ever try to fool you as to which one is who?"

Kel thought back to his wife and their conversation the other night. "Yup," he said, trying to interject a laugh into the tone of his voice. A little levity at the moment couldn't hurt.

"Bet they can't do it for long. Me and Ray Junior used to . . . different as night and day we was, but we looked exactly the same. We used to try and fool folks from time to time. Could do it for a while too, but never for too awful long. People always figured it out." He turned his right hand over and back, seating the revolver's grip better in his palm. "What do you know about mockin'birds?"

Kel didn't respond.

"Funny damn birds. Mockin'birds don't have a song of their own. You know that? They try to sound like other birds." Elmore paused and took a deep breath. "It's funny, but that's how you can tell it's them. Even if you can't see them, just listen long enough and they give themselves away in the end by mockin' too many birds. They can't keep it up. They can't sing like just one, they can't be happy with one identity."

Kel watched him closely. He rubbed his own moist palms on his thighs. His leg started thumping again.

"It's the same thing, this was—Jimmie Carl and Ray Junior tradin' places—same thing, really. I've been waitin' forty years. I knew that someone would finally figure it out, someday, someone . . . I'm sort of surprised it took this long."

"That why you searched my room the other night? It was you, wasn't it? You needed to find out what I was piecin' together. You knew I worked for the CIL and figured I was onto somethin' about Ray and Jimmie and Vietnam."

"Don't flatter yourself, son." Elmore spat loudly.

"Where do we go from here, Sheriff Elmore?" Kel emphasized the word *Sheriff*; he thought it was good to keep reminding Elmore that he was a sheriff, a man of civic responsibility and service. He only hoped he was sober enough to remember that.

"Why don't you tell me, Mr. McKelvey. You and that Levine seem pretty intent upon rakin' this compost pile out into the sun to dry. I don't see it. What you goin' to gain from it, Mr. McKelvey? What's anyone to gain? My daddy's dead.

He was a good man—a right good man. You gonna trash him up? For what? 'Cause you can? My brother Ray Junior is dead too. Whatever he did, he paid for it—he atoned himself to God—ten times over. Men are alive today because of him. You need to pull him out of his grave so you can drag him through the mud? And Jimmie Carl . . . he ain't comin' back neither, no matter what you do. Miss Grace is an old woman with nothin' but her son's memory; he's gone, but he died a hero to her and this town. You gonna tell her that he wasn't? You gonna make the world better by tellin' her that he died wrestlin' a drunk Negro out by a lonely levee? Is that what you're all about? No, Mr. McKelvey, I'm not sure I can stand to see that."

Kel could think of nothing to say. Seconds seemingly drew out to minutes.

"Dr. McKelvey . . . that thing I said about your father . . . he weren't second string to nobody. My daddy felt honored to know him. Thought you should know that."

Before Kel could answer, Sheriff W. R. Elmore raised his revolver to his own temple and in one single movement fired.

Kel screamed. Elmore's body spasmed back onto the hood of the car. The bullet had emptied his head of everything important, and the contents were sprayed across the windshield and hood in dark-bluish clumps. Kel jumped off the hood and ran to the driver's side of the car. He pulled Elmore off the car onto the ground where he groped in the dark for a pulse.

Already there was none.

And then someone bowled him over. He cartwheeled and sprawled into the dust, but quickly rolled to his feet. In the dim moonlight he could make out Levine's body, bent over the dead sheriff, looking just as vainly for a pulse. He thumped the sheriff's chest repeatedly, as much out of frustration as in hope.

"Levine. What the . . . when'd you get here?" Kel was talking way too loudly, he knew, but the crack of Elmore's gun was still ringing in his ears and damped his hearing. He returned to Elmore's side, trying to do something; but he didn't know what or how.

Levine didn't answer. He pushed Kel aside and placed his head on Elmore's chest, listening for a spark.

"Anythin'? Anythin'?" Kel kept repeating loudly. Levine wasn't answering.

Goddammit. Goddammit, Kel thought. Why hadn't he seen this coming? Because he'd been so worried about his own skin, that's why. "Anythin'? Anythin'?"

Levine slowly rose up on his knees, looking at what was left of W. R. Elmore's head. Then he stood up.

Kel looked up at him. He had his answer. There was nothing. He too stood up. Neither of them spoke. Finally, Levine reached through the car window and ejected the tape from the player. Even with the ringing in their ears, the silence that now stood on the floodplain grabbed them physically.

"God. Oh, God, oh, God, oh, God . . ."

Levine angrily flung the cassette into the field. "Oh, God is right," he said.

"How long? . . . I mean . . . did you hear . . ." Kel stumbled. His hearing had started to return.

"How much did I hear? Enough. Most of it."

"But, how . . ."

"How'd I get here? Luck, I guess. I saw the sheriff's car at the motel when I left—I thought it was Deputy Bevins at first, watching us like he had been. But then Bevins shows up trailing me out of the county, and I realized maybe it wasn't him at the motel. I didn't like the feeling I was getting so I drove back." Levine put his hands in his pockets and drew a deep breath, which he held for a moment. He looked at Sheriff Elmore's body again and then turned away to face the dark shadow that represented the levee. He exhaled and then continued. "You weren't in your room, so I asked Sam if he'd seen you. He said that you and Sheriff Elmore had driven off together a few minutes earlier—headed south, he thought. South. I took a guess."

It took Kel a minute to digest. "But where the hell'd you come from?"

Levine pointed vaguely to the northwest. "Over there about a half-mile. Fortunately, you had the headlights on and the radio blaring—not hard to find you people. Easy to walk up on you undetected as well."

"Then why in God's name didn't you stop him? You stupid sonofabitch. You could have—if you were here all this time . . ."

"Why didn't you? You were standing right next to him. You're right, I should have. I thought I could . . . intended to if I thought you were in danger, but I didn't want to spook him as long as he was talking so freely. I wanted to nail his ass so bad . . . I . . . I wanted to hear what he had to say . . . I . . . I thought I'd be able to intervene if he threatened you—or . . . I . . . I didn't see this coming."

Both men stood silently, staring into the darkness. In the distance they could hear a lone whippoorwill.

Kel motioned to Elmore's body. "Christ." He closed his eyes and took a couple of steadying breaths of his own. "I guess none of us did," he finally said.

"You're wrong, Doc. You're wrong. I think he saw this coming for a long, long time."

The silence returned.

"Now what? We need to report this . . ." Kel said quietly.

Levine didn't respond.

"We need to report this," Kel repeated.

"I wonder . . ."

"What do you mean? We've got to report this."

"Yeah, we do. I guess the question is how to report it." He turned and faced Kel squarely. "He was right, Doc . . . Kel. He was right about what he was saying. All of it. You weren't in Vietnam, were you?"

"No, but I don't see . . ."

"That's just it," Levine said. "You don't see. You can't. You weren't there; I was. You know what kind of guts it must have taken to do what Ray Elmore did over there? The Navy Cross, Doc." He took a slow, deep breath. "What good will it do? He was right about that. Kill that old woman? Wreck her world? Do we need that? Does the war need to take another casualty? Do we need to trash Big Ray Elmore's ghost? Is anything improved by showing up Leon Jackson as a drunk? It's time to tuck the snakes back in their box and hammer down the lid forever."

Levine reached out and grabbed Kel's shoulder. "I came down here to bring a murderer to justice. You look around—what do you see? I don't see a murderer. Do you?"

"But truth is truth, no matter how ugly it may be," Kel protested.

"And no matter who it hurts? . . . No, you're wrong, Kel. Truth is what people like you and me write in our reports. That's the truth. The rest . . . no, the rest is just . . ." Levine looked down at the dark form of Sheriff Elmore's body. He could hear the crickets resuming their night chatter and the faint feather brush of a breeze was stirring the dust and smells. He looked up at Kel and then off into the dark, inhaling the working breath of the river. His mind recalled the sound of angry gunshots that rippled and skipped across another flood-plain and another river, in a land almost as foreign. He thought of a young boy in pajamas. "A man once told me that we should let dead men rest in peace. 'Let them sleep,' he said. A good man told me that. And that sounds like good advice."

CHAPTER 43

Donnie Hawk, Jr., the Locust County coroner, ruled that the death of Sheriff W. R. Elmore was an alcohol-assisted suicide; the final expression of a depressed, lonely, middle-aged man fueled by a fifth of amber-brown resolve who exorcised some personal demons, and a third of his brain, with a .357 hollow-point. The official cause and manner of death was listed as rapid exsanguination caused by a gunshot wound to the head. Ordinarily Donnie Hawk would have acknowledged his professional limitations and requested assistance from the State Medical Examiner's Office in Little Rock for a case like this—but not this time. This time the paperwork was filed quickly and quietly.

People in Split Tree arose and greeted the morning news of Elmore's death with surprise, but certainly not shock. Everyone knew that the entire Elmore family had been unraveling itself for some forty-odd years. First Big Ray, then his wife, who never got over the loss of her son in Vietnam, and now the remaining twin boy. Waymond Ray Elmore was buried less than thirty-six hours later in the Elmore-Wallace cemetery, in a plot recently vacated by Luke 15:31. Grace Trimble paid the expenses, and Donnie Hawk, Jr., his Pacific Funeral Home in ashes, arranged to have the body prepared by a rival mortuary in Helena.

Special Agent Michael Levine returned to his Bureau-decreed exile in Memphis. He told his supervisor that he had hit a wall with his investigation, and his final report, which had probably been round-filed in less time than it took him to print it out, recommended that the case be placed in an inactive status pending the generation of new evidence. His inability to crack the code on the Jackson–John Doe murder hadn't materially helped his chances of reassignment back East, but oddly he didn't seem concerned. The weather had begun to moderate somewhat—even if only a little—and he found some level of physical comfort in that. More important, his attitude had changed around the office. He affected an air of contentment that none of his colleagues could quite understand. It was as if he'd finally run his personal demons to ground.

Robert Dean McKelvey traveled home to an office littered with a dozen brush fires, all of which required a level of undivided attention that he found himself absolutely unable to muster. He'd hardly spoken to anyone and certainly hadn't mentioned the events of the previous week. When questioned about his moody silence, he told people that he didn't feel well, and that certainly was the truth.

He had only been back to work five days when the package arrived. Truth be told, he had been expecting it, though he hadn't known what he was expecting or what form it would take when it arrived. But he knew it would come. In fact, he was surprised it had taken as long as it did.

"You got a package from the F-B-I. Some guy named Levine." Peggy always entered his office as if she had just tripped on a raised threshold. Kind of a lunge and a hop mixed with a focused purpose. She was carrying a red-white-and-blue Federal Express box, which she dropped onto the topmost stratum of work on his desk. "I signed for it," she remarked—almost as an afterthought, just in case Kel thought he needed some clarification—as she turned and exited. It had taken her less than five seconds and now she was on to her next task.

D.S. passed her in the doorway. "You got a couple?" he asked, being sure to avoid colliding with the accelerating secretary.

"No," Kel replied, "but go ahead anyway."

D.S. moved a pile of reports on the swivel chair in front of Kel's desk, stacking them on the floor, and settled in. He'd been wanting to talk to Kel for several days but could tell that the time wasn't right. Now he decided to test the water. "You following this storm that's headed for Louisiana? Might hit New Orleans they say. Looks like a big one."

Kel didn't answer.

"Suppose we'll get called if it does? I mean, like we did with the tsunami over in Thailand . . ."

Kel sighed. "Doubt it. I suspect FEMA and the folks in Louisiana have got it covered."

"Still, wouldn't hurt to have some of our guys on standby."

"Tell me, D.S., you come in here to talk about some storm, or you got somethin' else on your mind?" Kel's voice had an edge of impatience that he regretted but which he also couldn't control.

Davis Smart paused and then pushed ahead. "Actually, yeah, there's something else. While you were gone, I did a lot of thinking about the remains from the Evans and Trimble case."

"Maybe you shouldn't," Kel said quietly.

D.S. squinted. "You know something I don't?"

"You ever ask yourself who gave us the right to meddle in people's lives? Scratch open old wounds?" Kel asked as he opened the FedEx box. He didn't remove the contents, but dropped the box onto his desk and pushed it away.

"You asking that as a scientist or a philosopher?"

Kel snorted. "I'm neither. I'm just a man who writes reports."

D.S. gave that a moment and then responded. "Well then, what do you plan on writing in your report on this one?"

"You tell me."

"Wish I could. You know, it simply doesn't add up right. If you remember where we left off a couple of weeks ago, we'd agreed that Jimmie Trimble probably wasn't adopted—and I assume," he paused and looked closely at Kel, "I assume that if you found out something to the contrary while in Arkansas, that you'd share it with me." Reassured by the silence, he continued. "Okay, so where does that leave us? We've got remains out on one of our tables that don't match either the Evans or the Trimble DNA references. Right? But it has got to be someone. So, if it's not Evans or Trimble, then maybe it's someone that isn't listed as missing in Vietnam? What do you think the chances of that are?"

Pretty damn good. Kel kept this thought to himself. Out loud he simply vented an acknowledging sound.

"The way I piece it together," D.S. continued, "is this: we have remains from the Evans-Trimble loss location in Vietnam, we recover a dog tag for Evans, so we know it's a good recovery. Right location and all. The remains are those of a young male—definitely not an indigenous Vietnamese—and there are no other recorded U.S. ground losses within thirty or forty klicks of the site . . ."

He paused again but when Kel didn't respond—didn't even blink—he resumed. "I mean, think about it . . . it's not a local Vietnamese, and it's not Evans or Trimble. So it's got to be someone we don't even know is missing; someone we're not even looking for; someone who's not on our MIA list."

"Or a misidentification," Kel said quietly, still not making eye contact with his deputy. "Ever think about that?"

"You mean someone was misidentified during the war and taken off the list when he shouldn't have been? Yeah, could be. That'd explain why he's not on our list. That's sort of what I'm talking about. Whatever it is, we've got a case that involves someone we don't know we're supposed to be looking for; someone we don't have a record on. Somebody that isn't listed as even missing. Maybe a mis-ID, or maybe he's CIA, some sort of spook or something." He sighed and was quiet for a moment before leaning forward in his chair. "You know what really gets me about this case, though? What's so aggravating? I think of all the cases where we have absolute shit to work with—a couple of little bone fragments, maybe—and along comes this one. We have everything we should need to ID this guy—the location's right, the circumstantial evidence is solid, good remains, good DNA sequence—everything except a family blood sample to compare it to. Kinda pisses you off, doesn't it? A damn drop of blood. All we need is a drop of blood from a relative and we can put this one to rest. If we just knew who."

Kel didn't answer.

His thoughts were focused on the open FedEx box on his desk and the sealed plastic Ziploc bag visible inside. He didn't have to open it all the way to see its contents—a tan polyester-and-cotton sheriff's uniform shirt, covered with dried blood and crusty flecks of brain matter.

"Kel?" D.S. asked quietly. "Kel, d'you hear me? Said it's a real pisser, isn't it? Not having a blood sample."

"Yeah," Kel replied, his eyes never leaving the box. "A real pisser."

ACKNOWLEDGMENTS

This whole thing started in the San Francisco airport where I was waylaid for seven hours en route from Hawaii to Bosnia. Halfway through a particularly bad paperback novel that I'd purchased at an airport bookstore, I had the sobering vision that I could write a novel every bit as bad as the one that I was reading. Upon finally getting home, I shared my epiphany with my wife, Mary. Ever my soulmate, she expressed her belief that if I were to really put my mind to the task, she was sure that I could write a novel even worse than I had imagined. I think I have proven her confidence in me to be well-founded.

Few people knew that I was writing this book. My wife, of course, knew, as did my two sons, Pierce and Davis, who politely refrained from rolling their eyes in my presence—most of the time, anyway. Bob Mann knew. Bob is the deputy scientific director at the JPAC, and I ventured out on a limb and told him after learning that he was writing a book of his own. He kept my secret and wished me well when my spirits flagged. Jan Burke knew. She offered encouragement early on. Johnie Webb, Jr., the former deputy commander of the U.S. Army's Central Identification Laboratory, Hawaii (CILHI), also knew some sketchy version of what was going on, but that's about the extent of it—except, of course, for the slew of literary agents who rejected the manuscript with constructive criticism such as "unimaginative," "boring," "trite," and (my favorite) "don't make me get a restraining order because I will." If anyone is to blame for your reading this today, it's Linda Kenney and Michael Baden. Put on the spot, they agreed to mention me to their literary agent. Which brings me to Leigh Feldman. Why Leigh took a chance on me, I do not know, but I'm glad she did. I won't forget.

And while on the list of people who should have their heads examined, David Rosenthal, publisher at Simon and Schuster, should be near the head of the line. Once again, I don't know why he took a chance with me, but I won't forget.

A lot of people overlook the nuts-and-bolts end. That's shortsighted and ill-mannered. Tara Parsons, Alexis Taines, and Al Madocs of Simon and Schuster and Michele Mortimer, Ros Perotta, and Kristin Lang of Darhansoff, Verrill, and Feldman showed great patience in dealing with my literary procedural ignorance. Adrian Cronauer provided legal advice. My brother Jim drove around some back roads of rural Arkansas with me without pressing too hard about what we were doing or why we were doing it. Hugh Berryman has unwittingly been supplying rural Tennessee expressions for years—many much more colorful than any I ever heard growing up in Arkansas—and Lowell Levine has done much the same for Brooklyn.

Having read quite a few novels (during many hours in base camps, aboard aircraft, and sitting in airports), I have often seen acknowledged praise for nearly superhuman editors who, if you can believe what you read, managed to take a pile of disjointed notes scribbled on the backs of napkins and gasoline receipts and somehow managed to craft a novel. Being sophisticated and cynical, I never believed it—until now. Thank you, Marysue Rucci. (Now that this is finished, I need those receipts back.)

For the record, the CILHI is no more. Having existed, off and on, in one form or another since the late 1940s, the CILHI was decommissioned as an army command on September 30, 2003, only to reemerge the next day as part of the larger Department of Defense Joint POW/MIA Accounting Command. The mission—to recover and identify America's war dead—

remains the same; we just use different letterhead. It is the most intellectually and emotionally satisfying job that I can imagine.

This is a fictional story, albeit inspired by cases and situations that I have been involved in over my career. But it is fictional. That means that it originated in my feverish brain and does not reflect reality or, for that matter, the views, opinions, policies, desires, wants, hopes, dreams, aspirations, or fundamental doctrine of the U.S. Army, U.S. government, or anyone remotely connected to either. Characters in the story are just that—characters. They are composites of individuals I have known and encountered, and while some people may, out of ego or paranoia, think that they can spot similarities, I can assure them that it's all fictional and that any resemblance to persons living or dead is entirely coincidental.

Don't miss the page-turning suspense, intriguing characters, and unstoppable action that keep readers coming back for more from these bestselling authors...

Tom Clancy
Robin Cook
Patricia Cornwell
Clive Cussler
Dean Koontz
J.D. Robb
John Sandford

Your favorite thrillers and suspense novels come from Berkley.

penguin.com

Penguin Group (USA) Online

What will you be reading tomorrow?

Tom Clancy, Patricia Cornwell, W.E.B. Griffin,
Nora Roberts, William Gibson, Robin Cook,
Brian Jacques, Catherine Coulter, Stephen King,
Dean Koontz, Ken Follett, Clive Cussler,
Eric Jerome Dickey, John Sandford,
Terry McMillan, Sue Monk Kidd, Amy Tan,
John Berendt...

You'll find them all at
penguin.com

*Read excerpts and newsletters,
find tour schedules and reading group guides,
and enter contests.*

Subscribe to Penguin Group (USA) newsletters
and get an exclusive inside look
at exciting new titles and the authors you love
long before everyone else does.

PENGUIN GROUP (USA)
us.penguingroup.com